People in Glass Houses

CHARITY BLACKSTOCK

People in Glass Houses

HODDER AND STOUGHTON
LONDON SYDNEY AUCKLAND TORONTO

0397604

I

"THE POST COMES LATER and later," said Mrs. Fielding.

It was a curious coincidence that the six tenants of Curran House had all come down at the same time. It was half past nine in the morning, and Dr. Macek was presumably on his way to Harley Street, but Veronica seldom appeared at so early an hour, Mrs. Parsons never had any mail at all, and Nina and Andreas Photiades tended to scuttle round the house in a furtive manner, refusing to speak to the other tenants, and bestowing frozen, almost hostile, smiles on them if they met on the stairs.

Rose pulled Tom back from grabbing something out of Mrs. Fielding's carrier bag. Mrs. Fielding was presumably on her way to the Darby and Joan Club, where she worked two days a week. It was work she enjoyed, for she was a cosy, warm-hearted woman who loved people, provided they were not too complicated, she always said she adored the old folk, and came back in the evenings to Len and Lulu, resplendent with the happiness of it all. Rose thought ungratefully that, if she were an old woman, she would resent Mrs. Fielding's kindness bitterly: it would somehow relegate her to being a baby like Tom, she would be forced into being awash with gratitude. There could be nothing more diminishing than having to say thank you non-stop.

A little ashamed of herself for these unpleasant thoughts, she looked out into the street and saw that the postman was now five doors away. There was unlikely to be much for her

5

unless Gerard had decided to write to her again. This chilled her, stirred her stomach. Once, a long time ago, she had hardly been able to wait before tearing his letters open, she had read them all the way back to the flat and, when a letter did not arrive, dared not even go to the lavatory for fear the phone would ring and he might not hold on long enough for her to answer. And now she was simply terrified of what she would read, and the thought of this made her jerk Tom's arm more sharply than she intended so that he started to grizzle.

Mrs. Fielding said, "That's all right, Rose. I get on quite well with little boys, you know. Tom and I are old friends, aren't we, little fellow?" She stooped to pat his cheek. "You know something, Tommy, I think I've got something here that might just interest you." She smiled back into Tom's now beaming face, for he liked Mrs. Fielding, and with a grand gesture pulled out a bar of chocolate, which he at once put into his mouth without removing the paper.

Rose cried out, "Oh no, Tom!" She was aware as she spoke of the shrewishness in her voice. She saw that Dr. Macek was surveying her in his usual impassive manner. She was sure that he was registering disapproval. Of course he specialised in children's diseases, so no doubt he considered himself an authority on their upbringing. It was true that he seldom spoke to her, whether to register approval or disapproval, but she was nervous enough at that moment to feel nothing but dislike for him: she shot him an icy glance, then removed the bar of chocolate from Tom's mouth: he naturally burst into a roar of rage.

"He's got out of bed the wrong side," said Veronica, surveying him with some distaste, for she did not like children, indeed she did not like anyone. She uttered the trite words in her beautiful, ringing voice. It was a magnificent voice, full-throated and deep, it belonged to the stage, though Veronica had never acted in her life. She looked as if she had got out the wrong side, herself. But then she was never at her best in the morning, and seldom appeared before mid-day. She was still in her dressing-gown, which like herself, had known grander days: it must have cost a bomb many years ago, and was now dirty, stained and tattered. Her hair was hanging

6

round her grim, battered face in witch-locks, and she had evidently not even bothered to wash, for traces of last night's eye shadow were smudged on to her cheeks. Mrs. Fielding, looking at her sideways with a professional eye, thought she was about due for one of her seasonal bouts: she was an inquisitive woman and, living on the first floor, kept an austere watch on what was going on. She had not missed the frequent visits from the local wineshop, nor the innumerable bottles which were carted out with the rubbish. Lady Matford — she did not think of her by her first name—was already wandering round the streets at night, which was always an ominous sign.

However, she said nothing, and Rose too ignored the comment. She saw to her relief that the postman was now only two doors away. She wished Mrs. Fielding would not give Tom chocolate, which was really not good for him, and which he always smeared all over himself, but there was nothing she could do about it now, so she began to undo the damp package, saying as soothingly as she could, "All right, lovey, all right. Hold on. It's just coming."

She was aware, as she was beginning to be all too frequently, of the aura of disapproval around her. It was strange how even in these permissive days the woman living apart from her husband was regarded with distaste. Even Veronica, the only one among them who could be termed a personal friend, was regarding her with a kind of cynical derision. She and Veronica had not been on really friendly terms for some time now, yet she was in her own way an ally, if only because she had met Rose before her marriage. This unfriendly look was somehow the last straw, on top of the usual sleepless night, her aching eyes, Sally's temperament, and the extraordinary presence of Gerard who, for all he was seventy miles away, seemed in some strange way to be standing behind her shoulder. She popped a piece of the chocolate into Tom's avid mouth, and silently cursed the postman who, instead of making his way to Curran House, was gossiping with someone in the Studios next door.

She said crossly, "I don't know why we're all waiting like this." She addressed the remark to little Mrs. Photiades, but received nothing but the usual blank smile in reply. She

7

wondered occasionally why the girl was so uncommunicative. Perhaps it was because she was so far from Athens, her home. It was certainly not a question of language; both she and her husband spoke excellent English.

It was Mrs. Fielding who answered her. She said happily, "I'm expecting a letter from Amanda."

Mrs. Fielding, who was a moderately devout Catholic, had a family of three girls. In the friendly days, when Gerard was her husband and her lover, Rose had seen a great deal of the Fieldings, and met all her daughters. It always struck her as strange that the girls were so markedly different, almost as if they represented the opposing facets of Mrs. Fielding's character. Amanda was the eldest and the good girl of the family: she had married an office executive in the whitest of white weddings, owned two cars, a smart flat and a country cottage, producing two children, one boy and one girl, as a kind of pleasing sideline. Whatever Amanda did was right, in her politics, her behaviour, her choice of husband and her substantial income. It was always, Amanda says this, and Amanda does that. The rare occasions on which she visited her mother, in the smaller of the two cars and accompanied by the children and a well-clipped poodle puppy, were red-letter days for Mrs. Fielding, something that she talked about for weeks after. Gerard had always detested Amanda, who was a plump, dark young woman with an aggressive manner and without much charm, but then she had made it plain that she did not care much for actors either, especially when they were chronically out of work: she remarked once in that voice of hers that carried so well, "These good-looking types always think they are so fascinatingly sexy. It makes me sick, actually."

Gerard overheard this and, not surprisingly, never forgave her. It struck Rose with some irony, as she glowered at the back of the talkative postman, that Amanda must be one of the few people who would be on her side, but the thought of Amanda as an ally was so dismaying that she refused to pursue the matter.

She really preferred Monica, the next in line. Monica was the bad girl who, like Veronica, had raced through several husbands, and who was now galloping through innumerable

8

young men, all much younger than herself, whom she took into her flat and who stayed the course normally for a couple of months at the most. Mrs. Fielding tried not to consider this aspect of her daughter's life, which was to her incomprehensible, and Mr. Fielding said loudly and angrily that she was an utter disgrace, she needed a good hiding and he was ashamed to be her father. Monica, however, was unabashed, and came home dutifully each time to display the newest young man. Each new boy had longer hair than the last, frillier shirts, a bigger beard and sandals: Mr. Fielding grew more and more apoplectic, and Mrs. Fielding adopted a helpless, resigned expression, while oddly enough the resemblance between herself and her naughty daughter grew more and more marked as time went by.

Perhaps, Rose thought, Mrs. Fielding had been naughty herself when young. It was hard to believe. Monica used to repeat, giggling, how her mother had always counselled her to have a nice game of tennis with her young man if she were feeling you-know-what-I-mean-dear. It must be the Fielding equivalent of a cold bath, and unfortunately Monica had never played tennis in her life.

Rose found Monica, however naughty, warm and genuine, if a trifle silly: there was at least nothing censorious about her. She was a pretty, foolish young woman, wearing the most outrageous clothes that somehow suited her and, if her taste in young men was deplorable, she always enjoyed herself so much that it was hard to be cross with her. At one time she called in frequently at Rose's flat, to tell her all the more lurid details about her newest young man: she drank more whisky than Rose could afford—nowadays there was no whisky, but then Gerard had still been with her and there was a little more money—and she always stayed so late that she had to have a taxi home. However, unfortunately the day came when Rose, taking a long time in coping with a tricky casserole in the kitchen, came out to find Gerald and Monica on the sofa in a close embrace.

"It doesn't mean a thing, darling," said Monica quite unabashed, and indeed it did not, as Rose knew better than most. Gerard was the most tentative of philanderers, indeed,

9

he was scarcely a philanderer at all, and the kisses he had bestowed on Monica were simply to spite his wife, for they were already on the verge of separation. He would never go further than a kiss, and Rose sometimes had horrid suspicions about him that so frightened her that she pushed them to the back of her mind and refused to consider them. None the less it was still intolerable: no woman cares to find her husband kissing another girl, even if the girl were an amiable whore like Monica. The friendship after that declined, and since their last conversation a few months back, Rose suspected without much regret that it had ended for good.

Monica was a great gabber on the phone, especially when she had found herself a new lover, and on this occasion continued in her small, high, breathy voice for what seemed to Rose like an hour. Most of it was concerned with some marvellous man she had just met, who was *fabulously* wealthy, took her out to all the most expensive restaurants and who had promised her a mink coat.

"I expect it will be a rabbit stole, darling," Monica said, "but it's the thought that counts, isn't it, and he's got a marvellous Mercedes, and our dinner last night cost twenty pounds, I know because I peeked at the bill."

And so it went on, and Rose grew monstrously bored, then Tom fell down and began to howl, while Sally, instead of picking him up, went on determinedly with her reading: she had just discovered the ecstasy of books and could not bear to be distracted.

Rose began in some desperation, "Monica—" but the implacably sweet voice continued to tell her that the new man was just marvellous in bed, she had never known anything like it, he was the most sexy thing she had ever met. It was only a few minutes later that Monica, always enmeshed in herself, was forced to realise that her audience was no longer as enthusiastic as she expected. An edge came into the high-pitched voice. Monica could never tolerate lack of appreciation. "Oh, I'm talking too much, I suppose," she said, and Rose was exasperated enough not to answer, so that the pause grew and stayed. Then Monica exclaimed, "I'm so sorry. I didn't mean to bore you."

Rose said, "Monica, I've just got to pick Tom up. You can probably hear him." And indeed she would be deaf not to hear Tom's bawling, which had now reached a crescendo. "The front door bell's gone too. I really must go. I'll ring you back."

"Oh don't bother," snapped Monica. "I know when I'm de trop, I'm sure." And she rang off, plainly setting down the receiver with a bang, while Rose gathered her yelling son into her arms, kissed his bumped knee several times with unnecessary emphasis, and said crossly to Sally, "You really might have put that book down for one second. Didn't you even notice that Tom had fallen down? I was on the phone after all."

"I was too busy," said Sally and went on reading. It was her favourite phrase.

There had been no word from Monica since, though this probably meant she was entangled with her love affairs: she was not a girl to bear a grudge. And now that Gerard was gone, Mrs. Fielding seldom asked Rose in. Rose was learning fast that the unaccompanied woman, especially one who had left her husband, was not the most welcome of guests. Mrs. Fielding made it plain from the very beginning that she had little patience with people who messed up their marriages, especially when the husband was as devastatingly good-looking and charming as Gerard.

"He really is a golden boy," she said several times, and Rose, then frantic with nerves, misery and loneliness, wanted to reply that it was a pity golden boys could not occasionally pay the rent, and a pity too that Mrs. Fielding did not occasionally experience the tempers and quarrels and cruelties, provoked no doubt partly by herself, but largely due to a young man who believed himself to be God, and who could not endure to be thwarted in any way whatsoever.

Now she mostly met the Fieldings on the stairs, except for Lulu, nice, plump Lulu, the youngest daughter, sixteen and still at school. Lulu was christened Louise, and God knows why they gave her such a revolting nickname. She was a friendly, good-natured child, and still invited herself in, sometimes to baby-sit, and sometimes to watch the colour television that Gerard had bought with Rose's money, and which they could not possibly afford. Rose liked Lulu very much, listened to her troubles, gave her advice—how easy it was to advise other people—and heard sympathetically about her boy-friends, her adolescent difficulties with her parents and tiresome friends at school: sometimes they talked a soothing girl-talk about clothes and make-up, for Lulu shared Monica's way-out tastes, if not unfortunately her figure, and went in greatly for eye-shadow and lurid lipsticks. It was pleasant, and Rose could hardly regret either Amanda or Monica. But it all contributed to the sad ostracism and now, with that bloody postman still gabbing away, she turned to speak to Mrs. Parsons, from the floor below her, who was so uninterested in the other tenants that she possibly did not even know that Gerard was now in Chichester with his sister, Claudine.

Mrs. Parsons was the odd one out, partly because of her age, which must have been in the late sixties, partly because of her class which, from the Fieldings' point of view, was well below the Mason-Dixon line, but chiefly because she was a controlled-rent tenant. She had lived in Curran House since the end of the war, paid three pounds a week, and refused to move, despite the efforts of the landlord who was panting to get her out. Curran House was in a good neighbourhood where it would be difficult to harass her in the traditional manner, but he did all he could in a negative fashion, refusing to repair the roof when the rain came in, and ignoring the atrocious plumbing, while Mrs. Parsons, brought up in the East End to stand out sturdily against persecution, religiously paid her rent, plodded in and out for her shopping, and mostly stayed indoors watching the television and, as far as anyone knew, receiving no visitors.

Once, for no known reason, Mrs. Parsons asked Rose and the children in. Her flat was extraordinary, jammed so tight with possessions that one could hardly move. The children were fascinated by it, and Tom was always asking when he could go again, tugging insistently at Rose's arm when they passed the landing. Mrs. Parsons made a powerful, black brew of tea, and talked of her childhood: she had been born in Stepney, with a vast number of brothers and sisters, all now dead, and she held forth on this and her grandchildren for nearly an hour, while Rose watched her, fascinated, and the children, apparently stunned into silence, sat at her feet, chewing the sweets that Mrs. Parsons automatically distributed to them, much as she might have put out bread for the birds.

Rose said at last, seeking her way through Ted (pneumonia), Maria (heart), William (cancer, suffered horrible) and the other defunct members of the family—they must by now have a churchyard to themselves—"Mrs. Parsons, you really must get the landlord to do something about your roof."

She was by nature a practical, kind-hearted girl, and throughout the necrophilic recital, had grown painfully aware of the drip-drip-drip in the adjoining bathroom, where two buckets stood permanently under the broken slats. The rain was now pouring down outside, and really it could not be good for an old lady, even one as tough as Mrs. Parsons, to continue living in such damp. Indeed, she had been quite shocked by the horrid little bathroom, with its stained, broken lavatory: the seat was almost in two. She had seen this, for she had to rush Sally into it: Sally as usual left everything to the last moment, and had to be hurtled to relief, clutching herself, hopping up and down, and crying desperately, "Got to, got to!"

However, Mrs. Parsons was still continuing the death-roll, so it was only at the very end that she managed to slide her remark in.

Mrs. Parsons broke off. She was describing her monthly visit to the cemetery: she always laid flowers on every grave. It must cost her a pretty penny. For one moment Rose feared she had offended her. The old woman surveyed her in a brief silence. It was a craggy, solid, working-class face, heavily lined, a paintable face, thought Rose: death, disaster and the Luftwaffe had none of them made the faintest dent in so indomitable a frame. She could not help wondering about the late Mr. Parsons, who had died from a stroke. He must have been a brave man, but then it was all a long time ago: perhaps the young Mrs. Parsons was softer, more tender.

Then the old lady remarked in her rough, Cockney voice, "He wouldn't do a bloody thing, dear. Real bugger, that's what he is. Real bugger."

Rose saw Tom mouthing the last word. He was a late talker,

and mostly preferred to squeak, bawl and gesture, but he could talk when he chose, he was picking words up fast, and this would obviously now be included in his vocabulary.

She had to agree. She did not like the landlord herself, for she had already remarked a distinct difference in his manner, now that Gerard was no longer there. Gerard, when he chose to turn on the charm, could have softened Rachmann himself, and sometimes, when the rent was overdue, seemed almost to convince the landlord, arriving in militant fashion on their doorstep, that it was a personal favour for him to be owed money by such delightful people. The landlord, come to threaten, stayed to drink whisky, and the rent would be forgotten until a couple of weeks later. But now, with no Gerard, and Rose the woman on her own, it was very different. Only last week she had rung the office to report that the bath water was not running out properly, and his manner had been both evasive and impudent. She was about to say all this when Mrs. Parsons, rising heavily to her feet as if to end the session, said unexpectedly, "You're better off without him, dear."

"What!" Rose, also on her feet, could not believe her ears. Mrs. Parsons must surely still be talking about the landlord, but really, it made no sense, and she couldn't possibly mean what it sounded like—.

"He's a bugger too," said Mrs. Parsons, handing Sally some more boiled sweets, apparently as a farewell gift. Obviously, nobody bothered about children's teeth in Mrs. Parsons's young days. Rose, determinedly modern, cut out almost all sweets and sugar. It was one of the many causes of quarrels between herself and Gerard, who brought back toffees and chocolates in his pockets, and used to tease the children into trying to get them out. However, this was no moment to discuss tooth decay, and she hesitated, not sure whether to leave or to pursue this extraordinary turn of conversation. She had always been so sure that Mrs. Parsons never noticed what was going on outside: the outer walls were thick, and any quarrelling sounds could hardly penetrate, especially as her television was on all day and full blast.

Mrs. Parsons looked down into the young face below hers. Rose was small, and she was a big woman. Whether or not she saw the pain and strain revealed there was impossible to say, for her own weather-beaten face showed no kind of emotion. She only said, opening the door, "That sort's no good to any woman. Don't you fret, Mrs. Menusier. There's plenty more where he comes from, and a great deal better. You're a nice looking girl. You won't have no difficulty in getting yourself another man."

And with this she shut the door behind her, leaving Rose and the children standing on the landing. They heard the television come on. Mrs. Parsons had obviously bought herself a good set, for there was hardly any pause at all.

It is always disturbing to be observed, especially by a person hitherto regarded as unimportant. Rose found herself unnecessarily upset. It did not matter a damn what Mrs. Parsons saw or thought, and at least she appeared to be on her side, which made a change, but she realised at this moment what she should have realised long ago, that everyone in the flats knew all about her affairs, had always known. At this point she had never believed that the general opinion was so against her. It astonished and dismayed her, it was as if she led some grossly immoral life, bringing in lovers like Monica, neglecting and ill-treating her children. She began to see that if she had spread her woes around, she might be receiving more sympathy. But then she had been too distressed and humiliated to do so: the only person who occasionally received her confidences was Veronica, to whom she once or twice turned, with a propitiatory bottle of wine. And Veronica, with her three rotten marriages, her drinking and her bitterness, did not really care, only listened with her mouth curled cynically down, and doubtless related the incoherent story to her own misadventures. The only comfort was that she was unlikely to repeat anything, for she had no friends, and perhaps was not really interested, simply listened because there was nothing better to do.

Rose had met Veronica nearly seven years back, on a train from Marseilles to Paris. She was running away from her second marriage, and Rose was running into her first. She was never sure how much she liked Veronica, but in those days when she was younger and drank less heavily, she could be an amusing, unshockable and stimulating companion. One could hardly, even then, call her a friend. Now she was nearly always drunk and not amusing at all: from time to time she had to be taken into a nursing home when the alcoholic bouts became almost insanity. She was probably a wealthy woman, but all her money went on whisky, and she then tried to borrow money from Rose that she could not possibly afford to lend, and when refused, fell into a silent huff, sometimes not speaking to her for weeks on end.

Her final marriage—surely it must be final, she must be nearly fifty, and she had lost all her looks—was a disaster, but at least a titled disaster, for she married a small, negligible peer who endured her for two and a half months, then walked out, never to be seen again. He did however pay her rent regularly, on the basis that she left him strictly alone. Rose remembered Veronica telling her about the wedding: inconsistently she was a violent snob, and Gerard had found it very funny when she remarked idly, "My new name will be Matford. Actually, I shall be Lady Matford. So amusing, don't you think?"

But then Gerard was a snob too.

Two months later, with the marriage already on the rocks, she asked Rose in her grandest manner to lend her fifteen thousand pounds. As this to Rose was equivalent to the National Debt, she could only greet the request—it was almost a command—with a stunned silence.

"Well, you can always borrow it, can't you?" Veronica snapped.

"No, I certainly can't," said Rose flatly. Then, her voice rising in exasperation, "Are you completely crazy? Where on earth do you think I could raise such a sum? Gerard's had no work for months, we're already up to our ears in debt, Sally will be going to school, and I don't know how we'll even pay the rent. I haven't got fifteen thousand pence, much less pounds. Oh Veronica, don't be so silly. You must know how things are. What do you want it for?"

"That," said Veronica in a clear, harsh voice, "is my business." It was the tone of the aristocrat putting the serf in his place, it held all the arrogance in the world. It also held a great deal of whisky, but then this was customary, she was never entirely sober. She turned her fine eyes on Rose, the eyes that like her voice revealed a great past beauty. They were of a light, clear grey, with long, curling, black lashes: the whites were bloodshot now, but they were still startling. She added in a condescending manner, explaining the obvious to a palpable idiot, "The bank would of course lend it to you."

Rose said wearily—there had already been several strained interviews with the manager, where for once Gerard's charm had not worked at all—"The bank would certainly not. I'm sorry, Veronica. It's quite out of the question. In fact," she added almost hysterically, "it's plain bloody ridiculous." And seeing that Veronica, her face now purple-red with temper, was preparing to argue it out with her, she turned away into her own flat across the landing.

Veronica shouted after her in a voice that must have carried across the street, "You're a fucking awful friend. I can't think why I ever bothered with you. Next time you want advice for free, you can bloody go somewhere else." And then, as Rose, now shaking and on the verge of tears, closed her door, the razor voice shrilled after her, "You bitch! You mean, lousy bitch! No wonder you can't keep your husband—"

This came well from Veronica, but Rose was too shattered to say a word, only went into her room and sat crying on the bed, for violence always annihilated her. However, Tom needed changing, and Sally was eyeing her tears with a frightened expression, so she managed to pull herself together, even gave Gerard a semi-humorous, if censored, version of what had happened when he came in.

Gerard for once was sympathetic: a mean man himself he resented being dunned. He threatened to bang on Veronica's door and, in his own phrase, beat her up. He would have borrowed from her without the least compunction, but Rose had never known him lend anything to anyone, though he always refused in the most delightful manner.

There was naturally a great neighbouring silence after this, and Rose and Veronica passed each other on the stairs without speaking: this upset Rose who did not bear grudges, but there was no point in trying to make it up with someone who swept past you with a look of contemptuous disgust. Now of course

Veronica was talking to her again. The friendship had never quite recovered, but then it had never been much of a friendship at the best. Rose knew at that moment that she did not like her very much, that she never had really liked her, only she was sorry for her: Veronica between bouts was an oddly helpless and vulnerable person, desperately in need of the love and the help she kicked aside.

She saw to her relief that the postman was now at last making his way to Curran House. She said, "Thank goodness," and gave a faint smile to little Mrs. Photiades, who merely responded with her own kind of smile, which was blank and without meaning. Rose thought she could not be more than twenty. She and her husband never attempted to mix with the other tenants. Gerard once remarked that they were flitters, and certainly since their arrival in England, just under a year ago—Andreas was getting experience in an advertising firm—they seemed to have changed flats three times. There were always bills in their pigeon-hole: perhaps Nina was waiting for the next batch.

The postman looked a little surprised at the reception committee, but doled the letters out. There was nothing for Veronica or Mrs. Parsons, both of whom immediately went upstairs. There was a great sheaf for Mrs. Fielding, one obviously from Amanda, for she beamed triumphantly, remarking, "They're good children, you know. They always keep in touch. There's nothing like a family, really."

Rose did not answer this incontrovertible statement, but took her own three letters. Two were bills, and the third was in Gerard's unmistakable flamboyant handwriting. The sight of this made her start to shake: she saw her own disgracefully trembling hand and thought, This is absurd, I'm far too nervous, I really ought to go to the doctor—

She turned to go upstairs, then caught sight of Dr. Macek's face. She had forgotten about Dr. Macek, who had been standing there all this time, a little back from the others. She thought that one tended to forget Dr. Macek, and at the same time was possessed of the curious idea that of all the people in this gathering they were the two misfits, whom the others did not like. Mrs. Parsons, for all she was defiantly working-class among the bourgeoisie, plainly did not care what anyone thought of her: this was well expressed in the ramrod back as she turned the corner of the staircase. The other tenants might believe they despised this obstinate old woman: she certainly despised them. Veronica went her own way, caring so little about the world around her that it hardly existed, while the little Greek couple had no doubt their own circle of friends where they could make fun of the silly English around them, and toast the colonels with every glass of retsina. As for Mrs. Fielding, still gloating over her letter and surveying proudly the photos enclosed, she would fit in with almost every gathering, provided there were babies to tickle, children to play with, parents with whom to exchange family anecdotes.

But Dr. Macek, standing there, tall, thin, very still, staring down at the letter in his hand, was different. Rose thought for one second that a look of something like fear crossed his face. The next second she was sure she was mistaken, for he was as impassive as ever. He was a refugee from some central European country—she believed it was Czechoslovakia—but he had established himself here, he was a Harley Street specialist, he had probably taken British nationality, he could not have many worries. Perhaps he was crossed in love, though it was difficult to imagine him in love at all, much less crossed. He was not a bad-looking man in his own way, with the high cheekbones and the dark, rigidly waving hair receding over a forehead like a precipice, but there seemed to be no warmth in him, and Rose, whose mind wandered perpetually over things that did not concern her, wondered what he was like with children who, someone, probably Mrs. Fielding, had informed her, comprised his patients. She thought he must frighten them, and saw at this moment that Tom, who was bored and making an unsteady way up the stairs with a great display of bottom, brushed against him and caught at his jacket to balance himself.

Dr. Macek instantly looked down at him, and then to her amazement, Tom, who on the whole did not care much for anyone, put on what she always called his poor-Tom's-a-cold act, buried his head against Dr. Macek's leg, peeped up out of one eye and bestowed on him a beaming smile.

Dr. Macek plainly did not frighten children, and the answering smile altered his face in an extraordinary manner.

Rose was fascinated enough to stare, then grew aware that Mrs. Fielding had removed her gaze from her letters and was looking straight at her. In that instant Rose read her thoughts as clearly as if she had spoken them. Her mouth was a little open, her eyes were bright, she was gazing at Rose almost in fascinated disgust: the unspoken words were, So you've driven your own man out, and now you're making eyes at another one, you're obviously mad for anything in trousers —

It was so plain that Rose could hear the words. She flushed scarlet and opened her mouth to answer, then came to her senses and began to follow Tom and Dr. Macek up the stairs, while Mrs. Fielding, behind her, backed into her first-floor flat.

Then suddenly resolved to prove how right Mrs. Fielding was, she looked up at the doctor and smiled. "Hallo, Dr. Macek," she said, pronouncing the name English-style. "My Tom seems to have taken a fancy to you. You should feel honoured. He doesn't care for people much."

He looked down at her, a few steps above. It was hard to believe that he had ever smiled. He only said, "The name is pronounced 'Mahtzek'. But I am delighted I meet with your little son's approval."

Rose, disconcerted and furious, thought, Bugger you! She answered coldly, "I'll remember that. I'm so sorry. My name is always mispronounced too. Everyone calls me Mrs. Menuseer. It sounds like some disgusting tropical disease."

And running up the stairs to pass him — Tom was now on the next landing and looking wistfully at Mrs. Parsons's door — she was pleased to see that Dr. Macek too looked taken aback. Only he seemed to be one who must have the last word, for the tall figure paused, and the deep voice with its foreign intonation — he spoke excellent if stilted English — came down to her. He lived on the top floor, directly above her. He was a very quiet man who never seemed to entertain. She never heard a sound from him except once when she supposed he was having a sleepless night; she heard his footsteps pacing to and fro the whole night through. It was very disturbing: at one point she had the crazy notion that she ought to go up to him and offer him a cup of tea. But of course she did not, and so far it had not happened again.

Dr. Macek said, "My own name is not much better, Mrs. Menusier." He pronounced it impeccably, except for the rolling Slav "r". "It means in your language 'tom-cat'."

And with this he was gone. Rose, beginning, despite herself, to laugh, heard him close his door.

A more unsuitable name she could not imagine. Now if it had been Gerard—But whatever Dr. Macek was—she must remember to pronounce his name properly in future—he was certainly no tom-cat. It was hard to imagine his having a woman at all. Or perhaps that was a little unfair—yet it seemed to her that there was something aseptic and asexual about him, though of course she did not know him at all: they met on the stairs only occasionally and had never exchanged more than routine greetings.

She was so busy thinking about this and steering Tom up the last of the stairs, for there were fifty-three of them, and it was something of a labour for his short legs, that she almost forgot about Gerard's letter, still clutched unopened in her hand.

But Sally must have extra-sensory powers, or else something in her mother's face betrayed her. Sally was at home today, with one of her nervous stomach-aches that seemed to arrive whenever she did not want to do something. She put down the book she had been reading, and said instantly, "Has Daddy written to us?"

"Yes, darling, he has. I'll tell you about it in a minute. I haven't read it myself yet." And Rose stifled an exasperated sigh as she spoke, and went into the kitchen, while Tom began to stamp round the flat in the peculiarly busy fashion of his age, his brow furrowed in concentration, and his eyes alert for anything to eat. Soon he would begin to shut doors he could not open: Gerard in their happier days had once declared that Tom's idea of heaven was a small, confined space with seven open doors on a spring: as fast as they were shut, they would open again, and so ad infinitum.

Sally called out again, "Mummy, where's the letter? Isn't there one for me too?"

21

"I expect there is. Just a moment—" But Rose stayed there, standing by the sink, butter and cheese in her hand, ready to go into the fridge. Tom scarcely appeared to notice his father's absence, and often greeted him now as a stranger, running to hide his head against Rose's knee. But then he was little more than two, and Sally, now five and a quarter, had always been Gerard's favourite, he said he infinitely preferred little girls. She missed him badly, as Rose had to recognise, and Gerard still wrote persistently, "Let me have Sally, and I'll divorce you, I'll do anything you want. You can keep Tom, but let me have Sally. My sister will look after her, you know that, and you know too she loves me, she isn't happy without me." And again, always, always, "Let me have my Sally."

There was as yet no real talk of divorce. Gerard, though he no longer lived with her, and at times seemed to hate her, refused to consider the matter, and Rose felt too depleted and too anxious to pursue it, though she saw plainly that this was an absurd life for both of them, they were both after all quite young, and what was the point of a marriage that was not a marriage at all? At the moment they had what theoretically was a civilised arrangement: they lived apart, but Gerard paid the rent, came up whenever he could to see the children, and Rose went down once a month to the small village outside Chichester where he lived with his sister.

Only the rent was never paid until she had asked him for the money half a dozen times, his visits upset her and Sally for days afterwards, and the work she managed to get at home was never enough to pay the bills. It always meant asking Diana for help again, and that was becoming undignified and intolerable.

"I must go to the solicitor," said Rose aloud, as she had said a hundred times before, and the very thought of it was like a leaden weight in her belly, for she was not convinced that she had sufficient grounds for divorce. Gerard after all would come back, given half a chance, and though his behaviour was to her utterly unreasonable, she did not see how she could prove he was intolerable to live with.

Yet Sally was becoming more and more difficult, rude and

insolent to her mother, disobedient, having tantrums, and always having these stomach pains, which the doctor said were purely psychosomatic, as if that helped in any way at all. Sometimes Rose, who loved her dearly, thought she should give in and send Sally down to Chichester. It would be like tearing off a limb, it would be a kind of death: to meet Sally always as a stranger would be unbearable, never mind the tantrums, the rudeness, the deliberate insolence. And she thought of Claudine, Gerard's sister. Claudine had never liked her from the beginning. The pair of them were half-French, with an English mother, but while Gerard had always spent most of his time in England, Claudine until recently had lived in Paris and spoke English with a strong accent. To Rose she was cold and, despite her good looks, an old maid: she would never give Sally the warmth and fun and tenderness she so desperately needed. So once again it was, No, no, no, and never mind the constant pressure put upon her. Besides, Gerard would not make a good father, he was too mean, too turned in on himself, his beauty, his talent, the magnificence that was Gerard Menusier. He had always been a mean man, mean in money, mean in emotion: he wanted a pretty little girl he could cosset and cuddle and dress charmingly, but he would never begin to understand her, as he had never begun to understand Rose.

And thinking this, with a sickness in her stomach, and the feeling that was becoming habitual to her, that she could not cope, that her brain would burst with the conflict, Rose opened the letter.

Sally called out to her again, and Tom was making the urgent sounds that indicated that a shut door would not open on its own, but Rose paid no attention, only read the dramatic scrawl in front of her.

It was typical of Gerard that the first words informed her that he was on the box this evening. It was a repeat of course, and only a small part at that, it was something that Rose had already seen, but she knew that she had to turn it on. She and Sally would watch together, the little girl passionately intent: tomorrow she would be more difficult than ever, and the stomach-ache would perhaps be so bad that Rose would have

23

to send for the doctor, knowing perfectly well that there was nothing he could do.

"It was quite a challenge," Gerard had said at the time.

Actors always said a wretched part was a challenge. It was not a challenge at all. But then he had never really been able to act, only his looks—looks that Sally had inherited—were flamboyant enough to persuade innocent producers that there must be some talent behind the beautiful façade. There was the magnificent, leonine tawny hair, the bright speedwell-blue eyes, all straight out of a romantic novel, and in addition the really superb profile, so photogenic that at the beginning he was offered parts completely beyond his scope. He was in looks the complete film idol, plus beautiful body and soft, caressing voice: unfortunately, in these days of dramatic competition, a little ability was required as well, and that he did not possess.

Perhaps this too was that strange, deep-rooted meanness that Rose was unaware of until they married. Gerard was mean, even in his acting, incapable of surrendering to a part, of displaying genuine emotion. The television especially betrayed him at once. Gerard making love on the screen was ridiculous, and in real life, for all he professed an adoration of women, never, as far as Rose knew, went beyond the kissing: she was certain that he had never been unfaithful, and it was only, much later on, that she realised that her own sex life with him was utterly disastrous. Perhaps love would commit him to sincerity, and sincerity was something he did not seem to have. She often wondered why he had married her, and now believed that, like Peter Pan, he longed to show that he was a real, grown-up man who could have a wife and children, like everybody else.

She looked again at the letter. Inside was a small note for Sally. There was always a small note for Sally. Rose had a dreadful urge to open it and read it, and an even worse compulsion to tear it up. There was SALLY written on the outside, in capitals, and it would be typed so that it could be read easily. She called out, "Sal! There's a letter for you from Daddy."

Sally came running, her face flushed with joy and excitement.

24

If there had really been a stomach-ache, it was now gone. She really was, even allowing for a mother's partiality, a most lovely little girl, and incredibly like Gerard, except in temperament: the world would hurt Sally, Sally would always care to excess.

She grabbed the note without a thank you, shot her mother a strangely defiant look, then, like a dog with a bone, retreated to her own room. Rose heard the door slammed, tightened her lips and went on reading the letter.

"Why the hell are you so obstinate?" Gerard wrote. "Sally doesn't like you. She's always been her Daddy's girl. Let me have her. You can keep Tom. If you agree, I'll do anything you want, I swear I won't bother you again. You know she'll be well looked after. Claudine adores her, and Sally loves her so much that when she's down here, she won't let her out of her sight."

Such nonsense—you're hamming it again, boy.

"I won't give up, Rose. You're a fool not to listen to me. I want my little daughter, and I'm going to have her, if I don't I'll make life such hell for you, you'll wish you'd never been born." And finally, after this outburst, which was like a gout of spittle in the face, "We are expecting you down tomorrow as usual. Claudine is making that creamed chicken that Sally likes so much. We are having Trudy to lunch as well, she is so fond of Sally, and afterwards we are meeting some friends from the theatre . . ."

Rose folded the letter very carefully, and picked up the gas poker so as to burn it to ashes. But for some reason she did not do so, only, with a guilty look on her face as if she felt she were doing wrong, she put the letter at the back of the cutlery drawer. Then, quite calmly, as if nothing had happened, she came into the sitting-room to open the door for Tom, who was scowling at it and patting it. She gave him a kiss, which he received with his murderer's look. She told Mrs. Fielding once that Tom on the door-prowl always made her think of Crippen, muttering to himself, Where the hell shall I put Belle? Mrs. Fielding had not found this at all amusing: it probably confirmed her view that Rose was a poor sort of mother. She said, "Now, Tom, don't shut that door again because I

25

shall be busy in the kitchen and I won't have time to open it."

Then she switched on the television, though there was nothing on but a lesson in Hindustani; he was too young to watch for more than a minute, but he enjoyed the colours, and sometimes sat there, gazing fixedly at a picture he could not possibly understand.

The ruling passion, however, was stronger than television. She heard the sitting-room door shut almost before she reached the kitchen. She said aloud, "Okay, boy. This time you've had it," and to harden her heart against the imploring little squeaks that Tom was already mouthing as he stroked the heartless door with a coaxing hand, shut her own door, and sat down by the kitchen table, lighting herself a cigarette, and preparing to make the dinner: perhaps she could then get on with the review books that still had to be done.

But she did nothing except lay out the food: she sat there with potatoes on the table before her, some lamb chops and a lettuce which had fallen to the floor and which she left there by her foot.

She thought grimly of tomorrow's visit. It would be at the best boring, at the worst disastrous. She would talk with Claudine who cordially detested her. Gerard might take the children for a walk, as he usually did on his London visits. They would all come back for tea, Tom rather over-tired, and Sally flushed and exalted, at desperate high-doh, hardly speaking to her mother, following Gerard with adoring eyes everywhere. On the way home she would burst into frantic tears, and probably arrive with a temperature: she would not be able to eat her supper, and might even be sick. The day would be full of tension, with Gerard secretly gibing at her in the way that only he knew how, and at the same time making a pretence of loving her, putting his arm round her shoulders, complimenting her on the non-existent hair-do, turning everything he said to her into a covert insult. Claudine would be frigidly polite, and as for Trudy, the official imitation girl-friend of the day, she was blonde and plump and German, with not a brain in her head, and openly jealous of the intruder.

And then there would be the heart-to-heart, with the rent

money as the bomb enclosed, with the two girls dismissed to the kitchen so that husband and wife could be together.

"Oh God, oh God!" said Rose aloud, lighting a fresh cigarette from the stub of the old one. She really must give up smoking, she simply could not afford it. She could hear in her head that relentless voice saying all the things he put into his letters, and many more beside.

You're not looking at all well, you know. I suppose those eyes are worrying you again. It's obviously too much for you having the two kids with you all day, and I know how difficult Sally can be, I really do, but it's not my fault, Rose, the child just adores me, little girls always do prefer their father, besides, there's always some psychological difficulty between mother and daughter—

And then viciously, at the end, *Give me Sally, and then you can have your bloody divorce. If you don't, you'll be sorry. You'll probably go blind anyway, then you won't be able to look after either of them.*

Rose rubbed at her eyes, partly because the weak, angry tears were moistening them, but partly too because of the headache that was once again threatening her. She was sure there was nothing really wrong, she probably just needed glasses. But it was true that the headaches were growing more and more frequent, and her eyes, as Gerard had frequently pointed out, were large and therefore more prone to infection. Sometimes in moments of panic it seemed to her as if her vision were already blurring, then she would frantically rub them, making them worse. The only sensible thing to do was to go to an oculist, but she was becoming so frightened that she dared not do so.

She thought again, in a sudden craven weakness, Oh I ought to let Sally go to him, he's quite right, she's not happy with me. Have I the right to deprive her of the father she really loves? She'll grow up all psychologically twisted, and it will be my fault.

And she knew as always, deep within her, that she could not do this, any more than she could ever again set up house with Gerard. The very thought of his presence beside her, those mocking eyes that seemed to read her every weakness, the savage, semi-humorous little remarks that he dropped like poisoned darts, the constant tension that perhaps emanated

27

from both of them, made her sick and shivering, almost in terror.

Then she stood up, put everything neatly away, washed the dropped lettuce and set about peeling potatoes. Perhaps she could go out one evening, just to get away from this enclosed atmosphere. She could arrange for a baby-sitter or ask Lulu to come and spend an evening in front of the colour television. The children both loved her, for she possessed a warm simplicity that enabled her to understand them; she in no way shared her mother's hostility against Rose. She had never really known Gerard, who had in any case no time for lumpy schoolgirls, and she probably had heard little of the situation, for Mrs. Fielding still regarded her as a child, and would probably prefer not to discuss such sordid matters as errant wives in front of her.

Besides, she loved Rose. Rose knew that. She had said once, after a long account of some boy-friend who had let her down, "You are the only person I can really talk to. You never make fun of me. When you're my age," said Lulu, in this burst of confidence, "people never take you seriously. You always do." And Rose had listened to the long, sad little story and dried the angry, self-pitying tears: Lulu had never forgotten. "If you ever want any help, Rose," she said afterwards, "you can always depend on me. I don't care what it is. I'll do anything."

Rose could not think how Lulu could possibly help her, but she was very touched, and she thought that in any case she would invite the child round soon, to see one of the thrillers she so adored: she was a fanatical addict of Sherlock Holmes, Peter Wimsey and Maigret, and once confided in her friend that when she was older, she would like to be a private detective. Rose never even smiled, which was another big mark in her favour.

However, the thought of ringing friends up or booking theatre seats was too much effort, even if she could have afforded it. She came back into the sitting-room to open the door at last for Tom, who was gazing at it as if he would mesmerise it, and saw that Sally, her eyes like stars, still clutched her father's note in her hands.

She whispered, so excited that she spoke without her usual hostility, "Oh Mummy, Daddy's on the box tonight. Can I stay up and watch, please, please?"

On the box—the theatre child. "Of course," said Rose, and was instantly affronted by her own eagerness: it was as if she were trying to placate this child of hers who was only five years old. The play did not start till eight-fifteen, it was much too late for Sally when they were going to Fishbourne next day, but she knew that she could not possibly have said no, and so they would sit together, watching Gerard's ten minutes or so, in which he played extremely badly a comic Frenchman in a boarding-house, who waved his arms about and employed a monstrous accent that no decent Frenchman would be seen dead with. Gerard was completely bi-lingual, with a natural talent for languages: it was even more alarming that he should accept such a part.

Then, as Sally, enchanted, ran back to her book, Rose felt she could no longer bear it at all, any of it: defeat crashed down on her so that she once more retreated to the kitchen, and sat there in a huddle, as sorry for herself as even Gerard could have wished, only to be roused from her self-pity by an agitated Tom, who had shut every door around him, so that he was completely closed in, by doors that would not open, a heartless mother shut away from him, and a brutal sister who completely ignored his squeaks for help.

Rose heard his frustrated howls of, "Open, open!" for squeaks were no longer sufficient, and saw immediately what had happened. She burst out laughing, and the depression vanished. She opened the kitchen door, pulled the now affronted Tom inside, and popped a piece of carrot into his mouth, now squared for one grand, final bawl.

"You're a bloody, damned nuisance, little boy," she told him, as he chewed the carrot and scowled at her. "You and your doors—one day you'll shut one too often, and then you'll be locked in for ever and ever. The trouble really is," she went on, now addressing his back, for he was already wandering off in a determined manner to shut more doors, the back rigid with the weighty responsibility of it all, "that doors have been shut on me too, and I don't know how to open them. It's all right for you, buster," she said, though Tom had now disappeared, making his unerring way towards the door at the far end, "but there's no one to come to my rescue. It would be agreeable," said Rose, continuing her monologue, which now sounded to her quite insane, "if there were someone to help me, someone I really could talk to, instead of Veronica, who's half smashed most of the time, and married friends who all think I've got designs on their horrid husbands, who call me, poor old Rose, while secretly thinking I'm an incompetent ninny not to be able to hold such a handsome man."

And this made her feel better, for no reason at all: there must be thousands of women in her situation, even if their marriage were not so frightful as hers, young women who were the odd ones out at parties, whom all good wives regarded with suspicion, and whom the unmarried sneered at for their incompetence.

"Bugger them!" said Rose cheerfully, and started her cooking. Tom, who had so far left the kitchen door open, wandered back to bestow upon her a small, cool, prim kiss, and for a while the blackness receded: even Gerard's threats seemed unimportant.

2

THE OTHER TENANTS OF Curran House went about their business during the day, and Mrs. Fielding that evening settled down with her husband and Lulu to watch Gerard in 'Breakfast and Bed', a comedy series about a sexy landlady and the various people who rented her rooms. It had been running for a long time, the critics unanimously panned it as stupid, vulgar and corny, Mrs. Whitehouse complained about it, and viewers adored it. It was a series of a quite remarkable imbecility, with not the faintest resemblance to real life: this particular episode, in which Gerard briefly appeared as the new French lodger, was neither better nor worse than any of the others, indeed, worse it could hardly be.

Mrs. Fielding was not a stupid woman, only one enclosed in her own small world, and she watched Gerard's antics a little dubiously. Lulu, who had more highbrow tastes, wrinkled up her nose and said, "He's absolutely lousy, isn't he?"

"I don't think it's his sort of part," said her mother a little sadly, for the sight of Gerard with an absurd moustache, crying out, "Mon Dieu!" at frequent intervals, and making jokes about knickers, was not edifying. Len—poor-Len with a hyphen, as Rose called him—actually laughed twice, but then he was a simple man and an easy laugher, only violent on the subject of politics: he had had an exhausting day and watched the television simply for relaxation. Halfway through he fell asleep, and Mrs. Fielding smiled benignly at him, and turned the sound down a little.

31

"I don't think anything's his sort of part," said Lulu. "I just don't think he can act."

"Of course he can act," said Mrs. Fielding. "He's so terribly good-looking." And she repeated her pet phrase, "He really is a golden boy."

"I think he's a bit queer," said Lulu, who was a far more intelligent girl than most people gave her credit for being. She was a little too fat, made up her face badly, and wore her hair in a kind of Afro-tangle, but beneath the confusion there was a perfectly sound brain, and her bespectacled eyes did not miss much, especially when she was interested. Besides, she had never forgiven Gerard for making fun of her: he had gibed at her for her overweight, and exclaimed, "Oh, oh!" in mock-admiration when he saw her with some new, exotic make-up. Lulu had been his enemy ever since.

Mrs. Fielding said shortly, "You have no right to say that. I don't like you saying such things. Besides, you know nothing about it."

"Of course I do. I'm not in the kindergarten. I just don't think he's a nice man. And he's horrid to Rose. He really is, Mum. I've heard him say the most dreadful things. She's frightened of him. I think he's a beastly sort of person. The sooner she divorces him the better."

"Now, listen here, young lady," said her mother. She was careful not to speak too harshly, for one must never snub the young, but these unprovoked remarks astonished and displeased her. However, she did not allude to the remark about being queer: it was not at all nice, and where young girls learned these things, she did not know: she thought it best to ignore it. She said with great seriousness, for she meant every word of it, "Marriage is a very precious thing, Lulu. Not that any marriage is perfect—" She glanced at her sleeping husband, whose mouth had fallen open and who was snoring lightly. She sighed then laughed. "We've had our ups and downs too, you know. There have been times—when I was much younger, of course—when I wondered if I'd done the right thing, and there have even been moments when I've been attracted by someone else. I bet that surprises you!"

"Not really," said Lulu. She jumped up and switched the

television off. She gave her mother a teasing, affectionate smile. "You're not such a bad-looker. You could knock spots off some girls I know."

"Now really!" But Mrs. Fielding was delighted, and even permitted herself a faint giggle: she had been a pretty girl, just like Monica — not in disposition, of course—and it was true enough, she still provoked the occasional whistle in the street.

"Well, it's true," said her daughter, "and anyway I don't see what all these confessions have to do with it. I think Gerard's a pig, that's all."

"Lulu!"

"Well, he is. I've seen him in action. You're forgetting how many times I used to baby-sit for them. There's nothing wrong with my hearing, and you'd be surprised at some of the things that were said when they thought I wasn't listening."

"You shouldn't have been listening," said Mrs. Fielding sternly. "I daresay there have been difficulties. There are in every marriage. He's such a handsome man, and Rose really is a plain little thing."

"She's nothing of the kind," cried Lulu. "She's a marvellous person. She's got gorgeous eyes and lovely hair. I wish I had hair like that. If she doesn't dress very well, it's because he never gives her any money."

"You've no right to say these things. You don't know anything about it. She's got plenty of work, hasn't she? Her reviews and serials and things. And I'll tell you this, my girl. A woman should stand by her man—"

"Oh Mum, you sound like the magazines!"

"Well, I'm glad they write so much sense. Of course she should. I don't suppose it's easy for Gerard either. The theatrical profession is a hard one, and there's a terrible amount of competition. I expect he hasn't earned much lately. I'm sure he's a good husband to her, when she lets him, and he's always been faithful, which is more than you can say for some."

Lulu turned up her eyes, which created an odd effect beneath the round glasses in her round face.

"Yes, he has. I know that, and you needn't ask me how I know it, because I won't tell you. But he has, and he's a good father too, absolutely devoted to Sally. I have no patience," said Mrs. Fielding with some heat, "with women who're always grumbling, and I don't think much of them either when they sacrifice their own children, just out of sheer selfishness. That little girl is pining to death for her daddy, and I honestly think Rose just doesn't care, she's so full of her own grievances, she probably doesn't even notice. Moping about the place all day, when he's just dying to come back to her, and making eyes at other men too—"

"Who? Rose or Gerard?"

"Louise," said Mrs. Fielding, "I will not have you talk like that. Please don't let me have to speak to you again."

"Okay, okay," said Lulu not very penitently. "But you might tell me what other men, Mum. Good on her, that's what I say. Who is it? Oh go on. You can't leave it like that."

"I am not telling you, and that's flat. And I wish you wouldn't use that horrid phrase. It's so common. But I'll tell you one thing, and then you'd better go to bed, because it's late, and you know what you're like in the mornings—"

"Damn it all," said Lulu sulkily, suddenly looking like a child again, "I'm sixteen."

Mrs. Fielding ignored this, which was indeed repeated almost every night. She said, "I think—it's terribly sad, really—I think Rose is going a little off her head. I don't think her behaviour is at all normal. I've noticed this for some time, and so has your father. No, I'm not going into details. But I've done a lot of social work, you know, and I can recognise the signs. I think myself the sooner Gerard gets his hands on those poor children, the better. I don't think she's fit to look after them. I'm not excusing her behaviour, but I honestly believe she's a very sick girl."

"I suppose Gerard's told you all that," said Lulu in a small, cold voice.

Mrs. Fielding suddenly flushed scarlet. But she chose to ignore this, so obviously that Lulu knew at once it was true. She said, "Never mind that. It's none of your business. But I'd rather you didn't baby-sit for her any more, Lulu. I mean that. I don't think it's a healthy atmosphere, and I don't want you mixed up in it. And now," she added in her cheery mother's tone, "bed for you, my girl, and don't you go on

34

reading till the small hours, you'll just ruin your eyes. What about a nice hot drink? Some milk or a cup of tea—I'd rather fancy a cuppa, myself, and you can take yours to bed with you."

"I'll put the kettle on," said Lulu with unusual meekness. The short-sighted eyes, round behind the strong glasses, fixed themselves on her mother's face for a moment, then she went into the kitchen.

But she did not immediately light the gas, though she filled the kettle. She stood by the sink, gazing out of the darkened window, a plain, bulky girl, with the frizzy hair flopping over her face. Mrs. Fielding completely under-estimated her. Those myopic eyes were very observant. They noticed for instance that Amanda seldom came to visit her mother unless she wanted something, that Monica, with whom she had always got on well, was by no means the self-confident young woman she appeared to be, that she was sometimes frightened, that she longed desperately for a more permanent love. It had not escaped Lulu's attention that Gerard, when he came up to see the children, always stopped for a brief gossip in their flat, and usually with a bunch of flowers in his hand, flowers that were not for Rose. Usually she was at school when he came, but one day she had been in bed with flu, and heard the unmistakable voice on the landing. It was only too obvious where Mother, who really was awfully silly sometimes, got her information. A faint flush came into Lulu's plump cheek, for she was by nature both kind and protective, and she was deeply sorry for Rose whom once or twice she had seen in tears. Rose was not going off her head, Rose was simply worried half to death, what with her horrid marriage, the children and lack of money. Rose was a nice, kind person, and Lulu never forgot how sympathetically she had listened to her troubles, treating her as if she were an adult, giving her sensible, understanding advice. Rose did not know how stalwart an ally she had in this schoolgirl who splashed make-up on until she looked like a clown, who had pashes on pop-stars, and was convinced that one day she would be a private detective. Lulu was now determined to do Gerard down to the best of her ability, Rose was not nuts at all, and Gerard was a stinking bastard.

"And I'll baby-sit just when I want to," said Lulu aloud.

35

Then she lit the **gas,** lifted down the teapot, and waited for the kettle to boil.

Mrs. Parsons spent her evening in front of the television as usual. She kept it on most of the day. She watched Gerard in his play. He neither shocked nor disgusted her, for she accepted this as she accepted everything else, nor did it strike her that he was grossly over-acting. She simply thought he was a rotten, cheap creature, acting was not a real man's job anyway, and she wondered without much interest why a nice young lady like that Mrs. Menusier had fallen for such a lousy fellow. Halfway through she switched on to the other channel where 'The Good Old Days' was on, and this she enjoyed, joining in the choruses, and thinking it was a pity they couldn't write songs like that nowadays.

Opposite, the Photiades ate an exotic meal, for Nina was a good cook, and all the food they ate was on tick, for by now in this district alone they owed several hundred pounds, having long ago discovered the value of an account at one of the big stores. This did not worry them at all. They had lived this way throughout the two years of their married life. Soon Andreas would have finished his advertising course, and they would then go back to Athens, where angry landlords and debt-collectors could not touch them. It never struck them that the police might keep a record of their debts, but then they were unlikely to return to this dull, damp country where people presumed to speak against their own government, and where there were communists everywhere. Even Gerard, who found Nina a beautiful girl, with what he called her expressionless Greek face, and who had invited the young couple in one evening, was probably dangerous: in an effort to defrost them as they sat awkwardly side by side on the settee, hardly speaking and looking furtively at each other, he had put on the Theodorakis record of 'Zorba the Greek'.

"Marvellous stuff," he said in the very English accent he sometimes affected, beamed at Nina and wondered why the devil the girl couldn't unbend a little, instead of sitting there so stiffly and refusing to smile.

Nina turned her huge dark eyes upon him. She was small

36

and olive-skinned with a great curtain of night-black hair. She was twenty and Andreas was twenty-three. She said coldly—they both spoke excellent English—"His politics are bad."

"But the music is lovely," said Rose, wishing that Gerard would not always ask in people who so obviously did not want to come. He had these moments of violent hospitality. Things between them were not so bad just then, and she was aware of a certain malicious satisfaction in seeing that Nina Photiades was not going to be one of his conquests. She did not find the young couple in the least attractive. They did not seem to like the children, they had nothing to say for themselves, and throughout what could be best described as the interview, they wore a faintly outraged expression as if they considered they should never have been invited in the first place.

Nina Photiades only said more stiffly than ever, "We do not play him in Greece."

There seemed to be nothing more to say, and Gerard, for once a little extinguished, took the record off and put on Piaf's 'Je ne regrette rien'. This met with no more approval than the dancing Zorba, and after another chilly quarter of an hour the young couple left, with plainly no intention of extending a return invitation, and with so obvious an air of relief that Rose, while entirely sharing it, wanted to slap them.

"What did you ask them for?" she cried out, when the door had shut.

Gerard put on 'Zorba's Dance' again, probably in defiance. He answered angrily, "One has to be sociable. You English are so cold and formal. In my country we always try to be friendly to strangers."

England was Gerard's country as much as it was Rose's, but when quarrelling he always became insistently French, even down to the accent, which was the purest affectation.

Rose, clearing the glasses into the kitchen, looked at him in silence. Her experience of France was that people avoided strangers like the plague, but there was no point in saying so, and she could see that Gerard was furious at being rebuffed by a pretty girl.

He would have been even more furious if he had been able

to follow the Photiades into their flat. Once they were home, they were both immediately convulsed in giggles. The stiff, pale little girl who had not so much as smiled in answer to Gerard's flirtatious blandishments, now struck an attitude, ran her hand through the black hair, and declaimed in a mock English accent, "Mahvellous stuff, mahvellous stuff!" while her husband who had throughout been so correct, called Gerard a very rude name in Greek, then proceeded to imitate Rose in a dreadful refined accent that was really not deserved. He cried in falsetto, "But the music is lovely," and at that they both went off again, only breaking their mirth by making fun of Gerard's artistically curly hair, Rose's rather dull sweater and slacks, and the extraordinary habit of the British of gulping down quantities of whisky at the smallest provocation. At last, weak with laughing, they fell into bed and drowned the abominable English in their love. The letters Nina had carried up earlier, and which were all bills, lay in the wastepaper basket, to be thrown away with the rubbish next day.

Veronica sat by herself, as she always did, and drank a great deal of whisky. She had not had a really bad drinking bout for some time now: the last occasion had frightened even her, for in a fit of raving madness she had almost set fire to the flat, and would perhaps have been burnt to death, had it not been for Mrs. Fielding who, for once in league with the landlord, kept an eye on her, prepared to ring the nursing home the moment things seemed beyond control. The landlord had given her the number: he did not care what happened to Lady Matford who was nothing but a confounded nuisance, but he did care about the flats, and a wild drunken woman, stoned out of her mind, was a liability. All this had happened some months back, but now, with half a bottle inside her, Veronica's perceptions were dulled, the bottle stood beside her, and would certainly be empty before the night was through.

She had grown accustomed to her loneliness, though she resented it: she would have resented even more anyone who tried to call on her. There was no man to ring, no man to knock at her door: of the three marriages she had embarked on, each one was worse than the last. Lord Matford, thankful to be rid of her, paid her rent when she defaulted, and paid her also an allowance which he would have doubled rather than see her again. She never saw him these days: on the rare occasions when she rang him, he was always out. She did not really care: his title and his income were the only things about him that interested her.

She sprawled on her bed, with the television at the foot of it. There was a great crack across the frame where she had once thrown a bottle at it. She watched Gerard glassily, grinning from time to time, for he really was quite bloody awful, though undeniably good-looking in his poufy way.

Rose knew her as entertaining at her best, bad-tempered and unscrupulous at her worst: not being a mischief-maker herself, she never fully appreciated the extent of Veronica's malicious nature. The malice was partly due to having nothing to do, she had no need to work, there was no man to distract her, consequently she beguiled her time by watching everyone around her and without charity. She was perpetually and endlessly bored: it was her only outlet. Curran House would have been appalled by the extent of her knowledge, for she had no scruples and enormous natural cunning, especially when drunk. She knew for instance that the Photiades were up to their slender necks in debt. Some of the bills that came in were not stuck down, and these she had taken to her room to examine: the amount of money owing made her whistle. It was not much according to her own extravagant standards, but constant demands for twenty pounds, thirty pounds, forty pounds, for so young a couple, were to put it mildly revealing. She now eyed the two of them with great delight. Their prim, correct faces amused her, and the fact that young Nina so plainly despised her for her drunken and battered appearance, sometimes made her laugh out loud. Mrs. Parsons of course did not interest her, for she was nothing but a common old woman who probably in her youth worked in a shop or did office cleaning.

As for the Fieldings, Mrs. Fielding was the type of suburban housewife she abominated: it never struck her that she might have owed her life to Mrs. Fielding's observing eyes, nor did she know who was always responsible for ringing the nursing-home. Monica, whom she saw occasionally in her absurd way-out clothes, with her bright smile and over-sweet voice— "Oh hallo, Lady Matford, how are you?"—she dismissed as another whore, and not an interesting one. And with Amanda, Veronica contented herself with using the odd four-letter word, answering the cool, genteel greeting with anything that came to her mind as crude and shocking: she knew well enough that if she had not had a title, Amanda would not have spoken to her at all.

Lulu she dismissed entirely, but fortunately for her eager malice there was always Dr. Macek and Rose. And Dr. Macek interested her very much indeed, as did the situation between Gerard and Rose. She had known for a long time that Dr. Macek, despite his cool, correct exterior, was a harassed and frightened man, but she still had no idea what it could be about. His letters were always securely stuck down, he usually collected his mail before she was up, and the one letter she had caught a glimpse of was in some strange foreign language, of which she did not understand one word. Once she had invited him in to have a drink with her, but he had declined, civilly enough, but in a firm fashion that inhibited further invitations. She found him very difficult to pin down, and this intrigued her more than ever. He never seemed to have any visitors, he hardly ever went out in the evenings, and despite his perfect politeness, she sometimes had the uneasy feeling that he read her better than she could read him.

But there certainly was trouble, and Veronica, switching off Gerard's incredibly boring crap, considered as she had done a hundred times before, what it could possibly be. Blackmail, almost certainly—Doctors were vulnerable to blackmail, especially unmarried ones, and there was no sign of a Mrs. Macek. He was a children's doctor, of course, but children had mothers, and perhaps some woman had fallen in love with him and was now putting pressure on him.

The fact that however much she tried, Veronica could find out nothing, drove her almost wild with curiosity. Sometimes, full of whisky and boredom, she had almost gone upstairs to bang on the doctor's door, to say, Come on, boy, what's all this about, you know you'll feel better if you tell me about it.

40

But there was something about Dr. Macek that stopped her. Veronica was accustomed to getting her own way, but she could not quite face that impassive appearance, besides, she was sure he would never ask her in.

Her thoughts turned therefore to Gerard and Rose, and here she was on happier ground, for it was plain that Rose—bloody little fool she was—was scared to death of her husband, and this could only mean that he was threatening to take her children away from her. Why anyone should want children at all was beyond Veronica's imagining, but Rose was plainly devoted to her two spoilt brats, and Gerard was equally plainly all hell-bent on getting them into his hands.

Veronica thought it would be fun to stir things up a little: tomorrow she would have a talk with Rose, and see what she could do. But the whisky was at last taking effect, so she rolled over, buried her face in the pillow and fell asleep.

And as Veronica slept, Rose, who had watched her husband's performance in a kind of weak fury—he really was awful!— was preparing for bed, while Dr. Macek, unaware of the curiosity he had aroused, looked once again at the letter he had received, saw only too clearly that he was not going to sleep that night, and began to pace up and down his room.

Rose heard him. It was not that he was making much noise, indeed the muted footfalls suggested that he had his slippers on, but there was one creaking board that he seemed to encounter every other minute, and there was a relentlessness and regularity to the sound that beat savagely on her nerves.

She had put Sally to bed, a grossly over-excited and emotional Sally, who had astonished her by flinging her arms round her neck to give her a good-night hug. Rose, moved nearly to tears—she must do something about these preposterous nerves, they weren't good for the children, and really, if an ordinary good-night kiss had this effect, she had better go on to tranquillisers—returned the hug with all the warmth and heart in her. Sally lay back on the pillows, looking up at her. It was as if there were a moment of real understanding between them, and this after so many tantrums and scenes, moved Rose to such a degree that she stood there in silence, not daring to move lest she should ruin a moment so precious.

41

Sally said sleepily, "It wasn't really like Daddy, was it?"

Rose knew at this moment that she would not part with Sally, if Gerard brought in a battalion. She forgot how nervous she was feeling, forgot the eyes that were always worse after watching the television. She said calmly, "Well, Daddy's an actor, love. He has to play all kinds of different parts." She added with a mendacity that staggered herself, "The fact that it didn't seem like him means that he's a good actor."

And she said good-night, wished Sally happy dreams, and softly closed the door, while before her eyes came the picture of Gerard anticking up and down like an organ-grinder's monkey, waving his arms in what was presumably a Gallic manner, crying, Mon Dieu, and Ma foi, and putting on that dreadful accent: Vot ees zees? which in this case was a pair of frilly panties. No doubt it brought Surbiton down in a roar—

You're a silly, lousy bastard, said Rose aloud as she undressed, then with the damnable inconsistency of human memory, thought of Gerard as she had first known him, when he seemed to her the most handsome, wonderful and perfect man in the whole wide world. She slipped on her dressing-gown—it had given at both elbows, but really she could not afford a new one—and peeped into Tom's room, ostensibly to make sure he was asleep, but really to comfort herself.

He was fathoms deep in slumber, sprawled there in the vulnerable innocence of the very young. This little angel would never go around, shutting one door after another, dance with temper, yell if crossed, spit out his food if it did not please him. This was a little Victorian prodigy, so destined for heaven that it was a wonder the earth could hold him. Rose gave a faint laugh, bent over to kiss him, then returned to her own room and climbed into bed.

She had been sleeping badly for a long time now, but she felt drowsy, it had been a pleasant evening, she thought tonight she might fall asleep almost immediately.

Then she heard those bloody footsteps again. For God's sake was this going to go on all night as it did last time? Surely the man could make himself a hot drink or take a pill or something. Pad, pad, pad, creak—it was as if he were a caged animal, pacing from one end of the room to the other and back again.

Sometimes Rose herself, when she could not sleep, got up and went into the sitting-room, but usually she read for a little or made herself a cup of tea. But she never walked up and down, up and down, as this impossible man was doing. She pulled the bedclothes over her head to muffle the sound, and tried to will herself to go to sleep.

But by this time she was wide awake. It was as if those footsteps, still going pad, pad, pad, creak, jostled afresh the ugly thoughts in her brain: it seemed to her as if every nerve in her body were on edge. Her eyes ached and burned, she was sure that the vision was worse, then the terrible thought came to her that one day soon she would go suddenly blind. She would be looking at something in an ordinary manner, then everything would swim away from her in a dizzy haze, in a second there would be nothing.

She would never see again.

Pad, pad, pad, creak!

"Oh Christ!" cried Rose in a frenzy. "Shut up, can't you? Shut up, shut up, shut up!"

She flung the bedclothes off, and switched on the lamp. She picked up her library book, and began determinedly to read. It was a poor sort of book, a tough thriller where everyone kicked and gouged and tortured, it was in no way a soothing read. And always above her head sounded those relentless footsteps. The man must cover several miles in one night, it was like someone on a treadmill.

At last, her hair wild, and her face flushed with rage, she got out of bed and went into the sitting-room. She opened the cupboard hopefully, to see if there were anything to drink. But there was nothing except some cheap cooking sherry which she felt she could not face, so she padded into the kitchen on her bare feet—no one surely could complain of her—and heated up some milk. She drank this, shivering, for the September night was cold, and there was skin on the top of it that stuck to her lip. This disgusted her so much that she could not finish it, and poured the remainder down the sink. It was a terrible waste, and she would have scolded the children for doing something so wicked, but she could not bear the sight of it, the very look of it made her feel sick.

She looked in the fridge to see if there were something she could eat, but there was nothing but some cheese and the stewing steak for tomorrow's casserole. It was the end of the week, her budget was down to rock-bottom, and even the spare tins in the food cupboard consisted of nothing but peas and butter beans and, of all things, golden syrup.

She saw that she would have to ring Diana. It was hateful, disgraceful, but there seemed to be no choice.

She came back into the bedroom, after going to the lavatory, sponging her face and swallowing down an aspirin. She had never felt more wakeful in her life, and in her feverish state it sounded as if those bloody footsteps were pounding up and down in jackboots, crash, crash, crash. Rose could have screamed: it was obvious that this was going on all night.

Suddenly she made up her mind. She would go upstairs and speak to him about it. It was two in the morning. By this time she was in such a state that it did not even strike her as an extraordinary thing to do. She pushed her hair back, wrapped her dressing-gown tightly round her, snibbed the lock of the front door — Tom's mania for shutting doors had made her wary, and there was the one chance in a hundred that he might wake up and come out to see what was happening — and ran up the stairs.

Halfway up she stopped, one foot poised to go higher. She saw then that not only was this at its best a strange way of behaving, but also that it might well be misconstrued. She was at heart a conventional girl — "une bonne bourgeoise," Gerard had called her without affection, in one of his French moods — and no good bourgeoise should come out in her dressing-gown at two in the morning, to burst in on a gentleman she hardly knew. But, even as she turned a little disconsolately to go downstairs again, she heard once more those footsteps, and the sound broke down all the conventional embargoes within her.

She stood outside his door, shivering with cold and apprehension. It struck her inconsistently that she might at least have pinned up her hair. Then she knocked. It should have been a fierce rat-tat-tat, but it emerged as a timid little

44

sound and, when she heard the approaching footsteps, she all but ran away.

Dr. Macek stared at her in understandable amazement. He was fully dressed, and looked precisely as if he were about to set out for his consulting room. His hair, which was thick if receding, and possessed waves that in a woman would have been made by old-fashioned irons, was undisturbed, his tie dead in the middle, and he still wore his jacket. His only concession to the hour of the night was a pair of big, old-fashioned bedroom slippers, and the only indication of tension the nicotined forefingers that held a cigarette.

Rose was silent because she could think of nothing to say. She realised now with a sinking feeling in her stomach that she had made a complete idiot of herself. She felt as she had sometimes done at school when she had given an absurdly wrong answer in front of the whole class. The colour roared into her cheeks so that she was dizzy with the heat of it.

Then Dr. Macek spoke. He said, "One of your children is ill—If you'll wait just a moment, Mrs. Menusier, I'll come down with you."

He turned, presumably to fetch his stethoscope, or whatever doctors carried with them, and Rose, now ashamed and conscience-stricken, cried out, "No, no, please—you don't understand. I'm sorry to have bothered you. I should never have come up, I know, but I just couldn't stand it any longer."

She saw from Dr. Macek's face that he was beginning to think her mind unhinged, and continued more calmly, even with a hint of temper. "Dr. Macek," she said, pronouncing his name with the utmost accuracy, "you have been walking up and down for the past two hours or more. Your room is just over my bedroom. It's driving me absolutely mad. I just can't sleep. I—I thought perhaps you were ill, and I could make you a hot drink or something. I'm really sorry if something is wrong, but I couldn't bear it any longer, I had to come up and speak to you about it."

Then she saw that Dr. Macek was human after all. The frozen look vanished from his face, and a faint tinge of colour appeared in his cheeks. He looked embarrassed and disconcerted. He said at last, "I do apologise, Mrs. Menusier. It is

45

extremely thoughtless of me. I did not realise that your room was directly underneath and the sound carried so far. I have been most inconsiderate. I assure you, it will not happen again."

Rose said a little weakly, "It really doesn't matter. I'm sorry to have made such a fuss." Then she said, "Is—I mean, it's none of my business, but is something wrong, is there anything I can do?" She added, remembering the depleted state of her store cupboard, "Would some hot milk help or—or perhaps some soup? I'm afraid it would be packet soup, but it would at least be hot, and sometimes when one can't sleep—"

Then he smiled at her. The smile, as she had noticed before, transformed his face. Dr. Macek must once have been quite a good-looking young man. "You are a kind-hearted lady," he said, "and it is more than I deserve. But thank you, no." He looked away from her as he spoke. "I fear I suffer from insomnia. Doctors are as prone to ailments as anyone else, but we must not talk about it, it destroys the image. However, I have no right whatsoever to give you insomnia too, and once again, I apologise. I suggest you return to your bed, Mrs. Menusier. If you wish, I could perhaps give you a tablet. It would be very mild but it might help you to sleep again."

"I think," said Rose, returning the smile a little wryly, "you had better take the tablet yourself. I'm sorry I came up. I don't usually behave in such a neurotic way, but what with one thing and another, I just got a bit frantic. You're sure I can't make you that hot drink?"

"Thank you, no. My apologies again. Good night, Mrs. Menusier," said Dr. Macek, made her a little formal bow and turned back into his hallway. Rose, now going downstairs again, heard the click of the latch. She came into her own flat, and stood for a moment in the hall before climbing back into bed. There was no sound from upstairs. She had to see that Dr. Macek had been very calm and civil in the circumstances, then she thought that there had been an odd air of desolation to him, as if he were in some lonely place, away from the comfort of humanity. And she lay unsleeping for a while, half listening for the repetition of those footsteps. But the house was silent, and presently she slept. Only it was as if the doctor's desolation crept into her dreams, for when she woke up some four hours later she found she had been crying in her sleep, and her cheeks were still damp with tears.

Dr. Macek did not walk up and down any more. He sat in his armchair, chain-smoking, wished for the first time in his life that there were all-night television as in the States, then poured himself out a large Scotch. He was a temperate man, and the drink in his cabinet was mostly for his rare, occasional guests, but since he must not move about for fear of disturbing that poor young girl with her pretty hair, he thought the alcohol might help to calm him.

If Rose had known it, he had all but accepted her invitation. The letter, open on the table beside him, was imprinted on his brain, he had no reason to read it again, yet perpetually picked it up and devoured its contents as if this were the first time he had seen them. It would have been good to talk with someone, drink the hot soup she offered him, feel for a while as if he were an ordinary human being again, whose main troubles were no worse than a difficult case, the high price of a new piece of equipment or that tiresome clutch in his new car, which he had no time to have mended. He thought Mrs. Menusier was a charming little thing, really pretty in her own way, and with a kind, gentle manner that pleased him very much. Certainly she was better off without that husband of hers, though he seemed to come back far too often. Dr. Macek had no illusions about Gerard. It was the Gerards of this world who had produced the letter that haunted him. Gerard was a cheap, weak, sexually twisted man: how strange that so pleasant a girl should ever have married him.

But it was no good. The problem was his alone, somehow he must resolve it in his own way. Hot drinks with a kind-hearted girl would not help him at all. She could, thank God, have no conception of the world he moved in: she probably would not believe that such evil existed.

In this he underrated Rose who was not as simple as she looked, and who was confronted with evil herself, but then he did not really know her except as a young mother with two nice children, who would soon no doubt resolve her marital

47

difficulties. Dr. Macek dismissed her from his mind. He sat there with the letter now on his crossed knee, twirled the glass between his fingers, hardly touching the contents, and so he remained until the dawn light came through the windows.

One person in Curran House was a witness to what had happened. The Photiades were asleep in the deep slumber of sexually satisfied youth, wrapped in each other's arms, oblivious of everything: it was after all a glorious world, and who cared about a pile of silly old bills? The Fieldings also slept, including Lulu who, in defiance of her mother, had read till nearly one o'clock: it was a reprint of some of the Sherlock Holmes stories. As for Mrs. Parsons, whether asleep or not, she was not concerned with her neighbours, and only a fire—if she had been aware of it—would have brought her on to the landing.

But Veronica, after three hours of whiskied coma, woke up as she always did, and her mood was bitter and savage with the hangover headache pounding through her skull. Lying there, looking as old as the hills, with her hair wild, her face raddled and her eyes sunk back into her head, she travelled back along the three-forked road of marriage, each of which had ended in anger, recrimination and hate: the gross injustice of it all weighed down upon her, the wickedness of these three men, none of whom had even tried to understand her, all of whom had walked out on her, leaving her furious, bereft and alone. Particularly she detested Lord Matford, who had endured her for only two months: he was old, a little mad, and he drank as much as she did, but to leave her after so short a time seemed the final insult.

Veronica crawled out of bed, and made straight for the whisky bottle. But there was none left and, though she went frantically through the cupboard, she could find nothing but some beer and the dregs of a sherry bottle. She finished the sherry. It made her gag, but afterwards she felt a little better. She decided to take a walk. She slipped her feet shakily into shoes, wrapped her dressing-gown around her, and came downstairs. It did not strike her as odd that she should come undressed into the street in the middle of the night, but then Veronica, even when sober, prided herself on being unconventional. Once, after a similar jaunt, she had decided to ring Rose on the front door inter-com. She had yelled up at Rose to come down immediately, and continued screaming and swearing until a frantic neighbour called the police.

"I can't see what all the fuss is about, officer," she said haughtily to the rather young policeman who had arrived.

She was drunk and wild and, on this occasion, actually dressed, though the term was perhaps a little all-embracing, for she wore trousers with the fly open, a filthy, torn shirt, and over that a long, black cloak that made her look like a vampire. She was, however, from the policeman's point of view, unmistakably a lady: the beautiful voice pealed out at him in an awe-inspiring manner, and the great eyes flashed so that he felt as if he were confronted with some mad kind of royalty.

He said, "Madam, you are waking the whole neighbourhood," to which she replied in the same grande dame manner, "And do you think I fucking well care?"

He was appalled, but in an odd way the language seemed to make her more unapproachable than ever: only a lady would dare to swear in such a fashion.

He said sternly, backing a little as he spoke, "Give me your key, please, and I'll open the door for you. You'll feel much better after a good night's sleep, and we can't have you waking everybody up, can we?"

By this time windows were opening everywhere, and angry voices were shouting abuse, but Veronica did not care, she loved embarrassing people, and it was only because she felt cold and in need of a drink that she at last permitted the policeman to open the door for her and almost push her inside.

He heard her fall up the stairs. He shrugged his shoulders. He muttered, "Christ!" and walked quickly away.

The police by now knew Veronica only too well, and mostly gave her a wide berth. She was after all in her own way harmless, a bloody nuisance, certainly, but when she was caught up in real D.T.s, the ambulance took her away. If she were left alone, she usually did nothing worse than upset passers-by, who heard her muttering to herself as she sloped along, and kept well out of her way. Once she nearly landed herself in the police station when another constable found her by the roadside, with her skirt raised to the waist. "I'm doing a wetty," she announced triumphantly in her ringing voice, and so indeed she was, like a waterfall, but there was no one else in sight, and the policeman was so embarrassed that he turned aside to find, when he peered round again, that she had gone.

This time she behaved with reasonable decorum, and there was no police constable for her to worry. She walked quickly and unsteadily, talking and swearing to herself in a growling monotone. Once she leaned against the wall to light a cigarette, and once she lurched against a passer-by, who quickly stepped off into the road. She wandered round the block, by the car park and the fire station: one of the firemen on night duty saw her and grinned: he said out of the corner of his mouth, "Here comes Lady Dracula again." She walked for a few minutes up the High Street, peering into the unlighted shop windows, then met a cat. She crouched down to talk to it, and the cat, recognising another solitary night creature, arched its back and rubbed itself against her legs. Then, suddenly exhausted, she made her way back to Curran House.

She saw that the light was on as, after several boss shots, she managed to open the front door. It was a time switch: anyone who pressed the button on any landing illuminated the whole house.

She came to the first landing, and peered up the well of the staircase. She saw Rose in her dressing-gown running up to Dr. Macek's flat. It could only be Dr. Macek, for he was the only tenant on the top floor. Veronica was so fascinated that she stood there, gaping. For her there could be only one explanation. But none the less it seemed to her extraordinary, for she thought of Rose as a silly, tame little thing, useful for the odd loan, and the one person in the house whom she could speak to, but completely without spirit — why else could she let herself be bullied by that show-off bum actor husband of hers? And to think that this little idiot was running an affair with the doctor! Rose, if she had known it, now shot up several degrees in Veronica's estimation.

Veronica waited for a moment, heard the upstairs flat door open and the sound of Dr. Macek's voice. Then she turned slowly into her own flat, pondering over this new strange situation and wondering how she could make use of it. It would certainly be fun to tease Rose about it, preferably when Gerard was there: unfortunately, Gerard could not stand the sight of her, so the confrontation seemed unlikely.

However, it was all quite amusing, and Veronica, distracted for once from her own unhappiness, brooded on the matter for nearly an hour before falling asleep.

Rose, preparing herself and the children for the day's visit to Fishbourne, thought that it was all becoming more and more difficult. She was tired after her almost sleepless night, her eyes were worrying her, and Sally, as if regretting yesterday's show of affection, was as impossible as only Sally could be. Rose had to tell her everything twice, and once or twice was so exasperated that she only just restrained herself from slapping her. Sally, half-dressed, slouched on her bed, reading the book of the moment: Rose in a moment of temper snatching it from her, saw to her surprise that the little boy-hero, who flew over the rooftops in his dream, was drawn with the full equipment. She supposed she was old-fashioned to be even mildly astonished, it really did not matter one way or another and, when Sally tried to grab the book back, dismissed it from her mind.

She said crossly, "Sally, we're supposed to be there by lunch-time. It takes at least two hours to drive down, and it's already nearly ten. Will you please put your shoes on and go into the bathroom and do your teeth."

"I want my book," said Sally, looking so sulky that the beautiful little face was all down-drawn lines.

"Well, you're not having it," retorted Rose, forgetting all her careful self-training, "and if you don't hurry up, I shall ring Daddy and say we're not coming. And if he asks why, I'll tell him you're being too naughty to take out."

This of course did the trick, but even then Sally managed to take much longer than was necessary and, then, having recovered her precious book, fell to reading again so that Rose had to jerk her arms to fit her coat on. Tom at least was no trouble, apart from closing doors. He consented to be dressed with comparative amiability, and looked so cosy in his hood and anorak that Rose's heart lifted a little, and she gave him a hug. It looked now as if they were all ready, Sally with her book under her arm, some drawings from school to show to Daddy, while for Tom there was a bag of toys and picture books to distract him, and perhaps prevent him from distracting Claudine who, though she did her best, had little patience with small children.

She was just going down to get the car, the small Mini that was about all that was left her of the old and more luxurious days, when the bell went. She said, "Hell!" energetically, and Sally at once subsided on to the nearest chair and began reading again.

It was the landlord. Rose's heart sank. She had never particularly disliked him, though recently his manner had become more insolent, but there is an inevitable withdrawal from people to whom one owes money, and the rent was overdue by a fortnight.

She said a little wearily, "We are just going out. Could I perhaps make an appointment to see you when we come back?" She added unnecessarily, for he could not be in the least interested in her affairs, apart from her financial ones, "This is the day we visit my husband in Fishbourne. He likes to see the children regularly."

The landlord looked her up and down, and she knew at once that her coat was shabby, and her hair already falling out of its pins. He said with the little smile she was beginning to dread, "It's about the rent, Mrs. Menusier."

"Look," said Rose in sudden exasperation, "it's Saturday morning and I can't get to the bank. I've just told you, I'm seeing my husband, and he'll give me the rent money. I'm sorry to keep you waiting, but it's only a few days after all—"

"A fortnight, Mrs. Menusier."

Dr. Macek would possibly be amused at the pronunciation. Or perhaps not—what a pity Gerard was not called Smith. She said, trying to keep herself and her voice calm, "Well, that's not so long after all. But I really am sorry. I promise you'll get it next week."

She saw out of the corner of her eye that it was now a

quarter past ten, that Tom was trying to unzip his anorak, and that Sally had kicked off one shoe so as to curl her foot more comfortably beneath her. She wanted at that moment to murder both her children and the landlord, who was still wedging himself in the doorway so that she dared not move back lest he slide into the room.

He said, "Well, I hope so, I'm sure." He was still eyeing her up and down. "I can't help it, Mrs. Menusier. I appreciate that you are having difficulties, and I don't want to dun you, but I run a business, see, and times are hard for all of us, especially with this Labour government. I'm sure you see that—"

"Of course. Of course I do. But if you'll excuse me, we're supposed to be at Fishbourne at—"

"Perhaps we could discuss it more comfortably next week. If you'd like to look in at my office on Monday morning—"

"I hope to have the rent for you by Monday," said Rose, her voice grown small and cold.

"Of course, dear. I hope so, I'm sure. And how is Mr. Menusier? I saw him on the telly last night. He must be earning quite a packet."

"Look," said Rose again, "I've got to fly, so you must excuse me. Thank you for calling, and I apologise for being late with the rent. It won't occur again. Goodbye."

And she gave the door a determined push so that he had to move back. She only hoped he would not wait for her outside. However, she was certainly not the only overdue tenant, so he might have other things with which to occupy his time. Veronica never paid any bills on principle, never mind the rent, and her phone was always cut off for at least a week after the final demand. Poor Lord Matford—whatever possessed him to marry her?—would certainly be lugged in, but probably he could afford it. Rose ran back into the room, zipped up Tom's anorak, then unceremoniously lugged Sally to her feet so violently that she dropped the precious book to the floor.

Sally began to whine, she was in the mood that Rose most detested, and at that her temper broke. She gave her a shake, shouted—if the landlord was still there, he must be having an earful—"Oh for God's sake! You are absolutely impossible,

I don't know why I put up with you. If you don't put that shoe
on this instant, you'll go straight back to bed, and you'll stay
there all day, and we'll go down to see Daddy without you."

How not to deal with children in one easy lesson—But
fortunately Sally, however temperamental, was too young to
recognise that the threat was impossible to fulfil. The angry
tears rolling down her cheeks, she put on her shoe, as slowly
as she dared, picked up the book, and followed her mother to
the door, sniffing and scowling, while Tom selected this
moment to shut one more door, presumably just for luck.

The happy party went down the stairs. There was no hope
of hurrying, for Tom could not run down the steep steps, and
would have resented it instantly if Rose had picked him up.
He went down his own laborious way, sometimes jumping with
both feet and several times going backwards, while Rose hung
on to his hand, and wondered why any woman wanted
children, much less a husband. Sally was now in her dignified
not-speaking-to-mother mood, and Rose herself was shaking
with a kind of chill despair at her own inadequacy, and at the
prospect of a day that always seemed to turn into a nightmare.

When she almost ran into Lulu, very prinked up for some
occasion, and with far too much blue shadow on her eyelids,
she stopped resignedly to smile at her, for this was a nice child,
perhaps the nicest person in the block, and they were going to
be horribly late anyway, a few minutes more made no
difference.

"I'm going to see Monica," said Lulu, adding, "You look
super, Sal. Is that a new coat?"

It was not a new coat, there was no money for new coats,
but it was Sally's best and she loved it with all her heart.
Gerard had bought it last year, it would not fit her much
longer, and to Rose's mind it was in the worst possible taste,
being trimmed with imitation leopard-skin and bright red
buttons. But Sally adored it and, unless the weather was too
hot, the coat had to be worn when she went to see Daddy.
The compliment removed the last of her sulks: she fell quickly
into temper but her moods changed with the weather, and
instantly she was all smiles.

"Very smart indeed," said Lulu. "You look like a film-star.

54

Shirley Temple Menusier, that's what you are." She said to Rose, "Monica's got herself a new beau. Didn't she tell you?"

Rose was amused by the old-fashioned word, so at variance with Monica's character. She shook her head, smiling. "What's he like? Is he another of the young ones?"

"Oh Christ, yes," said Lulu. Mrs. Fielding would never have permitted her to use such language, and the words came strangely from that childish mouth, for all it was rouged with some kind of shiny orange that Rose remembered seeing advertised in a magazine. Then she giggled. "He's about nineteen."

"Oh no!"

"I told her she's old enough to be his mum."

"I don't imagine that went down very well. Besides, it's just not true. How old is she?"

"Twenty-eight. He's a real freak-out, Rose, honestly. He's got hair down to here." Lulu gestured at her undefined waist. "And a beard and droopy moustaches. He never wears anything on his feet, he's got one ear-ring, and his shirt's open to the navel. I think he must be terribly cold in this weather. He's quite nice actually and he plays the guitar. But Mother will have a fit when she sees him, and he does look awfully queer."

"Well, he can't be queer," said Rose, "not if Monica likes him." She added, "We must be going, Lulu. We're going to see Gerard, and I'm supposed to be in Chichester by mid-day. We haven't a hope, of course, but we'd better get cracking." She smiled again at Lulu, thinking the hair style terrible and the make-up almost grotesque, but feeling full of warmth towards her. "Come in one evening," she said, "when there's a good thriller on the telly. You haven't visited us for ages."

"I'd love to," said Lulu, and sounded as if she meant it. But she watched for a moment as Rose continued on her way downstairs, and on her face there appeared a secretive, conspiratorial look that would have immediately warned her mother that she was up to something. Then she tore down the stairs, past Rose and the children, tweaking Tom's hood as she did so, and making a derisive gesture of farewell to Sally.

However, once she was out in the street she remembered that she was now a young lady, not a schoolgirl, and she walked

55

sedately on to Monica's flat, forgetting about Rose in the excitement of the visit, for the two sisters, despite the difference in their ages, got on very well indeed. Neither of them cared much for Amanda, and Amanda disapproved of both of them— Monica for her appalling boy-friends, and Lulu, because she was young and awkward and did her little credit among her suburban friends. Occasionally Lulu acted as baby-sitter for her niece and nephew: she was good with children, and of course one did not have to pay her. But otherwise, except on birthdays and at Christmas, Amanda hardly saw her, and as for Monica the two girls could not meet without bickering. Even Mrs. Fielding, with her passion for family reunions, saw that it was better to keep them apart. The times when the whole family was assembled together were red-letter days for her, but they were few and far between.

But Lulu enjoyed the daredevil wickedness of meeting Monica, hearing all about the new boy-friend, what he was like in bed, and other intimate details that made her feel both grown-up and sophisticated. As for Monica she was touched by the obvious admiration, and perhaps more than the rest of the family appreciated the good heart and loyalty of this little sister, who would rush round at once if she were ill, and who could be depended on never to repeat anything that was said to her.

Rose drove along the A24, on her way to Chichester and Fishbourne. Tom sat at the back with Sally, harnessed into his seat, and gazing with rapture at the moving world outside: he loved cars, and the greatest excitement of his life was to be in one. Sally fell once more with absorption into her book, ignoring everything else, and Rose was free to think her own unhappy thoughts.

These visits to Gerard frightened her badly, and because of this she was always compelled to dress up for the occasion. She wore now her best trouser suit, which was three years old, she had made up her face, and she had taken great trouble with her hair, the thick, soft hair that was so unmanageable, and which was now piled into a great coil at the nape of her neck. It would certainly fall down before the day was out, and this offended her, but she could not afford to have it cut, which

56

would mean regular visits to the hairdresser. She had always been a neat girl, and this was one of the foolish things that even at the beginning had been a source of argument.

"I am as I am," she told Gerard indignantly if without much originality, when he made fun of her for always brushing her hair, and making sure that her clothes were clean and tidy. "I don't mind people dressing like hippies if they want to. Let them wear their funny clothes and beads and things, and they can have their hair hanging down to their ankles, but it isn't me, I shouldn't be happy like that, and I don't see why you're always nagging at me. Do you want me to be dirty and untidy?"

"You're so suburban," Gerard would say. He himself would be wearing bright-coloured jeans and a flowing, open shirt: sometimes he let his beard grow and sometimes he cut it off, it depended on whether he had a job or not. The leonine mane came down to his shoulders, and sometimes he wore a bright-spotted scarf around his throat, as if he were John Wayne. He was a magnificently handsome man, and Rose, still moved almost to pain by his beauty—these were the early days—could only say a little sadly, "You've married the wrong girl, my darling. You look absolutely gorgeous, but if I went in for such flamboyant clothes, they would do nothing for me at all, they would simply eclipse me. You'll have to put up with me being suburban. At least," she added with some vigour, "I can cook."

And this was a nasty dig at Claudine, his sister, who lived in Paris those days and whom they sometimes visited. Now she could cook a great deal better, but then she tended to burn or undercook everything she produced for the table. No doubt, now that they had set up house together, Gerard, who liked his food, insisted that she took more trouble. Rose sometimes suspected that the bad cooking had been largely on her behalf, for Claudine had never made the faintest pretence of liking her, and had shown her jealousy all too clearly. For Gerard on his own it was doubtless different; for Rose it was undercooked chicken with neither stuffing, sauce, seasoning or gravy, or a sad, burnt casserole, with the juices blackening the bottom of the dish. Even now Claudine seldom made much effort for the unwelcome visitor, and Rose thought that the dinner—she was quite looking forward to it, for she seemed to have no energy to cook for herself these days—would be at the very best dull and conventional.

She believed now, in these disillusioned days, that Gerard was more suburban than herself. The bright clothes were actor's clothes that suited him, the long hair was worn by everyone nowadays, and his defiance of convention was mainly verbal. She could still remember the day they went to an avant-garde play, full of nudity and four-letter words: it was Gerard who declared loudly that it was disgusting and threatened to walk out in the middle of it. The fact that he did not do so was mainly due to his being recognised by someone in the row behind, who at once informed her friend, so that they both gazed adoringly at the back of his neck.

Rose looked down a little drearily at her far from avant-garde trouser suit, and felt that the coil of hair was already slipping: one hair pin trickled down her back. Sometimes, she thought, I would give anything and everything—"Yes, Tom, that's a lovely little dog!"—for enough money to buy occasional new clothes for myself and the kids, to keep a bottle of whisky in the cupboard, and—"Aren't the leaves pretty, Sal? It's nearly autumn, in another couple of weeks they'll be all red and gold,"—and buy myself some really expensive perfume. And how suburban can you get! No culture, no self-improvement, just feminine self-indulgence—

She turned at last onto the A27. It was the longer way round, but she was never quite certain of the way if she went through Chichester, and anyway, they were so late already that it hardly mattered. She peered at Tom through the driving mirror, wondering why he was so quiet, and saw that he had fallen asleep, lolling against his harness like a little doll, his eyes tight shut, his mouth a little open.

I hope he hasn't got adenoids, thought Rose, the worries seizing her again, then over her shoulder, "Okay, Sally? We're nearly there. I expect Daddy's wondering what's happened to us."

But Sally barely raised her head from her book, and only made a non-committal grunt in reply. It was all affectation, thought Rose a little crossly: she had already read that book a dozen times, she could at least answer civilly, instead of mumping away like that, I think her manners are getting terrible. But anything was better than a scene, so she let it pass and, driving now in the direction of Fishbourne, her thoughts turned to Trudy.

Lulu once asked her what Trudy was like, and Rose, stung to a sudden rage, answered, "She always looks as if her knickers are dirty."

Lulu probably assumed that she was Gerard's girl-friend, and that they were sleeping together. Rose doubted very much if they were. She had known for a long time that Gerard had to have girl-friends, but simply as it were to keep him company. She thought many times that the most remarkable piece of acting he ever achieved was during their courtship, when he played the gallant lover: it was entirely convincing, but then perhaps she wanted it to be so. That he had managed to beget two children was a miracle too, but since Tom's arrival, he had only slept with her twice, and the last time, a dreadful occasion, was just before they parted.

Perhaps one day he would really fall in love, and forget the main obsession of his life, which was Gerard Menusier. Rose, turning at last into Fishbourne—my God, we're nearly an hour late, Claudine will be furious—was aware of an inconsistent pang of jealousy, and it was strange, dog-in-the-manger strange, for not only did she no longer love Gerard, she even sometimes despised him and was always afraid of him. Yet the thought that Trudy, dirty knickers and all, might be the one to arouse a real emotion in him, made her quite sick with anger, so much so that when they came at last into the Close, and Trudy, hand in hand with Gerard, came out to wave to her, she stared at them as if they were her enemies, and it took a moment for her to recover her senses sufficiently to wave back.

59

3

THE BUNGALOW WAS SET in a housing estate, ugly outside, comfortable within, and there was a communal lawn for each group of four; to Rose, who liked above everything else her privacy, it was nothing she would ever have chosen, but then to be fair, if Gerard had lived in some historic home, she would have disliked it equally, if only because of his presence.

She parked the car outside the bungalow, and Sally at once leapt out and ran into her father's arms. He lifted her high in the air, an indignity she would have tolerated from no one else, and laughed uproariously, tossing back the great mane of hair which was, Rose noticed, considerably longer than when she had last seen him.

She knew this signified that he had no work. Once, in the horrible, countless quarrels that occurred before they separated, Rose, staring at the tangle of tawny hair, called him a jobless Samson. He did not really take this in, but understood it enough to shout at her that all this stupid Eng. Lit. stuff merely proved what a dowdy academic she was, with neither grace nor charm, just one of those blue-stocking, women's lib. females.

It was for him the ultimate insult, for women to Gerard were supposed to be pretty, sexy, provocative little things without much brain. It was actually merely silly, for Rose could hardly be called an academic: it was true that she had longed to go to college, but this ambition had been denied her, Diana sharing Gerard's views on the matter. But she was more hurt by this than she knew she should be—after all, she had started it, and it was an offensive thing to say to him—and she contrived to laugh, saying, "Hardly Eng. Lit., Gerard. Don't you know your Bible?"

Then he slapped her, and at that moment Sally, then Tom's age, wandered through, and for one small, strange moment, husband and wife stared at each other in horror, as if for the first time they saw the chasm between them.

Trudy at least could not be called an academic, dowdy or otherwise, and Rose had to wonder why Gerard liked her, for she was not pretty either: perhaps there was some bizarre sexuality in her lack of conventional attraction.

She came up to Rose now, saying in her thickly accented, slightly grating voice, "How are you, Rose?" And she extended her cheek to be kissed: the ritual peck was exchanged in a cloud of unappealing perfume, then she said as she always did, "Did you have a good journey down?" She added, "Oh, the sweet little boy, how good he looks."

Tom, as Rose lifted him out, looked neither sweet nor good, being cross after his deep sleep. When Trudy said winningly, "A nice little kiss for me?" he scowled at her and, when she tried to draw him towards her, stalked away with an expression of loathing that would have made his fortune in one of the tougher thirties' films.

"He's always a bit grizzly when he wakes up," said Rose, too entertained to sound as apologetic as she should have done. "He'll be all right in a few minutes." Then she added, compelled for some odd reason to gabble, "Boys are like that, you know. At the beginning they run like hunted deer if anyone tries to kiss them, and then later they rush to kiss everyone in sight."

Trudy received this in silence, the light, slightly protuberant blue eyes moving over Rose's face. She was a big girl, and as German in appearance as her name; the yellow hair, so pale as to be almost white, was plaited around her head, and her face, which was round, was devoid of both make-up and expression. She wore the clothes that she always seemed to wear, summer and winter: a tight-fitting sweater and a dirndl skirt that was at least three inches above the knee, revealing stocky, big-calved legs with surprisingly neat ankles and small feet. Her age, Rose thought, must be about thirty, virtually her own, and the mini-skirt was not becoming. She repeated now, "Did you have a good journey down?"

I don't think you're my husband's mistress, but I know you'd like to be. He is still my husband, you know. I wonder sometimes if this kind of behaviour is as civilised as it is supposed to be. I think it might be just vulgar and silly. It would make more sense if I smacked your fat, stupid face and told you to get the hell out of it—

And she said aloud that the journey had been very easy, with only one hold-up at Dorchester, and reflected again that, though the knickers were doubtless white as snow, there really was something grubby about Trudy. Perhaps it was the square, ugly little hands with the chipped red polish and the bitten nails, or perhaps it was her bulkiness, with the full skirt gathered deeply into her waist. Certainly there was a slight smell of sweat about her, mingled with that perfume: if Gerard found that attractive, the best of luck to him.

And as she thought this, she suddenly laughed, so that Trudy looked at her in surprise and said in an offended way, "Do I say something funny?"

"Oh no," said Rose, making her way towards the kitchen where Claudine was presumably cooking: she had not come out to greet her. "Oh no. I'm just thinking horrid thoughts, Trudy, that do me no credit at all."

And seeing that she might as well speak in Greek for all she would be understood, she laughed again and suggested she would go first to the bathroom to tidy up.

In the bathroom she stood for a moment in front of the mirror, without seeing herself at all. It was very much Claudine's bathroom, though there was a small heap of things in one corner that must belong to Trudy. This included a very dirty comb, thick with grease and scurf, and a bottle of the perfume Rose had smelt on her: she recognised the brand, it was cheap, sexy and had a poor fixative, it was eminently suitable. On the other side was Gerard's electric razor, and a handful of bottles for his personal use, for he appeared to indulge himself in some of the more advertised men's after-shave lotions, deodorants, perfumes and hair-oils. There was quite a pile of these, Rose noted: in the old days he had seldom used such things. Claudine herself obviously used nothing at all, not even eau-de-cologne, even the soap, though expensive, was unscented, there were no bath-oils or talcum powder, and not a sign of make-up. Rose herself made up hardly at all these days, but the bathroom at home was always full of bits and pieces, old lipsticks, almost empty bottles of perfume, and the various bath essences — 'smellies' Sally always called them — that had been presented to her for Christmas and birthdays.

She tidied her hair, pushing the pins back in: the mirror was too high for her so that she had to stand on tiptoe. Then she washed her hands with the expensive soap, and still made no effort to come out. She was feeling now that she could not bear it, any of it, from Claudine's frigid greeting, to the poor dinner, and the dreadful talk with Gerard afterwards that must take place, whether she liked it or not. If only Trudy were not here it might be better, somehow her presence was so insulting, never mind the bloody permissive society: it was not decent that she should sit there, holding Gerard's hand, stroking his hair, shooting him adoring glances.

She had never quite understood how Trudy came to be there at all. Certainly she had come over from Berlin to be an au pair girl — and God help the family who employed her, unless she got on better with their children than she did with Sally and Tom. How she met Claudine, Rose did not know, but the two girls now seemed to be staunch friends, and Trudy, though officially living in Chichester, spent most of her time in the Close, doing some kind of part-time teaching job that only took up the weekday afternoons. Rose, from the moment of their first meeting, had found her heavy and dull, detested her habit of calling Gerard "Poops" — where on earth did that come from? — then grew to dread her continued presence, for she never left Gerard's side until the moment came for the confidential talk, and her lowering silence — she talked very little — hung over her like a black thunder cloud.

Claudine's voice came through: "Rose! Rose, where are you?"

"Coming!" said Rose, banged her hand twice on the rim of

the bath as if in exhortation, then crossed the hallway into the kitchen.

Claudine was a great deal older than Gerard—Rose had never found out her exact age—and there was a marked family resemblance, only the glory and the glow were not in evidence. She was small and handsome with the same coloured hair and eyes, a little ice model of her leonine brother, so cold, so indrawn that one knew she could never have been in love, perhaps never loved. Having spent the greater part of her life in France, she still spoke English with a French accent: there was a provincial air to her, in a lower class of life she would have dressed in dusty black and ruled some trembling family with an iron hand.

She greeted Rose with the usual lack of enthusiasm. She had never even pretended to like her, and Gerard often repeated her derogatory remarks. "I should have taken her advice," he said. "She said from the very beginning that you were not right for me, you'd be no help in my career."

(*"Is that why you married me? To advance your career?"*

"Of course. I thought you were intelligent. I thought you knew the right people, would make a good hostess at my parties.")

Now that the marriage was virtually ended, any faint pretence that had ever existed, was gone. Claudine plainly despised this ridiculous little Englishwoman who had deserted her beloved brother, and occasionally the repressed temper broke through so that she could no longer speak with civility.

Yet even now she and Rose kissed. They had always done so from the first meeting: it was after all the continental fashion, and nowadays everybody kissed as they would once have shaken hands.

"You look tired," Claudine said, and there was contempt on her face, contempt for a poor creature who could not even control her own health.

You're not exactly bursting with vitality yourself, thought Rose's unhappy inner self—oh God, what's happening to me, I'm becoming so vulgar—"I am a little. I didn't sleep well last night."

Then she could have strangled herself for this admission, for Claudine would understand at once how she dreaded the visit to Fishbourne, and Trudy, pressing her fat carcase against Gerard's side, shot him a meaning look, God knows what it meant, but it provoked an instant grin that he immediately altered to a look of unnatural solemnity. Soon he would be making his guttersnipe faces at her, and the children would laugh and get out of hand, there would follow that dreaded, all too familiar sensation of hysteria, welling up and up and up so that perhaps one day, oh Christ no, please no, it would break and she would make some unpardonable scene, perhaps even burst into tears.

You are growing a bit crazy, Rose. Crazy and blind. I really do not feel happy about leaving the children with you. Have you seen a doctor? Claudine knows the name of a specialist, not far from you. Why don't you go? It would reassure all of us.

Rose answered calmly Claudine's query, "Why didn't you sleep?" with comparative truth. She said, "There's a strange man who lives above me. A Czech—"

"Oh," said Gerard, "one of those Commy foreigners. I can't think why they all come over here. They should be sent back to their own country."

It was true that Gerard was British, but this was a bit much all the same, especially when the remark was delivered in such an exaggeratedly English accent. Rose looked at him, and even Trudy said, "Oh Poops!"

He at once stroked her hair. With all those plaits it must be quite painful. "Not you, petite. You can stay here as long as you like."

Petite, indeed! Trudy must weigh all of ten stone. Rose, watching Claudine straining the vegetables, said in the same calm voice, "He's a doctor. I think something must be worrying him, because he walks up and down his room all night. It's just over my head, and last night it drove me frantic."

"You'd better complain to the landlord," said Gerard, looking bored.

Rose said in a crisp voice, "I'm hardly in a position to complain to anyone."

He looked at her. The smiling, derisive look was replaced by something more ugly. He said, slurring his voice, "Shall we perhaps discuss our personal affairs later on?"

E   65

"As long as we don't leave out the little matter of the rent," said Rose, knowing perfectly well as she spoke that this was stupid and unnecessary, that she was provoking the very brawl she so passionately longed to avoid. She felt herself beginning to shake. She lit herself a cigarette and prayed that Claudine would offer her a drink.

Nobody spoke. She could not be unaware of the combined hostility, and felt as if even Sally, who was staring at her, was against her. They all despised her, these women: Claudine, Trudy and her own daughter. Oh, thought Rose, he's right, I'm going crazy. Am I? Am I really? And blind, he said. And blind. It seemed to her at that moment that her vision was blurred, and the sheer shock of this brought her to her senses. She raised her head, blowing a smoke-ring that brought Tom running to her side with cries of excitement. He had just shut the kitchen door, and was looking round for another one, but this beautiful distraction made him stand still, gazing up out of wide, admiring eyes. Rose thanked God for Tom, beamed at him, then turned to Claudine, saying, "Are you going to offer me a glass of your nice sherry? I don't know why, but driving always makes me long for a drink. I hope you don't mind my asking."

And really, it was incredibly rude, but she felt she had to have a drink or scream, and perhaps the rest of them felt the same, for Gerard, without a word of protest, took the bottle down from the sideboard.

They all drank their sherry and made desultory conversation. Yet it was all somehow not quite real, even Sally's wild affection for her father, the way she clutched him round the thigh and buried her face against him. The colour in her cheeks was too brilliant, there was far too intense an excitement bubbling from her. There would be tears on the way home, she would probably be sick, certainly there would be a scene when she got back to the flat.

Rose said nothing, for what could she say? She watched Gerard tickling Sally, ruffling her hair, kissing the top of her head, teasing her so that she giggled and squealed: he was bent on showing what a wonderful father he was, proving with every word and gesture how wicked Rose was to deprive him of his child. He hardly looked at Tom, who was now squatting on the floor, playing with his coloured bricks. Once or twice Trudy addressed a word to him, speaking to him in an affected, cooing way, but Tom completely ignored her and, when once she tried to arrange his bricks for him, pushed her hand away.

Gerard, noting this, said to Rose, "He seems very withdrawn."

"I don't think he's withdrawn at all," returned Rose sharply, and nearly added, He doesn't like Trudy any more than I do, but restrained herself just in time.

They sat down to lunch. It was, as she had expected, a poor meal. There was the creamed chicken for Sally, probably leftovers from the day before, but by now she was over-excited, and could hardly swallow a mouthful.

"Surely she eats more than that," Gerard said. "I think the child should see a doctor."

It seemed to be his slogan.

For the rest of them there was roast lamb, rather undercooked, with boiled potatoes and a salad. There was wine. There was always wine at Gerard's house, it was one of the things he insisted on. The meal ended with a cream cake, bought from the local village shop. It was none of it very appetising, and Rose, for all she had felt so hungry, found the utmost difficulty in eating it. And the conversation continued, largely about Gerard himself. Occasionally a remark was addressed to her, usually by Claudine, and it was always thrown over her shoulder, as if to intimate that Rose's intelligence was so limited that one could only ask her questions of an impertinent simplicity.

"Have you seen any good television lately?"

Rose wanted to answer simply, No, but said instead, without giving a direct answer, "We watched your play last night, Gerard."

"Oh Poops, it was so wonderful," said Trudy with an ecstatic sigh.

"Well," said Gerard with a considering look, putting his fingers together and gazing up at the ceiling, "I wouldn't say that. No. It was quite a challenge, of course, but not really my

67

sort of play. It didn't really give me—how shall I put it?—scope. That's the word. Scope. It was too much in one key. Don't you agree with me, Rose?"

Rose thought of the jokes about frilly panties, and saw again Gerard making a monkey of himself, gesturing wildly, shooting his eyebrows up and down, heard him using that dreadful accent. She said yes, she agreed with him, it wasn't much of a play.

Gerard said huffily, "Oh, I wouldn't say that. I think it's quite a clever series. Naturally, I would never have accepted the part if I hadn't liked it. One has to preserve one's integrity. But the production was poor. You wouldn't understand that, Rose, not being interested in the theatre, but if I had directed it, I would have made something quite different of it. The author agreed with me. He was very disappointed, poor chap. For instance—do you remember that scene where—"

And away he went, describing banality and stupidity, turning it into Shakespeare with his beautiful voice, making a Greek tragedy out of a wretched piece of smut. It at least took them all through the roast lamb—"Sal, why don't you eat your chicken? Tante Claudine made it specially for you,"—to a second helping of now cold potatoes.

Suddenly they all concentrated on Sally and the creamed chicken. Rose could have told them it was no good. Sally was far too excited to eat, and the combined attention of everyone was already bringing the tears to her eyes. Tom, a far better trencherman, was stuffing food messily into his face, with Rose's slightly shaky direction, but Sally's plate was almost untouched and, when Trudy, treating her as if she were a baby, tried to push a forkful through her lips, she burst out crying.

Rose looked accusingly at Gerard, and he at her. He said grimly, "I really do worry about that child," then rose to his feet and gathered Sally into his arms, seating her on his knee and pressing her head against his chest.

"She is very nervous," said Claudine heavily. "She is highly-strung, like me."

Rose said nothing, for there was nothing seemly to say; she looked at her daughter and thought of the journey home: as she thought this, she wished passionately that a bomb would descend on the bungalow, wiping out Gerard and his two attendant witches.

Claudine turned to her. "And how is your health, Rose?"

"Oh, it's fine."

"You do not look well. You seem very overwrought. What does the doctor say?"

"Doctor? I don't need a doctor. I daresay it's just my face," said Rose, then a little desperately, "How's work, Gerard?"

He was still stroking Sally's hair. "Very promising," he said. "I really do believe I've made a good contact with the theatre in Chichester. I fancy there's going to be a part in the next production. You'll have to come down and see me. If," he added, with a black look, "it is not too much trouble for you. Have you seen the new photo in *The Stage*? No, I don't suppose you have. It wouldn't interest you."

"It is very beautiful," said Trudy.

"Superb," said Claudine.

Rose, mopping up Tom and removing the spoon from his fist with which he was liberally bespattering the tablecloth, glanced at the three of them, and a shudder ran through her. Perhaps Gerard was right. Perhaps she really was going crazy. They did not at that moment seem to her to be human beings. There was no communication between them. Have you seen any good television lately? Once it would have been, Have you read any good books lately? There was no conversation on such a level. Perhaps it was her own fault. Perhaps she was the wretched blue-stocking creature Gerard told her she was, a kind of crabbed, academic old maid. After all, 'old maid' was a character description, it had nothing to do with virginity. It seemed to her that they were all staring at her with dislike, possibly hate. Claudine's cold and beautiful face never smiled in her direction, while Trudy, when not gazing soulfully at Gerard, stared out of those pale eyes as if wishing to God she would go home. As for Gerard, he seemed to her to have changed beyond recognition. A kind of shocked horror convulsed her when she remembered how much she had loved him: it seemed a blasphemy that love could turn to a non-feeling that was perilously near disgust. She wondered what would happen if she turned on them and said, What is the matter? I am a human being too. We are all reasonably intelligent creatures, we do not see each other very often, surely we could make some attempt at a conversation that is conversation, speak civilised words that might draw us a little closer together.

And then she became angry, mostly at herself for being so easily set-down, and she began to talk with a kind of defiant gaiety, ignoring the silence that greeted her remarks. She talked about politics, though she knew that Gerard was not remotely interested, discussed a film she had seen on a rare occasion when she had managed to go out and, when all this was greeted with bored monosyllables, fell into gossip: Monica's new boy-friend, Lulu's new make-up, Veronica's latest insanity.

At least it passed the time, though the sound of her own voice beat painfully on her ears. Only when the coffee came, she fell silent once more, and for no known reason her eyes moved away from what she now thought of as the coven — there was certainly something remarkably witchlike about Claudine — to, of all people, Dr. Macek. She could not imagine why. She did not know him, she did not find him particularly interesting or in any way attractive, and her only personal meeting with him was something she preferred to forget. Heaven knows why she had behaved in that stupid, neurotic way, he must think her a complete idiot. But she had to remember that his immediate reaction was to assume that one of the children was ill, and his instant offer to come down — after all, he was a consultant, he must be pretty high up in his profession — somehow warmed her, as something generous and kind and not mean.

They were all so mean, these people. There was no warmth in them, no charity, in the oldest sense of the word. Gerard was somehow not a real man: the frame was magnificent, the features beautiful, but the ingredient that would make him a human being was not there. It had been lost in the mixing, it was like the time she made a cake and forgot to put in the eggs. Claudine must love her brother, but she had no pity for this young woman who was sitting there, isolated, no wish to recognise her difficulties, while Trudy, it seemed to her, was

70

almost a non-being, a fat, stupid whore of a creature who wanted food and drink and bed, who probably disliked her own sex, whose knickers were dirty, and whose comb was thick with hairs and grease.

Then Rose suddenly laughed, and they all looked at her in astonished disgust, as if she were indeed mad.

"I don't think I said anything amusing," said Gerard.

"I don't think you said anything at all," said Rose, "but I was not laughing at you, only at myself."

"And why do you laugh at yourself?" demanded Trudy, screwing up the pale eyes in an effort to understand something so incomprehensible.

Because your pants are dirty, and your comb revolting—"Because I was thinking of something silly. It doesn't matter." She turned to Gerard. "Tell me more about the theatre," she said. She supposed she sounded almost propitiating, but at that moment did not care. "What part is this you were talking about? Is there any other work in the offing?"

She saw that he did not like this, though the questions were surely unexceptionable. He said airily, always caressing Sally, who now huddled against him like a lost kitten—could she in the primitive depths of her mind understand anything of the situation, oh God forbid—"There's always work. I just can't take anything that comes along. It is bad professionally, if you understand what I mean."

She understood only too well. It was as she suspected. There was no work. But determined still to keep her cool, to be civilised, she nodded and waited.

"I do the odd bit of dubbing," he said, "just to keep my hand in. And of course there's my commercial. If you're interested, you can see me on I.T.V. next week."

Sally cried out, "Oh Daddy!" and then it seemed he had grown tired of her, for he gave her a little push and said, "Go and read your book, my darling. Daddy and Mummy have to have a little talk when we've finished our coffee. Do you want a brandy, Rose?"

"That sounds rather ominous," said Rose, then, "Yes, please."

Gerard got to his feet and tried to open the door that led to the sitting-room. For a moment it seemed to be stuck. Tom, performing his usual routine, had slammed it and somehow shifted the bolt along. He suddenly swore. He looked so angry that both children stared at him, and Claudine, for the first time a little flustered, came towards him. Only Trudy remained unmoved, smiling, enjoying the prospect of a scene. Trudy would be a great one for public executions, and certainly enjoyed bull-fights, for she had once been on holiday in Spain, and had recounted the experience with the nearest approach to animation that Rose had ever seen in her.

Gerard said in a snarl to Rose, "Have you no control at all over that child? This shutting doors business is becoming ridiculous."

Rose said quickly, "Please, Gerard, he's only two. He's too little to know what he's doing."

"He's old enough to know better. It's always the same with these kids when they're deprived of proper family discipline."

Rose saw the look in Tom's round eyes. He might not speak much, but he understood almost everything, and now his face raised from the bricks he had been playing with, wore a strange idiotic look that she had never seen on it before, a retreat from a violence he had never so far experienced. She exclaimed, "You're making an absurd fuss over absolutely nothing. Please don't go on like that. You're frightening him. It's a perfectly natural thing to do, most children are the same."

He said heavily, "He obviously needs a psychiatrist. He is shutting himself off from something that frightens him."

Rose said in a controlled voice, "May I have my brandy, please?"

Claudine, who so far had remained silent, said, "I think we would all like a brandy." Then, turning to Sally, "What is this little book you are reading, chérie? Show it to Tante Claudine."

Sally too looked a little drawn. Children were intuitive like animals: they picked up quickly any tension in the atmosphere. But without a word she handed the book to her aunt, while Gerard who appeared to have forgotten his anger—had his moods been always so mercurial?—strolled across to look over his sister's shoulder. Rose, thankful that the crisis was past, knelt down beside Tom to fiddle with his bricks: anxious to comfort him she put her arm round him and began to set the bricks in their appropriate patterns. When he indignantly pushed her hand away—he was an independent little boy who liked to sort things out for himself—she saw that all was well, and was delighted. Then she perceived that all was not well at all, for Gerard gave a sudden shout of rage that brought her violently to her feet, standing between him and Tom in case the anger was again directed at him.

It struck her afterwards, a long time afterwards, that the one thing everyone here had in common was a lack of humour. She saw that Trudy, though she laughed frequently, would hardly know what a sense of humour was, Claudine never seemed to laugh at all, and as for Gerard, one of the many things that had sent their marriage on its sloping path, was his complete inability to laugh at himself. Herself, she was at that moment as humourless as could be imagined: she stared at Gerard, who was waving Sally's book wildly in the air.

She said below her breath, "Oh what is it now?"

He answered, suddenly quiet, "Is this the kind of thing you let the child read?"

Sally was beginning to cry, and Rose at that moment could have murdered him, but she was so astonished that she simply said, "What!"

"I said, is this the kind of thing you let your child read."

Rose for a second was silent, looking at the three of them, now standing together, for Trudy had come up behind Gerard to see what was the matter. They all stared at her as if she were some kind of monster. She understood then that they all hated her, and this was so ridiculous that she managed to speak quite calmly.

She said, "You tell me I'm going mad, but I think you're all absolutely nuts. What's wrong with the book? It's just a children's book. I think it was very well reviewed. Sally likes it. I've forgotten what exactly it's about, but I think the little boy in it has some kind of dream and flies over the town. You're as bad as politicians who see reds under every bed, you seem to see something frightful everywhere."

Gerard strode over to her, the book still open in his hand,

and jabbed his finger at one of the pages. "What about this?" he said.

Then Rose remembered. She had noticed it herself with a mild surprise. The little boy-hero flying over the town was stark naked and had, as she herself had put it, the full equipment, penis and all. She looked up at Gerard, almost in contempt. She ignored the two women who wore the air of crusading missionaries about to burn a witch at the stake. She said, her voice chill with restraint, "I don't know what you're making such a fuss about, but I do know you're being extremely silly, and upsetting Sally into the bargain. I think it's time we had our talk, Gerard, and I suggest, if Claudine will excuse us, that we go into the sitting-room and discuss whatever has to be discussed in private."

He was taken aback. In the old days, when she had stood up for herself, he had always been surprised. He was a steamroller by nature, and a bully as well: he could never take a direct confrontation. He hesitated, obviously torn between a wish to have his allies about him, and the awareness that he had hardly distinguished himself, with his daughter crying and his son staring at him with accusing eyes. He shot Rose a murderous look, but said calmly enough, "Okay, if that's how you want it." He turned to his sister. "We shan't be long. Afterwards we will take a little drive, and then we are meeting some friends of mine and having tea together."

"I'd like to be home by seven," said Rose.

"You grudge me even the little time I have with them!" They were walking across the hall as he spoke. A united glare from Claudine and Trudy followed them. "After all, I don't see much of them, and they are my children too, in case you've forgotten."

"Tom is only little and he'll be over-tired."

"What absolute rubbish. As if it would hurt him for once—"

They were in the sitting-room now. It was a room that Rose had always detested, perhaps because it so clearly bore Claudine's imprint. It was fusty and airless and crowded with heavy furniture. It reminded her of a certain kind of French boarding-house. Everything seemed to be covered by everything else, the tablecloth was velvet with bobbles at each corner, the chairs all had lace (handmade) antimacassars, and were heavy and uncomfortable, the walls were smothered in bad pictures and family photos. Rose longed to fling open the windows, for all it was a cold day: the atmosphere choked her and she longed for fresh air. The final horror, from which she now steadfastly averted her eyes, was a small urn on the mantelpiece, which contained the ashes of the late Madame Menusier. When it was first pointed out to her—it was Claudine's idea to have it there—she had hardly been able to believe it, but she knew now it was perfectly true, mother had the place of honour in the room, and sometimes it seemed to Rose as if something living stirred within that abominable urn, watching her with disapproval, this little English girl who had ensnared her handsome son.

Rose always tried not to look at it, but naturally it held a macabre fascination, and, like the celebrated eyes of the Laughing Cavalier, it seemed somehow to follow her wherever she was. She never forgot the hideous occasion—it was two visits ago—when Tom, at the stage when he clambered on to everything and grabbed at anything within reach, whether it was an electric plug or a piece of rare porcelain, chose to climb on to one of the chairs and reached out for the urn with an eager, fat little hand. Her shriek of horror came out before she could stop herself, and Tom naturally fell off the chair with, after a stunned pause, a howl of fury and a cut forehead.

Now she picked her way between the cupboards, chairs and occasional tables, to sit by the window, her back carefully turned towards the mantelpiece. She looked across the lawn, desolate this autumn day, and longed passionately to be home, away from this alien atmosphere, away from this alien creature who had once shared her bed, who was her husband and the father of her children. She pushed back the heavy hair, coming down again and in wisps against her cheeks, and said in a clear, distinct voice, "I would like the rent, please, Gerard. Unless, of course, you are calling off our agreement. The landlord called just before I left. It wasn't very nice. He was amiable enough, but that won't last, and anyway it's overdue, he's perfectly entitled to make a fuss about it."

She thought he was going to create a grand scene, and

instinctively braced her shoulders against the back of the chair. But instead he made one of his guttersnipe faces at her, jutting out his lower lip and pulling down the corners of his mouth, then smiled and dug his hand into his pocket. To her astonishment he pulled out what seemed to her dazed eyes at least a hundred pounds in fivers: he proceeded to count them on to the table. When he had laid out the full rent, he peeled off one more fiver and put it by the side of the pile.

"That," he said, "is for you, my darling, to buy yourself some pretty little thing. A present from your loving husband. I'm so good to you, don't you think? I hope you appreciate it."

Rose put the rent money in her notecase. She ignored the extra fiver, saying, "Thank you, Gerard, but I don't think I need pretty little things. But if you really want to buy something, Tom could do with a new pair of shoes, and Sally's jeans are disgracefully shabby."

He shouted at her, the colour rushing into his face, "You're a fine one, I must say. Why can't you ever be feminine and gracious? I'm making you a present, aren't I? After the way you've treated me, you ought to be glad I even bother to speak to you. Are you going to take that money or not?"

"No, thank you," said Rose, her voice small and cold. The face she turned on him was expressionless, but her hands gripped the seat of the chair so hard that she broke one of her nails.

"Oh very well," he said, "very well." He was smiling again. He picked up the fiver, and tore it neatly into tiny pieces, then scattered them on the carpet in a delicate fashion, rather as if they were rose petals.

Rose averted her eyes. A sob of anger and wretchedness was rising in her throat, but she choked it down. I mustn't cry, I won't cry, I won't give the bloody shit the satisfaction. But she could not help thinking of what a fiver could do: something for the children, an extra-special joint for Sunday dinner, even a new vegetable rack for the kitchen, to replace the old one that was breaking everywhere and spilt potatoes every time she opened the door.

She was painfully aware of Gerard's gaze moving hopefully over her, the mobile mouth grimacing, the eyes alight with anger and malice. She said, her voice miraculously under control, "We can't go on like this, can we? It's not decent."

"Why not?" he said. But he was not quite sure, so his voice grew loud and over-confident. The sound must carry to the Furies next door. What were they doing, those two bitches? Looking hopefully at each other? Giggling? Shocked? "I'm not deserting you, Rose. I would never desert you. I'll come back with you now. You've only to say the word."

"Oh no!" The words jerked out before she could stop them. The spontaneity gave the words a bitter conviction that Gerard at his most dramatic could never achieve. The impact of them brought the colour to his cheek again, and the grimacing smile was replaced by so ugly an anger that Rose was suddenly appalled: he looked as if he would murder her.

He said thickly, "Don't imagine I want to. It's only for Sally."

"Is that the only reason?"

He was silent for what seemed to her an interminable time. When he spoke again, he did not answer her question. He said, "The thought of living with you again makes me sick. But—" And here the smile returned. "Nobody will know that. I'm not an actor for nothing, my darling."

Rose said, trying to make herself sound calm, even friendly, "Gerard, what sort of life is this for you? Never mind me—"

"I don't."

"Oh, don't be so childish! We're both in the same jam. I've no money, I shall have to ask Diana for help, and you know how much I hate it." Then she saw that these were the wrong tactics, for Gerard was plainly delighted. She went on, "What sort of life is it for you, then? You're married and not married, you're tied down with kids you hardly see, you pay my rent because you're frightened not to—oh yes. I know that perfectly well."

"We made an agreement. I always keep agreements."

"Do you?" But she did not pursue this, only asked suddenly, "Do you want to marry Trudy?"

"Christ, no!"

There was no doubting that. If Trudy imagined she would ever be the second Mrs. Menusier, she would soon find out her

77

mistake. Rose said, "At least you surely want to be free. And I might want to marry someone else. Why not?"

"That's your problem." He was lounging back now against the mantelpiece. The urn was behind one broad shoulder. A sudden sick horror came upon Rose that he might upset it, and the contents spill on to the carpet. If this happened, she would run from the room. But her imagination refused to calm itself: she could picture Claudine scooping the ashes up with a shovel, and this thought was so terrible that her colour changed.

Gerard noticed this. He said, almost indifferently, "You look quite ill. How are your eyes?"

"Fine".

"I saw you rubbing them, and blinking. I know someone who had the same symptoms and went blind. Your eyes have a blind look."

"Would you mind keeping to the point? My eyes are my concern, not yours."

"They're my children's concern. You know, Rose," said Gerard, gazing ahead, "this is all becoming too much for you. Why are you so obstinate? Give me Sally. That's all I want."

"All!"

"Well, you obviously don't like her."

"I love her, Gerard."

"She certainly doesn't seem to love you. I'm very worried about her. I have never seen her so nervous."

Rose thought of the stupid fuss over the book, saw Gerard tickling and teasing her, but said nothing. The hysteria she had so far repressed was boiling within her, and her one desire was to get away, take herself and the children home.

He said, suddenly coaxing, "Give me my Sal. If you do that, I'll leave you in peace. I'll divorce you. There. Ah come on, my darling, my little Rosie. For old sake's sake. It's a fair bargain."

Rose said quietly, "It's a rotten bargain. It's blackmail."

And it was the first time she had uttered the word, which had somehow been in her mind for a long time. As she mouthed its syllables, her fluttering mind, turning and revolving in a desperate desire for help, protection and security, moved briefly to Dr. Macek and those monotonous footsteps pacing eternally overhead.

Perhaps he was being blackmailed too.

Gerard was shouting, "How dare you use that word?"

And perhaps Gerard too — perhaps Sally represented his last hold on normality.

She said, "It's true." She forgot about Dr. Macek. She rose to her feet and came towards him. Her voice was shaking with anger, and with fear too, for he looked so ugly, and in a way he still had all the weapons in his hand. She said, "You don't really want Sally. You look on her as a toy. She's not a toy, Gerard. She's a human being. She wants more than being cosseted and teased and — and tickled. I wouldn't leave her with you, whatever happens. I wouldn't trust you. If you really loved her, you would see that the best thing for her would be to divorce me and get things settled so that we can all live decent lives again. You say you pay the rent. You don't. I have to ask you every time. You know perfectly well that I'm broke, and I suppose you're pleased, but it's the children who suffer in the end. I can't get them new clothes, I have to scout round jumble sales, and if it wasn't for my mother, I mightn't be able to feed them properly. The work I do at home isn't sufficient, and how can I get any kind of job with things as they are? Oh Gerard, what is the point of all this, for either of us? I know you're trying to wear me down, but you won't, you know. And you'd be much happier free of me."

"That's true enough," he said more quietly. He was chewing his lower lip, which was always an indication of temper. "But don't be so sure you'll get your own way. You're not well, Rose."

"Oh, you always say that! You just want to make me out so ill that I can't look after the children. I'm as strong as a horse. If I wasn't," said Rose bitterly, "I'd have given in a long time ago."

"Those eyes of yours—" he said thoughtfully, looking her up and down.

"Oh damn my eyes!" Then this sounded so absurd that she burst into an angry laugh. "There's nothing wrong with my eyes. I'm just overtired, and that's mostly your fault."

"Claudine was saying how hysterical you were." He waited for her protests, then as they did not come, went on, "You're becoming quite unbalanced. I don't imagine you notice it yourself. It's one of the symptoms. But other people notice."

"What other people?"

He looked at her slyly, then made another of his grimaces. "Oh," he said airily, "just people. You'd be surprised. Naturally, I hear about it, because I'm still your husband, and they think they ought to tell me. You've no idea how marked it is. Even Trudy—"

"I think we'll leave Trudy out of it," said Rose. She was beginning to shake again: she was sure he noticed it.

"You're just jealous of her. She's a sweet girl. It's a pity you're not more like her. She'd make a wonderful mother."

"Well," said Rose bluntly, "she's not being mother to my children, and I'm not going mad, Gerard, however much you hope I am, and I'm not going blind either."

He said, in an unexpectedly soft voice, "Do you remember when we first met, Rosie?"

"Oh no! Gerard, all that's one hell of a long time ago, and really—"

"You were a pretty girl then," he said. His voice was gentle, but his eyes seemed to her as sharp as daggers. "I thought this was really it. I thought we'd prove that there are some happy marriages. It's a bloody shame that it should have turned out like this." Then his voice shrilled out. "It's all your fault. You never really loved me. You've never given a damn for anyone but yourself. You've ruined my life, and now you want to take my children from me. But I'll get even with you. You'll see. I'm not accustomed to being thwarted. I've tried to be nice to you, because I was sorry for you, but I see I was mistaken. Give me Sal, Rose. If not, I'll take her, and the little one too. I'm warning you. I'm not just playing games. I've been far too kind, and it's going to stop, you're going to get quite a surprise. I've got friends, you know. They're all on my side. You'll see, darling, you'll see. If you're sensible, you'll leave Sal behind you today."

"So you've already said," said Rose wearily. "If we're going out, I suggest we do it now, because I would like to get the children back before dark."

"Is this a challenge?"

"Oh, stop being so ham, Gerard. It's not a challenge, it's simply commonsense." She looked at him in sudden desperation. "Can't we stop quarrelling? You know perfectly well we could never live together again. We'd simply drive each other mad. I think we're just born to get athwart each other. It'd be death for the children, and for us too. Why don't you come up to town one day and take me out to lunch so that we can talk things over in a civilised fashion?"

"Civilised!"

"It would surely be possible."

But it was not possible, and she knew it. She could see that Gerard, for all he was silent, was in a towering rage, and she was frightened again, his rages always frightened her, besides, her eyes were aching badly. She said weakly, "Ah come on, Gerard. This is doing nobody any good. Give me another brandy, and let's shake hands, as we used to do when we quarrelled and made it up."

She held out her hand, and he turned his back on her. She supposed she deserved it. It was a silly kind of appeal between two people who so plainly hated each other's guts. However, he poured out the brandy, saying in a tight-lipped fashion, "You're drinking too much."

"I'm not!" Her voice rose, then sank again. "I never drink at all at home. Where do you think the money would come from?"

"Perhaps that's where the money goes. I thought you were supposed to be working."

She said carefully, "I am working, after a fashion, but publishers never pay you for at least a couple of months, and magazines are just as bad. Besides, reading manuscripts and cutting serials doesn't pay much at the best of times. However," she said, sipping the brandy, and speaking in a deliberately conversational tone, "there is a new batch of reviews come in, and the pay won't be too bad." She looked up at him, and managed a smile. "I might even manage to buy myself a bottle."

He said nothing. She began to wish she had not asked for the brandy. She had not swallowed much of the unpalatable lunch, and the unaccustomed drink was making her a little dizzy. She put the glass down. She said, "Well, I don't think there's anything left to say. Shall we go?"

"I suppose so. If you are sure it won't tire my poor, ill-used children too much."

This she did not answer, and presently they were all driving into Chichester, with Claudine at Gerard's side, and herself in the back with Trudy and the children.

It was a silent drive. As they were leaving—Tom very excited at the prospect of once more being in a car, and Sally unusually quiet and pale—Trudy said almost coyly to Gerard, "And did you have a lovely talk together?"

Rose saw Gerard's face tighten, then Trudy and Claudine exchanged commiserating glances, and Trudy slipped her hand through Gerard's arm. Gerard patted her hand and brushed past Rose as he stepped into the car. It was like being sent to Coventry. The weight of the united disapproval was such that she felt as if she were being physically pushed aside. However, the drive soothed her a little, and presently they reached the theatre, where Gerard pointed out all the details, telling the children that Daddy would shortly be on the stage there, and they must all come and see him.

Rose knew this was nonsense. Gerard had not had a stage part since he had left her: if he had, he would certainly have rung her to boast about it. There had been the occasional commercial, and once some dubbing, but that she believed was all. She wondered where all that money had come from: there was a surprising amount of it. But it was none of her business: the only thing that mattered was that she had the next quarter's rent and could spend a few months in peace.

The tea that followed was not a success. By this time both children were tired, and Tom, who had behaved so well for almost the whole day, now became cross and difficult, refusing to stay in his chair, shaking his head violently when offered a cake, and finally upsetting his glass of milk. When Gerard, forgetting his role of loving father, snapped at him, "For God's sake, behave yourself," he began to cry, and Rose saw that for once their departure would be welcomed.

The two young men, who appeared halfway through the tea, astonished her a little, for they were much younger than Gerard, and spoke an affected stage jargon that badly jarred her aching head. They were both handsome, about twenty apiece, and certainly one of them, whom Gerard called Terry, was the most beautiful young man she had ever seen in her life. She looked at him almost in dismay, for he seemed to her typecast as the perfect Nazi: his thick hair was an ash-blond, the features almost Greek in their perfection, and his face with its ice-blue eyes so cold that it might have been carved in marble. From time to time his gaze met hers, and she found that she was frightened of him: the beauty was almost inhuman. Terry might have goose-stepped through Berlin, singing the 'Horst Wessel' song, Terry would regard Jews as if they were cockroaches for his foot to step on, Terry could have appeared on any poster picturing the Hitler youth.

The other young man, called Ray, was a paler copy of him, and the two of them talked interminably in that strange cleft-palate twang so popular among young actors, and mostly they talked gossip and scandal: afterwards she could not remember either of them saying one kind word about anyone. She thought that she would never use the endearment 'darling' again. She was by now too exhausted to make any social effort, but she could not ignore the ironic glances turned on her. It seemed that her monstrous reputation had preceded her even here: this was the fiendish wife who had deserted her handsome husband, and who now tried to estrange his own children from him.

The hanging jury had now been augmented by two.

She found that in defiance of commonsense she was vulnerable enough to care, though God knows what it really mattered if Terry despised her and Ray sneered at her. They were silly boys, probably both queer, and the magnificent looking Terry, from his expression, had a heart as small as a pea. It should have consoled her to see that Claudine and Trudy were as ill-at-ease as herself, for the young men paid them no attention, confining most of their remarks to Gerard, a few needling ones to herself, and the odd endearment to the children who were

83

by now, as she noticed with a faint pleasure, regarding them as if they were something at the zoo. But she could only feel cold and desolate then, as she drank her tea and averted her gaze from the over-luscious cream cakes, she grew aware that this was reviving a memory of her childhood, an æon ago.

The first day at school, and the Paris model dress that Diana insisted on. She was accustomed to the company of grown-ups, her education had been with a governess, and while her French, English and history were excellent, her science and mathematics were non-existent. She was no good at any sport, except tennis, she had no idea how to cope with the little barbarians who surrounded her, and the day turned into a black nightmare of sideways glances, giggles and jibing remarks.

It did not last, of course: After a terrible scene with Diana— "What the hell is the matter with you, darling, that dress cost a bomb!"—Rose reappeared in a plain dress that she compelled her mother to let her buy, and became her normal friendly self: for the first time in her life she became one of the gang.

But now she remembered the awfulness of being the odd one out, feeling like an animal in a cage with people prodding her and making fun of her. Only here it was worse: she was not only the outsider, she was the enemy.

She wondered idly what they had all heard of her. Certainly she was a miserable kind of wife and an impossible mother. Perhaps she beat her children and starved them, locked them up in their rooms while she went gallivanting, possibly whoring and drinking whisky. She knew it was ridiculous to take this all so seriously. They were none of them important people. Claudine was a strange, handsome old maid, and Trudy, for all her mini-skirts, well on the way to being an old maid too. The boys were nothing, while Gerard—She raised her eyes from her plate where she had been crumbling her cake to pieces, to find him staring at her with such hatred that it chilled her blood.

Then she knew she could stand it no longer. She could only thank God that she still had her car: if she had to depend on Gerard to get her home, she would be sunk indeed. She had thought of selling it many times, but somehow it was a lifeline, for all it was old and dilapidated and half the time in dock. The thought now that she could jump into it and within a few minutes be away from this horrible place and these beastly people, was such a wild relief that she almost burst into tears.

"Come on, children," she said in a brisk, bossy voice that did not sound like hers at all, "it's time we went home."

Naturally it was not as easy as all that. Sally had to go to the lavatory, Tom, who had been behaving like a fiend, suddenly decided that he wanted to stay, and over all this hung the black cloud of disapproval from everyone, especially Claudine, who said, "It's a pity, Rose, you can't stay a little longer when you've come all this way. We expected you for supper, and I have made something special."

It probably has arsenic in it — "I'm sorry, Claudine, but it'll take two hours to get back, and the children must go to bed."

"You could stay the night."

Oh no, God forbid — "I have to be up early tomorrow morning. I've got work to do."

And throughout this exchange, Rose saw the boys with their bright, sharp eyes, giggling and whispering, thinking no doubt, Poor Gerard, fancy saddling himself with such a bitch, while Trudy snuggled up to him as if to comfort, even putting up a square-fingered hand to stroke his cheek.

Gerard said very little, only watched. He saw them to the car which fortunately was parked just round the corner. He made a great performance of his goodbye to Sally, who burst into tears and clung round his neck. Tom, it was true, paid no attention to him at all, and was so overjoyed at the prospect of yet another ride that he forgot his tantrum and climbed happily into the car, holding out his arms for Rose to buckle him in.

Gerard said, "Goodbye, my darling. You'll be hearing from me. I shall probably be up next weekend. I hope you'll think things over."

Then he clasped Sally once more in his arms so that her sobs became hysterical, then deposited her in the car with such dramatic reluctance that a passer-by stopped to stare.

Rose said between her teeth, "You bastard!" and started

85

the car so violently that they were all flung forward. She saw Gerard laughing as she turned the corner. That at least was language he understood. He would go back to his family and friends, and they would all have a wonderful time, pitying him and tearing Rose to shreds.

But she was so relieved to be away that for the moment she did not care. She saw thankfully that Sally stopped crying almost at once, and saw too with fury how exhausted and pale she looked. It was far too big a burden of emotion for someone so young. The thought of what she might be like when she got home, cramped Rose's stomach. But it was so marvellous to be shut of them all that she pushed her apprehensions away, and for a while drove almost in peace.

4

By now it was dark, and there was considerable traffic. It was also beginning to rain. Rose found that the wipers were not working well so that her vision was blurred: she rubbed the glass over but it made no difference. Then panic overwhelmed her, such panic as he had never known. It was not the window, it was not the wipers, it was not the rain. It was her eyes. She slowed down, her mouth dry with terror and her heart thudding: she rubbed frantically at her eyes as if this might clear her vision. It made no difference, it even seemed to make them worse. The traffic was rushing past her, each car in its passage sounding like the crack of a gun. Then Rose could take it no longer, indeed she dared not, not with Tom asleep in the back and Sally sitting very upright, staring out of the window, the book open and unread on her knee.

She could dimly perceive a layby, so she turned on to it and shut off the engine. She did not offer any explanation to the children. She simply sat there, lit a cigarette with a badly shaking hand, and tried to compose herself to think out what she should do.

It's nerves, she told herself, it's been a ghastly day from beginning to end, I'm over-tired, I'm upset, and Gerard deliberately makes me self-conscious about my eyes. She became a little quieter. She wondered if she should try to stop a passing motorist, or ring the A.A. to get someone to drive her home. They would probably think she was drunk, they would smell the brandy on her breath. Then another thought came to her mind, an idiotic thought that really seemed to prove she was going mad after all. That coven in Fishbourne, Claudine, Trudy, Gerard as presumably the arch-warlock— perhaps they were ill-wishing her. It was the purest nonsense, ridiculous in someone of her age and education, but the malice had blown from them like a bitter wind, there was no mistaking hatred, and Gerard had once or twice looked murder. Rose found the tears welling up in her eyes, and at that moment longed in a weak, feminine way for someone to comfort and advise her, some broad-shouldered, faceless creature from whom she could take strength.

Certainly Gerard at his best had never been a person one could lean on.

It was strange to remember now that the first cracks in her marriage—they had come so soon—were revealed in a battle of wills. She had never considered herself a dominant person, and Gerard, so large and handsome and brilliant, was simply masterful as a proper man should be. It took a little while before she realised his deep, innate weakness. But like all weak, spoilt people, he had to have his own way and, when Rose, stung to surprised action, answered him back, he grew hysterically angry, called her unsexed, unfeminine, told her she was always trying to bully him. In the early days the quarrels blew over, later on they did not. Already after one year of marriage there were bleak periods of silence in which they stalked about the flat, not exchanging one word, shooting ugly looks at each other, obstructing each other as if they were children.

Am I a bully, Rose asked herself, her head bowed, the unsmoked cigarette burning away between her fingers. Then she thought of the bullying she had received this afternoon, the relentless pressure, and a sad, futile rage surged up in her again so that she wanted to cry out, to swear, to batter Gerard with her fists.

A wretched, exhausted little voice broke in upon her.

"Mummy, what's the matter? I want to go home. I'm tired."

Rose, horrified at herself, muttered, "Oh my God!" and swung round to meet Sally's accusing eyes, magnified and shining in the light of the passing cars. She immediately came to her senses. She forgot about Gerard and her eyes and the horror of the day. She said quite briskly, "Oh love, I'm so sorry. I felt a bit sleepy, so I thought a cigarette might wake me up. I'm all right now. It won't take long to get home." She threw her cigarette away, and started up the engine. Then she said, almost diffidently, "Would you like to come in front for a change? I see our Tom's fallen asleep again."

There was a pause. Then Sally climbed over the back of the seat, and slid in beside Rose: after another moment she leaned against her.

Rose absurdly grateful, put an arm round her, then drew out once more into the roadway. Her vision, thank God, had cleared. It must have been exhaustion after all. Presently Sally said, "I don't like Terry."

"Neither do I. He didn't say anything to you, did he?"

"No. He just kept on looking at me. I think he's funny." Then she said, "Mummy, I don't want that book any more. It's a silly book."

"Then we'll throw it away," said Rose cheerfully, thus disposing of one pound and seventy-five pence, regardless of her own quicksand finances and the fact that the book had been a present from a magazine editor.

"Can we throw it away now?"

"What! This very minute?"

"Yes!"

"All right. Why not?"

Why not indeed? A daft thing to do in a nutty world, a fitting end to a crazy day — Rose reached back into the back seat and pulled the book from under Tom, who had slumped against it. She slowed down: it would help no one if she caused an accident by a book whizzing through space. She looked down at it almost reluctantly. She never liked to discard books, and this really was such a harmless affair: at the beginning Sally had been enchanted with it. Then she saw that Sally was looking fixedly at her. She began to laugh. She dropped the book from the window so that it landed on a grass verge. The rain was still mizzling down in a determined and dreary way: soon the book would be unreadable, and serve it right for its wicked and pornographic corruption.

Sally, delighted, began to giggle, and Rose said, "It's an awfully naughty thing to do. I don't know what's got into us. But it's done now, so it's no good wanting to read it any more."

"I never want to read it again," said Sally.

And with this she huddled up against Rose's shoulder, and presently like Tom fell asleep.

They reached home earlier than Rose expected, and both children went to bed without fuss. Tom was so sleepy that he hardly woke up when Rose lifted him out, and Sally, from whom she had expected tears and tantrums, ate her supper meekly and let herself be tucked up without protest.

Rose did not trouble to make herself anything, though she had eaten almost nothing throughout the day. She brewed herself a coffee, wished once again there was some drink in the cupboard, then knelt down on the rug by the fire, immeasurably thankful to be back in her own home. Tomorrow she would ring Diana so that she could go round to see her: now she wanted only her own company, even the television would be an intrusion.

When the knock came at the door, she was almost dozing off. At first she decided not to answer. It was half-past nine, early enough, but she could not think of anyone who would call at such an hour, besides, if she made herself some more coffee, she might begin to read the typescript she had to cut for serialisation. But when the knock came again, she rose crossly to her feet, still wondering who the hell it could be. Curran House seldom indulged in neighbourliness, it was not the kind of place where people popped in for a pint of milk or a screw of tea. At one time Veronica occasionally called, usually hoping for a drink, but she knew now that there would be no whisky on the premises, besides the friendship between them had almost died.

Perhaps it was Dr. Macek, returning her crazy call.

But it was not Dr. Macek, it was Mrs. Fielding, and Rose looked at her with some lack of enthusiasm as she stood there on the landing, with the naked bulb illuminating a drawn and worried face. Then the time switch went out, and Mrs. Fielding's voice came disconsolately from the darkness.

"Am I disturbing you, Rose? If you're just going to bed—"

"No, of course not." Rose heard herself speaking in what was positively a welcoming manner. There was no one at that moment she wanted to see less than Mary Fielding, but there was obviously something wrong, and it would be unkind to vent her temper on this amiable woman whose only crime was that she disapproved of her. "I never go to bed before midnight," she said, "and I was just going to make some more coffee. Do come in. I'm afraid the flat is dreadfully untidy. We got back late and I just bundled the children into bed. It's a funny thing," she said, babbling on in the face of Mrs. Fielding's silence, "but whenever people call, the place always seems to look just like a slum."

And as she spoke, she whisked up Tom's anorak, Sally's shoes, and kicked a pile of magazines and papers under a table.

"Oh, of course you went to Chichester today," said Mrs. Fielding, seating herself in the only armchair, and blinking a little as Rose switched on the lamp.

Rose nearly said, And how do you know that, then thought that Lulu must have told her. But she resented this intrusion on her privacy, and instead of going into the kitchen to make some more coffee, stood there looking down at Mrs. Fielding with a faintly hostile apprehension, as if she sensed that this visit was not entirely a social one.

Mrs. Fielding must have been a lively, good-looking girl. Rose noticed again the marked resemblance to naughty Monica, coming strangely but unmistakably through the middle-aged spread. Monica would be lucky if she wore as well as her mother by the time she was fifty. And I'll be lucky too, thought Rose, I'll probably be some thin, leaky old lady, always rushing off to the lavatory, and bad-tempered and neurotic into the bargain. And perhaps blind—but Mrs. Fielding was still comely, over-plump, but pink-cheeked and bright of eye: one could imagine her telling a naughty story, then rocketing with laughter. The only oddity about her was her family, and Rose wondered as she had done many times before how she had managed to produce three such extraordinarily different daughters.

She said, "Now what about that coffee? I think there's some cake if you'd like it—"

"Oh no thank you, my dear. I daren't drink coffee at this hour. I wouldn't sleep a wink."

"Well, tea then? I'm afraid I can't offer you a drink. We seem to have run right out." And as she spoke these words, she saw at once that Mrs. Fielding was branding her as either a liar or an alcoholic.

"No, thank you, Rose. I don't want anything. We only finished dinner an hour ago. I really came to see you," said Mrs. Fielding, "for two reasons." There was a faintly embarrassed air to her, and seeing this Rose's heart sank: Mrs. Fielding had always had a tendency to lecture her, and tonight she could not endure it, she would certainly lose her temper.

But the first words were harmless enough. "I'm so worried about Lulu," said Mrs. Fielding, adding irrelevantly and much to Rose's surprise, "If you'd like something to drink, my dear, we've plenty downstairs. I'll just pop down and get a bottle. What's your fancy? Len likes his little tot when he comes in, but I don't usually touch it much myself."

"No, thanks. It's very kind of you, but I really don't want anything. Why are you worried about Lulu? She always seems to me such a level-headed kind of girl."

And she sighed a little, for really, she would have loved something to drink, only she was not going to be bought in this fashion, and it was only too evident that Lulu was part one of the programme, with herself in the second half.

"She's gone to see Monica," said Mrs. Fielding.

"But surely—"

"And she hasn't come back."

"Well," said Rose soothingly, "it's not ten yet, and to-morrow's Sunday, so she can have a lie-in. I expect the girls are having a nice sisterly gossip."

"That is the trouble," said Mrs. Fielding.

Rose remembered Lulu's conversation on the stairs. No doubt she was hearing all about the bedworthiness of Monica's new lover. She could not believe this was very serious. Lulu was over sixteen, many girls of her age already had lovers of their own, whether bedworthy or not, besides she must have heard this many times before, what with Monica's three husbands and God knows how many lovers. She said, "Oh I don't think it will hurt her. I don't suppose she listens to half of it. At least it's nice that the two girls are on such good terms."

And she nearly added that it was more than one could say of Amanda who liked neither of her sisters, but then remembered that Amanda was Mrs. Fielding's favourite, so she held her tongue.

"You wait till you meet the new young man!"

"Why? Is he worse than the others?"

"Yes."

"Heavens! What's he like?"

"Terrible. Just too terrible for words. I can't think what's happened to boys nowadays. Apart from the fact that he's half her age—Len nearly had a fit when he saw him. Of course Len's such a man's man, if you know what I mean."

Rose thought of poor-Len, poor hyphened Len. He was a nice little man in his own way. She could not remember exchanging more than a dozen words with him. He was inclined to be flirtatious in the mildest possible manner, and Mrs. Fielding's mama, if a snobbish lady as she probably was, felt no doubt that Mary had married beneath her. A man's man suggested a tall, strapping fellow in a Burberry, smoking a pipe while tramping the Scottish moors, and Len was certainly not that.

She said, "Well, they all wear their hair long these days, and dress peculiarly. It doesn't mean anything."

"You haven't seen him. He has hair almost down to his waist."

"I think Monica likes them like that."

"She usen't to," said Mrs. Fielding, a little aggrievedly. "She was all right till she divorced Martin. He was her first, you know. I always liked him myself. I daresay if they'd had children they'd be together still. Children somehow make a marriage, bless them."

Rose saw that this, in Mrs. Fielding's most tactful fashion, was a method of introducing topic two. She flushed with anger, but managed to say quite calmly, "Who did she marry after that?"

"Oh, there was Guy. We didn't like Guy. Len said the

marriage would never last. Len's very sharp, you know, he doesn't miss much. Besides, he was such a Bolshy, a real red. And you know what Len thinks of that."

Rose's memory, which was an irrational one, dredged up a sudden small cameo, and the thought of this nearly made her laugh and so restored her temper. It was during the election before the last, when the Tories romped home. For three days after Len Fielding sported a bright blue shirt. He said it was his little tooraloo of victory.

"And then of course there was poor Paddy. But you met Paddy, of course. He wasn't her type at all. I can't think how she picks them. You did meet Paddy, surely?"

"Once, I think. A little man."

"In every sense of the word," said Mrs. Fielding. "He worked in a bank. Can you imagine? Not even in a grand manner, just behind a grille. I gave the marriage six months. It lasted two years, I can't imagine why. But at least," went on Mrs. Fielding, plainly girding her loins for topic two, and now not to be deflected, "they were married, and it counts for some-thing, even in these days. I suppose I should be glad really that there are no children. Kiddies do need both parents, and you can't pretend it's a good idea to have a new daddy arriving every other month or so."

"I pretend nothing of the kind," said Rose, both head and temper raised, "and if that's what you are accusing me of, Mrs. Fielding, I can only suggest that you mind your own business. There's no new daddy here, and there's not likely to be. In fact, there's not likely to be a daddy of any kind, the way things are going."

"Oh my dear, please!" Mrs. Fielding's house-worn but well-manicured hand came down on Rose's knee. "You would never behave like that. Why, if someone said such a thing of you, I'd be really very cross, and so would Len. We're both so fond of you, you must know that."

Rose could have answered that she knew nothing of the kind, and was convinced that any such report on her conduct would meet with an enthusiastic reception; perhaps, however, Mrs. Fielding had as many facets to her character as her daughters. There were days when she eyed Rose as if she had three heads and all of them revolting: now she was playing the role of motherly neighbour, and Rose was sickened, would have told her to go to hell if she had had the energy.

She really ought to eat something. It was ridiculous starving herself like this, she'd only make herself ill. A sudden strange urge came upon her to confide in this woman, perhaps simply because she was a woman. She began in a subdued voice, "Mrs. Fielding—" but her companion, set on delivering her little homily, did not hear her, was never to know the opportunity she had missed.

"You see," said Mrs. Fielding in a wise, motherly fashion, "I do know a bit about these things. I daresay you think I'm an old fuddy-duddy, Rose, but then I'm used to that." She gave a little laugh. "I have three daughters after all, and they all think old mum is past it, but you'd be surprised, really you would. Dear, I've been meaning to speak to you for some time." She eyed Rose's bowed head. She could hardly miss the lack of response, though fortunately for herself she did not appreciate the blazing anger whirling through Rose's heart. She sighed, then went on determinedly, "I wouldn't talk like this if I wasn't fond of you. But you're still so young, and you have those two lovely kiddies. And Gerard's a good man, you know."

She paused. Rose knew what was coming. It did.

"Really quite a golden boy—I always call him that, and it makes Len laugh. Of course I don't know what's happened between you—"

"No," said Rose in a small, cold voice.

Mrs. Fielding waited hopefully, but there was only silence. Then she began again. "Of course I know you've not been very well. It's natural enough in the circumstances. Have you seen a doctor? I think perhaps you should, we go to the man at the corner of the High Street, he's really very good. Anyway—I can't help feeling if you talked it over—I like Gerard, you know, and of course he's absolutely devoted to you and the children. Especially little Sal. He thinks the world of her, and she misses him so much, you must know that. I am sure if you would just try again—for the kiddies' sake. Of course I'm not suggesting you're like Monica. I'm afraid

95

there's bad blood in her, and really, she is so irresponsible that it quite frightens me. Sometimes, with all those boys she just takes home with her, I think of all those things one reads in the paper. But you could never behave like that, you're too sensible. Only I do so hate to see young people drifting apart when it could all be so easily mended. It's not a very happy world," said Mrs. Fielding, shaking her head, "what with this permissive society and coloured people and trade unions and things, but I have the odd feeling that one little bit of personal happiness puts things into the right perspective. I see that in my Darby and Joan Club, you know. Some of these old people are really happy, and with so little. I expect that all sounds rather silly to you."

"It sounds bloody silly," said Rose. She did not mean to say this, it was not her way of speaking, but she was choked with emotion, a kind of wild mixture of grief and anger and desolation. It was as if she and Mrs. Fielding stood on opposite banks with a widening river flowing between them. It was even worse, for not only did the river flow wide and deep but also there were other people on the far bank, there was everyone on the far bank, there was the world on the far bank, and she was alone and lonely, so lonely, with all of them hating her, and the river carrying her away. She raised frantic, furious eyes to Mrs. Fielding, who could not interpret their message: because of this and the language, she grew flustered and said what she did not mean to say.

She said, "Gerard says he would come back here tomorrow if you'd only say the word."

Then she realised the implication of this, and for the first time was at a loss for words: she went very red and looked for the moment an uncertain woman who was meddling in matters that were not her concern.

Rose knew now who the 'other people' were, the people who noticed that she was becoming unbalanced. She said quietly, "When did you see Gerard, Mrs. Fielding?"

"Well," cried Mrs. Fielding in a suddenly girlish voice, "I was going to tell you, my dear, but what with all this—oh, you know how it is." She moved her hands as if she did not know what to do with them, then clasped them firmly together.

"You see," she said, "Gerard's always inviting me down to his sister's little bungalow, and of course Amanda's cottage is only about fifteen miles away, so the other day—you don't mind, do you? I was sure you wouldn't, you're such a sensible girl—well, the other day, I was down with Amanda, and Len said, 'What about calling on old Gerard?' So we drove over, just like that. We only stayed for an hour or so. Such a nice place they have, and I really took to Claudine, charming girl, Len said she was a real Frenchwoman, but then he's so sharp, Len is, he always says things like that—"

Mrs. Fielding stopped for breath, still very red. She was babbling, and she knew it; she knew too that she had no right to call on Gerard and claim Rose as a personal friend. But she had committed herself now and Rose gave her no help, indeed she did not speak a word, only continued to kneel in front of the fire, the untidy hair hiding her face.

Mrs. Fielding went on more calmly in her normal, sensible tones, "You needn't worry about Trudy, you know. She's a nice enough girl, but she doesn't mean a thing to him. She's just a friend of Claudine's. I'm sure Claudine would never encourage any hanky-panky, she's just not that kind of person. I thought she was rather splendid, Claudine, I mean." And here Mrs. Fielding made a strange gesture that Rose had remarked in her before, which apparently expressed acute appreciation, holding out her hand with the four fingers tight together and the thumb wide apart. It looked as if she were making a shadow-wolf on the wall. "Really splendid. And so fond of you."

Rose had had more than enough. She stood up. She found that she was trembling, so she rested her hand on the back of the chair. "Thank you, Mrs. Fielding," she said. "I expect Lulu will be back by now and you'll want to hear all her news."

Mrs. Fielding could hardly ignore this, so she too rose to her feet. She said, "Don't be too angry, Rose. There are not many good men in this world. When you find one, you should hang on to him."

"When I do find one," said Rose, "I'll do just that."

But Mrs. Fielding was too guilty and disturbed to stop

herself from speaking, and because she was angry with herself, she turned the anger on Rose. Walking towards the door she exclaimed, "Divorce is ugly and so bad for the children. I really think you're being very selfish. What about poor little Sal? And Tom needs his father —"

"Good night, Mrs. Fielding."

Mrs. Fielding exclaimed, "Oh!" then because there was plainly nothing more to say, came out into the hall, shutting the door very carefully behind her so that she could not be accused of slamming it. She was a little ashamed of herself. She hoped that Rose would never repeat this conversation to Lulu. And because of this she did not, when she found that her daughter had at last come home, reproach her for staying out so late, only asked amiably for news of Monica and the new boy-friend. She did not mention that she had called on Rose, and neither did Len, though he knew it perfectly well: Lulu at once burst into a long account of Donny, the boy in question, and for a time nothing else was discussed.

Donny, apparently, was even nuttier, Lulu said, than the rest of them. Both her parents exclaimed at the horror of it, and both were fascinated. Lulu always thought that Monica provided a great deal of the excitement in their lives, and she enjoyed describing her sister's new fantastic clothes and the staggering costume jewellery she always wore, so heavy that it must have weighed her down. She omitted to mention, however, that she had borrowed fifty pounds, for this would have shocked her mother beyond belief, and if either parent had had the least idea of what she proposed to do with it, it would have created a situation that even Lulu would have found impossible.

She said, an hour and three cups of tea later, "How did Rose get on at Chichester?"

"It's Fishbourne, not Chichester," said Mrs. Fielding, and for a moment the colour glowed brightly in her cheeks.

"Well, it's almost the same thing. Was it too awful for her?"

"I have no idea," said Mrs. Fielding, still a little red, for she was a poor liar, "but I'm sure Gerard and Claudine were charming to her. He's such a nice man, he couldn't be rude if he tried." Then, as Lulu remained silent, she went on, "I know

98

how fond you are of her, Lou, but I think myself she's terribly wrong, and your father agrees with me, don't you, Len?"

"She's a silly bitch," Mr. Fielding said. "She's got herself a good husband, the sort most girls would sell their eye-teeth to have, and all she does is moan. I can't bear a moaner. I think myself she needs a good hiding. He's too soft with her, that's what it is. Women are all the same. They need to know who's boss."

"Ah come on, Len," said his wife, seeing the resentful anger in Lulu's face. She knew it was all talk. Len was as soft as butter, and he had never bossed her in his life. She said to Lulu, "Your father doesn't really mean it. He wouldn't hurt a fly. But she does moan, you know. That's quite true. And it's the children who suffer. They should always come first."

"I think she's got plenty to moan about," said Lulu, then she cried out explosively, dumping down her cup of tea so hard that she all but broke it, "I just don't understand you. I don't understand any of you. It's always women who get the blame—"

Len Fielding, not the most tactful of men, started humming, 'Ain't it all a bleeding shame,' but his wife checked him, shaking her head, then looking rather despairingly at her daughter.

"Well, it is," insisted Lulu, though no one had contradicted her. "Look at Monica now. You all go on about her as if she was a whore or something—"

"Louise!" said her mother, and this briefly checked Lulu: her mother only used her full name when she was really angry. But then she went on again, ignoring her father's surly murmur of, "And so she is. Sometimes I'm ashamed she's my daughter." She said, her voice rising, "If a man sleeps around, no one says anything, it's just sowing wild oats or something, but if a woman does, she's called a real bad lot, people make horrid remarks about her and cut her dead when they meet her."

"Lulu," said Mrs. Fielding earnestly, "you're getting excited over nothing. And what you say just isn't true."

"It is true. It is!"

"Do you think Monica would really mind?"

"That's not the point," said Lulu more quietly. She knew

99

that Monica would not mind at all, she would love the drama of it, make a grand story of it for her boy-friend. But Rose would mind. Rose would mind everything, and Rose, unlike Monica, was not to blame.

She said this. She said, "Rose minds. And Rose isn't a scrubber."

"I don't know where you pick up those words from," said her father, looking at her in fascination. Lulu was his favourite daughter, and he always told everyone how clever she was—'a real good brain, our Lou, oh she's sharp all right'—but he had never heard her talk like this, he could hardly believe this was his little girl.

Lulu ignored this. She said, "You're all down on her. Everyone is. You all think it's her fault. Just because Gerard is handsome and charming and butters you up, you assume he's the perfect husband. Well, he isn't. He's an absolute bastard."

"Look," said Mrs. Fielding, "I know how strongly you feel, and I know you mean every word of it, but you're really quite wrong—"

"How do you know? From that crabby old bitch, Claudine, I suppose. She's as sour as a crab-apple and madly jealous."

"I don't like you swearing like this, Lou. It's not necessary."

Lulu opened her mouth to protest, then saw that she was doing Rose no good by her outburst, so she fell silent, wondering how on earth the conversation had become so violent and involved.

Her father remarked, "I like Claudine. Real little French bird, oo la la!"

Lulu could not imagine a more inaccurate description of Claudine. Perhaps she was the kind of woman who came to life in the company of a man, though one could hardly see Father, nice old boy as he was, as a spark-striker. She said at last, "Okay. It's no good arguing about it. But I still think it's peculiar that when a marriage breaks up, all the women think it's the woman who's to blame. You'd think it'd be the other way round. I suppose it's a kind of jealousy, a kind of she can't hold her man, so she must be no good. But I think it's awfully unfair. I bet if Rose's marriage goes completely down the drain, you'll all be frightfully sorry for Gerard. Well, there'll be a minority of one. I'm not sorry for him at all. I hope he rots."

Neither of her parents answered this, so she exclaimed defiantly, "There might even be a minority of two. I think that foreign doctor knows what a pig Gerard is. But then he's a man. He can see through him."

"If you're talking about Dr. Macek," said her mother, "I can't see what he's got to do with this."

"It's just that I think he's rather nice," said Lulu. She could have added that from the way he sometimes looked at Rose—she had noticed this once or twice—he thought her rather nice too, but saw that to say this would only provoke a new and worse situation.

"I've hardly spoken to the man," said Mrs. Fielding. Then she gave a little laugh, saying, "We do land ourselves in for some peculiar conversations, don't we? I can't think how we ever started this. Well, Lou, as it's Saturday, what about the late-night movie?"

And they all settled down to watch, only later in their bedroom, the two Fieldings returned to the subject of Lulu's odd behaviour.

"I can't imagine why she champions Rose like that," said Mrs. Fielding. She had already given her husband an expurgated version of their conversation earlier on. "I know the young know everything these days, but what can she know about marriage and men? And why does she hate poor Gerard so? Do you think he made a pass at her?"

Her husband shrugged sleepily. He adored his little daughter, but there was no denying that she was still a schoolgirl and looked like one too—pity she threw the eye make-up on like that—and he really could not see a sophisticated chap like Gerard wasting his time. And on this thought he fell asleep, but Mrs. Fielding remained awake for some time, and what with her own conscience and her bewilderment at Lulu's reactions, grew angrier than ever with Rose, and decided that her daughter must be kept away from her as much as possible.

5

THE PHOTIADES WERE LYING in bed, discussing their next flit. They had thrown all their bills into the wastepaper basket as usual, but were too experienced not to recognise the warning signals that it was time for them to go. As Nina, always the practical one of the two, remarked, "Once they get all legal, it's time for us to run." And having said this, she kissed her husband passionately, and for a while all difficulties were forgotten. However, later on she said again, "We must go soon. We needn't tell that horrid landlord. We'll do just what we did last time." She added, "Our usual time of night. It always works." And she giggled happily at the thought, for flitting was easy, the furniture all belonged to the landlord, and all they had in the world were their clothes and some oddments that would go into paper carriers.

And once again they fell to kissing, forgetting all about the furious letter from the bank, pointing out that their overdraft was now nearly five hundred pounds and that their account would be frozen. With this letter was another from a gardening firm—the Photiades were fond of pot-plants, and Andreas always said that Nina had green fingers—another for the stationery that Andreas used in his office, and a largish bill for a sheepskin jacket that would accompany them back to Athens. None of this would have worried either of them, for bills had accompanied them the whole of their married life, even down to the diamond ring on Nina's finger, but that morning, coming back with her shopping (on the overdraft),

Nina had nearly run into a dark-haired, smiling gentleman wandering about the landing in front of their door: as she hastily retreated she heard him ask Mrs. Parsons if she had any idea how he could contact Mr. Photiades.

Mrs. Parsons answered curtly that she had no idea, which was the literal truth. She was in no way interested in the foreigners who lived opposite her, except that she did not like the smell of the hot, spicy food they were always cooking. She stumped back into her own flat, glancing once over her shoulder at the gentleman who instantly smiled again, trying to look as if it were the most natural thing in the world that he should be loitering around, leaning against someone else's door.

He said ingratiatingly, "You wouldn't know, I suppose, at what time Mr. or Mrs. Photiades are likely to return?"

Mrs. Parsons recognised a debt-collector as surely as Nina, though she had not had so much experience. These foreigners were all the same, coming over to this country and spending other people's money. Mrs. Parsons did not like foreigners who to her were only one degree better than those dark people who arrived in droves from Africa and would obviously take the whole place over. But she believed firmly in minding her own business, so she did not even trouble to reply, simply shut the door.

The smiling gentleman who was smiling no longer, sighed and wondered why he had chosen a job where people were somehow never in to see him. He looked at the sheaf of bills in his brief-case, and presently, after banging the knocker several times, made his way down again. He did not notice the pretty, black-haired little girl who was gazing earnestly into the shop window opposite, but then he was not really interested in people, only concerned in hunting them down in terms of l.s.d.

"He'll be back," Nina told her husband, then, "I wonder which one he is."

"I expect it's the jacket," said Andreas, "it was very expensive." And he smiled as he said this, for it was a beautiful affair, made in Scotland and so cosy and warm: it would be splendid for mountain holidays and all his friends would envy him.

"I don't think so somehow," said Nina reflectively. "He had quite a lot of bills in his hand. I think it must be that plant shop. I never liked them. I always thought they'd turn nasty. I suppose we'll have to leave all those lovely pots behind." She glanced back at the window-sill. It was the one thing she always regretted, and really, this lot had done splendidly, the dwarf pineapple, the little orange tree and that gorgeous lily. It seemed such a shame to bequeath them to the landlord who would certainly forget to water them and who would know nothing about fertilisers.

He said comfortingly, "We can always get some more."

And so they planned their next move which by now was pure routine: they would wait until the rent was due, then creep downstairs with their suitcases and carrier bags into the waiting taxi.

Their combined debts, during their stay in England, amounted to over two thousand pounds.

Sunday was one of Veronica's nights for wandering. Perhaps she sensed that the drink was overcoming her again, that the time was coming when she would have to be taken away, sobbing and shaking and screaming, to the nursing home which had already received her so many times. She did not put the premonition into words, she did not even consciously think of it, but she could not ignore the violent headache that now never seemed to leave her, the shakes that convulsed her the moment she needed a drink and the feeling of being hideously out of control. Sometimes the very walls shivered as if they were alive. These times she savagely hated people, could hardly speak to them without shouting, and felt always as if there were something unspeakable just behind her shoulder, prepared to leap on her and strangle her.

Dr. Macek met her on his way back. He was very late. Being a conscientious man with a strong sense of civic duty, he had sworn never to pace up and down his flat again, but he could not endure the thought of sitting there with no possibility of sleep, he was too disturbed to listen to his beloved music, and drink was no comfort to him: he had never drunk much which perhaps in the circumstances was fortunate.

After that appalling lunch with the man from the Embassy, he had no desire to eat any more for the rest of the day, but when he had seen the last of his patients, he decided to go to a restaurant simply for the sake of company and something to do. He had a meal that cost too much money, then took himself to the cinema to see a Czech film he had seen a long time ago in Prague. With Marika—He did not realise until the film started that it had been Marika. It was a pity. He nearly walked out, then the thought of his lonely room kept him there, though he hated every minute of it. The film had never been much and was now completely out of date. The story was slow and old-fashioned, the technique poor, and the actors mouthed and strutted as they would never do these more modern days.

He was thankful when it ended, and appalled, for there was now nothing else to do. Dr. Macek knew nothing of London's night life, which would not in any case have interested him; he wanted nothing more to eat or drink, and the only thing to do was to walk, which he did for an hour and a half. He strode up and down the Embankment, a part of London that always pleased him: when eventually this palled, he walked the whole way home, through Fleet Street, up Southampton Row and in and out of the Bloomsbury squares. Rose, as exiled as he was, had felt as if she were on the bank of a fast-moving river, but to Dr. Macek it was as if he were isolated on some frozen mountain peak, perhaps in his beloved Krkonoše, with the world moving beneath him and himself fettered there by chains.

He thought of Rose, and this was strange, for after Marika had left him he had seldom thought of women at all. He knew nothing of Rose's private life except that she appeared to be separated from her husband; he had passed Gerard on the stairs several times and saw him clearly for what he was. The poor little girl was better off without him, but it was tough luck being there on her own, with two small children and probably not much money. He liked the look of her, and it seemed to him that somehow she was as lost as himself. She was not exactly pretty, though perhaps if she were happier and had more time to herself, she would become so. The long brown hair was lovely, she had a neat if too thin little body, and the eyes were quite magnificent, though—Dr. Macek's clinical gaze had remarked this—they seemed to worry her, for she was always screwing them up and rubbing them.

As he thought of Rose he was aware of quite a warmth within him, and he knew that he wanted to call on her. It was after eleven, a ridiculous hour to call on anyone, much less a young woman he hardly knew, but Rose like himself kept late hours, and he suddenly decided that if her sitting-room light were on—it was easy to see from the pavement outside—he would tap on her door and ask if she would like to have a drink or a coffee with him.

After all, she could always refuse to answer.

It was at this moment, as he was crossing the road to Curran House, that he saw Veronica.

It was plain that she was drunk again, but then she was hardly ever sober. Soon the ambulance would draw up outside, she would be carried in screaming, not to reappear for three or four weeks. Then for a time she would be quiet and dull and comparatively well-behaved, keeping to her own flat, never going out, probably sedated and sleeping her life away. But then it would start all over again, for she was lonely, and the lonely have few means of distraction. Once Dr. Macek, after visiting some friends, had seen her leaning against the railings, so drowned in alcohol that it was like a sea between them: she did not even recognise him. Perhaps she did not see him. He could see her even now, huddled there, her head thrown back, great blurred eyes unfocused, and a thin thread of saliva trickling from the corner of her mouth. She looked to him like a gaunt, shabby wolf, for even in drunkenness her predatory nature showed through: that would be why she was always alone, for not even the most faithful of friends could let themselves be eaten alive.

He did not feel much pity for her, but then for a long time now his emotions had been concentrated on his practice and his young patients. With them he was gentle and compassionate and kind, knew how to make them laugh, knew how to comfort when they were afraid. But Veronica he found a tiresome,

106

self-indulgent woman, and the flirtatious glances she sometimes cast at him, disgusted him so that he hurried past.

He would have hurried past now, only she saw him, and was sober enough to recognise him.

She was dressed more outrageously than he had ever seen her. Once she must have been an attractive woman, for the features were good, her figure still striking: there was a style to her, one could never ignore her. But the constant drinking had coarsened her complexion, the fine eyes were bloodshot, and her hair, grey at the parting where the tint had grown out, was down on her shoulders. She could hardly be badly off, living in Curran House and drinking so much whisky, but she seemed to pick her clothes off some rag-and-bone man's cart: the black skirt was torn, the old sweater filthy, and round her shoulders she wore a tattered bright shawl that could have served as a stage prop for some Dickensian slattern.

She greeted him in a great clarion cry that made him jump, and echoed down the street.

"Why, it's Dr. Macek," cried Veronica, and he had to notice that she pronounced his name correctly. "Come in and have a drink with me," she said, and moved unsteadily towards him.

He shook his head and opened the front door. As he did so, he glanced up at Rose's window. The light was still on.

"So I'm not good enough for you," said Veronica, then her gaze followed his. "Ah," she said, "Ah! So it's little Rose again, is it? Good luck, boy. I daresay you'll need it. Oh, I know she comes up to your room, but I shouldn't depend on her, I shouldn't depend on her at all. She's lonely, that's all it is, and no doubt she wants to make that fat sod of a husband of hers jealous. You'll find yourself a co—a co-respondent any day now, dear doctor. She's that sort of girl. The clinging kind who runs like the wind the moment there's trouble. Besides, she's too young for you. You'd do much better with me. But never let it be said that I'd spoil anyone's fun. You go to her flat, boy, and I hope you enjoy yourself. I hope—"

And here followed such a stream of obscenities that Dr. Macek, not particularly shockable but with old-fashioned ideas about ladies, especially those of a certain age, could hardly believe what he was hearing, and swung round to stare at her.

She burst into a great shriek of laughter. "Oh poor Lothario," she spluttered between the peals of mirth, "have I embarrassed you? Do say I have. I adore embarrassing people—"

Dr. Macek opened the door, shut it in Veronica's face, and walked upstairs. He did not stop at Rose's flat. The idea that this dreadful woman, and perhaps everyone else, had seen Rose come knocking on his door, shocked him. Once he would not have cared, he would even have laughed. But this on top of his lunch with the Embassy official, and the appalling situation he was now in, was more than he could take. He pushed away from him the idea of a pleasant chat with Rose, went into his own flat and prepared, as he had done many times before, for a long and sleepless night.

Veronica forgot the conversation as soon as the words were uttered. She had always been malicious, even as a young girl, but nowadays it was something automatic, to be instantly expunged from her mind. It never entered her head that she might hurt people, damage them, but then in a sense her malice was unmalicious, it spurted from her, it was like urinating before the police constable. She felt now hazily satisfied. She had wanted to get back at Rose, and this in a way she had achieved. She looked at the shut door, swore, then continued walking round the block, staggering home some two hours later.

And Dr. Macek, for the first time in his life, faced its possible conclusion. In his flat with its cheap, shabby boarding-house furniture—he rented it furnished, for all his belongings were in what had once been his home—there was little warmth or comfort. A woman might have cosied it up: he had not made the slightest attempt to do so. The chairs were uncomfortable and did not match, the settee was some fifty years old, the curtains were a vulgarly patterned cretonne. There was a rented television which he only used for the news. Only the record player and books were his. It was to him now utterly cheerless, and he slumped down in one of the armchairs, his feet catching in the worn carpet, threadbare from the shoes of other occupiers. He poured himself out the drink he had planned to share with Rose, but he did not touch it, left the glass on the table beside him. He thought he might switch on the late-night movie, but it was a tough thriller of a kind he could not stomach: his own life had become a tough thriller, and he had no wish to see it portrayed on the box.

He was in most ways a practical man. He did not possess much sense of humour, but there had always been gentleness and compassion. He loved children. Perhaps if he and Marika had had more children, things might have been different. There was always Pavel, of course, but possibly he would never see Pavel again. And now, whichever way he looked, he could see no future. Either he branded himself as a traitor—a melodramatic word, but then it was a melodramatic situation—or he betrayed his old father, living now in some poverty but at least peace, and even perhaps Marika, now married again with another child on the way. He was not sure about Marika. It was impossible to believe she would ally herself against him, but not quite impossible after all, it was something he preferred not to think about. In any case he would never know.

It seemed to Dr. Macek at what was now two in the morning, that cold, dark hour when despair becomes hard and clear, that the answer to all this would be to finish himself. As a doctor he had ample means at his disposal, but he found within himself a certain clinical disapproval at being found untidily dead by some innocent person. The best thing would be to take another walk along his beloved Embankment, in the middle of the night when there was hardly anyone there, and quietly disappear.

Then his living mind began to argue with him. There was that little boy with polio. There was the baby girl called Cicely, a spina bifida with distracted parents. There were so many, they depended on him, there were a thousand other doctors, but the mothers used him almost as a priest-confessor, which was ironic in itself as he held no religion. They would not leave him alone, they nagged at him, their foolish, sad, persistent questions rang in his ears. It won't be permanent, will it, doctor? I mean, these days, medicine is so wonderful, I'm sure there's something to be done. It's not a question of money. We'll raise it somehow. We just want to feel there's hope.

We just want to feel there's hope.

There was no hope. What hope could there be? It was, when you looked at it squarely, utterly ridiculous that in the twentieth century, when the days of prejudice and brutality should sink into the archaic past, an individual could be hopelessly trapped on a matter of ideology, not by torture or execution or savage poverty, but simply by a sophisticated webbing of lies and pressure and politely uttered threats.

And so the night passed. Dr. Macek still sat there, with the untouched glass in front of him: it was too late for suicide, it was too late for anything. The dawn light brightened, and Rose, thinking of her own problems and of Dr. Macek not at all, made the children's breakfast, and prepared to ring her mother, whom she had to call Diana, but who was her mother after all.

She rang the bank manager the moment the bank opened. He was one of those men who look tall when sitting down, and when standing, reveal short, stumpy legs. She dialled the number without the least optimism. She could see his point of view and, if he were a tiresome little man, that was neither here nor there, he was simply doing his job. Her account, never much since she married Gerard—one of the few sensible things she had done was to refuse a joint account—was now permanently in the red. To ask for a further overdraft was nonsense, and the bank manager would have been an incompetent idiot to listen to her. He was to her way of thinking an idiot, but certainly he was not incompetent.

She said once explosively to Lulu, always sympathetic in any crisis, "I never was a woman's libber, but two minutes with that man and I'm burning every bra within sight."

He was now predictably tiresome. "And how are we today, Mrs. Menusier?"

"Broke," answered Rose, too miserable to remember to put on an act. Then, realising that this was entirely the wrong approach, she said quickly, "I know I'm overdrawn—"

He quoted the exact figure at her. She suspected from this that he had been about to write a letter, and had her account sheet on his desk. The figure was worse than she had expected. To think she could cover this with her serial and reviews was purely silly, but she said at once, "I've quite a lot due in. There's a nice batch of work just arrived. I was wondering if—"

He did not let her finish. Perhaps that was decent of him in his own way. But then, just as she was aware of a faint kindly feeling towards him, he began to talk to her as the little woman, using a teasing, flirtatious tone that somehow chilled her blood, it was so damned insulting, it relegated her to the teacups and cress sandwiches, it seemed to strip her of all human dignity.

"Now, my dear Mrs. Menusier, if you'll take my advice—"

Rose listened. She had heard it all before. A settlement— surely a talk with her husband, forgive me if I seem a bit personal. "You see, we really can't go on like this, can we? I always want to help, but you must appreciate my difficulties. In the present financial situation with this dreadful government in power—it is not even a majority government, at least then one would know the enemy."

She wondered what he would say if she told him she was one of those who had voted the dreadful government in. Fortunately he could not see her expression, of combined guilt and amusement, and he went on, "Now perhaps you would like me to have a nice little chat with Mr. Menusier. I don't think he appreciates how difficult things are—"

He bloody does, mate. He appreciates it all right. If she spoke to him like that, he would probably have a coronary and, when he had recovered—if he did recover, which he probably would—freeze her account. Rose continued to listen, said she did not think the chat would do the least good, assured him that she would be paying in shortly.

"May I ask how much?"

"Oh, I don't quite know, but it's a fair sum."

She knew that he did not believe her. He fell once again into the flirtatious manner, and the threat shimmered perceptibly under the coy words. There was no question of cashing another cheque. Rose went on listening, for there was nothing else she could do, answered his enquiries about the children, and knew that he had no patience at all with silly young women who left their husbands and could not cope with the cruel outside world. When the conversation was over, she was nearly in tears through rage and despair, and it was half an hour and a cup of strong coffee later that she summoned up enough energy to ring Diana.

After that she would have to pay in her rent, and the landlord, as contemptuous of women as the bank manager, but a couple of echelons further down the social scale, would probably make a pass at her, as he had done several times before.

It was definitely not her day.

At least with her mother, there was no need to pretend. "Broke again, darling?"

"That's right."

A sigh, half a laugh. At least, whatever you could say of Diana—and she and Rose had little in common—she was not mean. There was plenty of money, Michael had ensured that, but then people with money could sometimes be the meanest of the lot. She said in that husky, stagey voice of hers, "You really are a bloody silly little nit, aren't you?"

"I suppose I am."

"I can't see why the hell you can't go back to Gerard, as you don't seem to be divorcing him. I know he's a bastard and a pouf, but he is a kind of man, darling, all women need a man, and you're not really the self-sufficient kind, are you? Not that I want an old dyke for a daughter—"

"You don't have to be a dyke to be self-sufficient, surely," said Rose wearily, then perceived that Tom as usual had shut himself in, and that Sally, her eyes raptly bent over her book, was listening with all her might. She said quickly, "Let's talk it over when I come."

"You'd better come to dinner on Wednesday. Michael will be out. Some freemason do, little aprons and things. Men are such babies, darling, it's time you learnt how to manage them."

"I will if I can. I have to get a baby-sitter, and they charge forty-five p. an hour."

"I'll pay for it, darling. For Christ's sake, let me stuff some decent food into you for once. You're as thin as a pin. It's not becoming. Christ knows why I have to lumber myself with a daughter who looks as if she's in the bloody workhouse."

"All right," said Rose without much enthusiasm. "But I may be a bit late. I have to get the kids to bed. Baby-sitters don't do anything but watch the telly. I'll probably be there about eight. Will you speak to the children? They're dying to have a word with you."

This was no longer really true. Diana was wildly generous with presents, but detested her grandmotherly status, and the children had to be firmly instructed never to call her Gran, but always to address her by her first name.

Sally said, "Why can't I call her Gran? Other children call their grannies Gran."

Rose said, "Well, she's still quite young, and Gran would make her sound so elderly. Besides, Diana's such a nice name. Don't you think so?"

"No," said Sally. "I think it's a silly name. I'd rather call her Gran."

Rose now heard her mother heave an exasperated sigh, but refused to be bullied: she laid the receiver down on the table and gathered the children round. Tom of course was delighted, indeed, he could hardly be kept away from the phone at any time: next to shutting doors it was his ruling passion. His sole conversational gambit, however, was, "Bye-bye," so this was soon over: with Sally it was more difficult. She no longer used the term 'Gran' but nothing would induce her to say 'Diana', so the conversation became a monologue on the part of Diana herself, who recounted in an impatient voice the dinner party she had been to, and the film show that followed it, none of which was of the slightest interest to a five-year-old.

Sally looked bored, which did not matter, and sounded bored, which did. Rose was thankful when the whole thing was over, shook her fist at her daughter, and wished Diana goodbye.

Twenty minutes later she set off for the landlord's office. She dropped Sally off at school—it was very late, but it would not matter for once—and took Tom with her, thinking he might prove an inhibiting influence on gentlemen who made passes.

It was only a few blocks away, but it took a long time, for

Tom was interested in everything, had to stop at every puddle, had to stroke every dog, and frightened passing cats to death by grabbing at them with the best of all possible motives. It was only people he did not care for, and kindly ladies who stooped down to speak to him were greeted with a terrifying scowl as he rushed to hide his head in a theatrical manner against Rose's leg.

"He's very shy," said Rose apologetically, and knew at once that the ladies did not believe her: they probably believed she was a kid-basher or that Tom was in some way mentally disturbed.

The landlord fortunately behaved himself. This was partly due to Tom who, for all he liked so few people, suddenly decided to be coy with him, peeping up, his face half buried against Rose, and giggling when the landlord winked at him.

"You have no taste at all," she told her son on the way home. "The man's an absolute horror, and there you are positively flirting with him."

However, the rent was now paid, there would be peace for three months, and Diana would help as she always did, offer a permanent allowance as she always did, deliver an exasperated lecture as she always did. There would be money to buy food again, something could be knocked off that bloody overdraft, and so in this undignified fashion life would go until the next crisis.

But it was all very depressing, and when Wednesday arrived Rose would have given anything to cancel the dinner. She was so tired that in the privacy of the kitchen she burst into tears while preparing Tom's lunch: she wondered dismally if she would ever again feel happy and carefree. She told herself fiercely that this was just self-pity, and wept all the harder so that her eyes ached and misted: then she did stop crying in a kind of terror as if the next moment she would suddenly go blind.

She watched Tom devouring his bacon and sausages, and ate nothing herself, only drank yet another of the endless cups of coffee. She knew this non-eating was becoming a dangerous habit, but tonight there would be an excellent meal, as much to drink as she wanted, and probably a bottle to take home.

It was as if Diana, who gave so little of herself, compensated by lavishing material things on her daughter. All this should have been comforting, but Rose could only see herself going once more cap in hand, and the depression grew so strong that she was delighted to exchange a few words with Lulu whom she met on the stairs as she was putting out her rubbish.

"One day," said Lulu, who from her general appearance was going out to a date, "that rogue boy of yours will lock you out."

For Tom, drawn irresistibly by the open front door, had already placed his two hands against it and slammed it to.

"I always snib the lock," said Rose, smiling.

"He's a terror, isn't he? You!" said Lulu with a great theatrical roar to Tom's beaming face as he peered at her through the slit of the already opening door.

"Where are you off to?" asked Rose. "Shouldn't you be at school?" And noticing again Lulu's over-dazzling make-up, and the new cape she had bought recently, which came down to her feet so that she looked like a nurse about to make some pocket-money on the side, "You're playing hookey, aren't you? Is he nice?"

"Oh, he'll pass," said Lulu airily. A hot colour was creeping into her cheeks and Rose, noticing this, wondered if perhaps the new boy-friend was really serious at last.

She asked, "Which one is it this time?"

"Oh, his name's Derek."

"I thought it was Stephen."

"That was last week, Rose."

Rose began to laugh, leaning against the side of the door as she did so. "You make me feel terribly elderly," she said. "No, Tom! This is becoming an obsession." Then she said suddenly, "Do you think it's really psychological?"

"What? His shutting doors? Oh rubbish," said Lulu in a healthy, hearty manner. Then she said, "That's Gerard, isn't it?"

"That's right. No prizes," said Rose a little bitterly.

"He really is a bastard. You ought to divorce him. I'm sure you've got grounds. I know that sounds like coffee or something, but you know what I mean."

"Your mother would have my guts for garters if she heard you talking like that. Swearing and all."

"She's out with her Darbys and Joans," said Lulu, unimpressed.

"Is that why you're not at school?"

"Oh Rose, you're being preachy. Well actually," said Lulu, flushing again, "I ought to be at school, but there's something else I've got to do, something important." Then, the years dropping from her, she said anxiously, "You won't tell on me, will you?"

"Of course not. But won't the school find out?"

"I got Monica to ring them," said Lulu, still pink-cheeked.

"You're quite thorough, aren't you? I suppose I mustn't ask where you're going."

"I'd rather not," said Lulu, looking at her then away. Then in a rush, "Goodness, I'll miss my train. 'Bye, Rose. 'Bye, little horror."

And she rushed downstairs, calling back as she did so, "Do you like my new cloak?"

"It's lovely." And Rose went back into the flat, wondering what exactly was going on. Mrs. Fielding would not be back from her club till the evening: Lulu was safe from discovery. But obviously she was up to something. The bright-blue eye-shadow and the carefully tangled curls with the wisps at the side seemed to indicate a boy-friend, but despite the joking Lulu had never so far fallen seriously for anyone: there was always the odd Derek or Stephen, but it was usually a joshing, giggling kind of business that only lasted a couple of weeks.

"Well, it's none of my business," Rose told Tom, which as it happened was by no means true, but fortunately for her peace of mind she had no idea of Lulu's destination.

Lulu was thankful she had no idea, as she sat in the train for Chichester, with the fifty pounds, minus the fare, snug in her purse. She had borrowed the money from Monica, and for the first time in her life had seen her elder sister genuinely shocked. "Fifty pounds!" Monica repeated, "That's one hell of a lot of money. What do you want—" Then in a shriek of horror, "Oh Lou, no!"

Lulu saw at once what she was thinking and answered

calmly, "Don't be silly, Mon. Anyway I could get it on the Health." Then she begged her sister not to enquire any further, and Monica, relieved that it was nothing worse than some intrigue—it never entered her head it could be anything else— did not press the matter.

Only Lulu remembered her shock with some surprise, for she believed Monica to be unshockable. The memory obviously remained for, as she left, her sister said urgently, "You are telling me the truth about that fifty quid, aren't you?"

"Of course," said Lulu in astonishment, and Monica looked carefully at that round, youthful face before permitting herself to be convinced.

But now Lulu had other things on her mind. She was excited and terrified, for she had never done anything like this in her life. It was only when she thought of Sherlock Holmes—'the game's afoot, Watson!' that she calmed down a little: none the less when she arrived at Chichester, her heart was beating wildly, and she wondered for the first time if she were being really wise.

6

Rose rang the baby-sitter agency without enthusiasm. Lulu was obviously out for the day, and she was too proud to approach any of the friends Gerard had so successfully antagonised. But she was never entirely happy about the agency, and their prices were high: it was a pity Mrs. Fielding was so hostile to her, for the children adored her and she was utterly trustworthy.

The car chose this moment to break down. It was a very old car, and the drive to Chichester had probably been too much for it. It was something to do with the gears. Rose, who was not mechanically minded, had no idea what, but she had to take it round to the garage and leave it there. This meant going to her mother by tube, it also meant being very late, but then Diana was unpunctual herself, and such things did not bother her.

The baby-sitter arrived on time, a brassy, middle-aged woman whom Rose did not take to, but she looked efficient though she was plainly irritated at not being offered a drink.

"I've left a casserole in the oven," said Rose, "and there's plenty of coffee. I hope there's a good programme on T.V."

"I suppose it's mono," said the baby-sitter sourly: she looked around her with a disparaging eye.

"No. It's colour."

This obviously improved matters, and the baby-sitter looked more cheerful. Rose wondered if she were a barmaid in her working life, for she wore a mild-and-bitter air. "I wouldn't say no to a drink," she said, confirming this impression.

"I'm so sorry," said Rose. "I've none in the house."

She saw that this was not believed, and that she was branded as mean. However, as it was unhappily true, there was nothing to be done about it, and if the woman chose to investigate, as she probably would, she would be disappointed. As she was at last going, the baby-sitter, ensconced in front of the fire with the television already on, remarked, "Are the kids likely to be a nuisance?"

"Certainly not," answered Rose hotly. The heat was partly due to the fact that Tom and Sally had indeed been a vast nuisance, as always when she had to go out. Tom, usually sleepy and amenable, insisted on playing interminably with his Mothercare fish in the bath, demanded an extra song when tucked up, while Sally wanted two stories read to her instead of the usual one. The goodnight hug had to be repeated at least half a dozen times, and when at long last she managed to dab on some perfunctory make-up—Diana would comment at once if she did not do so—and pin up her impossible hair once again, there was the inevitable cry for a glass of water and then, from Tom, a completely unnecessary demand for the potty.

Rose, aware that her hair was already coming down, and her nose shining, said, "They should sleep the clock round. If they do wake up, just tell them I'll be home in a little while. Tom might want his potty. He'll go straight to sleep again."

"You'd better leave me a number in case anything goes wrong."

"It's written down on the pad by the phone," said Rose. It was ten past eight already, she had promised Diana to be there at eight, and she had no money for a taxi. Damn the car, it would go wrong today of all days—She thought the baby-sitter was rather disagreeable, and wondered why she had chosen this particular kind of job: the pay, though well beyond her own purse, was not exactly extravagant, and there did not seem to be the least feeling for children.

She ran down the stairs. She could hear her own television at the front door: the baby-sitter must have switched up the volume. There would probably be complaints in the morning.

Apart from this the house was completely silent, and she paused for one second, wishing oddly for some friendly communion, perhaps Mrs. Fielding relenting enough to pop out to ask where she was going, or even Veronica suggesting she might come in for a drink.

But there was no sound from anyone, and presently she was hurrying towards the underground station.

Mrs. Fielding heard her footsteps, but did not immediately comment. She was as usual worried about Lulu, who had not yet come home.

"She didn't say she was going out," she told her husband crossly, "though I suppose I should have guessed it from that ridiculous cloak she was wearing. But I do wish she'd let us know." Then she spoke the words crawling within her mind. "You don't think she's becoming like Monica, do you?"

Len grinned at her. "Mary love," he said, "she's just over sixteen."

"Well," said Mrs. Fielding dubiously, "that's nothing these days, and there are those teddy bears and things —" She did not embroider this strange statement. She said, "Monica started so early."

"Oh for God's sake," said her husband. "You've only got to look at her. She's just not the sort. For one thing she's got too much sense."

He looked at Mrs. Fielding as he spoke, and she stared back at him. They both adored Lulu, perhaps more even than the perfect Amanda, but both at that moment saw her clearly, with the deplorably frizzy hair, the over made-up eyes and the air of utter innocence. She was a darling girl, and one day might be very attractive, but there was no comparison between her and Monica who even in her pram was already a determined flirt with an eye for the men and a contempt for females who wished to kiss her. Mr. and Mrs. Fielding burst out laughing in unison, the latter saying at last, "Well, I suppose it's all right. But she ought to let us know when she's going out. She must have gone straight from school." She added thoughtfully, "If she was there at all. I don't quite trust that young lady. I agree it's not a boy, but she does get up to the oddest things."

She poured out a Scotch for her husband and a sherry for herself. When in surprise he asked if it was some celebration he had forgotten, she did not trouble to answer. She said, "Rose has just gone out."

"Well, she doesn't have to ask our permission, love!"

"She really is the silliest girl," said Mrs. Fielding. "I know I shouldn't have spoken to her like that, and I will try to make it up, but she does make me so cross. She's got herself a really lovely man, and she lets him go. I think I'll never understand the young people of today."

Her husband did not answer. He seldom argued with his wife. He had enjoyed the visit to Fishbourne, and he thought Claudine quite a piece, but he found Gerard less devastating than his wife. He had put up a spirited defence of him to Lulu, but in his heart he could see that this actor chappie might not make the ideal husband, with his flash clothes and the charm that was as slippery and removable as a polythene bag. However, he was not particularly interested, and soon he settled down to watch the television and wait for Lulu's return.

Veronica heard Rose on the stairs too, but was now too near the point of no return to want to see anyone. The boy from the wineshop had delivered three bottles that morning, and two were now finished. He had given her a sly grin as he removed the empties. He knew her very well, as all the local shops did: he told the manager when he returned that Lady Matford wouldn't be wanting much more for a few weeks, they'd be taking her away any day now. It seemed to him very funny, though he had had a bit of a shock when he came in: she was pacing up and down the flat like a caged animal, her hair down her back, her dressing-gown open so that he could see her breasts. The face she turned upon him as he set the bottles down, was fallen in as if she had not eaten for days, the eyes bloodshot and enormous, and the hand instantly stretched out to the bottles, shaking as if she had a palsy. He was glad to get away. There was a dreadful desolation in the flat that chilled him: he could not have put this into words, but there was a damned air to her as if she were already in hell. However, the old girl always tipped generously: in fact he half believed she simply did not know what she was giving him. This time it was a pound note. He wondered where all her money came from.

The landlord could have told him. The rent had not been paid for over a quarter. He did not call in to ask for it. The truth was that Lady Matford scared him. He was prepared to bully Rose, who was a silly, soft little thing, but Veronica's wolfish grin, her pealing voice and the language she used, appalled him. In any case the rent would eventually be paid, by her poor old sod of a husband, he would do anything to keep the old bag out of his hair. When she came back from the nursing home, she would behave herself more or less for quite some time. He was far more concerned with the Photiades, who also owed him a quarter's rent: he had suspected for a long time that one day they would just disappear: he always called in at the flats once a week before the tenants were up, and he had noticed the pile of bills that always filled their pigeon hole. He wondered if he could put pressure on them, to frighten them into paying, but then of course this might accelerate the moonlight flit.

If he had known it, the Photiades were frightened already. "I suppose we have been rather extravagant," Nina told her husband, but he only laughed, told her not to be such an old silly, and gave her a shake and a kiss. Despite the laugh, however, he never opened the flat door these days unless they were expecting friends, and even then he always made sure who it was. There were too many knocks both early in the morning and late in the evening, too many smooth, smiling gentlemen lurking on their landing. "It gives me the creeps," Nina said. "Sometimes I just don't dare go out." She had had another narrow escape that very day, for a man—a different one this time—called just as she was going downstairs, and even this evening—they too heard Rose go out, for they were always listening—there was an insistent banging on the door just after nine o'clock.

Andreas exclaimed, "I've half a mind to go out and knock him down. What an hour to call! Don't they ever stop spying?"

But Nina did not respond laughingly as she usually did. She was thinking of the sheepskin jacket, the new Revelation suitcase, and the television they had just got on approval, to—

as they put it—test the colour. After the correct period of time they would then return it as unsatisfactory, and try another make. She said suddenly, "Oh Andreas, let's go now. I don't like it here. I don't like the people. That dreadful drunk woman terrifies me, and the creature opposite is so common, I can't think how she ever got into this block. Let's go tonight."

"We can't do that. I must notify the office. Besides, they owe me a month's salary."

This of course was unanswerable. The Photiades would never lose a month's salary. But Nina said, "Well, at least we can start packing." And despite Andreas's protests she went instantly to the cupboard where they kept all their paper carriers: these, plus the beautiful, brand-new suitcase, would see them through the flit, so that they could once again start a new and exciting life in another part of London.

Rose arrived half an hour late, breathless and dishevelled. Her mother, dressed in a black and white velvet trouser suit, her hair immaculately rinsed and set, greeted her with a resigned, smiling sigh. They bestowed on each other the ritual kiss, and Rose flung off her jacket. The lining was torn under the arm. She saw it, and Diana saw it too. However, there was no comment, and Rose sank down gratefully into an armchair, and accepted the large drink offered her.

"You look bushed, darling," Diana said.

There was no particular sympathy in the endearment. It was simply theatrical. Diana Morley, who had left Mr. Morley when Rose was seventeen, had once been on the stage, mostly in musical comedy roles, for she had been an extremely pretty girl with magnificent legs. Her acting career had finished a long time ago, but she still moved in theatre circles, and spoke of well-known actors by their christian names. Sometimes she was invited to a first-night party, she knew a number of television actors who dropped in from time to time, and there were several signed photos on the piano that she so seldom played. However, Michael fortunately was waiting in the wings, and there had always been a comfortable family income: Rose, though she had never been close to her mother, had always found her generous, sometimes wildly so. Money was not only forthcoming but offered, and even Michael, who was a company director and wealthy, was always willing to help.

"You make me feel like a poor relation," said Rose rather ungratefully, looking first at her mother's outfit, which certainly did not come off the peg, then at the flat, almost as if she were viewing it for the first time. It was not at all to her taste, and the children, on their rare visits, terrified her for fear they would break or dirty something, but it was lush and plush, the furniture was covered in brocade, the carpet was furry and white, and there were bright silken cushions every-where, sometimes with dolls on top of them, and matching satin lampshades. Pink was the predominant colour, the lights were carefully shaded, and mantelpiece and tables were covered with small pieces, some antique and many rare.

"Well, so you are, darling," said Diana, refilling her glass. "So I expect you'd better have this straight away." She pushed a folded cheque into Rose's hand. "That's what you want, isn't it?"

"Oh Mother — Yes, I'm afraid it is." Rose unfolded the cheque and looked at it in shame and bewilderment. "But I— I don't want all this. It's so much. I mean—"

Diana walked over to the mantelpiece, a glass in her hand. She leant against it, looking across at Rose. She was still an extremely pretty woman, and the soft pink light flattered her as it was intended to do. Rose thought she looked younger than herself, then she glanced down again at the cheque and burst into a flood of tears.

Diana heaved a theatrical sigh. She made no attempt at comfort or consolation, but then that had never been her way: she was not a maternal person, she had never wanted a baby, and her grandchildren bored her after five minutes of their company. She only said, "You are a bloody mess, darling, aren't you? You'd better tell me all about it. And for Christ's sake, stop calling me Mother. You make me feel all bosomy. I can't stand it. I'd give you another drink, but you don't look to me as if you've been doing much eating lately, so you'd better come into the kitchen and let me feed you up. We're being all informal. I couldn't be bothered to lay the dining-room table."

"Won't Michael be in?" asked Rose in a choked voice, mopping at her eyes.

"I told you, he's gone to this freemason thing-ding. He won't be in till the small hours, and he'll be pissed to the wide."

"Are you happy with him?" asked Rose, preparing to follow her.

"Christ, darling, what a bloody silly question to ask me. I'm still with him, aren't I? I don't have to be. We're not married, thank God, and he's not the only man in the world."

"That doesn't sound very loving," said Rose. She had now recovered herself, indeed the tears had simply been the product of strain and exhaustion: she already felt better if a little ashamed of her lack of self-control. She met her mother's amiable if cynical gaze. Diana was on the whole a good-natured woman, without much feeling but also without malice: she had nothing of Veronica's wildly destructive nature. Rose reflected that she must be well into her fifties: she did not know the exact age for that was something that was never mentioned. Michael was certainly very much in love with her, gave her everything she wanted, and was always begging her to marry him. Why she did not marry, Rose could not imagine. She was in no way a promiscuous woman, not even a highly-sexed one, she loved security and, for all her talk of other men, had surely reached the age where she could no longer pick and choose. She had now lived with Michael for ten years, it was virtually a marriage, it might as well become a legal one. And thinking this, Rose followed her into the bright, modern kitchen filled with every kind of gadget that money could buy: it always made her sadly envious when she thought of her own poky little affair, with the old gas stove, the sink that always blocked up, and the fridge that was far too small.

"You're being very sentimental and boring," said Diana. "Do you really expect me to fall into girlish transports? Sit down, darling. I'm trying out a new recipe on you. I think it smells rather gorgeous, don't you? Here's your little starter. That's something new too. You see, I'm doing you proud."

For Diana was a magnificent cook: perhaps this was the only maternal outlet she allowed herself. Rose thought briefly of the scrag-end and mince and kippers and eggs that made up her home menu, then discovering she was wildly hungry, began to eat the shrimp-avocado mousse that was placed before her, enchanted with the way the table was laid, with its hand-sewn serviettes, the fine glass, the china that matched, and the openwork tablecloth. Her mother's idea of informality was something she herself could never achieve for the most exotic party, but it gave her a feeling of remoteness so that this, coupled with two large drinks on an empty stomach, made her feel misty, floating and, for the moment, at peace. For a while she simply ate in silence, having two helpings of everything and drinking glass after glass of wine. This Diana entirely approved of, and she watched her daughter with the nearest approach to affection that was in her, refilling her glass and trying to make her take a third helping of the wild duck casserole.

"Oh I do feel better!" said Rose, with an explosive sigh that was half a belch, then she apologised and laughed. The colour was back in her cheeks, and her eyes shone with satisfaction and repletion.

"You're half-starved," said Diana. "Let's go back to the sitting-room and I'll make some strong coffee."

Rose drank two cups of coffee, and looked down at the glass of brandy placed before her. "I haven't had such a meal in years," she said, then looking at her mother's velvet-suited body, "How on earth do you keep your figure if you always eat like this?"

"Michael likes his food, and I never put on an ounce," said Diana. Then settling herself artistically on the settee like Madame Récamier, for she always contrived to look decorative —"even on the loo, darling, someone might look in"—she said. "Now what the hell is all this about, darling? I gather you and Gerard haven't made it up yet."

"No, and we're not going to," said Rose a little grimly, and some of the glow and pleasure left her so that she twirled her glass round in silence, staring down at the floor.

"I think you're a bloody fool," said Diana calmly. "Now listen, Rose. Just forget I'm your mother, and let me talk."

"Okay," said Rose with a faint smile, and thought how strange it was that Diana was indeed her mother, for the relationship between them, even when Rose was a child, was at its best that of cool, detached friends. It seemed to her, as she watched Diana in the soft, pink light, that there was something oddly sexless about her, with her beautiful clothes, her unlined face—did she have it lifted, oh certainly—and the elegantly arranged hair that was neither too young nor too old. She had divorced Rose's father in the same calm, almost bored fashion that was hers in everything, it had all been done quietly and without scandal, and Mr. Morley had courteously died some eighteen months later so that there was never a tug-of-war between parents. How Michael came on the scene, Rose never knew, for she was then away from home. But she came back to find him ensconced as official lover, and he too seemed a quiet, amiable person, who accepted his new daughter with perfect good nature.

To Rose, who lived her life in an untidy welter of emotions, who loved the wrong people, who in her extreme youth flung herself wildly into causes, who had never seen where she was going, it was a kind of fairy tale of the more macabre kind, with a changeling mother who bore no resemblance to her at all. She said suddenly, before Diana could embark on what was plainly to be an oration, "You don't understand me, Mother—"

"I do wish you'd call me Diana, darling. How often do I have to tell you?"

"I'm sorry. You don't understand me, but I don't begin to understand you. Okay, okay, we'll talk about Gerard, but what are you doing? Why don't you get married?"

"Oh for Christ's sake!" Diana gave the little tinkling laugh that Rose disliked, and lit herself a cigarette. Then she said in a different voice, "It's a bloody silly thing to ask me, you know, but I'll tell you. Why not? I think I've drunk too much— You're not drinking yourself to death, are you? You seem in that sort of state of mind."

"I can't afford it!"

"How you do go on about money—"

"One always does when one hasn't got it."

"Well, all right, I'll make you a present of a bottle when you go. Why don't I marry Michael?" Diana paused again, and for that one moment, despite the pink shaded lamp, the charming clothes and the elegance of her posture, she looked old. "First of all, why should I? He wants to, of course. He's a funny old maid in some ways. Respectable as they come. But it's not that. I don't want the permanence. I couldn't stand the permanence. As things are now, I can walk out whenever I please."

"And so can he."

"True, true. Though I doubt he ever will. But if we got married—oh God, just the thought of it makes me puke—I'd be tied down. I can't bear that. It makes me feel so old. It would make a cock-up of everything. I'd probably walk out on him in a matter of weeks. I should never have married your father, darling, and I shouldn't have lumbered myself with a baby either."

"That's a nice thing to say to me," said Rose, but she smiled as she spoke, for she had heard this many times before.

"Well," said Diana, "you can't pretend I made much cop as a mum. Loving arms and bedside stories and sweeties and things—you were better off with your nanny. But I always got you nice clothes, and you didn't even wear them, you ungrateful bitch."

Rose remembered that episode at school, and laughed.

Diana went on, "And if I may say so, darling, you look quite deplorable. Where on earth did you buy that trouser suit? And when?"

"Oh never mind," said Rose crossly. "I know you don't like my going on about it, but I'm as broke as hell, and well you know it. I like nice clothes just as much as you do, but I don't have the money to buy them. And please, please don't offer me anything, because that's not why I'm saying this. It's just that you asked. The cheque you've given me I have to take—"

"Gracious little pet, aren't you?"

"Oh I'm sorry, I didn't mean to sound so beastly. Only—"

"You're getting emotional again," said Diana calmly, and leaned over to put some more brandy into her glass.

"Dear, you'll make me so drunk I won't be able to get home."

"You can stay the night if you like."

"Of course I can't. What about the children? The baby-sitter will probably walk out at midnight." Then Rose thought suddenly how strange it was that her mother had not once enquired about Tom and Sally.

She did not do so now. But then she had never pretended to be in the least interested. She sent lavish presents for birthdays and Christmas, occasional gifts of beautiful, expensive and unsuitable clothing, and that was all. Rose in the early days had given her photographs: what she did with them her daughter had no idea, they probably ended up in the wastepaper basket. They were certainly never on display, though Sally especially was a beautifully photogenic child.

Diana, dismissing the subject of the children, started again. "I think you were going to tell me you're in an all-fired bloody mess."

"I don't know if I was going to say that," said Rose sadly, "but God knows it's true."

"Then you'd better go back to Gerard."

"I couldn't."

"Oh balls, darling. Sometimes you make me so tired. Now listen, Rose. I realise that you and I are quite different people. I can do without a man if I have to. I never have had to," said Diana, with a twitch of a smile, "but it may come yet. I'm not sure that I really like them, you know. They're all right in bed, and one has to have an escort from time to time, but they're mostly bloody bores, and sometimes I think I ought to have been a business woman and lived on my own. I've an excellent business head, you know. I really am frightfully good at money."

Rose was a little bewildered by this, for it did not go with the pink satin room: Diana must have sensed her reaction for she went on, "You're thinking this is hardly a business girl's pad? Of course it isn't. I like my comforts and I like luxury. I don't have to live in a permanent office, do I? I'm not a butch lesbian after all."

"Oh Mother, really—"

Diana looked as if she were about to protest, then changed her mind. She said firmly, "Now you, darling, you're the sort who needs a man. You've just gone to pieces since you left

Gerard. And you don't seem able to find anyone else. I know he's a bastard, and as queer as a coot—"

Rose said wretchedly, "I suppose he is. It took me a long time to accept it, though people threw hints around like confetti. But I don't think he—I mean, I think he's tried to get over it. He even seems to have a girl-friend. Of sorts—"

Diana looked at her silently for a moment, then said in a restrained voice, "You're so bloody innocent, darling. He was your first, wasn't he?"

"Yes. He still is, if you know what I mean."

"My God, and you my daughter! Don't you like men?"

"Of course I do," said Rose with more spirit, "but it doesn't mean I have to hop into bed with the baker and the milkman. I'm not a glove, after all."

Diana broke into a laugh at this, saying, "Sometimes I think there's hope for you yet." Then more seriously, "I never approved of your marrying him. But even if I'd said so, you wouldn't have listened, and I don't interfere in other people's business. You'll grant me that, I hope. I mayn't be much of the cosy momma type, but at least I've always left you alone."

"Yes," said Rose, and reflected that sometimes it would have been agreeable if Diana had interfered a little more. The lack of interference was not really a virtue, it simply signified lack of interest.

"You've married a rotten bastard," said Diana. "I always knew he was AC/DC. If I'd told you, you wouldn't have understood. If you'd anyone else, I'd say good luck to you. But you haven't, and he's better than nothing. What's going to become of you? You won't let me settle an allowance on you—"

"No. Thank you, no."

"I think you're just being silly. All right, darling. And what then? You've got the two kids. You can't go back into a full-time job. You're not divorced, you're not married. You don't seem to do anything about another man, and if you go on looking as you did when you came in, you won't get one. Men don't like dreary females. So what? I don't suppose you'll be particularly happy with Gerard, but at least he'll provide for you in his own way. He seems to have plenty of money, as long as one doesn't ask where it comes from."

"I don't know what you mean by that," said Rose in a chilly whisper. She did not quite understand what all this was about, but there was an edge to Diana's voice that frightened her.

"Well, it certainly won't be acting, darling. I saw that god-awful play of his. That poor devil couldn't call the register at school. Still, he has to live, and I daresay some people fall for that bogus charm. I'm not holding much brief for him, Rose. I'm sure he's treated you abominably, though you're such a bloody doormat these days you do ask for it. But what the hell are you going to do? Now don't start crying again. I get so bored with people who cry. Just answer me. What are you going to do?"

Rose said after a pause, "I don't know. In a way you're right, and in a way you're terribly wrong. I can't go back to Gerard. The very thought of it makes me sick. He frightens me."

"Don't tell me he knocks you about."

"Oh no. He's not that sort of man. There are other ways of hurting people. But of course you're quite right about what I'm to do with myself. You know," said Rose with sudden energy, "I'm not really a women's lib type. I've no desire to burn my bra, even if I could afford to—but the woman on her own is really in one hell of a spot. Wives don't really like you—"

"They never liked me," said Diana smugly.

"I bet they didn't. But they don't like me either. I don't think it's anything to do with whether one's pretty or sexy or anything like that. They just don't want unattached females around their husband, it somehow seems dangerous. I used to go out a lot, you know. I don't now. Well, it's partly my fault, I suppose, and of course it's Gerard's fault too. He was always so horrid to my friends, flirted with them in a kind of phoney way and then, when he saw they didn't like it, was so rude that they just didn't come again. I'm sure they'd come running if I said I needed help, but somehow I can't, it looks so feeble. So I seldom see anyone. Besides—you divorced my father. I don't know whose fault it was, but I'm sure all the other wives said it was yours."

131

"It was actually, darling!"

"They'd still say it even if it wasn't. The people in the flats all think me dreadful because I walked out on Gerard, they tell me I'm selfish and don't bother about my own children. I met a man the other day who used to know both of us, and was always popping in for drinks and so on. I called out, 'Hallo', and he crossed over to the other side of the road without so much as acknowledging me. Oh, I expect that's just an extreme example, but it was quite horrid. It made me feel like a whore."

"Not in that sweater, pet," said Diana. "You really must let me give you something. I've got a blue pullover that's quite new. It might be a bit big for you, you're so skinny, but I think it would be all right."

Rose ignored this. She went on, "And of course the woman on her own is regarded as the natural prey by landlords and bank managers—"

"Yours being sticky?"

"He's an absolute bastard. Well, I do have an overdraft— but he doesn't have to flirt with me."

"I should tell him to fuck off, darling," said Diana.

Rose, always a little taken aback when such words crossed her mother's lips, said austerely, "You don't tell people that when you're wildly in the red. Oh well, all this is very silly, but it's nice to get it off my chest."

"Not much of a chest either," said Diana.

"Oh come now—I'm not as bad as all that. Am I?"

"You look ghastly. Well, you look better now because you've had a good meal, but really it's a bit much to see one's daughter looking positively older than oneself. Well, Rose? So what? Landlords bully you and wives avoid you. What you need is a nice boy-friend, but I suppose I'm just wasting my breath. What are you going to do? Are you going to divorce Gerard?"

"I think so. But I'm such a coward, I'm so frightened it won't come off. After all, he hasn't technically deserted me. He wants Sally, you know."

"And you won't let him have her?"

"Of course not. How could I? But you're quite right, I

132

can't go on like this. It's bad for the children as well as me. Only I just seem to have lost all my energy—and my eyes bother me. I know it's nothing—"

"I'll give you the address of my oculist. He's marvellous."

Rose was about to say she could not afford it, but stopped herself in time. She fell silent, looking at Diana, who lay there as beautifully as a cat, who was so composed, so reasonable, so full of impeccable advice—and who had not the least comprehension of the appalling muddle her daughter was in: how could she be patient with a weakness and indecision that was totally alien to her? Rose wondered for a silly second what it would be like to have some cosy, conventional mother who would say there, there, and cradle her against her bosom. Like Mrs. Fielding—Mrs. Fielding would rush to her daughters' defence, even if it were Monica had up for soliciting, or something equally discreditable. There would be no reasoning, no cool, dispassionate consideration of the situation. She would be instantly bursting with protective emotion, it would be my daughter against the whole, wide world.

Rose exclaimed in a sudden, clear, high voice, "Oh Mother, can't you help me?"

"Help you!" Diana was so outraged that she sat bolt upright. "What the bloody hell do you think I've been doing the whole evening? Really, darling, sometimes I think you're out of your tiny mind. I give you a whacking big cheque, a gorgeous meal and the best possible advice. I think you just about have the bloodiest nerve—"

"Yes," said Rose more quietly, "I have. I'm sorry. You've been marvellous." She glanced idly at her wristwatch as she spoke, then leapt to her feet with a cry of dismay. "Oh my God! It's nearly twelve o'clock."

"Does it matter? You're not Cinderella, darling, though the type-casting wouldn't be bad at all. You can always pick up a taxi."

"It's the baby-sitter," said Rose, grabbing at her jacket. "She charges forty-five p. an hour."

"Well, you've got the money now, so I don't know what you're going on about."

133

Rose did not point out that taxi-drivers do not accept a cheque, however magnificent. But reckoning it up swiftly in her mind, she thought she would have enough for both baby-sitter and taxi, so she said nothing more about it, only kissed Diana's cheek again and made swiftly for the front door.

She looked back as she came down the steps. There was a bottle of Scotch under one arm. Diana had insisted, Diana who stood there in the doorway, beautiful, immaculately groomed, and remote as the North Pole. Rose wondered in a confused way how she had ever done anything so inelegant as to give birth to herself. It was impossible to imagine her sweating and straining, for once as dead common as the rest of her sex. She said, "Thank you so much. You've been a darling. I can't tell you how much better I feel, especially after that miraculous meal. I'll give you a ring tomorrow."

"Get yourself a lover," said Diana. "If you can't do that, go back to Gerard. He's not much, I grant you, but he's better than nothing."

"I'll think about it," Rose called back gaily, then ran down the street, making for the main road where she should be able to pick up a taxi. The tears were pouring down her cheeks. She felt so lonely that she believed she could die. She stood there on the pavement, shamelessly weeping: when a taxi at last pulled up, she directed him in a choked voice, then huddled on the seat. The cheque was in her handbag, and in her heart was a blank bewilderment that two people linked by the closest blood tie should be so utterly apart. She had grown within Diana, she was part of Diana's beautiful body, and the whole evening could have been conducted in two dissimilar languages for all the communication that existed between them.

She arrived home at half past midnight, to find the baby-sitter pacing up and down. The late-night movie was on, but apparently that was not enough. Rose could see dirty plates and cutlery in the kitchen, so she had obviously eaten her supper.

She said, "I'm so sorry. I'm afraid I forgot the time. Do forgive me. Were the children good?"

"You didn't tell me you'd be so late."

"I'm really sorry, but you know how it is—"

What the hell am I apologising for? I pay her, don't I? Then Rose was panic-stricken lest she did not have sufficient money, but fortunately there was just enough, four hours, four times forty-five, oh, about two quid—

"I think it's most inconsiderate," said the baby-sitter. Rose realised that there must be a strong aroma of brandy about her, and of course there was the bottle of Scotch. Doubtless she was now branded as an alcoholic.

She said, ignoring this, "It's four hours, isn't it? I make that—"

"Four and a half."

"Oh, of course. Well, that's—that's—"

"Two pounds, two p. and a half."

Rose thought, Don't forget the half whatever you do, but said nothing, only counted the money out—there was, thank God, enough, just—and dropped the halfpenny into the avaricious palm with a little bang. She said, "I hope you don't live too far away."

The baby-sitter told her the address. Rose knew it very well. It was a big block of flats two minutes' walk away, just across the High Street.

She said, "Well, thank you very much, and I'm glad the children—"

"I want the money for my taxi, please."

"What! But it's only just across the road!"

"It's one of the rules of the agency," said the baby-sitter, "that we always have to have a taxi."

"But forgive me, that's ridiculous—"

"It's the rule, madam."

The 'madam' was slung in like a stone. Rose stood there, her purse in her hand. There was two and a half p. in that purse. She thought mistily, What the hell am I to do? Then she remembered Sally's piggy-bank. She went silently into the bedroom where Sally was sound asleep. Feeling like a burglar, she shook the money out. There was just over twenty pence. It must be replaced next morning, or there would be the devil to pay. She came back into the sitting-room and, still without a word, handed the money over.

She could see that the baby-sitter thought her horribly mean but, as the money would simply go into her pocket as a bonus, she felt nothing but a spiteful satisfaction. She said, "Good night," in her crispest tone and, once the door was closed, nearly ran to the window to see if the woman was crossing the High Street.

However, this would be silly for obviously there was nothing else she could do. No taxi would accept a fare across the road. One thing was certain: she would never contact this particular agency again. Then Rose flopped down into the nearest chair. and took Diana's cheque out of her bag, to look at it again. It was for two hundred and fifty pounds. It was almost the National Debt. Two hundred and fifty pounds, and she had to rob her poor little daughter's piggy-bank—

Rose, for the first time that evening, broke into helpless, spontaneous laughter.

7

LULU ARRIVED IN CHICHESTER at mid-day. Her first thought was lunch. She was a practical girl, and it seemed to her stupid to conduct what was obviously going to be a tricky assignment on an empty stomach. She had not so far met Gerard's entourage, but from what Rose had said, knew well enough that Claudine was unlikely to welcome her to a meal. Besides, she was already nervous, and a good solid lunch would put some stuffing into her, in every sense of the word.

And it was not going to be a salad either. Lulu was painfully aware that she was too fat, and was always trying different diets, much to Mrs. Fielding's irritation. There was the grapefruit diet, which lasted for two weeks, then Lulu, bored to death with sour fruit, tried some strange new device that involved honey, orange juice and eggs. This made her sick, and she abandoned it after one day. There was then the rigid calorie diet, but she grew exhausted with the perpetual counting, besides it gave her an appetite. There followed the milk diet, the all-protein diet, and then something that involved two fast days a week, sustained only on fruit juice, water and black coffee. This last was the most disastrous of all, for Lulu had a healthy appetite, and halfway through the second day she could stand it no longer, and rushed into the kitchen to help herself to a large hunk of bread and butter and jam, thus adding far more than she could possibly have taken off.

"I don't know why you worry so much," her mother said a little wearily, for Lulu on a diet was invariably in a bad temper.

"In another year's time you'll drop all that weight. It isn't as if you take no exercise. I was just like you at your age. I know I'm a bit overweight now, but as a girl I was as slim as a reed. You ask your father."

"I want to lose it now," said Lulu. "People laugh at me because I'm too fat."

"Oh nonsense," said Mrs. Fielding, and because she loved her youngest daughter very much, forebore to say that the way-out clothes in imitation of Monica, were disastrous for the fuller figure, and that Lulu's real trouble was not the quality of what she ate but the quantity. If she could have been persuaded to have one helping and not three for dinner, a piece of toast for breakfast instead of bacon and fried potatoes, she would probably lose weight in a painless manner. However, bringing up three daughters had taught her that it was no use saying anything, so she sighed and prepared to accommodate herself to the newest fad; it would probably be expensive and upset her household accounts, but then all dieting was and did.

Lulu now decided to ignore her weight problem altogether. She found herself a pleasant little restaurant, quite empty because it was still early, and ordered herself a luscious meal, starting with soup and going on to steak and chips—the last did give her a twinge of conscience, but the chips were so good that she dismissed it—and ending shamelessly with ice-cream. This made her feel a great deal better, and she wound up by smoking a forbidden cigarette: this was the one thing Mrs. Fielding would not permit, and Lulu only dared buy a packet when she was out.

But even the meal, though it made her feel stronger, could not allay the trepidation inside her. She was not even certain of what she proposed to do. Sherlock Holmes would of course have his plans already laid, but Lulu was an immature sixteen, Gerard, much as she detested him, frightened her a little, and to go like this into the lion's den required as much courage as she had in her, and Lulu was in no way a coward. She stubbed her cigarette out, paid her bill, telling herself fiercely that she had to do this for Rose's sake, Rose who was always so nice, who never laughed at her, who sympathised with her problem and treated her like an adult. There was a gentleness in Rose that Lulu had not met often in her life: the adult woman stirring beneath the puppy fat, the schoolgirl speech and the inappropriate taste in dress, told her intuitively that here was a lost and vulnerable person, who was being terrorised by people utterly beneath her.

Perhaps this visit would do no good. It might even do harm. Certainly she would not be welcome. Gerard had no time for schoolgirls and made it only too plain: the sister no doubt would share his views, and as for that other ghastly girl—what was her name now, oh Trudy, German, she would have to be German—she sounded quite awful and might even be jealous. But at least she might hear something that would give her a handle against Gerard, something to help Rose start her divorce, something to stop her being persecuted. But it was a pity that something that had seemed so terribly exciting when she asked Monica for the money, should now, oddly enough, sound almost silly.

But it was too late to go back now. Lulu paid a visit to the cloakroom, for nerves were stirring her inside, then came out briskly, a squat little figure, rather over made-up about the bespectacled eyes, the frizzy hair blowing in the breeze, and the cloak billowing behind her. A passing boy whistled at her, and this restored some of her confidence. She walked back to the station, found herself a taxi, and directed it to Fishbourne Post Office which, Rose had told her, was near the estate.

The blank surprise on Gerard's face when he opened the door, was, though in the circumstances only to be expected, not encouraging. For a minute the two of them stared at each other in silence. Lulu, a little breathless, thought that he had changed a great deal: she had not after all seen him for several months. The good looks, the unmistakable good looks, were somehow—the word floated into her mind—raddled. The mane of tawny hair was as dashing as ever, the features were impeccable, and the teeth displayed in a swift and brilliant smile, every dentist's dream. He was dressed in corduroy slacks, a scarlet pullover and a white shirt open to reveal the strong, muscular neck. It was all magnificent, he was, whatever one thought of him, a handsome man, but to Lulu, her perceptions sharpened by fright, he possessed as much reality as a tailor's dummy. There was something mean and shabby about him, as if the beautiful façade concealed rottenness within. And she was afraid of him, not for what he could do to her, for he could not touch her, but for what he could do to Rose: the thought of living with such a man, sleeping with such a man, made her flesh crawl.

All this barely touched her conscious mind, but it made her speech jerky, and she wished furiously that she could control her breath which was doing the oddest things, calm her bumping heart.

She said in a quick, flustered way, quite unlike her usual method of speech, "I say, I hope you don't mind me calling, it's awful of me, only I was in Chichester, and I suddenly thought it's such a nice day, it's a pity to go back so early, perhaps I could call on you. Of course if I'm disturbing you—"

"Come in, come in!" said Gerard jovially. "Rose's friends are always welcome."

He was thinking she really was a revolting child. Thank God he didn't have a daughter like that. He looked at the bright blue eyelids, magnified by the glasses, and suppressed a giggle. And that hair—He did not see the intelligence in her face, the good nature and warmth that shone from her, for such things did not remotely interest him. Women, as far as they concerned him at all, must either flatter him non-stop, like Trudy, or else be beautiful, elegant creatures who would enhance his own good looks by their presence, prove his own impeccable good taste. But he could hardly leave Lulu on the doorstep, so he put his hand under her elbow to steer her in, talking effusively as he did so.

"And how is Rose?" he said. "I hope to come up to London shortly. To see my darling little girlie. Oh, I know you probably think me a sentimental old father—" He gave a boyish laugh as he spoke. "—but I do think my Sally has something I've never seen in another child. We are very close, you know. I think it happens sometimes with fathers and daughters. It is almost like twins. We should never be apart, both of us are somehow diminished by separation. I don't think Rose really appreciates this, but there is so often a kind of antagonism between mother and daughter. Don't you think so? I believe the mother resents the child who is lovelier than herself, it makes her feel old. And of course in such a case it is really better for both of them to be apart. Perhaps with your own mother—"

Here he spluttered into a quickly suppressed snort of mirth, for the thought of any mother, much less Mrs. Fielding, being jealous of a dumpy, plain little creature like this, was just too hilarious. He smothered the laugh almost at once, looking quickly at Lulu to see if it had registered, but he need not have troubled: she felt the laugh shiver through her arm, but simply thought he was a bastard, and probably high.

"Do come in," Gerard said again, referring this time to the sitting-room. "You haven't met my little sister, have you? No, of course not. Your parents came here, you know. We had such a nice day together. We have a guest today, too—"

"I'm so sorry," said Lulu, managing for the first time to slide in a few words. "If you're in the middle of lunch or something, I can always wait."

"Oh, we've finished lunch," said Gerard speaking with great firmness, so as to make it plain that Lulu, if she were hoping for a free meal, would be disappointed. He called out, "Chérie! We have a visitor."

And he opened the sitting-room door with a flourish, ushering Lulu in, and, as she suspected quite accurately, making monkey faces over her shoulder.

The three faces turned on her were enough to make anyone long to run home, but Lulu had a strong streak of obstinacy in her that reacted instantly against bullying, and the concentrated hostility even restored some of her courage.

Two of the people she recognised, though she had never met them. The small, handsome, chilly little woman must be the sister, indeed there was a faint family resemblance, though the eyes were dark, and the hair—tinted, thought Lulu—auburn. Lulu saw at once that this was a person with whom she could never have anything in common. Claudine plainly felt the same. She looked the intruder up and down, registering everything she despised: the make-up, the hair, the clothes, and the expression of distaste on her face made Lulu feel as if she were an insect to be stepped on and obliterated. The blonde was

of course Trudy, it could be no one else, and why she was
looking so disgusted, Lulu could not imagine, for she really
was an awful lump, mini-skirts had gone out ages ago, and
those coils round her head looked like ropes. They would fall
about with laughter in the King's Road to see such an old-
fashioned hair-do, that ridiculous skirt that showed her
bottom, and the over-tight bra that made her breasts stick out
like pineapples. Lulu was thankful for her own trousers and the
fashionably long grey cloak.

The two girls stared at each other with mutual loathing.
Lulu said, "Hallo," but Trudy did not even bother to reply,
only turned her shoulder, saying in a grating voice, "Oh Poops,
I thought we were going for a drive."

And to hell with you, thought Lulu, flushing a little, for she
was too young to accept such rudeness with the contempt it
deserved. Then the impact of that extraordinary nickname
struck her, and she almost giggled. Poops indeed! They'd kill
themselves at school if she told them. Then somehow it was
not funny at all: no one after all had even asked her to sit
down, she was simply left standing there in the middle of the
room. In an effort to distract herself, she turned her gaze on
the fourth member of the party.

His name was Terry. Lulu thought he might be a bit queer,
but perhaps that was because he was an actor. She noticed, as
Rose had noticed, his quite extraordinary beauty, and she
noticed too that—perhaps it was for this one occasion—he was
dressed in an impeccably conventional manner that, she
suspected, cost a vast amount of money, and which, coupled
with the amazing good looks, was far more startling than if he
had assumed the wild clothes of today. A white shirt, a plain
silk tie, a blue pullover, knife-pressed grey slacks. The glossy,
almost white blond hair was even cut reasonably short, and
brushed back from a wide forehead. Lulu was woman enough
to be staggered by the look of him, but the expression on his
face was something she could not accept, any more than the
contemptuously drawling voice. He did at last speak to her,
which was something, but the amused derision in his eyes
frightened her, made her wish fervently that she had not come.

"Why don't you sit down, ma'am?" he said, his eyes

roaming up and down her. "There is a chair behind you. It is all perfectly free, is it not, Gerard? We do not charge people for sitting down. Are you not going to offer the young lady a potation, someone? Or perhaps mummy does not permit you to drink."

Lulu had never met anything like this in her life. Such young men did not come into the Fielding circle. He was treating her like an absurd, gauche little schoolgirl, and that was exactly how she felt. She sat down clumsily, her trousered knees close together as if she were in church: she could not think of one word to say.

He persisted, "Drinky? Nice drinky? Milk, perhaps—"

Trudy giggled. Claudine concealed a smile. And Gerard threw back his head in a great guffaw of laughter.

Lulu summoned her scattered senses together. These were horrid people, all of them, they were not worth bothering about, she was not going to let them set her down. But her voice quavered as she answered, "I should like a drink, thank you." She looked fully at Terry. "Not milk, thank you. Mummy does not let me drink milk. Perhaps I could have a sherry."

This seemed to disconcert him. It was as if he had not expected her to answer back. He poured her out a drink in silence, then Gerard said, "And what brings you to Chichester, Lulu? Shouldn't you be at school?"

Lulu saw that they were determined to shove her back into the kindergarten. However, she had thought this all out on the train, so she answered readily enough, "We're doing a form project. On the cathedral cities. So I came up to see the cathedral here." She went on, for she had read it up, "The fifteenth century cloister is magnificent, and of course it has the only bell-tower in England. But what really impressed me were the sculptures by Bishop Sherbourne's tomb. They're quite lovely," said Lulu, who had not so much as set foot in the cathedral, and who was simply quoting from a guide book bought three days before. Her courage was slightly restored by the evident fact that none of them here seemed to have visited the cathedral either: she saw that she was boring them, and was so pleased that she continued. "You've seen them, of course," she said.

143

"Of course," said Claudine coldly.

"And what do you think of the paintings by Lambert Barnard?" persisted Lulu, the devil inappropriately working within her.

"Superb," said Gerard shortly, and Lulu knew that if she had asked him about the paintings by John Snooks, his reply would have been the same.

She let the matter lie, for her own knowledge was at its best precarious. She sipped her sherry, which she did not like very much, and at this point they all began talking at once. It was as if they felt that the balance had shifted, that this stupid schoolgirl was in the ascendant. Lulu did not feel in the ascendant at all. She was now frantic to get home, convinced that this was all a frightful mistake. Their conversation seemed pointless, vague and without cohesion. She saw that Trudy was in a great temper—was she the cause?—and her words came out in a sulky moan: she appeared to be urging her Poops—goodness, what a name!—to get his car out. Claudine was discussing some play they had all seen in the theatre, and the possibility of Gerard's taking over one of the parts. Terry, in his light, brittle, baritone voice, told a long and scurrilous anecdote about another actor, using several four-letter words, then leaning over Lulu, said mockingly, "Oh but I shouldn't say that in front of you, darling, should I?"

"No," said Lulu, and this direct, uncompromising reply silenced him more quickly than something subtle could have done: he stared at her in genuine surprise. But she made no further attempt to join in the conversation, only wondered how soon she could leave, it had all been awful and such a waste of time and money, Monica would be furious if she knew.

She looked round the room, and thought as Rose had done that it was quite frightful. All bubbles and bobbles and horrid tatty bits of lace and things. Somehow it smelt fusty, it looked unlived-in, quite unlike the shabby comfort of Curran House. There was a large pot on the mantelpiece, and she wondered what was in it. Perhaps Claudine was growing a plant, and because there were always pots of things at home—Mother was mad on all green things—she asked suddenly, "What's in that, Claudine? Are you growing something?"

144

This innocent question produced a staggered silence. Only Terry was suddenly shaken with a secret merriment. Claudine looked thunderous, Trudy flushed an unbecoming red, and Gerard, who had poured himself out another glass of something, made one of those urchin faces that always seemed to Lulu so extraordinary in a grown man.

Claudine did not really answer. She simply said, "No." Then rising to her feet she said, "We are shortly going for a drive, Lulu, so we will drop you at the station. I will make you a cup of tea before you go."

Short of a boot in the pants, thought Lulu, they could hardly make it plainer. But as she was now desperate to go, she was almost relieved and said she would love a cup of tea. She saw Claudine, accompanied by Trudy, go into what was presumably the kitchen, across the hallway. She was a little frightened of being left alone with Gerard and Terry: the latter's savage malice was something she had never up till now encountered, and she could not help having a slight conscience about Gerard, much as she detested him. She had after all come down to spy on him—and a fine mess she'd made of it too: if he had the slightest idea of what she was up to, he would probably murder her.

There was after all nothing to stop him. Lulu's imagination, heightened by wretchedness and fright, was working overtime. Nobody knew she was here, they none of them liked her, it would be quite easy—

Then she said firmly to herself, Nonsense! and at this moment the telephone in the hall rang.

Gerard at once went to answer it, and to her relief Terry strolled after him. Lulu, left alone in this nasty, fusty room, decided to satisfy her curiosity. She rose to her feet and went over to the mantelpiece to examine this strange pot that seemed to embarrass them all so much.

She had to stand on tiptoe to look in. The first thing she saw was an opened letter in its envelope, dropped there presumably by accident. She picked it up a little nervously and, as she did so, her hand brushed against the pot's contents. They felt strange to her, and she tipped the pot a little to examine it more closely. The letter was still clutched in her other hand. She saw that the pot was filled with soft, fluffy grey ashes. She did not for a moment realise what these must be. When she did, she was so horrified that she gave a little cry, and at this moment Gerard returned to the sitting-room. Lulu spun round and, as she did so, the pot slipped from her grasp and fell to the floor, breaking into small pieces and scattering those dreadful ashes everywhere. This in its way saved her, for Gerard did not see the letter she was still clutching, only the appalling spectacle of maman scattered over the carpet. And in that moment, Lulu, shocked into dynamic action, acting almost unconsciously, slipped the letter down the front of her sweater, this being the simplest and most inaccessible hiding-place.

Gerard said in so savage a voice that she jumped back, nearly falling herself, "You bloody, clumsy little idiot!"

The thud and crack of the broken pot brought Claudine and Trudy running in. Lulu, aghast, saw the colour fade from Claudine's cheeks, while Trudy flung her hands up to her mouth.

"Oh my God!" said Lulu, beginning to shake, "Oh, I'm so sorry, I'm so sorry. I don't know how I could be so stupid—"

"It is intolerable," said Claudine in a thin whisper, and at this Lulu began to cry: the furious accusation in all their faces, on top of this really dreadful day, was too much for her.

Her tears seemed to bring Gerard back to his senses. Terry, she was thankful to see, had not come back into the room. Gerard said roughly, "Well, it can't be helped, so stop crying, for Christ's sake." Then he snapped, "How the devil did you do that? Of all the clumsy things—"

"I'm so sorry," said Lulu again, mopping at her eyes, "I—I just slipped on the rug and put out my hand to catch at something to save myself."

It sounded remarkably lame, but there was a rug by the mantelpiece, and the floor beneath it was polished. At least no one seemed to doubt her word, and she could see that the catastrophe was so appalling that her clumsiness and guilt were the smallest part of it.

They were all standing there motionless, like statues. Then Claudine muttered, "I don't know what to do."

Lulu, whose mind functioned on various levels, understood her predicament and almost laughed out of sheer hysteria, only by now she was feeling so sick that nausea overcame this unseemly mirth. For after all, what was Claudine to do? These ashes presumably represented some close relative, probably mother, and really, it seemed a kind of blasphemy to sweep mother into a dustpan, though what on earth there was left to do, defeated her. Oh dear, thought poor Lulu, oh God, this is not my day, they'll hate me for evermore, you can't blame them, I couldn't have done anything more awful.

Claudine said at last in a thin, harsh voice, "I think you'd better go into the garden, Lulu, while I deal with this."

"I really am so sorry," said Lulu.

Claudine looked at her. There was no forgiveness in that look. Everybody would hear about this now—this aspect of the matter had only just struck her—and Rose would certainly be held responsible. There would be one hell of a lot of explaining to do, especially when she got home, for Mother would be bound to hear too, and what she was going to say, Lulu in her present shattered state had no idea.

She made an inglorious exit, indeed she almost crept into the garden, which was bleak and cold in the fading light, with a few regimented rose bushes by the french window. Of course the best thing to do would be to scatter the ashes on to the roses, and go all romantic about the ensuing blooms, but that would never be Claudine's way: another pot would be found, and Mother would be poured back into it, minus a few essential particles and plus a certain amount of ordinary dust. It would never be the same again.

I am a wicked girl, thought Lulu, beginning to sob afresh, and she sat down on the wooden bench that lay along the wall, and wished she had not been so silly as to embark on this crazy adventure.

Sherlock Holmes would simply despise her.

She huddled there for a while, so overcome by the awfulness of what she had done that she felt clamped down by her own disgrace: enveloped in the long grey cloak that no one had asked her to take off, she sat there frozen like a hunted animal.

147

Claudine and Trudy did not reappear. They were doubtless discussing the frightful crime that had been committed, and tearing their unwanted guest to shreds. Lulu felt she could not blame them. She was not herself of the temperament to collect people's ashes in urns, indeed the very thought of it sickened her, but if one had to preserve the dear departed in such a form, her clumsiness must be equivalent to rifling a grave or body-snatching.

Out of the corner of one downcast eye she saw a faint movement at the bottom of the garden. Perhaps it might be some friendly dog or cat. Lulu longed for friendliness, for someone to be kind to her, so she raised her head to see what it was.

It was Gerard and Terry, who oblivious of her presence — the cloak merged her into the shadows — were embracing, clasped in each other's arms. Lulu, her mouth fallen open, saw that they were kissing: Terry's head was flung back in an abandon of love as if he were a girl.

She was more shocked than she had ever been in her life. She knew of course about homosexuals, queers as she called them. Occasionally she and her schoolmates joked about them, and occasionally she had met strange, epicene people in the street, dressed up like women, even wearing make-up. But it had never really interested her: being a good-natured girl she was prepared to admit that there were all kinds, and if men chose to behave like women, it was their business, it hurt no one. Sometimes on the television there were comedians who spoke in a thin, affected way, made sly, dirty jokes and hinted at things that she did not fully understand. Her father always laughed a great deal at this, and her mother said it was rather disgusting, one should not joke on such matters. But that was the sum total of Lulu's experience, and nothing had prepared her for the sight of two grown men embracing, embracing moreover with so unmistakable a passion.

It was worse than spilling the ashes, far worse. The hot colour flooded her cheeks so that she felt dizzy, and she looked instantly away as if this were too shameful to bear, and the shame were hers. She huddled back into her cloak, her eyes fixed on the ground: when at last she dared to look up again

Gerard and Terry were gone, and Claudine, a cup of tea in her hands was opening the french window.

Lulu took the tea with a hand that shook so badly that she slopped some of it into the saucer. She saw that this only confirmed Claudine in her view that this child was an ill-bred moron. She whispered, "Thank you," then said again with great difficulty, "I'm so sorry. It was absolutely awful of me."

Claudine looked at her with what seemed to Lulu pure loathing. She shrugged. "It is done now," she said. "It can't be helped." Then she said, "We are setting off in five minutes. If you wish to use the bathroom, it's through there."

Lulu thought, She probably expects me to wet my pants or something. She said that she did not wish to use the bathroom. She found that she could not swallow the tea so, when Claudine went back into the sitting-room, she poured it on to the roses. It then struck her that hot tea might possibly kill them, and she gazed at them in horror as if expecting them to wither before her eyes. However, flowering so late, they were probably hardy and they received the baptism without any perceptible ill-effect. It really could hardly matter now. If Claudine returned to find her roses dead of tannin poisoning, she would merely tot it up to the account of this terrible child who arrived uninvited and virtually broke up the entire home.

The drive to the station only took a few minutes, but it seemed to Lulu to last for hours. Terry was not there, thank goodness, but Trudy, for all she seemed so stupid, must have sensed something, for she huddled in the back seat next to Lulu, sulking, and when Gerard addressed a casual remark to her, merely muttered, "Oh Poops!" and said nothing more. In the front Gerard and Claudine quarrelled in French. At least, Lulu assumed they were quarrelling, for they spoke so fast and so loud, but then all foreigners tended to sound angry, especially Italians who even when simply exchanging the time of day, resembled the Mafia in a vendetta. She was sure they were talking about her, and tried to make out what they were saying, but she had never been good at languages in school, and only caught the odd word here and there. Indeed, she was still in such a state of confusion that she could hardly grasp anything, she could not even stop herself from shaking, and her one intense desire was to be back home in her own room, where she could hide her shameful head beneath the bed-clothes.

Gerard opened the door for her at the station, but did not offer to accompany her on to the platform, much to her relief. Claudine snapped, "Goodbye," without turning her head, and Trudy refused to speak to her at all.

They are going to have a jolly evening, thought Lulu, then. And what a jolly day I've had!

Gerard called after her, "Give my love to Rose. And kiss my little Sally for me."

Lulu promised she would, then scuttled on to the platform, not caring whether a train was due or not, only wildly thankful to see the last of Gerard's Renault as it turned the corner.

The train, she discovered, would arrive in half an hour, so she retreated to the ladies' room, where she cried again for a few moments in shame and humiliation, then restored herself a little by making up her eyes afresh and combing the frizzy hair. She could not rid herself of that sight of Gerard and Terry, though she told herself repeatedly not to be so silly, she had always known Gerard was a queer, it was strange that he had married, but then she had heard that a lot of men were what her father called 'ambidextrous', were normal for a time then reverted. Oh, poor Rose—Lulu, screwing up her freshly blued eyelids, clambered on to the train, which was almost empty, found herself a corner seat in a smoker, and lit herself a cigarette.

It was only then, as she bent down to cradle the cigarette against the draught that something pricked her neck, and she remembered the letter. She said aloud, "Oh my God!" As if it wasn't enough to do unmentionable things to Mother's ghost, she had to steal a private letter—But her curiosity, which was the strongest element in her character, was too much for her, and after all she had behaved so disgracefully that nothing else really mattered. By now no doubt the ashes were deposited in a polythene bag, and the roses fading fast under their onslaught of tea. A bit of sheer, unprovoked snooping would hurt no one, and it was obviously impossible to return the letter.

She took it out of the envelope, first looking covertly around her as if Gerard or Claudine might suddenly materialise at her side. Then she began to read, the cigarette dangling from her fingers.

It was a love letter. It was from Terry. It was obviously addressed to Gerard. It started with endearments that brought the colour into Lulu's cheeks again, some of it was in French which she could only dimly understand, and it was all, only too plainly, entirely private. She was on the verge of tearing it up and dropping the fragments out of the window, when a sentence on the second page made her eyes widen.

"Make sure you get the little wench to live with us. Pay no attention to that silly bitch of a wife. She's frightened to death of you. If you put pressure on her she's bound to give in. At the rate she's going, she'll probably go out of her mind as well as blind, then she won't be able to keep either of the children. But get hold of Sally, if you have to kidnap her. I know you won't be happy without her. You are always so bloody respectable, my darling boy, though Christ knows why you worry about such things. I suppose I have to accept it as I accept everything from you, and if we have the child with us it will make the menage seem more conventional, then you will be happy and I will be happy. If you want me to get the girl away, I'll do so, but it would come much better from Rose. From what you say, she seems to be at breaking-point. I suggest that you—"

The letter from this point was in French, and Lulu did not attempt to read any more. It did not strike her that the letter was stupid and silly, that in England it is not so easy to kidnap little girls, and that courts take a poor view of such an occurrence. It only seemed to her an evil letter, and at first she was simply frightened for Rose for, though she might not be so near breaking-point as Terry and Gerard seemed to believe, she was unhappy and afraid, and perhaps after all she might give in, for the sake of peace and sanity.

Lulu had never so far come up against evil, and the blackness of it made her forget the terrible things that had happened that afternoon: compared with this they were unimportant. It was only after a while, as she sat there, the letter still clutched in her hand, that it struck her that it would not do Gerard much good if this letter were made public. It would not do his divorce any good, either—

That is blackmail, said Lulu's conscience.

But then he is blackmailing Rose—

The ticket collector came into the carriage at this point, and seeing this young girl with her startling make-up and childish, almost frightened expression, decided to have a little chat with her. And though this whiled away the journey very agreeably without solving anything, it at least postponed an intolerable decision. Lulu, arriving home about nine o'clock and very hungry, was still undecided, very apprehensive and rather subdued by all that had happened this long and alarming day.

"And where have you been?" Mrs. Fielding demanded in as angry a voice as her daughter had ever heard from her. She did not usually speak in such a fashion, but it was too bad of Lou not to say she would be back so late, besides there was an oddly strained air to her that worried her.

The cross, homely tones did more to restore Lulu than anything else. This was home, this was normal, this was cosy and warm as it should be, even if Mum was in a temper. She had by now decided to tell the truth, if in an edited form, for obviously her excursion could never remain a secret. She described her visit to Chichester in a rather agitated voice that did not escape her mother's attention, and told the lie she had made up for Gerard about the form project. Otherwise she described with reasonable accuracy her calling in at Fishbourne, though she made no mention of the urn, and did not refer to the episode in the garden.

Mrs. Fielding looked at her doubtfully as she set about heating up some supper. "You really might have told me," she said, then, "But what on earth made you call on Gerard? You always say you loathe him, and you seem to be so fond of Rose, she isn't going to like this at all."

"I don't know," said Lulu. "I just thought it might be interesting."

"And was it?"

"No! Will supper be ready soon? I'm ravenous."

"They must have been very surprised," said Mrs. Fielding,

reluctant to let the matter go. She knew perfectly well that Lulu was keeping something back from her, but she could not imagine what it was, it all seemed quite crazy.

"I think they were horrified."

"Now, now, don't exaggerate. But it must have seemed a bit odd you turning up like that."

"I suppose it was," said Lulu with a sigh. She began to eat her supper. Then she said quickly, "Don't tell Rose, Mum. Please. I'll tell her myself, but just leave it for the moment, will you?"

When Lulu addressed her in this childish way, there was definitely something very wrong. Mrs. Fielding said resignedly, "All right, though I don't see why you have to make such a mystery of it." Then she said, "You're up to something. I know you are."

"No, I'm not. I don't see why you think that. This stew is awfully good," said Lulu. "May I have some more potatoes?"

"I thought you were on a diet," said Mrs. Fielding. She did not press the matter. Only later she said to her husband, "I wish Lulu wouldn't always interfere. I've never really liked her being so friendly with Rose, and now she seems to be getting more and more involved."

But Len Fielding had had a tiring day and was not particularly interested, while Lulu, now in her own room, was sitting on her bed, the letter in her hand, trying to sort out her conscience, her duty to Rose, and a niggling fear in the pit of her stomach that she had landed herself in for dead trouble.

8

Rose, UNAWARE OF ALL this drama centred on her, was feeling happier. The overdraft was cleared: it would certainly recur, but at least she did have some money in hand, and there was no further letter from Gerard. She bought both children new shoes, made Tom a present of a puzzle, and for Sally there was a rather revolting yellow daisy, cut out of cloth with a tarty painted face on it. Sally had already seen this in the shop window and her heart had gone out to it. Diana would be shocked at such lack of taste, but Rose bought it without hesitation, and now it stood on Sally's table by her bed as a prized possession. She also made a special chicken dinner, and drank some of the whisky.

She met Dr. Macek on the stairs as she was coming back with her shopping, and Tom at once performed the poor-Tom's-a-cold act, hiding his head against her knee, and peeping up out of one eye at the doctor who, to Rose's amusement and surprise put his head on one side and peeped likewise. The two of them bobbed their heads coyly at each other, creating such a ludicrous pantomime that she had to giggle as much as her son.

"Honestly!" she said, then, "He really does like you. What have you done to him? And how are you, Dr. Macek? You see, I pronounce your name correctly."

He answered gravely, "I am well. I think you look a little better."

"Did I look ill or something? I'm all right. I usually am,"

said Rose, fumbling for her door key. She wondered if she should ask Dr. Macek in for a drink, now that she actually had a bottle on the premises, but decided not to, for though she was no longer so tired and her eyes ached only intermittently, she felt as if she could cope with nothing more, not even a kindly man who was such a success with her son. But she was a little taken aback when Tom, seeing his new friend begin to climb the stairs to his own flat, burst into tears and held out both arms to him.

Dr. Macek at once stopped, took the two little hands in his, and said in his quiet, correct fashion, "You will not cry, Tom. I will see you again. One day I will take you out with me and show you the boats on the river. We will go together to the Embankment, if your mother will permit."

Tom's tears stopped at once, and Rose, thinking that now she really had no choice, said, "Why not come in and have a drink? My mother has given me a bottle of Scotch, so you see I can really offer you something."

She thought he hesitated, then he thanked her and, much to Tom's delight, followed her in. He said, "The little girl is at school?"

"Oh yes. I collect her in the afternoon. She's very happy there, and doing quite well. I'm rather proud of her reading, actually. She's streets ahead of most of the others. You see," said Rose, setting out the bottle and two glasses, "I've become one of those boring, boastful mothers."

"She is a most beautiful child," said Dr. Macek, sitting down in a chair from which Rose had hastily whisked away one shoe, a teddy-bear and a picture book. "I think she is also very highly strung."

Rose found that she was still tired enough to take this almost as a kind of accusation. She began quite hotly, "Oh, I don't know. I think—" Then she broke off. "I'm sorry. I think I'm rather highly strung myself these days. Yes, she is, of course. Sometimes it worries me. I'm awfully sorry, by the way, that the flat is so untidy. It always seems at its worst whenever I ask someone in. Do forgive me. I never used to think of myself as a muddler, but somehow with two children— I'll have to make myself a system. Do you like water, or do you prefer it neat? I can get some ice out of the fridge if you want it."

"I like it straight without ice," returned Dr. Macek. He did not answer Rose's self-accusation, but looked round the flat with a deep pleasure. Rose was not to know, but this homely, untidy room, with toys on the floor, odd garments on the chairs, and examples of Sally's artwork Sellotaped on the walls, was more comforting and soothing to him than any beautifully appointed lounge. He thought of his bare, tidy flat upstairs which never seemed warm, even when the fire was full on, and bestowed on Rose a faint, ironic smile as he sipped at his whisky, then looked down at the picture book pushed on to his knee by an excited Tom, waiting to be asked the appropriate questions.

Dr. Macek at once responded. Rose thought he was plainly well-trained, wondered if he had children of his own, but did not like to ask.

"What," said Dr. Macek to the manner born, "is that?"

"Cow!" said Tom, bobbing up and down in ecstasy.

"He's slow in speaking," said Rose, hoping it was indeed a cow, for Tom's vocabulary was erratic, so much so that sometimes she thought he had a perverse sense of humour. "Sally was much better, but then I think girls usually are."

Dr. Macek did not answer this, only listened attentively as Tom enlightened him on the subject of sheep and hens and dogs, and really looked, Rose thought, as if he were personally interested. When Tom returned to his favourite pursuit of shutting doors, he glanced up at Rose and said, "I am glad to see you looking well. It is perhaps because I do not pace my floor at nights."

"Oh!" She began to smile. "It really was awfully rude of me." For the first time she looked at him fully. She thought he looked drawn and grey, and there were deep shadows under his eyes. She said, a little shyly, "Do you sleep better now?"

"When you get to my age," said Dr. Macek, not answering her directly, "sleep does not matter."

Rose thought he had the air of one who did not sleep at all. The skin of his face was taut, with the bones showing through. There was about him an aura of desolation, almost despair.

Once she would not have recognised this, for she was after all still very young, but what had happened during the past few months had sharpened her perceptions, and she believed she recognised here another human being weighed down by some intolerable burden. For one second there was a strange communion between them, almost as palpable as a thread, then Tom, refusing to leave his new friend alone, returned to the attack with the new puzzle Rose had bought him, dumped it into Dr. Macek's hands and began to rearrange the pieces.

Rose watched the pair of them as she sipped her whisky. It was nice of Diana to have given her the bottle. She wished she could feel more love for this remote and brittle person from whose womb she had come. She had rung her in the morning to thank her, but Diana sounded preoccupied and bored, hardly answered her, only, just as Rose was about to ring off, said, "Go back to Gerard, there's a good girl."

"Mother," said Rose, forgetting her instructions, "I can't."

"Then," said Diana, "you're a bloody fool, darling, and don't come running to me when things go wrong, for you'll get a kick in the pants, and it's all you deserve."

She said now to Dr. Macek, "Why do you talk like that? You cannot be so old."

"I am forty," he answered, and she was taken aback enough to open her eyes wide, at which he laughed.

"You think I am much, much older?"

"Of course not! I was simply thinking it's a bit silly to say sleep does not matter. You sound as if you're in your seventies."

"He is a very bright little boy," said Dr. Macek irrelevantly, watching Tom fit in the pieces with surprising accuracy. "Oh, I feel as if I'm in my seventies. And I must go. I have a lot of work to do. I should not be here drinking your whisky. My patients will smell it on me, and it will be bad for my reputation."

He rose to his feet. He was a tall man but far too thin. Rose nearly asked him to stay for lunch, then stopped herself. This kind of over-maternal feeling was foolish, especially between neighbours who hardly knew each other. She said, "Are you sure you won't have another drink?"

"No, no." He paused by the door. He said, "You will forgive

me, Mrs. Menusier, but I believe you are having a difficult time."

Rose said stiffly, for this unexpected intrusion into her privacy jolted her, "Oh no, I don't think so. Well, I mean, one does go through tricky patches and as of course you know, I'm separated from my husband, but—The children are very good, and work is beginning to come in again. I think I'm pretty well off, really." She looked at him, almost in hostility. What sort of man was he to say such a thing to her? This was the first time she had spent more than a few minutes with him, and here he was speaking to her as if somehow he knew her intimately. Perhaps he was regarding her as a patient—She saw the look on his face, and was suddenly ashamed of herself. On an impulse that she did not quite understand herself, she held out her hand to him, and he took it briefly in his. "I suppose," she said a little ruefully, "that one only becomes so prickly when things are difficult. You're quite right, of course. All sorts of things seem to be happening at the moment, and I really haven't organised myself at all. There are the children, you see, and I think I have a terrible conscience about my marriage, they always say it's the children who suffer, and sometimes I half believe it, only in this case I think they would suffer far more if I—what's the word?—capitulated. But I didn't think it was all so obvious. I've never had any kind of poker face, but it's a bit of a shock to know it's so revealing." She looked down at Tom who was reluctant to let his new friend go, and laughed, stroking his silky hair. "I'm as bad as the children. You should try playing games with Sally some time. If she has a good hand, or the draughts are coming out right, she positively thumps on her chest with joy, and laughs so much that any poker player would shoot her instantly. She must get it from me. You're not having a very good time yourself, are you, Dr. Macek?"

He said simply, "No."

"If there's anything I can do—"

"There is nothing. Thank you. Only," said Dr. Macek, preparing to go, as it seemed to her, reluctantly, "for me it is in a way my own fault, and I think there is no solution. For you it is different. You are very young, and it will pass. I

158

would say that if you wanted help, you should call on me—"

"As I did the other night!"

"Oh, it was unforgivable of me. We will forget that. Only I would always like to help you, it is a pity that I may not be here much longer."

"Have you found a better flat?" asked Rose. "I'm so glad, though we shall miss you. I'm used to this place, but it's a bit of a dump, and the landlord never does anything if he can help it. Only it's a controlled rent, so I don't suppose I'll ever be able to afford to move. Where are you going?"

He was now out on the landing. She could not see his face. "I don't know," he said, then again, "I do not know." With that he started to go up the stairs. Tom called out, "Bye-bye," but he did not seem to hear. Rose watched him. She was possessed of an extraordinary urge to run after him, call him back, to say, Don't go, stay here, have lunch and talk to me. But she did none of these things, only stood there until he disappeared round the corner of the staircase.

Tom was tugging at her, perhaps to show her something or to signify that he wanted his dinner, but she still stood there, not closing the door.

Then she saw Lulu on the landing below and called down to her.

Lulu did not, as she expected, come running up. She looked up silently at Rose who, a little surprised, said, "Are you just back for lunch? How's tricks?"

"Fine, fine," said Lulu in what seemed to Rose quite a surly fashion, then without another word turned into her own flat, shutting the door with a crash for which her mother would certainly reproach her.

"Well!" said Rose to Tom, "I don't know what's the matter with everyone, but I think they're all mad save me and thee. What do you want, boy? Is it dinner? I'm just about to dish it up."

But as she dropped the liver in the frying pan—another treat bought from Diana's cheque—she could not rid her mind of Dr. Macek's face, and wished she had somehow persuaded him to stay.

Dr. Macek wished it too. It was his hospital afternoon, and

his surgery was closed. It was always a bad day for him for, when he was busy, he could forget the threat that lay over him, besides, his receptionist, such a willing and unattractive woman, insisted on mothering him, and the exasperation this induced in him, took his mind off his worries. But to be alone was becoming intolerable. He was not by nature a melo-dramatic man. Once he had been calm and sensible, with a mildly ironic sense of humour, he had enjoyed his life with Marika and Pavel, his work, his numerous friends. It was a normal, quiet life, entertaining, going to concerts and theatres, working hard. The thought of killing himself would have been obscene and absurd. It still seemed so. They said that suicide was often a vindictive act or a cry for help, it was a way of getting back on society, of saying, Look what you have made me do, it is all your fault, I hope you are satisfied. In his case it would be nothing of the kind. Society would frankly neither know nor care, except for the children in his charge, and the parents who leaned so heavily upon him. The senders of the letter, the third letter, which lay now in his breast pocket, would simply shrug their shoulders. Certainly he was of more use to them alive than dead, but it really did not matter much either way, there were plenty of others, possibly far more willing and useful.

Dr. Macek thought of Rose, the untidy room with children's toys lying about, the beguiling little bright boy who played games with him. He was in no way in love with Rose, as far as he knew, but he found her warm and comforting and—that English word—nice. He thought he liked everything about her. Perhaps after all he would come to love her, if there were time. There was no time. It was a pity. He liked the untidy, soft, brown hair that was always coming down, the face that changed expression with every spoken word. He liked the shabby clothes, the sleeves rolled up for work, and the quick way she moved. He liked especially her voice which was soft yet emphatic. At first her looks had not particularly appealed to him, but now he found her very feminine and pretty: she would be even prettier if she did not always screw up her eyes, if she ate and relaxed a little more, and were not so plainly worried half to death. It would be pleasant to spend an evening

160

in her company, perhaps take her out to dinner, then at home play records and talk far into the night.

He did not contemplate anything more serious. But he was beginning to find out that he wanted her and needed her, and this in the circumstances was both impossible and ridiculous, so he pushed her out of his mind. And once again he looked down that long, cold, distant road where lay the end for Dr. Macek who had not the least desire to die, but who could no longer face the appalling dilemma of living.

And at this moment Gerard was travelling up to London, planning to arrive just after Rose returned from school with Sally.

The rest of Curran House went about its business. Mrs. Parsons, who had done her small piece of shopping early, sat as usual in front of her television, knitting a vest for the newest grandchild. Despite the fact that she kept herself to herself with a ferocity that made her home a fortress, she was secretly very interested in everything that went on around her, though nothing would have induced her to interfere: if that little couple opposite who were planning to skip any moment now, had set fire to the building, she would have done nothing about it. It was none of her business. Besides, she was certainly not going to help that bugger of a landlord. When he had called for the rent a few days ago, she pointed out to him that the lavatory roof was still leaking, the sink blocked up and the wood on the front room window-sill rotten.

He simply looked at her. He said curtly, "I'm busy."

"It's your job, and you ought to do it," said Mrs. Parsons, who had stood up to Hitler, and who was certainly not being done down by this little toad of a creature, Jewish too, they were always the worst. Mrs. Parsons had the lowest opinion of all Jews and foreigners, but quite without any personal ill-will: they simply represented something alien and outside her circle: she was perfectly prepared to be civil to them, provided they did not cross her path, but did not really regard them as human beings.

"Not at the rent you pay," he said, looking grimly down at the three pound notes in his hand. Mrs. Parsons did not pay quarterly by cheque like the other tenants, but put her weekly rent away in a china teapot every Friday, just as she used to do when her husband came home from work.

"It's not worth the half of it," said Mrs. Parsons.

He was as always a little nonplussed by this old woman who never conceded an inch and who would, he was certain, have coped implacably with any pressure he could put upon her. It was not the kind of district for savage dogs, bully-boys or glass on the stairs, and the landlord was not really the type to employ such means, even if he had been able to do so, but he had a horrid suspicion that if he did, Mrs. Parsons would somehow turn it all against him, the dogs and the bully-boys, then he would slip on the broken glass and cut an artery. She'd let him bleed to death too, then ring the office to come and clear up the mess.

He turned to go. It was no good arguing with her, you might as well try it on the Rock of Gibraltar. He looked round the appallingly cluttered room. How could the old girl live in such a confounded muddle? The television was on as usual. It was some soap opera. He said in an aggrieved tone, "You're living right in the West End. I could get thirty quid for this flat."

"You're a right bugger, aren't you?" said Mrs. Parsons.

She had called him worse before now. The landlord at that moment wished without any particular conviction that he could unleash a Doberman Pinscher on her. She would probably hand it a bone. He said nothing more. There was nothing left to say. When rents went up to fifty pounds a week, Mrs. Parsons would still be there with her bloody teapot. The only thing in her favour was that she paid her rent, such as it was, regularly, which was more than one could say for the other tenants, with the exception of the Fieldings and the doctor who always sent a cheque dead on the nail.

He stood on the landing, staring at the Photiades' flat opposite. He knocked on their door. There was not a sound, though he was convinced that Mrs. Photiades was in. He tried once more, with no result. He had rather liked the young couple when he first saw them, especially as Nina was such a pretty girl, but now he did not like them at all, any more than he liked the pile of bills in the pigeon-hole every morning, that were always removed almost immediately, but certainly not for paying. He would have to send them a solicitor's letter, not that they would answer.

He came reflectively downstairs, to pause for a second outside Lady Matford's flat. There was utter silence inside, but this time he knew perfectly well that she was in, knew too that at any time now they would be carting her away. There was no point in knocking. Even if she answered she would be in no state to pay him, or even speak coherently. He saw that he must get his secretary to write to the husband again—he was well shot of her, the poor bastard—and inform him that the rent was now owing for two quarters.

He passed Mrs. Fielding—nice woman—who greeted him cheerfully, and saw that two more bills had arrived for the Photiades. The other morning he had slit one open. It was a final demand for thirty pounds. It was obviously one of many. He muttered to himself, "Who'd be a bloody landlord?" and stepped into the street.

He looked up at the house once as he got into his car. He thought, as he often did, what a rum lot they were, the old soak with her title, the Czech doctor who seemed to live entirely on his own, the little Greek crooks, and that young woman with her kids and the poufy husband who had walked out on her.

And of course bloody Mrs. Parsons.

"You really are a funny girl," Mrs. Fielding said to her daughter. "I thought you liked Rose, and first you go and visit her husband, and now you're rude to her."

For she had heard the exchange on the landing, and found it odd, to say the least of it.

"I didn't mean to be rude," said Lulu miserably.

Her mother thought she did not look at all well. Perhaps it was her period, it sometimes played her up. She said, "Well, I don't suppose she noticed," and could not stop herself from smiling a little, for she had never approved of the friendship, and she hoped that this meant that Lulu had at last lost interest in this neurotic neighbour.

Lulu had not lost interest at all, nor had she wished to be rude to Rose. She had no idea, of course, that retribution in the person of Gerard Menusier was now well on its way to London. She longed to run upstairs and confess to Rose what she had done, but she did not dare, and somehow that beastly letter, now hidden away in her underwear drawer—it seemed the most appropriate place—frightened her so much that it was as if it were hanging in the air and Rose would somehow see it. For the first time in her life she had no appetite for lunch, and she trailed back to school, her head aching, wishing passionately she had never gone to Chichester, and wondering if she would ever, ever, summon up enough courage to confront Gerard.

Gerard was not concerned with the letter. He simply assumed it was lost. When that revolting little schoolgirl upset the urn, the letter, which he had casually dropped in because Trudy turned up while he was reading it, had probably got whisked up with the debris, or perhaps been blown away. It did not matter. There was no mention of his name, and it would mean nothing to anyone else. His thoughts, as he drove up the A24, which was jammed with traffic, were mainly concentrated on Rose. He was glad to be away from Fishbourne. Trudy was being extremely tiresome and making no attempt to hide her jealousy of Terry, while Claudine, normally so sensible, seemed to be taking her side against him. All women were bloody, the sooner he left the bungalow the better, and he only prayed that it would be soon when he could settle down with Terry, with little Sally to keep them company.

As for Rose—The temper welled up in him so that he took a corner far too fast, and the car behind him sounded its horn in agitation. It seemed to Gerard, slowing down a little for, when sober, he had an excellent sense of self-preservation, that Rose was responsible for everything, for the fact that he had no work, for his quarrel with his sister, for Trudy's jealousy, and certainly for the arrival of that ghastly child, undoubtedly sent there to spy.

Well, this time he would have it out with her. And thinking this, he arrived in the High Street.

Rose was still wishing that she had asked Dr. Macek to stay to lunch. The brief euphoria caused by the gift of the money had vanished, and she felt tired and depressed again, with a foolish feeling of foreboding for which there was no apparent reason. Her eyes were aching badly, and once more she noticed the disturbing symptom that occasionally her vision was misted over and obscured. She thought as she set out to collect Sally, with Tom tugging at his harness, that this was all just stupid, people did not go suddenly blind, and she had never until recently had the least trouble with her eyes. But the terror of what might happen dried her mouth and made her head swim: she had cooked the liver for Tom but had been unable to swallow a mouthful: even the strong coffee she made for herself was left mostly in the cup.

Tom was chatting away in his own fashion, exclaiming at intervals, "Man!" or "Dog!" or "House!" It was not precisely the kind of conversation to take up Rose's full attention, and she agreed mechanically while her frightened mind scudded wildly here and there: all the apprehension and unhappiness that she believed she had at last warded off, descended on her afresh and with greater force.

As they came up to the school, which was only a quarter of an hour's walk away, she struggled to calm herself. Sally was perceptive as a nervous child must be—highly strung, the cheek of it, but of course he was quite right—and she would sense instantly that something was wrong. Rose pushed her thoughts on to Dr. Macek. She stood there by the entrance, waiting for the stream of little girls and boys, holding firmly on to Tom's harness, for he was always excited by so many people, and would certainly dash off to meet his sister the moment he set eyes on her. She smiled mechanically at the other mothers, most of whom she now knew well enough to chat with, and wondered what could be wrong. Something certainly, to make a man of forty look over fifty, and now that she paused to consider this, she recognised well enough that despair that burnt within him: she had faced despair many times lately, there was a quality to it that could not be missed, it was as if it somehow was linked with the unhappiness within herself.

Married trouble?—"Wait a minute, Tom, wait a minute, she's just coming,"—probably. He had a married air to him. A wife at home who could not join him? A wife who perhaps had left him? But it must be much more than that, for she could have sworn he was afraid, and he did not strike her as a cowardly man. What a pity that there were so many barriers between human beings, barriers that only cracked in moments of intense emotional crises. How easy and comfortable it would have been to say, I'm frightened of my husband, I'm frightened for my children, I'm a weak kind of person, what am I to do? And you're frightened too, aren't you? Tell me about it, then we can comfort each other, it is always so much easier to solve other people's problems than one's own, I am sure we shall give each other the best possible advice.

Sally—"Hallo, lovey. You're nice and early."

Little fresh faces, pink and excited, little high-pitched voices, eager reunions as if after a year's parting. Passionate accounts of what had happened in class today, how Miss Somebody had said the composition was excellent, the painting had been hung on the classroom wall, the dinner was horrid, roly-poly—

And Sally, bubbling over with the intensity of it all, ignoring a persistent boy-friend who always followed after her and whom, in true female fashion, she treated like dirt. He was very attentive and even stroked her hair. Her drawing was very good, and she'd written a poem, and one of the little boys near her had had an accident, and Miss Thing had had to change his trousers—and much more, with Rose trying determinedly to listen as a good mother should, and the ominous apprehension knocking in her brain the nearer she came to home.

"What's for supper?"

"Liver. Tom had it for his dinner, so I've kept some for you."

"Oh, super!"

Super. Silly word. Even Lulu used it. Super, super, super, means nothing, could never have meant anything. When we were young, it was 'wizard' and that sounds even sillier.

"Mummy, I want to buy something."

"What's that?" asked Rose, steering Tom away from a rather nasty, yapping little dog who plainly did not care much for small boys.

"Want!" shouted Tom, a useful word that was among his first, then the owner of the dog, who markedly resembled it, pushed away his stroking hand, and snapped at Rose in quite a canine way, "Will you please keep your child under control? You shouldn't let him torment poor, dumb animals."

Rose almost gaped at her. Tom, bursting with love and friendliness for all animals had touched the creature so gently, and her main preoccupation had been that it looked the biting kind. But before she could say anything, Sally remarked in a clear, carrying voice, "What a rude woman!" so there was nothing left to do but scuttle away as quickly as possible.

But this at least made her laugh: rather pink in the face she dared not look back, but Sally did so, saying in surprise, "She looks terribly angry."

"Well, so would you if someone called you rude."

"She was rude."

"Well, I suppose she was. Perhaps she's got a tummyache. What's this you're going to buy? Never mind, Tom. It wasn't a nice dog. One day," said Rose, "we'll live in the country, and you shall have a dog of your very own, and two cats and a guinea-pig." And as she made this impractical prophecy, she thought how lovely it would be: herself and the children in some beautiful old-world cottage, with a nice garden, friendly neighbours and new-laid eggs for tea.

The old-world cottage would cost at least twenty thousand and have an outside lavatory, the garden would be over-run with weeds, the neighbours wouldn't talk to us, and the eggs would come from battery hens.

One can always dream. Let's throw in Dr. Macek as a neighbour. I would quite like to have Dr. Macek as a neighbour.

"What's this you're going to buy, Sal? Or shouldn't I ask?"

"It's a secret."

"Oh, I see."

"How much have I got in my piggy-bank?"

"Oh, about four bob—I mean, twenty p.," said Rose, her mind still on the cottage. "I don't quite know. I expect it will be enough."

Sally nodded, mouth pursed up, her face shining with secrets. She said, "It's going to be a surprise. If I tell you, will you promise to forget it?"

"All right," said Rose, smiling. "But perhaps you'd better not tell me at all, then it'll be even more of a surprise."

They were now crossing the road to Curran House. Once on the pavement Rose released Tom's harness, and he dashed as always to the front door. Gerard watched them from the opposite corner. He had been waiting for nearly half an hour. He did not propose to come in immediately, he wanted to wait until they were all safely there, sitting down to their tea. He had parked his car a couple of streets away, for Rose would recognise it and he did not want her in any way to be prepared. He saw Rose bend her head to Sally, who looked flushed and happy. Tom was already battering at the front door. It was a pleasant family picture, and it infuriated him. It was as if this were something that could never be his, yet this was his wife, these were his children, they had no right to cut him out as if he simply did not exist.

He lit himself another cigarette—he had been chain-smoking—and continued to wait.

Sally whispered, as Rose took out her keys, "It's a present for you."

"Oh darling, how lovely. What is it?"

"I'm not telling you, so there!"

"Mean bitch!" said Rose, made a face at her daughter, and opened the door.

They all clattered up the stairs, making the usual cavalry charge noise of small children. Rose, following them, thought how silent the rest of the house was. Of course they would most of them be out at work, but Nina Photiades was probably in—she could smell the spicy cooking—and it was not one of Mrs. Fielding's Darby and Joan days. The chill descended on her again. She thought, furious with herself, that really she must stop this. Perhaps she should go to the doctor and get some pink placebo that would help her control herself. As she fitted in the key of her flat door, with the children banging against her, wanting to be home, to have their tea, to watch 'Playtime', her eyes moved round to Veronica's door, where all was as silent as the grave.

The grave, indeed. Rose, like Mrs. Fielding, knew that Veronica was by now in her pre-nursing home state. She had known her for too long not to recognise the signs. She seldom met her these days, for she would be locked into her own flat, drinking herself to pink elephants and damnation, but sometimes when she came on to the landing, she heard her pacing up and down. Always, before the final insanity came upon her, she would set out on her moonlit walks, rocking from side to side, talking to herself in a growling monotone, insulting passers-by with catcalls and four-letter words, making obscene gestures, raising her skirts.

Rose, opening the door to a scramble of children—Sally at once put the television on, wasn't this the kind of thing parents were warned about?—thought how strange it was that she did not really know Veronica at all. She could never explain to herself how it was that someone from what used to be officially known as a good family, with so many advantages—striking looks, intelligence and money, not to mention three husbands—should have toppled into so sad a degradation. Rose had after all known Veronica in a fashion for the length of her marriage, which was six and a half years: at one time they had almost been real friends. Yet she now saw that she knew nothing of her, had only met the last husband once, a small, lost, balding man who had somehow lumbered himself with a tigress, and had no idea what had driven her into the abyss.

It must be loneliness, that dreadful loneliness of spirit, that nothing—marriage, friends, parties—could touch, but why she was lonely, why the bottle had become her only companion, perhaps Veronica herself could not say.

There, said Rose to herself, going into the kitchen to prepare supper, but for the grace of God—and a deep shudder ran through her, for perhaps not even the grace of God could always help one. She was lonely too and, if she had not hit the bottle, it might simply be because she could not afford it. Rose, who had been toying with the idea of a drink from Diana's whisky, of which there was still half left, changed her mind determinedly, and began cutting bread. And as she cut it, the silly words came into her mind, and she hummed softly to herself:

"We're poor little lambs who've lost our way,
Baa, baa, baa!"

Gerard knew the timetable. Twenty minutes to half an hour for the preparation of food — the children were always ravenous, and Rose usually did something quick like bacon and eggs or fishcakes or sausages — and they would all be sitting round the table, watching the telly, with Rose probably drinking a cup of tea.

He came in. He met Nina Photiades on the way, coming down to buy herself some cigarettes. She and her husband smoked the whole day long, and her hands, which were the least attractive part of her, being stubby-fingered and pudgy, were always stained with nicotine. She turned on him an almost hostile face, she barely returned his greeting. Gerard had never forgiven her for snubbing him, he thought her a cold, stuck-up bitch and nearly told her so. But she probably would not even have heard, for tonight was the flitting night, Andreas had at last received his pay. Her mind was concentrated on what they could take with them, such things as electric light plugs and bulbs, soap racks, brackets and a kettle which had been thrown in with the cooker. Nina up till now had always enjoyed the flits, which were so dramatic and necessitated creeping down the stairs late at night, but now she could not rid herself of the apprehensive feeling that this time it might be more difficult. She therefore slid silently past Gerard, who now stood on the landing and put his hand in his pocket for the key.

Lulu, back from school, saw him in the street and hastily retreated into a doorway. He was the last person in the world she wanted to see. She wondered what on earth he was here for, and her guilty heart at once informed her that he would be telling Rose about that disastrous visit. Then she began worrying about Rose, and what with this and that awful letter, still concealed beneath a pile of tights, became pale and silent. Mrs. Fielding, now convinced that she must be in love, shook her head at her, and wondered what on earth she could do with a daughter who drooped about the flat, and who was even for the first time actually losing weight.

9

Rose heard the key in the lock. The colour fled from her face. She might have known it. The premonition had been clear enough in her brain and in her belly. She was still not eating anything, but she had made herself some coffee. She was about to fry the liver, but now set the pan down. She was to her own astonished rage completely terrified, though Gerard had turned up unexpectedly before, and it might simply mean that he was up in town for some interview. But her pumping heart, vanished colour and indrawn breath contradicted this, absurd as it might be. It was a good minute before she summoned up the strength to call out, "Is that you, Gerard?"

"It is," he answered, straight on the cue for Act Two, and he strode in, almost as if expecting applause from the gallery. The expression on his face confirmed her fears, for she had never seen him look so savagely angry. However, Rose was of a temperament to respond to crises, so recovering, if not her courage, at least her commonsense, she called out quite briskly, "Children, here's Daddy. Isn't that a lovely surprise?"

The children did not respond as she expected, or indeed as Gerard expected. Sally, avidly watching some puppet show, did not run as she usually did into his arms. She turned her head, gave Gerard a little gappy smile—she had not yet grown all her missing teeth—said, "Hallo, Daddy," and continued to look at the television.

It was Tom who shocked Rose. He was normally a solemn,

reserved little boy, not given to rushing into people's arms, and he had never shown much enthusiasm for his father: it was as if he knew perfectly well that he was not appreciated. He now slid out of his chair, and Rose believed with surprise that he was going to go to Gerard, who held out his hand to him. But this he did not do: instead he ran towards Rose and buried his face in her knee.

She thought at first he was playing his peeking game then, as she put an arm round him, found that he was trembling. The fury that this aroused in her was such that her own fear vanished. She knew well enough that Gerard did not like Tom: during that last visit to Fishbourne he had been rough, even unkind. But that Tom, who was frightened of nothing, should be afraid of his own father and tremble in his presence, was more than she could take. She cuddled him for a moment, ignoring Gerard, who was almost standing over her, then she said calmly, "I gather you've come to talk to me."

"I have indeed," he said, with all the melodrama she might have expected, and his eyes flickered over Sally, who was still watching the television and paying no attention to him.

"Well," said Rose in the same calm tone, seeing very plainly that this was going to be some sort of ultimatum, "we'll leave the children to the telly for the moment: they don't like being disturbed, Gerard, any more than you or I would. I must make their supper soon, they're always hungry. But in the meantime I suggest we go to my room and discuss whatever you have come to talk about, and afterwards, while I do the supper, you can take Sally for her little walk. I can even offer you some whisky. Diana gave me some."

"And how is Diana?" enquired Gerard in the voice of one who could not care less. He had never liked his mother-in-law—even stranger to think of Diana as a mother-in-law than as a mother—for she made no attempt to conceal her distaste for him and, being as she was, he could never patronise or bully her. Rose remembered that he had been utterly taken aback at their introduction. He had of course expected some decent suburban housewife, rather like Mrs. Fielding, who would be cosy with him and offer him a cup of tea. The sophisticated beauty—Diana was then at the height of her

172

good looks—who stepped up to him, eyed him up and down so disdainfully, and who obviously knew the theatre world so much better than he did, had disconcerted him, for one of the few times in his life, into utter silence.

"She's very well," said Rose, gathering up the bottle of whisky and two glasses. It seemed a pity to waste the whisky on Gerard who would certainly finish the bottle, but she needed the drink far more than he did, seeing clearly that he had come up with the express purpose of making some kind of dreadful scene.

They went into her bedroom. She wished it did not have to be her bedroom, but it hardly mattered, for whatever Gerard had in mind, it would at least be nothing whatsoever to do with bed.

She motioned him to the one armchair by the window, where she sat sometimes when she had work to do. She sat down on the bed. She poured him out a drink, and one for herself. She said, trying to ignore the heart that was again beating too fast, "Well, Gerard? What is it? I can't believe this is just a social call, besides, we only met a short while ago."

He answered, "I want to take Sally back with me tonight."

Rose did not react as he expected. She sipped her whisky in silence for a moment. Her head was bent so that he could not see her face. She said in a cool little voice, "Now? This very moment?"

"That's right, darling."

"I see. So what do I do? Pack her things?"

"That's right, darling." The words, oddly coarse and common from that handsome face, fell out like stones.

"Oh. And what do I say to Sally?"

"You can leave that to me."

"So I simply back out, do I? Perhaps it would be better if I don't even say goodbye to her. I just push her into your arms, wave my hand and retire into the kitchen, or wherever decent women retire to. Are you sure you don't want me to throw in Tom too, as make-weight?"

Even Gerard, filled with the dream of his private rage, had to see that this was not going according to schedule. He drained his glass, refilled it then came over to Rose, who now raised her head to stare at him. Her face was quite white. For the first time he noticed, with the strange irrelevancy of such moments, that she did after all resemble her mother. There was nothing of Diana's brittle beauty here, yet none the less it could have been Diana, younger, softer, and a great deal angrier, who looked up at him.

He said fiercely, "Oh, cut this out, Rose. Are you trying to be funny? I am in no mood to be funny. I want my Sal. She's my daughter."

"And mine."

"She doesn't like you, darling. You must know that, or are you so bloody conceited that you won't admit it. She's not happy here, poor little pet. I want her. I need her. You've no right to hang on to her. You can keep the boy. I think he's a bit mental, myself, always shutting doors and hiding his face. I suppose you've made him like that. You're going crazy yourself, I've known that for a long time. Your sight's going and your mind. If you can call it a mind—I suppose you want to keep Sally so that she can look after you. But she's too good for that. She's too good for you. She's coming with me now, Claudine is expecting us."

Rose picked up the glass that she had hardly touched, and threw it in his face. It was a shocking waste of good whisky, but it was a purely instinctive reaction: if she had been big enough to reach up and hit him, she would have done that as well. Her voice came out in a thin whisper like a hurricane, and this so took him aback that he moved away, the whisky trickling down his cheek, and nearly tripped over the rug. He did not know that even in her temper she thought of the children and kept her voice down. He stared at her. He and Rose had quarrelled bitterly in their time, but he had never seen her as she was now, ashen-faced, hair half down, looking like a maenad. In that moment she did indeed look mad.

"Get out!" she told him in that thin, almost inaudible voice. "You're not taking Sally. You're not seeing Sally again. I'm divorcing you, and there's no court in the world that wouldn't give me custody. You think I'd leave her with that old maid of a sister of yours, that little blonde whore who hangs around you, and all your pretty boys? You don't want a daughter.

You wouldn't know what to do with her. You want a nice little doll you can show around, so that you can point at her and say, That's mine, aren't I clever? She's a person, Gerard. She's an intelligent, sensitive little person. She needs understanding—"

"Are you pretending that you—"

"Shut up!" Rose was completely beside herself, only she still remembered not to shout. She hardly saw Gerard except as a vast shadow standing over her, indeed she hardly saw anything for her vision was misted with horror and rage. "What do you know about children? You've never bothered about your own. Oh, you dandle her on your knee, you play little games that over-excite her, you ruffle her hair and give her sweeties. Do you really imagine it will always be like that? She'll be sick from too many sweeties, and then you'll have to clear it up—"

"You're the most disgusting bitch I've ever met," began Gerard. He was now as white as she was. He had never been able to look after the more ordinary needs of his children, he had always flatly refused to change a nappy, and when they were sick or messed themselves, he would make fastidious grimaces and immediately leave the room.

"It's you who are disgusting. But you'd better accustom yourself, Gerard. You'll have to clear up after her and cope with her tantrums and make her eat her dinner, and wash her and sit up with her when she's covered in spots or can't keep any food down. You've never begun to do any of these things. It doesn't interest you. You don't even begin to know her as a person. Why," whispered Rose so fiercely that she almost spat the words at him, "when she's reading a perfectly ordinary book, you snatch it from her so that she's frightened, and accuse her of reading pornography. Just because the little boy has a penis. You've got one, haven't you? Or perhaps you're impotent nowadays—"

He said in a kind of shriek, "Have you finished?"

And somehow this extinguished her so that the whispered vituperation stopped; she gaped at him as if horrified by her own words, then burst into floods of tears.

He began to laugh. It was his stage laugh, a kind of grand

ha-ha-ha, head flung back, the great hero deriding his enemy. And through her eyes, blurred with anger, wretchedness and tears, she saw him as a poor, cardboard thing: a magnificent profile, flowing hair, a tall, upright body, yet one could put a drawing pin through him and it would come out on the wall at the other side. And somehow this, which should have comforted her, frightened her all the more, for he was not entirely cardboard, he was a malevolent human being, he wanted to take Sally from her, and what he would do to her if he succeeded, God alone knew.

He spoke now in that coarse, ugly voice that always shocked her. He said, "You send your spies out, don't you, darling?"

She sobbed, trying with a shaking hand to pour herself another drink, and slopping it all over the bed, "I don't know what you're talking about."

"Oh yes, you do. Come off it. Only your supplies must be pretty low to send that fat little bitch from the kindergarten."

Rose, suddenly calmer though still shaking from head to foot, said, "What fat little bitch? What do you mean?"

"Lulu," he said. He almost sang the name, turning up his eyes as he did so. "Lulu! Dressed fit to kill in a cloak she almost fell over, with bright blue eyelids and hair like a nigger. Lulu! Well, she bloody didn't find anything out, I can tell you that, and she'll never come again. If she does, she'll be slung over the garden wall. Spilling maman's ashes—"

"Gerard," said Rose, "I think it's you who are mad. Maman's ashes! I just don't understand one word of what you're saying. Lulu? I never sent Lulu down. Why should I? She's far too nice a girl to get involved in that stinking pigsty of yours at Fishbourne. Why are you talking such nonsense? I don't know what Lulu's got to do with anything, and neither do you."

For some reason this appeared to enrage him completely. He began to scream. Rose had forgotten Gerard's hysterical rages, and for a second gazed at him aghast, her hands pressed tight against her cheeks as if to preserve her own sanity before this terrifying cacophony. Then she remembered the children. Those thin screaming cries must drown the television: Sally and Tom must be appalled and frightened half out of their wits. She cried out in desperation, "Gerard, please. Sally will hear you. She's always upset if people shout. If you love her as much as you say you do, please stop. Oh please—"

But he was far too angry even to listen. Perhaps that small, shaking voice did not even penetrate his hearing. The words continued to roar out at her, and she huddled away, her eyes on the door: she was praying that whatever programme was on would drown all this infernal noise, and knew only too well that it could not do so.

"You're out to destroy me," he shouted at her. "You spy on me. You spread dirty stories about me. Do you think I don't know why I'm never offered parts these days? Oh you think you're so clever, don't you? You and your little whispering campaign—ringing my agent no doubt, and getting that bloody bitch of a mother of yours to tell everyone I'm past it—"

She said very quietly, "Gerard, you're mad."

"I'm mad! I like that. It's you who're mad. You always have been. It didn't take me long to discover that. You're not fit to be out of a looney-bin, much less look after my darling little girl. I'm taking Sally with me, Rose, I can tell you that, and I'm taking her now. I wouldn't leave her with you. I'd never know what you'd do to her. You'll probably end by murdering her. You should be certified, it would be a kindness to yourself, and I'm going to see a doctor about it tomorrow. You talk of bringing a divorce action—you make me laugh. You just try and see what happens. Christ knows why I ever married you—"

"Sometimes," said Rose in a shaking whisper, "I've wondered, myself. And now you've said all this, Gerard, could you please—"

But it seemed that there was no stopping him. He looked so wild and white and frantic that she began to believe he might have a stroke. He burst out now into a flood of pure invective, as if he had no more accusations to bring against her and could only shout filth at her. "You're ugly! You're dirty! You're disgusting! I could vomit on the floor when I think that I—"

The door opened. He fell silent, his face suddenly twisted

M   177

and taut, wary as if he had been caught out. He swung round, very clumsily for someone usually deft in his movements, and almost lost his balance. Rose for a second closed her eyes. When she opened them, she found her vision so blurred that she could hardly see. But Sally's white, appalled face swung into her view, almost as if isolated from her body, and immediately she came to what was left of her shattered senses, rising shakily to her feet and saying in what seemed to her a dreadfully over-jolly voice, "Hallo, lovey. Have you come in to say goodbye to Daddy? He's just going."

Gerard said, "I thought you'd like to come back with me, Sal. You'd love that, my darling, wouldn't you? Tante Claudine has prepared a special supper for you, and we're putting you in the spare room—"

Rose took a step forward. Then she saw that there was no need for her to say anything, and somehow this, which should have been victory, appalled her. The look on Sally's face was unmistakable. She was staring at her father as if he were a hostile stranger. When he came up to her, with a kind of desperate smile on his lips, and tried to take her into his arms, she wriggled away from him, putting up her two hands as if to ward him off. Not even Gerard could ignore this. A look of black temper flashed across his face, and he opened his mouth as if to shout at her, then instantly shut it again, as if aware that this was hardly an advertisement for a loving father. He was left standing there with empty, open arms, then Sally, her face still pale with shock, turned to Rose and cried out in a loud, piercing voice, "You've stolen my money!"

The words formed themselves in Rose's mind: this is just about all I need. And because this was the last straw, because it was also entirely ridiculous, she did the best thing she could have done, she began to laugh. It was natural, unforced laughter, and Sally's face, as she heard it, began to lose that terrible shocked look. She glowered accusingly at her mother, who said soothingly, "Darling, I'm so sorry. I forgot to put it back. Yes, I did take it, it was awful of me, but I didn't know what else to do. That baby-sitter, the other night, wanted a taxi, and I just didn't have the change. Get your piggy-bank, Sal, and we'll settle the matter now." She turned to Gerard.

She was still smiling. Her face was as white as Sally's, but the battle-light gleamed in her eyes. "Give me some money, will you? Make it fifty p. You're becoming a millionaire, Sally. You're a rich girl. You're getting it back with interest."

And she held out her hand to Gerard who instinctively took some small change out of his pocket. When Sally came running back with the piggy-bank, Rose put the money in, shook the pig so that it rattled pleasingly, and handed it back, seeing with relief that a faint smile was appearing on Sally's face.

Gerard, she saw, was entirely at a loss. Then he turned again on Rose, who saw something at this moment that she had never before fully realised: he was fundamentally a stupid man. He was refusing to acknowledge that the real cause of Sally's distress was not the rifling of her piggy-bank but the screaming words that had come through into the sitting-room; by ignoring what had happened, he believed he could turn the whole thing to his advantage. This time he did not raise his voice, but the words were delivered in a theatrically cutting tone. "Really," he said, "do you have to rob the poor child's piggy-bank? I've never heard anything like it. And you have the nerve to ask me—"

Rose said clearly, "Oh, don't be so silly. Aren't you going to say goodbye to Sally and Tom? It's past their bedtime and I haven't given them their supper yet."

She saw that he was hesitating. But even Gerard at his most dramatic could hardly pick Sally up in his arms and carry her off, especially as she was backing away from him. He gave Rose a long, ugly look. He said quietly, "All right, my darling, all right. But I'll be back, and sooner than you expect. I suppose you are congratulating yourself on having won a famous victory. But we'll see. We'll see."

He turned again to his daughter. Rose, still unable to control her shaking, and feeling the sweat cold on her body, saw that the child did not respond to his embrace. She accepted the kisses on both cheeks, and made no attempt to move away, but the small body in his grasp was stiff, as if for the first time she was unsure of him, as if the love she normally bestowed on him like a fountain, were no longer there.

Gerard could hardly have been unaware of this, but managed to smile, as he called out, " 'Bye, Tom. Haven't you a kiss for Daddy?"

There was no sign of Tom, and Sally still stood there, staring at him out of wide, expressionless eyes.

He said bitterly to Rose, "You've done your work well."

She did not answer, only walked with him to the door. Gerard stood for a moment on the landing. She thought she had never seen him look so ugly. The fear consumed her, and she struggled to reassure herself. After all, what could he do? He could not kidnap the child, he could not knock her down and snatch the children from her. It would all make a monstrous noise and chaos, and even Mrs. Fielding could hardly ignore something so appalling. But she still did not say a word, only prayed that someone would come down the stairs, preferably Dr. Macek.

But there was no sign of anyone, and then Gerard said softly, the hamming for once not amusing, "I won't forget this. I'm having Sal to live with me, Rose. I know you think you've turned her against me, but you haven't. I'll do everything and anything to get her. You haven't a bloody chance, darling. I've got to know you at last. I once thought you really wanted the best for the children. I thought we could come to some civilised arrangement. Now I see I'm wrong. You want a fight, don't you? You'll get it. You'll get it, don't worry. You'll be hearing from me very soon."

Rose remained silent. Her knees were giving beneath her, so that she had to hold on to the door, but she stood there, her eyes fixed on him. She thought in the chaos of her frightened thoughts, This is my husband, this is the man I fell in love with and married. And she gazed mistily into that handsome, weak, implacable face, and saw nothing there, nothing but a spoilt, stupid little boy determined to get his own way, out to smash and destroy even his own daughter, simply to spite this young woman who was still his wife.

At last he tired of the staring match, or perhaps Rose's silence was too much for him. He muttered something in French—English was of course his language, but he still fell into French in moments of emotion—and turned violently on his heel to stamp down the stairs in a noisy rush, like a child in a temper.

Rose heard the front door slam behind him. It must almost have crashed off its hinges. The shame and humiliation of it all still convulsed her, coupled with a strange feeling of guilt as if somehow she were responsible for harming her own children. For a second she felt as if she were about to faint. It did not strike her that she had eaten nothing the whole day. But somehow she must calm Sally and see what had happened to Tom: she clenched her fists, told herself not to be a bloody fool, and came back into the flat.

The Photiades were packing in a frenzy. The flat was littered with carrier bags. The two suitcases—one was the new Revelation—that contained their clothes, were almost full. Nina was gathering up the oddments that she always collected from every flat they had rented. She told Andreas, who was removing the light bulbs, "We'll have our meal in a moment. I must take that big stewing pan. He'll never miss it. It was probably left by the last tenant, anyway. The car's coming about ten. It's a good time. People who're going out, will be gone, and they won't come back so early."

It was a regular routine. It had always worked. Only, as they were opening a bottle of wine for their last dinner in Curran House, Nina began to worry again and said, "I suppose it's all right."

"Of course it is, you silly little nut. Why shouldn't it be?"

"He never comes in at night, does he?" "He" was of course the landlord: landlords to the Photiades were natural enemies.

"Good God, no. Why should he? What are you scared about?" asked her husband fondly, and refilled her wine glass.

"I don't know," she said. She was dressed in black sweater and slacks. Her face was even paler than usual. Then she said, as she always did, "I've never liked this house. You know that. The people in it are so funny. And I've never trusted that girl underneath."

"She's all right," said Andreas. Despite that unhappy meeting, he rather liked Rose, though he never spoke to her, and he thought the children were sweet. He was a paternal kind of boy. One day, when they had stopped flitting, he hoped they would have a large family. But he was always careful to make fun of Rose if he mentioned her to Nina: she was a fiercely jealous girl, and it would be disastrous to indicate that he had the least feeling for a neighbour who was not only a female, but young and quite pretty.

"She could ring the landlord," said Nina.

"Why on earth should she? Anyway, even if she does, we'll be miles away by then."

"That dirty old peasant woman opposite might ring."

"Oh for God's sake!" said Andreas in a burst of laughter, then he got up, rushed round the table and kissed her. "She hasn't got a phone," he said. He stayed there, holding Nina tightly in his arms, and for a moment she hesitated before saying with obvious regret, "There's no time. I haven't finished packing yet. Oh Andreas, I shall be so glad to get away."

And after that they fell to packing again. The dirty dishes were left in the sink, only the stewing pan that Nina coveted was washed and stuffed into one of the carrier bags.

It was nine o'clock, and Dr. Macek was standing by his window, looking down into the darkened street. The whole situation seemed to him more and more ridiculous. It was the twentieth century, he lived in England, he was successful in his profession, he had no money troubles. He was moreover a quiet and rational man who did not care for histrionics, and he had no wish whatsoever to end his life. He again thought of Rose. It seemed particularly absurd—it was the word that always came into his mind—that now when, for the first time here, he had met a woman for whom he felt an extraordinary warmth, who really appealed to him as someone feminine and charming and lovable, he should feel obliged to end his existence, and in such an untidy sort of way. At least Rose would be unaware for a long time of what had happened to him. Perhaps it would not matter to her. And so he continued to stand there, struggling to make up his mind, wondering if he would have the courage to go through with it, and wondering what, if he did not succeed, the devil he was going to do.

He did not speak his own language at all these days. He

never associated with his fellow refugees, he found them on the whole intolerably right-wing. He even thought in English. He had come a long way from the stammering foreigner who thought he would never master such an impossible language.

But then he had come a long way from everything. And now he spoke aloud in his own language, saying, I just can't bear it, I don't know what to do.

"*Já už to déle nevydržím*," said Dr. Macek, and, "*Nevím co mám dělat.*"

And the last he repeated several times as if so weak-kneed a remark would somehow act as a talisman. It was nearly an hour later that he at last and irrevocably made up his mind. He looked once round his cold, bare, impeccably tidy flat. The pan he had used for his supper was washed and dried and up on the rack. There was so little in the tiny kitchen that it might have been unoccupied. In the small wall fridge provided by the landlord there was nothing but half a bottle of milk and some butter.

The quarter's rent was paid.

Dr. Macek put his keys in his pocket—this was purely mechanical, if odd in the circumstances—shut the door quietly and came downstairs.

Mrs. Parsons, on the floor below, was quite aware of all the disturbance in the flat opposite. She was convinced that the Photiades were preparing to scarper. It did not worry her, it was none of her business, let that bloody landlord cope. Her mind was concentrated on next Saturday's excursion to the cemetery, where she would travel with appropriate bunches of flowers for Ted, Maria, William and the various other members of the family who had passed over to the other side. She seldom went out, and this monthly jaunt was a great treat for her. She always put on her best black, including a special hat kept only for this occasion, and she travelled by a bus that dropped her almost at the cemetery gates. She felt no particular emotion about it. They had all died a long time ago. She would have had no sympathy at all for Claudine and her urn. She thought the cemetery, which was well-kept, very pretty with its neat rows of graves, and she often paused here and there to read the inscriptions describing people who were strangers to her. Then the ritual flowers had to be laid, and Mrs. Parsons would stand by each grave as if in meditation, though her mind was in no way concentrated on the dear departed: it merely seemed to her unfitting that she should drop the flowers and move instantly away. The whole proceeding took up about an hour, then she would get herself a meal, catch her bus back (it went at three minutes past the hour) and come home to watch the television as usual.

It made a nice change.

Rose, having come back into the flat, decided that the only thing to do now was to forget her own misery and do something about the children. On this she concentrated all the energy within her. She found Tom flat on his stomach doing one of his puzzles: he did not seem particularly disturbed and was soon shutting doors in his customary way. Sally, however, was looking cross and unhappy, and still apparently brooding on her piggy-bank, for all that Gerard's money clinked and clanked when she shook it. Rose decided that she was probably hungry, for it was long past supper-time, and went into the kitchen, where she made an especially nice meal with the liver and a pile of chips. It was sadly undietetic, but the children adored all fried food, and at that moment she would have done anything and everything to make up for that disgusting scene between herself and Gerard. She managed to ignore her own aching head, and the odd fits of dizziness that came upon her, and was so gay during the meal that both children seemed entirely recovered. She let them stay up late, she sang songs to them, she invented a new game that was gloriously noisy, but she did not think the Photiades would complain, indeed from the various strange bumps and noises coming through the window, they were not very quiet themselves. Perhaps they were having a party. Finally, when the children had had their bath, with a great deal of scented bubbles that Diana had given her for her birthday, she sat them down by the fire and read them a story, by which time Tom was almost asleep, and even Sally was nodding.

It was only when they were tucked up in bed that her own exhaustion and misery descended on her again. The fact that her fears were mostly ungrounded made no difference: she was in her own flat, she was surrounded by people, the children were safely in bed and probably asleep, and she was stark, staring terrified.

Of what? Why am I so frightened? It is all wind and bluster with Gerard. He cannot kidnap Sally, and if he did, he would be put in prison. But into her sick, exhausted mind came countless tales that she had read: once they had been merely newspaper headlines, now they assumed a dreadful reality. Fathers ran off with their children and hid them, they even left the country. It would be quite easy for Gerard to return to France before the police were notified. Rose knew nothing of extradition laws, she only knew that Sally was a nervous, sensitive child: to be snatched up by this egocentric maniac and whisked away might send her out of her mind. It seemed to Rose, huddled there, that the flat creaked and whispered, as if Gerard had somehow returned: so strong was this nightmare impression that twice she had to get up and make sure she was alone.

She put the chain on the door, and snibbed the lock, which made her feel better, only then she was overcome by a sudden panic that she had locked Gerard in with her, that he might appear behind her with a sleeping Sally in his arms. And so she had to get up again, and this time she walked over every inch of the flat, including the bathroom and lavatory. There was of course no one there, and the children were sound asleep, their breath coming evenly and peacefully as she bent over them, ostensibly to tuck them in, but really to satisfy herself that they were unharmed.

She came back at last, and poured herself out the last drops of whisky. She still had eaten nothing but a couple of chips fed to her by Tom, but she did not think of this, it never struck her that the pain pounding behind her eyes, and the weakness in her legs was due to the fact that she had eaten almost nothing for the past two days. She put a hand up to her eyes which were behaving oddly, seeing shadows where there were none, misting over when she tried to concentrate. She thought of turning on the television but, when she did, could not somehow co-ordinate her vision, so that it was all a coloured blur, a confusion of sound like scrambled telephones in a spy story.

If only there were someone I could talk to. I wish Dr. Macek were here.

And she all but went upstairs, only first she could not bear to leave the children alone, and secondly it seemed both neurotic and unfair to burden a comparative stranger with her silly vapours.

She decided to ring up Diana. Her mother would certainly not be encouraging but, though she lacked sympathy, she had plenty of common sense, and Rose felt that at that moment the common sense was more valuable. She dialled the number and held on for a long time. There was no answer. Diana and Michael led a full social life, of the kind that Rose herself found tedious; there were endless cocktail parties, little dinners and first nights. Rose knew little of her mother's private life, but imagined that there were very few evenings when she stayed at home. This certainly was not one of them. Perhaps it was as well. Diana would never begin to understand the fear and desolation and loneliness that now engulfed her daughter. Only it would have been agreeable to hear that husky voice, if only it said, Oh darling, don't be such a bloody fool.

Rose picked up her address book and leafed through it. She thought how odd it was that one should have a book full of names, and not want to contact any of them. There were old friends here, even one she had known at school. They were all nice people, they would be quick to comfort her, they might even suggest coming round, but Rose felt too raw to endure their sympathy: she wanted from them, oh Christ, what did she want—sympathy, no sympathy, advice, no advice, cheerful chat, exchange of confidences—No. No, no, no.

She shut the book with an angry slam, and dropped it on the floor. Since her marriage she had lost contact with almost everyone. It was probably her fault. At first they had come round, eager to meet the handsome husband, but Gerard's mixture of flirtatiousness and rudeness was such that they seldom came back. The only person who had stood up to him successfully was Diana, but then Diana would never be set down by anyone: she was as rude as he was, had an even more fluent vocabulary, and simply begged him, darling, not to be such an all-fired bloody bore.

Rose knew now what had after all been hinted at by almost everyone, that Gerard did not really like women, and had no intention of permitting her to surround herself with her own sex, who would side with her against him. At the time she merely thought he was being possessive, and was even a little flattered. Now, when she desperately needed friends, she found that in essence she had none left. They would be kind, but they would surely despise her. And she would never be able to tell them the full story: she was ashamed to admit her own fear and humiliation.

But she felt that if she did not communicate with someone, she would go mad. Gerard said she would go mad. And blind. It was true that her eyes were very strange, it was almost as if she had double vision. Rose, struggling not to contemplate this, rose to her feet again and wondered if she could ask Mrs. Fielding to look in for a while. Then she remembered the extraordinary account of Lulu's visit, and a weak rage overcame her: this little girl whom she had regarded as a friend, had double-crossed her, consorted with the enemy. There was nobody to trust, nobody at all. And Mrs. Fielding, though she would be sympathetic in her own way, would no doubt preach another of her homilies—Don't you think, dear, it would be best for both of you and of course the children to give it another chance—

It was a pity Mrs. Fielding had not been here a little earlier.

Rose decided in desperation to cross the landing and knock on Veronica's door.

10

MRS. FIELDING AT THAT moment was not thinking of Rose at all. She had been listening for some time to the odd noises that filtered down from Veronica's flat two floors up: she kept on coming out onto the landing, and each time the noises seemed more sinister. Now there was a dead silence. She knew perfectly well how things were, for she had lived in Curran House for over fifteen years.

She said to her husband, "I think we'll be ringing that nursing home any moment now."

Len was not particularly interested, though secretly he was a little frightened of Veronica who was like nothing he had ever met in his life and who, on the rare occasions when she met him, treated him like a servant, except that she had never so far offered him a tip. He professed to find her drunkenness rather funny. He shrugged and continued to watch the boxing match on the telly.

Mrs. Fielding hesitated, looked up again as if somehow her gaze could penetrate through two ceilings, drummed her fingers on the table, then went to the phone. This complete silence meant the worst; they would be lucky if it were not followed by thin, whining screams and the crazy crashes and bangs that made the place seem like a madhouse. She only hoped that there would not be another fire like last time, when the poor soul had nearly burnt the place to the ground. Besides, all this would be frightening for Lulu, who still did not seem at all well; it was frightening enough for everyone,

Veronica included, who was probably seeing the walls alive in her dementia, like that horrid film they had seen some weeks ago.

Mrs. Fielding, a little nervous now, took off the receiver and dialled the number she had been given by the land-lord.

Rose had forgotten about Veronica's bouts, for by now she was in such a state herself that it did not even cross her mind. She was only desperate for someone to talk to, and so she came out, leaving her door open: after all she would hear at once if Gerard or anyone else came, and perhaps Veronica would come back with her.

She found that Veronica too had left her door open. The flat was in darkness. It smelt bad, of stale drink, dirt and sickness. She called out a little shakily, "Veronica?"

There was no answer. There was not a sound. Rose knew where the light was, for the flats were all built on the same pattern, and switched it on.

Then she gave a gasping cry, and for the second time that day nearly fainted. Veronica was standing there so close that she almost touched her. The face staring directly into Rose's was that of a gargoyle, eyes enormous, mouth open, hair hanging over her like a tattered curtain. She neither moved nor spoke.

Rose, dry-mouthed, whispered, "Veronica, are you ill?"

There was no answer. Rose's eyes moved over the room, taking in the empty bottles, the appalling disarray everywhere as if the place had been ransacked, the filth, the chaos, the look of a place abandoned to hell. Then she understood, but she did not know what to do. It seemed wicked and cruel to abandon this wretched creature to her own despair, so she said in a choked voice, "Can I do anything? Would you like me to fetch a doctor?"

Then Veronica began to scream. Mrs. Fielding heard her, for her door was open. The nursing home was sending round an ambulance: thank God she had rung them. She hastily shut the door, hoping Lulu would not hear, even turned up the television, much to Len's disgust. And Rose, driven beyond the resources of her courage, unable to bear any longer the ghastly face and cries, gave a little sob and fled on to the landing.

Her door was shut, and she had no key. From the little movements inside she understood what had happened. Tom usually slept the clock round, but when he was upset, he always got up and made straight for her bed. The scene with Gerard must have disturbed him after all. When he found that she was not there he had fallen into his usual way of shutting any open door in sight: he was too little and probably too sleepy to realise that instead of being comforted by Mother he was in point of fact shutting her out.

"Oh my God!" muttered Rose, pressed the time switch on the landing, then said urgently into the letter box, "It's all right, Tom. Call Sally. Wake Sally up. Give her a good shake. I'll be with you in a minute, lovey, just wake Sally."

She could still hear Veronica's screams. This was becoming like a nightmare. Tom was beginning to grizzle, and she said again in as calming a voice as she could manage, "It's all right, pet. Just wake up Sally. Go on, lovey, then Mummy will be with you."

It was at this moment that Dr. Macek decided to come downstairs, and the Photiades, now packed and ready and full of loot, heard on their buzzer that the car was waiting for them, as arranged.

They came out into pandemonium. Nina was so frightened that she burst into tears. She sobbed, "I knew it would go wrong. What are we going to do?"

Veronica's screams carried through the house. Mrs. Fielding had run out on to the landing. Dr. Macek was too engrossed in his own grim thoughts to pay much attention to the little Greek couple with all their packages, and Rose, suddenly at the end of her tether, unable to think of such practical things as contacting the police, sat down on the bottom step and buried her face in her hands.

The Photiades, accustomed to slipping out in peace and quiet, found that everyone in Curran House seemed to be out waiting for them. Andreas whispered, "Leave all those carrier bags. Then it will look as if we're just going away for a few days—"

"But everything's in them," wailed Nina. "The light bulbs and the kettle—and that lovely pan."

Her husband did not answer this, simply grabbed the carrier bags with all their stolen contents, and dumped them on the landing. He seized hold of Nina's hand and ran her down the stairs, almost falling over Rose as he did so. At that moment, with Dr. Macek a few steps behind them, the time switch went out, and Rose raised her head to find herself in the pitch dark. Then she knew it had happened. She had gone blind. She was not even aware of the Photiades who, now foreseeing prison and possibly execution—the Colonels after all did not concentrate entirely on Theodorakis—pelted past her like rabbits, emerging at last to find an ambulance there and two white-coated men about to come inside.

It was the last straw. Nina thought they were police come to arrest them. She ran wildly into the street, Andreas at her side, and they both leapt into the car, still patiently waiting, so frightened that they could hardly direct the driver. Nina wept on Andreas's shoulder, sobbing, "I knew we should never have come here. Oh, I hope I never see this place again as long as I live."

Andreas could only hope that the place would never see them again either. But it was no good chopping logic with a woman, and nobody seemed to be following them, so he comforted Nina tenderly, and presently they were making their way to the small hotel where they would stay for a couple of days before settling into their new flat on the other side of London.

Dr. Macek touched Rose's shoulder. He saw that she was shaking convulsively. "Mrs. Menusier," he said, "what is the matter?"

She turned her face to him. She said, "I'm locked out of my own flat, and I've gone blind."

It was at this moment that Dr. Macek knew that he had not the least intention of committing suicide. Perhaps he never had. He pressed the switch so that the light flooded on, then sat down quite un-selfconsciously beside Rose, taking her hand in both of his. He paid no attention to the two ambulance men, now helping a silent Veronica down the stairs: she moved like a puppet, her feet dragging, and her face was sponged of all sanity.

Rose said, "There's light—I can see."

"The time switch went off," said Dr. Macek calmly, then as if he were speaking to an hysterical patient, "It's all right, Rose. It's all right." He did not realise he was using her Christian name. "So you're locked out. I suppose the door slammed."

She was staring at him, as if she still could not believe that she could see. She said in a whisper, putting up a hand to her eyes, "It's Tom. I thought he was asleep." Then, as if she had come fully to her senses, she jumped up, her voice suddenly loud and clear. "He's crying. What am I to do? I tried to make him wake up Sally, but he's too little to understand."

Tom was indeed bawling his head off, for he was furious that Mother was not there to comfort him: besides, the shut door frightened him and he began to batter on it with his fists. Only Sally, with her capacity for sleeping like the dead, could have remained unaware of such a noise.

Dr. Macek, who seemed to have an extraordinary way of remaining calm through crises, said, "There is a pass-key in the cupboard on the top landing. The landlord showed it to me, in case Lady Matford was taken ill." He paused briefly to look down the stairs. Veronica was being half-carried into the waiting ambulance, and Mrs. Fielding was bobbing about outside her flat, secretly adoring all the excitement and offering everybody cups of tea. "I will get it for you," continued Dr. Macek, "then we will open the door and you can comfort your small son. And then, I think, you will give me a nice cup of coffee, and you will tell me why you think you have gone blind."

"You really are very kind," said Rose a little unsteadily. She too was on the verge of tears. It was true that she could see again, only after that one terrible moment of blackness, she still could not quite believe it. She thought Dr. Macek was the most comforting person she had ever known in her life and, because she was still too shocked to know quite what she was saying, added, "You will come back, won't you? Please don't leave me alone."

"Of course," said Dr. Macek. "It will take one minute only to get the key." And in little more than that he returned with the pass-key in his hand: in a moment Rose was inside clasping a frenzied Tom to her, and assuring him that everything would be all right.

She was relieved to find that the tears were mostly due to temper and frustration. He had not yet had time to become really afraid, so she cuddled and kissed him, and presently tucked him up in bed again, sitting beside him for a few minutes until he started to doze off.

Then she came back into the sitting-room.

She looked at Dr. Macek, who was standing by the mantelpiece, examining Sally's art-work: the paper flowers, a crayon drawing, and an imitation stained-glass window with a Christmas motif, that Rose had inadvertently stuck upside down, much to Sally's fury. ("You're so stupid, Mummy!" "Yes," Rose had had to admit sadly, surveying the reversed Christmas tree, the stocking suspended in mid-air and a strange crescent moon the wrong way round.)

"The window is upside down," said Dr. Macek gravely.

"Oh God!" said Rose, beginning to laugh for the first time that evening, the first time for longer than she could remember. "Don't I know it! And it's stuck on with glue so it will never come off. I thought it was a shield. It's shaped like a shield. I suppose I just didn't bother to examine it. It only proves that I'm a rotten sort of mother."

"You are a very anxious mother."

"Yes. I suppose I am." Then she said, "Oh, I can't tell you how glad I am you're here. It's been a horrible day."

"I can appreciate that," said Dr. Macek. "It has been a trifle horrible for me too. I'm glad to be here, myself. I like your so cosy little flat. Mrs. Menusier—"

She nearly asked him to call her Rose, then decided not to do so. She forgot that in that one moment he had used her Christian name.

He went on, "What is all this about your going blind? Will you come nearer, please, and let me look at those eyes of yours. I am after all a doctor." And he repeated in a strange, almost angry way that she did not understand, "I am after all a doctor." He rubbed at his forehead as if this bewildered him. "Stand over there, please, so that the light from the lamp is on your face. Look straight at me. Now why do you think you are going blind?"

The tone made Rose almost smell the disinfectant. It was extraordinarily soothing. She obeyed him, raising her face to his, and blinking as she did so. She said, "Things go all blurry. I seem to have a permanent headache. Sometimes I'm sure I can't see at all, then I panic, and it all becomes much worse." Then she added, her voice so low as to be almost inaudible, "My husband tells me I shall go blind. I think I am beginning to believe him."

He made no comment on this, only moved his hands over her face, gently pulling down the corner of her eyes and looking intently into them. The nearness of a human face in so impersonal a fashion was strange, and Rose saw him as a collection of unrelated features, a nose, a rather large nose, dark eyes, very marked brows as if done with a pencil, and way beneath the lines and craters a firm, compressed mouth. Presently he moved away, pulling down the lampshade so that the glare was no longer upon her. He said, "When did you last eat?"

"What!" She had not expected this. She thought he would say something reassuring and perhaps suggest an appointment with an oculist. She stared at him.

"When did you last eat, Mrs. Menusier?"

Rose did not answer immediately. Then she said in a surprised voice, "I don't know. I think it must be some time ago." Then she said, "I haven't eaten anything today—yes, I have! Two chips. Tom likes to share his food in an unexaggerated sort of way, you know, ten chips for Tom and one for Mummy."

She half expected him to reproach her. After all, it was idiotic of her to starve herself, and she had no excuse now with Diana's lovely cheque, but he only said in the calm way that she was beginning to see was his customary manner, "I haven't eaten much either. Would it be impertinent of me to suggest that you now make us some little meal? Bacon and eggs, perhaps, or an omelette. I think we could both do with some nourishment. I find myself very hungry. I daresay you are hungry too, if you let yourself think about it. You will certainly find that your headache goes, once you have eaten. I do not," said Dr. Macek, in his slightly professorial way, "approve of these crash diets that involve starvation. What one loses on the fasting day, one invariably puts on the next."

"I expect you are quite right," said Rose dazedly. She thought it was considerate of him to suggest she was on a diet. She still felt very strange, almost floating, and the headache was blinding, but there was something extraordinarily soothing about Dr. Macek, it was almost as if she stood in some charmed circle of light where no evil could touch her. She said, making a rather dizzy progress towards the kitchen, "I'd love to offer you something to drink, but I'm afraid I haven't any left."

"It would, I think, be inadvisable in the circumstances," said Dr. Macek.

She left him sitting in the armchair. She did not think he would want to watch the television, so she found him a newspaper to read. It was only later that she realised it was three days old, but he did not seem to mind, only put on his glasses and perused it with great attention.

There was no bacon, but there were eggs and some cold chicken, so Rose made a large chicken omelette and tossed up a salad to go with it. Now that the word 'hunger' had actually been mentioned, she realised that she was famished, and once or twice had to hang on to the sink because her head was swimming. But she managed to prepare the omelette, and then put everything on the trolley that she normally used herself when alone, and wheeled it all through.

They made a kind of small talk while eating. They talked mostly about the children. Dr. Macek seemed genuinely interested, and heard about Tom's mania for shutting doors and Sally's brightness at reading, then threw in one or two stories about his own little patients.

When the meal was done, he offered Rose a cigarette and lit one for himself.

She said, "You're quite right. I feel much better and the headache's gone."

"Ah!" said Dr. Macek: it seemed somehow the only fitting comment.

"Shall I make some coffee?"

"I should like that." He raised his head from the newspaper he was again glancing at. He seemed to find the stale news absorbing. He said, "I think, Mrs. Menusier, we have a lot to talk about."

The formal address both amused and touched her. In an odd way it even pleased her. In Gerard's world and her mother's world Christian names were used from the very beginning, it was Johnny darling, and Mary my sweet, almost before the introduction. It was a world of nicknames, of endearments used as frequently and meaning as much as four letter words, a tinkling world where 'darling' could apply to one's dearest enemy, where kisses were bestowed like the dropping of ash on the carpet. Rose knew now that she was going to tell Dr. Macek things that so far she had told no one, knew too that she was going to hear similar things from him. For both of them this had been an evening of crisis, for both of them it had been a time of near despair. To talk to each other formally and at the same time to confide so intimately, was somehow right, the only way in which to conduct what might otherwise be an impossible confrontation.

She answered, "Yes, Dr. Macek, I think we have."

And she smiled at him as she spoke, the warmth flooding through her. In the kitchen, as she put on the kettle and slung the dirty dishes into the sink to wait till morning, she sang a little song to herself, not to give herself courage but because she felt happy.

She looked at the children once before she brought the coffee in. Both were asleep. She saw, as she came out of Tom's room, that Dr. Macek had observed this. She said, "Yes, I'm over-anxious. But when you hear the circumstances, you will understand. I'm sure it will pass. I hope so. Children are so damnably intuitive." Then she said, "I am too much alone. You are too, aren't you?"

He said, as she poured out the coffee, "So much so that tonight I believed I would commit suicide."

Rose did not exclaim, simply nodded: in this twilight intimacy of strangers it seemed somehow a perfectly natural remark.

He went on, in a reasonable voice, "Of course it was non-sense. I would not have done it. I can see that now very plainly. But I really believed myself. I even tidied up all my papers and left instructions with my receptionist, so that my patients could be passed on to another doctor and receive the right treatment. It took me a long time. I see now that I was simply trying to convince myself. When I saw you on the stairs I was about to walk to the Embankment."

"The Embankment?" repeated Rose. "That sounds very melodramatic. Were you going to throw yourself over a bridge?"

"I thought I was. But I will tell you what would have happened, for now I see it so clearly," said Dr. Macek. There was a small ironic smile on his lips as if he found his own self-deception comic. "I would have walked on to the bridge. I do not know which one. It hardly matters. And there I would have stood for a very long time, looking down at the water. And then—"

"And then?"

"Then I would have felt cold and in need of a cup of coffee. It would not be such good coffee as you are giving me, but there are—what do you call them?—coffee stalls which serve the down-and-outs as well as rich people coming out of their clubs. So—I should have bought myself a cup of hot, bad coffee and perhaps some kind of sandwich, then I should have come home. You see, I am not really the suicidal type. I am simply a coward, faced with something for which I see no solution. Tomorrow," said Dr. Macek, "I must get to my surgery very early indeed, in case my receptionist finds all the elaborate notes I have left her. I would not like her to see them. She might get the wrong impression. Will you please give me some more of your coffee? It is very good."

"Why did you want to commit suicide?" asked Rose, refilling his cup.

"I will tell you presently. I will lay my problems before you, and you will perhaps find the solution. Though I think there is none. But to kill myself would be a fantasy solution, as much as for that neighbour of yours who drinks herself into oblivion. I do not know why she drinks, but for her too there must be some immeasurable problem that she cannot face: she does not want to kill herself so she drowns herself. One day soon she will achieve both. I do not think you or I will take either way out."

"Why do you say that?" asked Rose. "You nearly did, and I might too, if it wasn't for the children. After all, I am responsible for them, I couldn't do such a dreadful thing to them. But you make us out such superior people. I am not superior at all. I am just frightened. I have been terribly frightened. I'm always in such a muddle. I have a mother—it seems strange to call her that because she isn't like a mother at all—but still she is, she gave birth to me. Sometimes I wonder how she ever did anything so vulgar. She seems to me a completely self-contained person. She never gets emotionally involved, she always knows what she wants to do. She has no time for me at all, she just gives me money. I don't mean I don't appreciate the money, God knows I do, I don't know what I'd do without it, but sometimes I feel all silly—how awful this sounds at my age!—and wish she'd cuddle me as I do the kids, and say, There, there. Poor Diana! She'd have a fit if she heard me talking like that. But she's somehow so strong, she'll never do stupid, idiotic things. I do them all the time, but Diana just organises herself and the world around her. She just can't understand my muddles. If I did commit suicide I think she'd just shrug her shoulders and say, Darling you always were a bloody bore. That's how she talks. Everyone's a bloody bore, and she just can't be bothered with them. She'll never even think of suicide. I do, quite often. Are you so sure I shan't capitulate one day?"

"You and I are survivors," said Dr. Macek.

"Oh, oh! As survivors," said Rose, "we don't seem to have put on much of a show tonight. You wandering off to the Embankment to throw yourself off the nearest bridge, and me—oh dear. Me sitting crying on the stairs, thinking I'd gone blind. Is that surviving?"

"We're still here," said Dr. Macek calmly.

"I wonder why we are."

"I've just told you. We are survivors. I do not know this mother of yours, but I would suggest she is far more likely to commit suicide than you ever will be."

"Diana? Oh no. Never."

"Why not? If you are correct, she has nothing. One day she will know that. How does she like your children?"

"Oh, she's no time for them at all. She likes buying pretty clothes for Sally, because she's a lovely little girl, but she doesn't have any feeling for her." A note of bewilderment crept into Rose's voice. "It always seems extraordinary to me, but she has never once played any kind of game with them or taken them out, and when their birthdays come round, she simply gives me the money to get their presents. I think she only tolerates them at all because they're decorative to look at. If they were plain or grubby, I don't suppose she'd so much as have them near her. And she's furious if they call her granny. Sometimes it makes me quite sad. I think she misses out. But of course she leads a far fuller life than I do. I suppose she just doesn't have the time." Then she said again, "Why did you want to commit suicide?"

"I did not want to. I simply felt I had to. I will tell you, Mrs. Menusier. You will be the first and only person to hear it. I think," said Dr. Macek, with a touch of emotion in the calm, even voice, "I should have told you before. There was one moment when I nearly did so. You will not remember, but you asked me in for a drink—"

"That was only yesterday!"

He said in astonishment, "You are right. How could I have forgotten? I think I have lost all count of time. Yes. Yes indeed. But now you will first tell me why you sit on the stairs thinking you are blind. You say you are afraid. Why are you afraid? I am afraid too. We will share our fears and look at them. Perhaps they will then disappear. What has frightened you so much? You seem to me a very courageous person."

"Oh, I am the world's worst coward."

"Then tell me about it."

Curran House was recovering after all the melodrama. Mrs. Fielding, who usually kept an eye on everything that was happening, was far too excited to pay the least attention to Rose. She rang up both Amanda and Monica to tell them the news, and was on the phone for over half an hour. She was

199

completely unaware of the remarkable source of gossip upstairs, that Dr. Macek was in Rose's flat, and indeed would remain so for the greater part of the night. She saw poor Lady Matford conveyed into the ambulance, and decided that next day she must go into her flat to clear up the mess for the time when she came back home. The poor soul, and a titled lady too—"I just can't understand it," she told Len as she had already done many times before. "With all her advantages and plenty of money—she must once have been quite a beauty too." She added, a little helplessly, for all this was outside her comprehension, "I just can't quite believe it. And what are you doing up, young lady?" she asked Lulu who had just emerged sleepily from her room, the cord of her dressing-gown trailing behind her.

"With all that row," grumbled Lulu, "you'd hardly expect me to sleep, would you?"

"Well, it's all over now, so go back to bed."

"Have they taken her off to the looney-bin?"

"Lou, you really mustn't say things like that. It's unkind. And it's not a looney-bin. I don't know where you pick these words up. It's a very expensive nursing home."

Lulu looked expressively at her, but did not trouble to argue. She had a vast store of sympathy for people she liked, but Veronica to her was simply a revolting old woman who went out of her way to be rude to everybody, who drank too much and was sick. She thought with perfect truth that her mother was simply enjoying herself. She retreated to her bedroom again, and once back there took out that horrid letter from her drawer, to read it through once again.

It seemed nastier each time she read it. If only there were someone to advise her—but the only person she could think of was Rose herself, which was ridiculous. Perhaps Monica— She suspected this was something outside Monica's range, besides it would be unfair to Rose to broadcast something so personal. She fell asleep at last, the letter under her pillow as if it were a billet-doux.

Mrs. Parsons naturally heard all the row: she could hardly avoid it. As far as Veronica was concerned, she was simply not interested. She had met plenty of drunks in her time, only they had neither money nor a title: they were not carted off to luxury nursing homes, they were simply dumped in a police cell, to be fined the next day. She was far more interested in the Photiades, and when all the shouting had died down, came out into the hallway to investigate.

She nearly fell her length over a pile of carrier bags. She looked at them, her long mouth going down at the corners then stooped rather laboriously — she was a big woman — to examine their contents. She saw at once that the young couple were not only flitters, as she had known all along, but thieves. The bags were full of the landlord's property: she knew this because she had gone into their flat one day before their arrival and while the builders were still working on it. Mrs. Parsons had an excellent visual memory. She remembered perfectly well the pan and the kettle; there was also a cushion, several light bulbs, and the soap rack from the bathroom, as well as a variety of other trifles. She emitted one brief snorting laugh. They must have had a fine old scare to leave all this loot behind them. They had even forgotten to lock the flat door, presumably left on the latch while they got the luggage out.

Mrs. Parsons pushed the door open and peered in. She had never seen such a muddle. There was chaos everywhere, the stove was covered with grease, the sink was chock-full of dirty dishes, and the bedroom looked as if an army had gone through it. They had even left the television on. She did not trouble to turn it off. Indeed, she hoped it would explode. She thought with the utmost pleasure of the landlord's face when he came to see this next day: he would certainly be there for that Mrs. Fielding, a real do-gooder if she'd ever seen one, would be ringing him up about the drunken old lady. Mrs. Parsons promised herself to be on the lookout for him: serve the bugger right for neglecting his decent tenants.

What with this and the proposed visit to the cemetery, it had been a splendid day.

Rose said, "I married Gerard over six and a half years ago. I was twenty-four. I am thirty-one now."

The words came out almost automatically. She did not

pause to consider whether this would interest Dr. Macek or not. She only knew that she was going to talk everything out from the smallest detail and, when she had done, he would do the same to her. She did not at that moment think of him much as a person. Dr. Macek, whom she had met only a few times, seemed to her a good, sound human being: she knew she liked him, perhaps she loved him. But now, sitting in front of her as she knelt by the electric fire, his face intent, almost expressionless, his eyes fixed on hers, his hands clasped round his crossed knee, he was a kind of exorcist, and Rose knew that she needed him, needed him more than anyone or anything in the whole of her life: he held her sanity in those broad, capable hands, he alone had the power to destroy the demons who had for so long tormented her.

When she had done and he had done, they could sweep the debris away, perhaps form some kind of life together, begin again inasmuch as anyone could ever begin again, at least face the world that had nearly defeated both of them. But now he was a listener, as she in her turn would be a listener, and so she went on speaking.

"I was a silly, innocent sort of girl. It seems odd nowadays, it was a bit odd then, after all, it's not so very long ago. My mother—I have to call her Diana, she hates being reminded that she's my mother—would have liked me to be daring and outrageous and beautiful, all the things she was herself. She was a great beauty, you know, in an odd twenties' sort of way.

" 'You should have lived in the twenties, it would have suited you, with the funny hair styles and your waist round your thighs.'

" 'Have a heart, darling, for Christ's sake. I was only born then. What are you trying to do, make me a hundred?'

"She met my father during the war. I didn't really know him. He was a regular army officer, and he wanted a son. Diana didn't want a child at all, of course, and I've never quite understood why she had me, after all, it's quite easy to get rid of a baby, and she wasn't the kind to have a conscience about it. I think it was just an interesting experiment. I mean, babies are funny little things anyway, all crinkled and crumpled and ancient-looking, they're messy and smelly and always

202

crying. Poor Diana! There wasn't much in the way of croonings and cuddles for me, not that it mattered so much, babies are so much tougher than one imagines. She got me a nanny. I was very happy. I still see the old girl sometimes. I haven't been down for some time, what with one thing and another, but we keep in touch. She was after all my mother.

"Diana didn't even behave like the Victorian mama who used to see her children once a day, all scrubbed and ironed and curled. I didn't see her for weeks on end, then she'd sweep into the nursery—I actually had a nursery, would you believe it!—and bring me fancy presents, and criticise the way I was dressed.

" *'Darling, what the hell have they done to your hair? And for God's sake, where did they dig that outfit from? You look like an orphanage bastard. Take it off at once! I can't stand the sight of it.'*

"Perhaps she'd have done better with a son. Mind you, she was never unkind to me. At Christmas she and my father always took me to the theatre, from when I was five. It was a grown-up play I didn't understand, but it was terribly exciting, and afterwards we went back-stage and everyone made a terrible fuss of me, and they gave me champagne and I was sick. I fancy Diana didn't like that at all. Still it was all quite fun, if a bit strange, and when I had my friends home for tea, they always found it funny that my mother was never there, and the tea was always so posh and formal, with beautiful little sandwiches and lace tablecloths.

"I think the oddest thing was my innocence. I don't imagine Diana was innocent from the moment she was born, and later on, when we could talk more—we always talked, you know, that was something—she would tell me about her affairs and the crazy things she did as a girl, then she'd give me advice that I couldn't take because I didn't understand it. I mean, it's no good telling a ten-year-old about contraceptives when she doesn't really know about sex, and in a way it put me off, it was all so fearfully matter-of-fact. Nanny never knew about this, she would have had a fit. Then when I was seventeen, I decided I wanted to go up to Oxford. Oh my God, what a carry-on—

" *'I'm not having any varsity girls in my family, thank you very much.*

All educated girls are bloody bores, men don't look at them. What do you want to be, one of those frozen up old spinsters wearing glasses and talking Latin? The next thing is you'll want to go and nurse lepers or something. Don't be a bloody idiot, Rose, you're quite pretty if you bother about yourself, get yourself a man. If you go up to college, you pay for it yourself, and you needn't come back, whining for a square meal, because you won't get it.'

"Well, I didn't get to college, and there were parties and dances and lots of young men, none of them serious, and I was marvellously sophisticated on the surface with the last word in clothes, and we always went abroad for holidays. It was an odd sort of life, quite out of period, almost pre-war.

"Only I did go to evening classes, and I paid for them myself. Diana never knew. I learnt shorthand and typing. It was one of the few sensible things I did, God knows what would have happened to me without it.

"But you'll understand that in a way I was just ripe for someone phoney like Gerard, because the whole thing was phoney, I never knew the real thing. I fell in love from time to time, but Diana never particularly liked any of my young men, she rather frightened them off, and I wouldn't sleep with them anyway, I don't know why, it's just how it was. I suppose I didn't love them enough. And then when I was twenty-four — from Diana's point of view that was virtually on the shelf — I met Gerard.

"It was at a theatre party. I told you, I was always going to parties. I thought he was the most handsome man I'd ever met in my life. Of course I know now he's a homosexual — I hate that horrid word 'queer' — but in those days I simply didn't know what a homosexual was. I don't know how I remained so simple, I think I just didn't want to know. I won't let my children be like that, it's no good. Innocence, if you can call it that, is terribly dangerous. In some ways it was as if I lived on two levels. I heard all the in-jokes, about sex and queers and all that, but it didn't really touch me, my mind was away on, oh God knows what, things like poetry and books, all of which were far more of a secret vice than any kind of sexual perversion. And then, bang, Gerard. He seemed to me the most perfect man in the world, and if people sniggered around us, I just didn't notice, I wouldn't have cared if I had. Now it's all changed, he hates me, he hates almost everyone, and his looks have gone. He's still technically handsome, but there's no substance to it. When I saw him today, when he said he was taking Sally away with him, he seemed to me a kind of cardboard monster, evil and dangerous, but not really human. With an ordinary person one can appeal to their humanity, even perhaps make them laugh, one can say silly, ordinary, common things like, Oh come off it, or, Don't be silly, or, You know you don't mean it. But not with Gerard. He's got an obsession about Sally, I don't quite understand it, but I think perhaps she makes him feel normal, he needs her to seem an ordinary, hetero kind of man. But when I first met him, he was marvellous. Do you know, even now when we hate each other, when we can't meet without being vicious and nasty and beastly, I still remember the glory of that first meeting. And it was a glory, it really was. He was so tall and beautiful and witty and, yes, kind—it seems strange now, when I remember our last night together when he was physically sick at my presence and called me every filthy name under the sun—"

Rose broke off for a second, then went on.

"I knew he was the only man I could marry, and I told him so. And Diana was horrified. Horrified!—

" 'He's queer as a coot, darling. But of course he is, everybody knows that. He had an affair with that boy who was in Macbeth, I've forgotten his name. And he can't act. You could act better than he can, and you're not exactly a RADA prizewinner. You bloody little idiot! Don't you realise what you're letting yourself in for? Yes, of course he wants to marry you. They always do. And in a year's time he'll be off with one of his pretty boys, and what the hell will you do then? I could kill you, Rose. Aren't there any ordinary men around that you have to choose yourself an old fag like that?'

"But of course I didn't listen, I knew everything. And the awful thing is she was absolutely right, this was the one time when I should have let her warn me off. At last she was so exasperated with me that she told me to balls up my bloody life any way I wanted—it's the way she talks—but she still tried to stymie me. I think in her own way she's quite fond of me.

For a time Gerard and I somehow never met, if I went to a party, he wasn't there, and so on. But this didn't work as she hoped it would, because it made me feel all romantic and secret, and we corresponded and he sent me reams of French poetry that he'd pinched from someone else. I found that out much later. Then he went to Paris where his sister was living, and he rang me at a friend's house, telling me to come over and get married. And so I did, so I did. You see, I was of age, I had plenty of money then because Diana made me a very generous allowance, and I was never supervised. Besides, I'd become quite a good liar, and I spun her some long story about a friend who had a villa and wanted me to stay, or something of the kind. I don't suppose she really believed me, but what could she do about it? So that was that, and I became Mrs. Gerard Menusier.

"I'm telling you all this," said Rose to Dr. Macek, "to get it out of my system. It's all pretty silly, and it makes me out a complete idiot, but you see, there really was nothing to prepare me for the marriage that followed. It was disastrous—disastrous! The glamour hardly lasted the honeymoon. I knew so little about anything that it didn't strike me at first how awful the sex side was, but after a time even I had to see this was not quite what I expected. Gerard got tired of me almost at once. I think at the beginning it amused him to trot me round as the little wife, but that couldn't last once the novelty had worn off, and soon we were quarrelling all the time, and he didn't come home at nights, and he was abominably rude to my friends when he did. Oh it was all foreseeable, and I must do Diana credit, she didn't say, I told you so. Now she thinks I ought to go back to him, because she says I need a man to be there, even if he's not a normal one. But she doesn't understand. I've just become frightened and completely alone. There are the children, of course—I sometimes wonder how we achieved them—but there they are, and I love them, and they've kept me more or less sane. But there came a point when I couldn't stand Gerard any more, and he couldn't stand me either. I suppose there were boy-friends, but I didn't know, though I think everyone else did; people used to make snide remarks and look sideways at me and giggle. That sort of thing. But I could never live with him again. He makes it so plain that I disgust him. He can't speak to me without being jeering or cruel, and the latest thing is that I am going mad and blind. I know it sounds ridiculous in a way, but when you're on your own most of the time, and worried about money, and tired and sick, it is quite easy for people to make you believe almost everything. And the more you insist you're all right, the crazier you sound. As for the blindness — my eyes aren't too good at this moment, but you're quite right, I don't eat much, and I worry all the time, and I suppose it's built up on me so that I can't see anything straight, literally or metaphorically.

"And then of course there's what you might call public opinion. The woman on her own is in a hell of a spot, really. And of course Gerard can turn on the most incredible charm when he wants to, and people think I'm wicked to even think of leaving him, especially as he likes to give the impression it's all my fault and he's so fond of me. So you see, I'm always being pushed on to the defensive, and there's nothing in the world more boring. And tonight I suddenly knew I couldn't bear it any more, I felt so utterly alone and so afraid. Before Tom locked me out, I think I really did behave like a lunatic. I even thought Gerard was going to leap out at me, snatch up Sally and carry her off to France. He has a key, you see. He can come and go as he pleases. I suppose in a way he's entitled, he does pay the rent."

Dr. Macek said, "He is not entitled to frighten you. Why don't you change the lock?"

Rose considered this eminently practical suggestion with a kind of incredulity. Then she laughed. She said, "Do you know, it just never struck me. I probably will. You're quite right. But even then he's so set on Sally that I could never trust him. He's very cunning. I don't really quite understand this obsession, because he doesn't care much for children, and he certainly doesn't know anything about them. He has a sister he lives with just outside Chichester, and she's a strange, hard, cold sort of person: I wouldn't like my child to be in her charge. The real answer to all this is to divorce him, and he swears he'll contest it and I won't have a chance and he'll get custody of the children. Of course this is nonsense, and in my better moments I know it. I've even kept the letters he's written me, and to put it mildly they're indiscreet. But I keep on thinking of the children. If they were taken from me I really would go mad. Oh, everything has become crooked and impossible — Diana's quite right. I'm a dreary idiot." Then she said, "You can have no idea what a comfort it is to say all this. I didn't mean to go on for so long, but I'm afraid, poor Dr. Macek, you've just got everything I've been holding in for so long. It's out now. I don't think I'll ever feel so frightened again. Loneliness makes one so sorry for oneself."

"I know that too."

"Well, thank you for listening to me. I'm going to make some fresh coffee, and then you will tell me why you proposed to throw yourself off a bridge."

He said, as she rose to her feet, "You have hardly mentioned your father at all."

She looked at him, surprised. "Haven't I? He divorced my mother when I was seventeen. She boasts that it was all her fault. I'm sure it was. He's dead now. He died a long time ago. No, I suppose I haven't. He never really impinged on me. That's an awful thing to say of one's own father. But I think Diana eclipses her men. She uses them as amenities, not really as human beings. Her present man, he's called Michael, he's a nice sort of guy really, but do you know, if you asked me for a description, I just couldn't give it you. I know he's quite good-looking, he's younger than she is, and he's got pots of money. I've met him several times. He's always very nice to me, and once or twice he's taken me out to lunch. I wonder sometimes what he and Diana talk about. I can't see that they have much in common. He's a freemason, she tells me. It doesn't sound important, but it's the kind of silly thing that sticks in one's mind. But about my own father I really know nothing. He was away quite a lot. Diana didn't like that. She doesn't care much for men, but she likes them around. Now I must make that coffee."

She made a fresh brew, and came back with it on a tray. The children were sound asleep, and Curran House was silent and still. Veronica, heavily sedated, was lying in her nursing-home bed, the Fieldings, worn out after all their exertions, were asleep, and so was Mrs. Parsons.

Nina and Andreas Photiades, in their hotel, had made frantic love to wipe out the memory of this appalling evening, and now slept in each other's arms. They were never entirely to recover from the shock of it all. Up till now it had all been so delightfully easy: a swift, silent scurry down the stairs into the waiting taxi, with such trifles as landlords, debts and over-drafts forgotten. To emerge into Bedlam, with everyone rushing around, was something they had never expected. When, a few months later, they returned to Athens, they tacitly decided never to visit England again. This was just as well, for the police would have been waiting for them. It is not so easy to diddle a bank as the Photiades fondly imagined, and in the end their debts from their various ports of call amounted to several thousand pounds.

Nina, just before they fell asleep, murmured wistfully, "I did want that pan. It was so big, and it was non-stick too."

"My darling ninny," said her fond husband, "I'll buy you another. I'll even buy you two!"

"It's not the same as getting it for free," said Nina.

It was, of course, because they never paid for anything. But it was in its way a kind of epitaph.

"I left home in 1968," said Dr. Macek. "I was married. I have a little boy called Pavel. He is quite a big boy now."

"I knew you must have children," said Rose.

He sighed. He did not comment on this. He went on, "I will not trouble you with the political situation, for you must know about it. Your television and radio did a most remarkable coverage. I was, as it happened, out before the Russians invaded, and then I thought I had better not come back, it would have been difficult, it might have been dangerous. I was over here for a conference, and I was advised to stay, by people who knew what they were talking about. And of course, Mrs. Menusier, the inevitable happened. Marriages, especially young marriages, do not survive on partings, and Marika, who was then my wife, was perhaps a little like this mother of yours whom you call Diana—was she not a lunar huntress?—she was gay and lively, she liked going out, she wanted a man to sleep with and to escort her, and—and. What is the use of a husband who is in trouble with the new government, who risks arrest if he returns, who is miles away in a foreign country? I tried to persuade her to join me, but this she would not do. I do not entirely blame her. I did blame her very bitterly at the time, but I can see now that ours was not a good marriage, it would probably not have lasted. I regret Pavel. I will always regret Pavel. But all that is not really the problem. It is—how does one put it—an unhappiness, a burden, a thing that remains with me always, but it happens to many other people, it is not the kind of thing to make one jump into the river. But now, Mrs. Menusier, there are other things, and they are not so easy to ignore. I have parents living. They are quite old, and my mother is retired. My father, since my departure, lost his job, though now he too is of retiring age. I am informed by the Embassy that as the parents of a dissident, a Dubcek supporter, they are likely to be put in prison unless I am prepared to compromise."

He fell silent, until Rose said at last, "What do you mean? I don't quite understand."

He did not answer for what seemed to her a long while, but she believed he was trying to marshal his thoughts, perhaps sort out what he was entitled to tell her, so she simply sat there smoking and waiting.

Then he said, "I really cannot tell you in detail. What I have to say is bad enough, for it sounds like a cheap thriller. Do you read thrillers?"

"Very little else, I'm afraid, apart from work. I find they relax me more than most other books."

"They are not so relaxing in real life. I am in the middle of one. In other words, pressure is being put upon me by my government. Unfortunately in the hospital where I work twice a week, I have access to information that is extremely valuable. I cannot obviously go into details, and I do not think it would mean very much to you if I did, but it concerns, shall we say, aviation medicine. A colleague of mine—I do not know how the Embassy discovered this, but one can assume there are a certain number of willing helpers around. We call them spies, Mrs. Menusier—and that is what they would make of me. You see, it does happen in real life, and in real life it is even more crude and vulgar and cheap than in your thrillers, if not so exciting. And now you will understand my personal situation. The dilemma is a simple one, like all dilemmas, but there is no simple answer. So I inform, in which case I become more and more embroiled. I have seen it happen. You have read about it in the papers. They start by asking for information that is not particularly important—I think it is so in this case—but then it progresses until the informant is so involved that he cannot and dare not stop, he becomes an official spy, and the ending is almost certainly prison. The police always find out in the end. Look at the Krugers. However clever people are, they always slip up, information vanishes, the police are alerted, and after a great deal of damage the spies are finally tracked down. And I do not think I would make a very good spy. That is the 'either'. And the 'or'—My father might go to prison. He is an old man. He would not survive. I do not know about Marika and Pavel. They have not so far been mentioned. I have often had the idea that Marika put them on to me."

"You can't really believe that!" said Rose in astonished protest.

"Oh you are too simple. Why not? I could not blame her. No doubt pressure has been put on her too. You have no conception of what it is like in an occupied country. Sometimes you may think that here we are no more free than anywhere else. But when I think this myself, I make myself see that I could walk out of Curran House this evening, stand in the middle of the road and shout with all the strength of my lungs, God damn the Queen and the Prime Minister! Do not mis-understand me. I am unlikely to do any such thing. But if I did, what would happen? Nothing. People would walk round me, thinking I was mad or drunk. If there was a policeman around, he would just come up to me and say, 'Now, now, sir, this won't do. If I was you I'd just go home and sleep it off'—You are laughing at me."

"No, of course not," said Rose, ashamed that she should laugh at someone in such terrible trouble. But she could not help smiling at the thought of Dr. Macek standing in the road and shouting such silly words; seeing she might have offended him, she told him so. "If you ever did such a thing," she said, "I would think I'd gone as mad as my husband says I have. I'd be more likely to do it, myself."

He accepted this gravely. She saw that Dr. Macek took life very seriously. Perhaps he did not have much sense of humour. But then in the circumstances that was hardly surprising.

He sighed, as if this frivolity were out of place, then went on, "In my country, which I love most dearly, to shout at the government would undoubtedly land one in prison. There was freedom once. There will be freedom again. But now such people as myself are necessary tools. Sometimes it is even easier, if for example one is a homosexual—but incriminating photos would not matter to me. And my old father does—That is all, Mrs. Menusier. There is no answer. I know that perfectly well. What do you think?"

It was three in the morning. Rose, getting to her feet because she was stiff from her crouching position, saw the clock on the mantelpiece. It did not really register. It was entirely unimportant. She walked over to the curtained window and stood there, her back against the sill. She said, "There is no simple answer for either of us. I know of course that my situation is infinitely better than yours. It probably isn't a situation at all. I just have to go to a solicitor and sort it out. It'll be horrid and depressing and sordid, but anything would be better than going on like this. Your situation is of course only too real. Only you can't go on like this either. I think you'll have to let it ride, and take the risk. It mightn't be as bad as you expect. Oh, I know that's an awful platitude, and the kind of thing people say, but it just might be a bluff after all. What's the point of chucking an old man into prison? It won't do them any good—I imagine their jails must be pretty overcrowded—and it'll remove their hold over you for good and all. You certainly can't get them the information they want, that's for sure. For one thing, as you point out, it would get worse and worse and you'd be found out, and that would be the finish of Dr. Macek, wouldn't it?—which would be a pity, because I'm sure you are a very good doctor. Besides, you haven't the right temperament. You'd make a rotten spy, if you don't mind my saying so. Your heart would never be in it, you're not interested in money, and the constant danger would get on your nerves. You'd have a terrible conscience too. It would be absolutely disastrous. You just must call their bluff and say no. What else can you do? I know it's frightful, I know you'll worry yourself sick about your father, but what else can you do?"

He smiled at her, a little to her surprise. He said, "You are a wonderful girl. How could I be so stupid? There is one thing I could do. And this is the first time I have thought of it."

"What is that?"

"I can go home."

"Oh no!" The words jerked out of her.

He too was now on his feet. He said, "I think it's always been at the back of my mind. It would at least solve the dilemma. And it is you who have made me see that. I can never thank you enough."

Rose, horribly disconcerted, asked in dismay, "What good would that do?"

"It would remove the weapon. You can never cure a wound until you have removed the weapon."

"And what would happen to you?"

"I don't know."

"They'd put you in prison."

"Perhaps."

"But this is ridiculous—"

"I wonder if it is. I am a British subject, you know. I have just become one. Unprotected, of course, what they call a second-class citizen. But it is a strange thing to leave your country, whatever the circumstances. You are always to some degree disfranchised. I love this country very much, but it is not my own, it never will be. Your people are not my people, your ways are not my ways. I shall never be entirely at home here. Perhaps that is why I think of things like throwing myself over a bridge. I am homesick, Mrs. Menusier, for my own, ill-used little country with its beautiful mountains, its grand history, and its shocking whisky at nine pounds a bottle."

She demanded angrily, "What has whisky to do with it, for God's sake?"

"Oh, I just mentioned it. English visitors always complain. It doesn't worry me. I can always drink vodka. Or water. But now, to be serious again, I see so clearly that there always remains one thing to do. You can retreat, you can go round in circles, you can procrastinate, you can compromise. None of that gets you anywhere. It is all temporary, impermanent. The wolf is always there, you can't weave circles round him for ever. So what remains for you to do? One thing only. You walk towards him."

"And he eats you up," said Rose. She spoke crossly, for she was sick with worry: it was as if the full responsibility for Dr. Macek's life had been laid across her shoulders.

"Not necessarily. By no means. He might run away. You never know with wolves. They say all bullies are cowards. And there is one more thing—"

"You sound as if you've already made up your mind."

"Oh no. Not at all. This is quite theoretical. I am merely saying that if I do go home—"

"Don't!"

He stared at her, taken aback. The sharp, harsh word cut across his gentle, reflective tones. He said, as if this were something that had never struck him, something incomprehensible, "But it can't matter so much to you—"

"Yes, it can. It does."

He made a brief gesture as if he would stretch out his hands to her. Then he turned a little away, saying, "Nothing is definite. I don't know. How can I know? But let me tell you about the one more thing. I am a doctor, after all. I am highly qualified, both here and in Czechoslovakia. I am a paediatrician. My country needs such doctors desperately. I am not so sure they would put me in prison, Mrs. Menusier, and I am a fool not to have thought of this before."

"Of course they would. You know they would."

"Just possibly not. We are precious commodities, and there are always unfortunately sick children. But perhaps this is all beside the point. It is the decision that matters, not the consequences."

"I think that is a silly thing to say," said Rose. "You're becoming all heroic, Dr. Macek. Do you think your heroism will sustain you in prison?" Then she said sadly, "Of course you must do what you think right. Only it seems so dreadful that I should have put this idea into your head, that I must be responsible for whatever happens to you. Do you think this would really be wise? At least here you're safe."

"Am I? I have not felt safe for a very long time. I think I have felt more secure this evening than since my arrival. Thank you, Mrs. Menusier. I will confess that for some time now I have wanted to talk with you, but I did not like to intrude. Tonight it seemed to arrange itself. I always had the idea that somehow it would be you who would provide me with the solution. Why do you look so distressed?"

"If anything happens to you," said Rose, "it will be my fault, and I shall never forgive myself. Gerard always told me I interfered. What about your father, Dr. Macek? If you go back, will he be any better off?"

"Of yes, of course," said Dr. Macek in the calm, reassuring voice she was beginning to expect from him. No doubt he used it with his patients. "He is quite unimportant, poor old fellow. He doesn't matter. He's just a useful hook with which to catch me."

"And now they've caught you!"

"Not yet. I tell you, I don't know. I will make up my mind tonight. I will let you know." Then he said, "How can I thank you?"

Rose said wretchedly, "I am beginning to feel I have done something dreadful to you. Must you thank me for that?"

"Dreadful?" He looked at her, then said in the same matter-of-fact way, "You have been my angel." Then, after this strange statement he looked at his wristwatch and said, "I must go to my consulting rooms."

"What! At this hour in the morning? You're crazy. It's not quite four o'clock."

He glanced up at her then down, in a way that oddly reminded her of Tom, when he had done something naughty.

He looked quite shamefaced. He said, "My receptionist—she is a nice woman, but she always frightens me so."

"Oh really!" said Rose, and despite her distress, began to laugh.

"She is a most formidable lady. She looks after me like—what do you call it?—a nanny. She protects me against my patients. She makes sure I eat my lunch, that I do not let my morning coffee, which is always terrible, get cold. If it is raining, she insists on my taking an umbrella, which I always lose, and when it grows colder, she makes sure I wrap up well. I believe sometimes she would change my socks for me, if it was necessary. I cannot imagine what she will say if she discovers the papers I have left on my desk. I cannot possibly let her see them. I will have no peace until they are destroyed and, as she is very inquisitive, I must take them home and tear them up there. I wouldn't put it past her to search my waste-paper basket. Oh, the very thought of it makes me shiver. I must go immediately and collect them."

Rose looked silently at this man who was prepared to go back to his country, who might face imprisonment and who would at the best have a tough and isolated time of it, yet who was so afraid of his receptionist that he had to go to his consulting rooms in the middle of the night. She said at last in a desolate voice, "You have helped me so much, so much, but what have I done to you?"

He was by the door now, and she came up to him. He said gently, "Everything. You have done so much that I will never be able to thank you. Now you will be a good girl, will you not, and see this solicitor of yours, and not let your husband bully you. You have nothing to be afraid of. The law is entirely on your side. You are the best of mothers."

"I am a horrible mother!"

"Don't be silly," said Dr. Macek, rather to her surprise. "And believe me, you are not going mad, and you are not going blind. I will give you the address of an oculist. He is a good friend of mine. He will look after you. I daresay he will prescribe reading glasses. You need not worry. Nowadays they are quite ornamental."

"I am not as vain as all that."

"All women are vain, and that is as it should be."

Rose could think of nothing to say to this pontifical statement but, "Oh dear!"

"Good night," he said. He looked at her. He said, "You are a dear girl. I will never forget this evening." Then he took her hand and formally kissed it, saying, "You are not to worry any more, Mrs. Menusier. Everything is going to be all right."

She heard him going down the stairs, making presumably for his consulting rooms. She was so dazed with all that had happened that she hardly knew what she was doing. A few tears rolled down her cheeks, but these were mainly due to exhaustion and the extraordinary emotion of the evening. She sat down in the armchair, and instantly fell asleep, to be wakened at half past seven by a highly censorious Tom, who had wandered out of his bedroom, and disapproved strongly of the spectacle of his mother in a dishevelled state, sound asleep in the sitting-room. Rose dragged herself up from a deep sea-bed of slumber to meet her son's accusing eyes only a few inches from her face, while his fingers stroked her cheek as if in enquiry.

I I

GERARD DECIDED AGAIN TO come to Curran House about five o'clock. It really made very little difference, for Rose would of course be there, but he thought it would give him time to apologise for his behaviour: he had decided to make a charming little scene which, he was sure, would disarm her. Rose had always been a soft girl. Then he could suggest taking Sally for the usual little walk and, to allay all suspicion, he would take Tom with him too. The little boy could then be thrust into the hallway with the door shut securely upon him: he would probably manage to make his way up to the flat or his protesting cries would bring Rose running down to him.

His plans were vague, though he had been thinking the whole thing over for several days. It was not until the Saturday that he fully made up his mind. He was not unaware—he was not after all an entirely stupid man, merely a self-centred one— that what he was about to do was illegal, dangerous and even foolish. But like a small, cold stone within him was the aware-ness that he wanted Sally more than he had ever wanted anything in his life: once he had her with him, he was convinced that somehow he could manage to smuggle her out of the country into France, where for no known reason he was sure he would be safe.

He had certainly no intention of taking her back to Fish-bourne. For one thing he was intensely bored with the female atmosphere there. He did not get on as well with his sister as Rose always imagined. Claudine would champion him against the wife she had never liked, whom she had always resented, but she was a deeply conventional woman, and not for one second would she become party to a kidnapping. Indeed, she was almost fanatically law-abiding, even in such small matters as parking tickets and the paying of bills. She did not in any case care much for children, though she dutifully put on an act with Sally and Tom, and Gerard could not see her acting as foster-mother to a highly temperamental little girl.

She was, Gerard thought, becoming a real old maid. There had never, as far as he knew, been any lovers or boy-friends, even when she was young. Her looks, though good, were tight and cold. He often wondered how much she suspected of the kind of life he led. She never spoke about it. She accepted Trudy as a kind of ally, and when Terry and his friends called in, treated them amiably enough as if they were casual acquaintances: only very occasionally had Gerard noticed her eyeing them with a kind of bewildered suspicion.

Trudy of course was simply a dead bore. At the beginning she had been useful enough, and she had amused Gerard by falling wildly in love with him. He had encouraged this: it was convenient and a cover-up, it harmed no one and it kept Claudine quiet. But now she was becoming both tiresome and stupid, besides she was jealous of Terry, and a sulking, aggrieved lump of a girl with her idiotic mini-skirts, was no joy to anyone. The very sight of her now with the plaited hair and doughy face so exasperated him that sometimes he wanted to hit her, to kick her out of the way.

Rose at least had never been a bore. At the beginning she had amused and flattered him. Even now, in his more reasonable moments, he was fair enough to see that it was not her fault that she disgusted him so much physically that it almost made his gorge rise to be in her company.

And she had given him Sally. Gerard loved Sally as much as he loved any female creature, though he knew nothing of children and how to look after them. He visualised some fantasy future, with himself and Terry living luxuriously on Terry's money, taking with them everywhere this beautiful little girl who would adore both of them and be happy, so that people would look sentimentally at the odd trio and envy them. It would be a charmingly idyllic existence, and there would be no need to worry about work, for Terry's father was very rich and wildly generous to his difficult son. Gerard always considered that if he really wanted to act again, parts would fall into his lap: he believed himself to be one of the greatest actors living, and that the lack of suitable parts was simply due to jealousy. But work would not be necessary: they would perhaps buy a villa in the south of France and live the kind of poetic, lazy life he had always wanted.

Gerard did not think of Tom at all. He had never cared for Tom, from the moment of his birth, perhaps because it was after that that the whole business of sex became something so unutterably revolting. Tom represented his final deviation. Rose could keep Tom and welcome. And so he drove once more up to London, so obsessed with his fantasy that reality disappeared altogether. It was all becoming an obsessive fairy tale, where there was no place for such mundane things as police and laws and courts. In his besotted mind it was now becoming entirely right that he should snatch Sally away: it was the only possible thing to do, everyone would agree with him and even Sally herself as a small child who might be frightened and scream and protest, was a dream-girl, not a real human being at all.

He did not tell anyone where he was going, though Terry must be aware of it. It was Terry who still occasioned a small doubt in his mind, for Terry was jealous, and for all he had urged his friend on, might in the end not take too kindly to a little daughter trotting around with them, especially when the little daughter became a big daughter as she must inevitably do.

"She's a lovely child," Terry agreed, as they lounged outside on the veranda. Claudine and Trudy were in the kitchen, talking some silly woman-talk. His eyes moved over Gerard as he spoke.

"She adores you," said Gerard.

The beautiful eyes, deep blue and black-fringed, sank down. Terry had his mother's looks, and her eyes were his. He made no comment. He loved Gerard passionately, gave him every-thing he wanted, showered his father's money on him, but

Gerard knew that there was a steely strength to this young boy that he himself lacked. If Terry decided that he did not want Sally—but of course he did. Anyone would want Sally. There might be the occasional scene—there were a great many scenes, sometimes hysterical and violent—but after all it was Terry who had suggested the kidnapping in that letter which seemed to have got lost, Gerard could not find it. It had probably been swept up with poor Maman's ashes. It would be all right, everything Gerard wanted must be all right, it was one of the natural laws of life.

Claudine asked him if he would be back for dinner. She had grown strangely silent these days: she seldom talked to him.

"Oh, I shall be back very late," Gerard said, and at that Trudy, who really was so boring it was not true, burst into tears, wailed, "Oh Poops!" in a petulant way like a child in a temper, and rushed from the room.

Jesus, how glad he'd be to be rid of the whole boiling of them—

"She is upset," said Claudine, quite unnecessarily.

"She's a bloody silly bitch," said Gerard.

"She's in love with you."

For a moment her eyes met his. He did not answer, then she shrugged and went into the kitchen, calling out as she did so, "There'll be cold stuff in the fridge, if you're hungry when you get in."

Those were the last words he heard from her. She did not realise they would be the last words, but then he was unlikely to see her again for a long time. It hardly mattered. He did not believe she would miss him. She and Trudy could console each other.

He put a brief call through to Terry before he left. He gave him no details. He only said, "I'll meet you this evening." He named a small hotel outside Chichester where they sometimes stayed. Then he said, "Bring some money with you."

Terry did not ask how much, nor did he make any protest at so casual a demand. There was, however, if Gerard had been in any state to notice it, a faint edge to his voice as he agreed, and it was a little odd that he did not ask what all this was about. But Gerard seldom considered anyone but himself, and at this moment his mind was entirely concentrated on his plans for Sally.

He arrived at Curran House, just as Lulu, returning from a movie with some friends, was running up the stairs.

Rose spent Saturday morning in a kind of daze. The days after Dr. Macek's visit had been extraordinarily strange. She had not seen him since. She was both happy and unhappy, living in a kind of dream void, with everything that lay before her as fluid and shifting as the sea. It was as if she had put an end to a certain period of her existence, as if she had thrown away so much that had frightened and appalled her, and now there must be a completely new existence in a new terrain that was so far unexplored. For the first time for many months she did not think of Gerard at all. She coped as usual with the children, taking Sally to and from school, washing and cooking, playing the appropriate games, and now she had taken both of them to the park before lunch, as she always did, and watched them running around on the grass, playing with other children and talking to any dogs or people that took their fancy.

And throughout all this she thought of Dr. Macek.

She sat on a park bench, her eyes moving to the children from time to time to make sure they were all right, but this was purely automatic. She would have registered instantly if either had been in the least danger or were running away, but with her eyes, her aching eyes — it was all right, Dr. Macek said she was not going blind — she did not really see them.

It was a beautiful autumn morning, but winter was coming and it was cold. She would have to move soon. It was all right for Tom and Sally, tearing about, but the light wind bit through her jacket, and she crossed her trousered legs, as if to preserve the warmth in her body.

I have never talked like this to anyone before. Never. We were like one person. And now, it seems, I have told you to go away.

"Tom! Tom, don't tease that little dog. Yes, I know, but dogs don't like being teased any more than you do. Sally, keep an eye on him, will you?"

I have told you to go away. You will go back to your own country. They may put you into prison. Even if they do not, you will not be able to come out again, you will be watched and supervised, they will make it plain they do not trust you. And it is my doing. I told you to go. I'll never forgive myself. It is so unfair. To meet someone like you, like this, when I felt there was nothing left for me, when I was so alone and so afraid. I felt I would never be alone or afraid again.

And now you may be going away.

"I should leave your jacket on, lovey. It's not very warm. Do his anorak up, Sal, please."

Perhaps you have no choice. If you stay here, you will worry yourself ill about your father, you will wait for the threatening letters, you might even give in to the pressure.

And what about me? I am thirty-one. I shall be divorced, I have two children, I shall be entirely on my own again. Do you really have to go? Stay with me. I'll look after you. I'm used to looking after people. It is always much easier when there are two. Stay. Don't go. It is too much to meet you like this and then lose you. We might never meet again. They may put you in some horrid prison. They may even kill you—

Must you go? It seems that I have told you you must. Oh for God's sake. I don't know what to do any more. I can't bear to ask you, I don't want to hear your answer, I will not say goodbye.

You really cannot sit here, snivelling in the middle of the park. That woman gave me a funny look, oh to hell with you, have you never done any crying, you silly old thing?

"Come on, children. We'll go home now. I've got some more washing to do, and then I really must get down to work. Yes, it's a lovely dog. You throw his ball for him. That's right. Say bye-bye."

Say bye-bye.

There was that strange call from Diana, just before she came out. Diana seldom rang until the evening, if she rang at all, chiefly, Rose suspected, because she could not be bothered to talk to the children. This time she rang after breakfast, and of course Tom had to speak to her, whether she liked it or not. One would have thought that a simple 'Bye-bye' would exhaust no one, and he was so delighted with himself, he adored the phone and went away, beaming, but Rose knew from the tone of her mother's voice that even this was too much.

She said soothingly, "He does so love to talk to you."

"He's not coming back, is he?" There was an unusually fretful note to Diana's voice: she always sounded bored, but this was different.

Rose nearly said, Well you could surely talk to your own grandson for half a minute, without killing yourself—but instead she said, "Is something wrong?"

"I'll say there's something bloody wrong!"

"What's happened?"

"Michael's upped and left me, that's all."

"Oh no!" Rose was genuinely shocked. She always believed Diana to be immune from such catastrophes: she accepted Michael as a stepfather and thought the alliance was a permanent one.

"Oh yes. Fuck him! After all I've done for him too—"

So even Diana was not above uttering the well-worn cry of the abandoned female. Somehow this hurt Rose. Her mother's coolness and apparent lack of emotion was often hurtful, sometimes repellent, but it made her an oasis in a weak and over-emotional world, one felt that here was a person who accepted life as it was and who therefore provided some kind of security for others less fortunate.

The furious, grumbling voice continued. "I've looked after him, haven't I? He owes half his job to me anyway. Entertaining his fucking, boring friends—Christ, those dinner parties! They're all stockbrokers and directors, darling, they've as much conversation as would go on a teaspoon, all they want is to get stoned and tell smutty stories. Apart from making a pass at me—I don't suppose they know what a theatre looks like, and they've certainly never opened a book. And now sir has just walked out."

"When did this happen, for God's sake?"

"This morning, darling. This bloody morning as ever was. 'I won't be coming back.' That's what he said, and out he trots with his little suitcase, his bowler hat and his umbrella. I could tell him where to put that umbrella—"

"But why? Did you have a row?"

"Oh no, darling. Nothing like that. No, his lordship has found himself a new bit of crumpet, and I know who it is too, she won't last long, and he'll come running back no doubt in a month or two. He'll find the lock changed, I can tell you that. No man runs out on me."

"Oh Mother, I'm so sorry."

"Don't fucking call me that!"

"I'm awfully sorry, it just slipped out. What are you going to do?"

"What am I going to do? I'm going to forget him, darling, that's what. He's not the only man in the world, and he was beginning to bore me, anyway. There's plenty more where he comes from."

Are there? You're well over fifty, love. You might be getting on for sixty. I wonder—

"Well, you're probably well rid of him. He always seemed a bit stupid to me."

"Stupid! He hasn't a brain in his head—"

Rose listened to the diatribe, stripping Michael of everything, brains, looks, potency. There was no missing the savage pain beneath. Some of it might be hurt vanity, some feminine pride, but there was pain there too. Diana was not so uninvolved as she always boasted. Perhaps if she had let him see that she too had feelings, that sometimes her head ached, sometimes she was tired, sometimes she had a pain in her belly—That beautiful flat with its shaded lights, its pink frou-frou, its charmingly appointed dinners—it was all lovely, but perhaps a tired man, coming home after a difficult day, wanted something a little more human.

Poor Diana.

She listened for a long while. She offered to come round, but this was rejected violently: she dared not offer again.

Diana at last paused, then said in her normal husky voice, "I'm going away for a bit."

"Oh, I think that's very sensible. You need a holiday."

"I've been invited to go on a yacht." Diana mentioned a rich young man, sometimes in the news. "When Michael turns up again, I won't be there."

"Serve the bastard right," said Rose without much conviction, and this was plainly the right thing to say, for Diana laughed very loudly as if this were some vast witticism, then suddenly rang off without so much as saying goodbye.

The conversation had an odd and unexpected effect on Rose as she went back to the washing machine. She could not quite explain it, but somehow her future did not seem so black any more: she suspected that she had as usual been exaggerating and dramatising herself. She was not after all violently in love with Dr. Macek, nor he with her. What she was to him she did not know, she only knew that for herself this was the first person she had met for a long time with whom she felt completely at ease, on whom—oh God, what would the women's libbers say to that?—on whom she could depend, even lean. In his presence she felt a comfort and warmth that she had forgotten even existed. She had not so far considered him as a lover, though he might well become one, but she wanted him to be there, and she was somehow sure he would continue to be there, whatever happened she would see him again.

Yet it was not quite so cool and calm. Rose knew that well enough as she sadly surveyed one of Tom's sweaters, a hand-down from Sally that was not going to stay the course. There was really no point in washing it—it would not be easy for him, either. It was going to be bloody awful for both of them, like being offered a drink of water when one was thirsty, then having it instantly snatched away.

But oh God, it was better than being Diana, Diana clinging to her youth, the memory of her past beauty, refusing to acknowledge her years, indeed concealing them so closely that not even her own daughter knew exactly how old she was. Diana. Diana, who would not be called mother, who swore at the designation of 'granny', and who therefore denied herself the delights and privileges that only her real status could accord her. Rose was still far too young to visualise herself as old, but she hoped that she would be happy with her grandchildren, be able to spoil them, take them out for treats, play games with them, baby-sit. To Sally and Tom Diana was as remote as the moon-goddess after whom she was named. On their rare visits to her flat, they were always given a preliminary lecture on how to behave, so they moved about almost on tiptoe, eyeing this strange woman who was Mummy's mother, they regarded her as if she were something in a

226

museum, a strange curiosity who smelt of perfume, who never hugged them or laughed with them or indeed paid any attention to them. They always behaved beautifully, it was completely unnatural. Rose wondered if Diana knew how lucky she was, to have such quiet little creatures who sat on the edge of their chairs and whispered to each other. It was as if they thought they were in church.

Only once, once in the whole of their lives, had Diana condescended to amuse them, and it was the most terrible fiasco. What got into her Rose never knew: it was so astounding as to be almost shocking.

Suddenly one afternoon she sat down at the piano, which she played quite well when she troubled to practise, and burst out, in a startlingly rip-roaring voice, into the old music-hall songs. "I'm always the blushing bridesmaid," sang Diana, and so she went on, waiting at the church, her golden hair hanging down her back, and ending up with "Now I have to call him father."

It was a magnificent display, it indicated that Diana had missed her vocation, and Rose burst into spontaneous clapping, while Diana, flushed and looking extremely pretty, bowed and smiled as if this were some public performance.

And the children—they should of course have run to her, wild with enthusiasm, and begged for more. They did not. Tom then was nearly two and Sally nearly five: they sat there like wooden images, their eyes round as marbles. Mummy had said repeatedly that Granny hated being mussed up, was revolted by hugs and kisses: don't grab at her, don't crumple her pretty clothes, don't put sticky fingers all over the furniture, she doesn't like it, if you do that, you won't be invited again. Why doesn't she like it? Oh, it's just the way she is, people are all different, it doesn't mean she doesn't love you.

And so, obediently, they did not so much as stir. Diana looked at them, flushed an unbecoming red, then slammed the piano lid down. "Christ, darling," she snapped at Rose, "one might as well sing to a ventriloquist's dummy. Take them away, for God's sake, I can't stand the sight of them."

Rose took them away in tears, and Tom howled dismally the whole way home. Rose had to stop at a sweetshop and fill him up with a forbidden ice-lolly before he could be pacified. She knew she could never explain why Granny was so cross, and Diana never referred to the matter again. What was there to say? The situation was entirely of her own making, and she lacked the imagination to see that if children are told to behave in a certain way, they cannot suddenly change as if given a new part in a play.

"I think Granny was just tired," she told the children.

"Is it because she's so old?" Sally asked.

At this Rose, who was as overcome as the children—it all seemed so unnecessary and so very sad—choked back a slightly hysterical laugh, and prayed that such a question would never be repeated in front of Diana. But she was sure that Diana never quite forgave Tom and Sally for their behaviour, and certainly the performance was never repeated, though the children talked of nothing else for days afterwards, and Rose had to try to sing some of the songs herself, which she did not do nearly so well.

Now it seemed to Rose that she could never be so badly off as this strange, cold moon-mother who had achieved little on the stage, but who acted so consistently that she no longer recognised truth or reality. Michael, whose face Rose still could not remember, had once been so much in love with her that he had left his wife and nine-year-old son for her. And with Diana it had always been, Oh really, darling, he's such a bore, and I know he adores me, but sometimes really, it's too much, I wish he'd find himself a popsy to distract him, and leave me in peace.

Rose, whose mind was functioning in the strangest way, wondered if she had ever told him she loved him.

Well, now he had found himself a popsy, and Rose was appalled by the desolation that Diana must be feeling, facing for the first time her own age, and the reality that men do not easily fall for women over fifty, that she who had always vaunted her independence, might be left with that independence as her sole support.

But of course this was nonsense. Diana was still beautiful, and sometimes young men preferred older women. She would always find herself a lover.

Even if she had to pay for him.

Rose pushed Diana out of her mind. She told Tom, who was playing with his bricks, "I am going up to see Dr. Macek after dinner. It's time I knew what he is going to do."

And the thought of this made her quite happy, so that she sang over the housework she never really enjoyed, and was quite unaware that Gerard was driving towards her.

Mrs. Parsons had set off for her jaunt to the cemetery. As she came out of her flat, all dressed in black, she saw that the landlord was standing outside the Photiades' front door, gazing glumly down at the row of paper carriers. The builders were already in the flat: he was certainly not wasting time.

"Bloody little crooks," said the landlord. "Christ knows what made them leave it all behind, but half the flat's in those bags."

Mrs. Parsons bestowed on him a smile that, he thought, was like that of a crocodile about to snap up its victim. But he was too obsessed with his troubles to mind. He waved at the open door. "Just take a look," he said. "Just take a look. Did you ever see anything like it?"

Mrs. Parsons had already taken a look, but she could not resist going in again. The flat looked worse than ever in the daylight, especially as the builders were already dismantling some of the fittings. Nina might be a good cook, but she had never dusted, washed or polished, and in the kitchen there were rotting remnants of food that must have been there for days.

"There's even a dirty sanitary towel under the bed," said the landlord.

Mrs. Parsons did not think this was a nice thing to say, especially in front of a lady, so her smile vanished, and she made stiffly for the door.

"And they owe me a quarter's rent, apart from owing money to half the shops in the district. Not to mention all the stuff they were proposing to take with them. You don't know where they've gone, do you?" he asked Mrs. Parsons, now sailing in a portly way down the stairs.

"It's none of my business," said Mrs. Parsons.

Gerard found his courage beginning to evaporate by the time

he reached London. He had never been a brave man. He parked his Renault near Curran House, and bought himself some more courage, in the shape of a bottle of Scotch from the local off-licence, then climbed back into the car, to sit there drinking until five o'clock, when Rose would be preparing the supper.

He knew this was foolish. He had always drunk a great deal, but in the old days, when he was still working, he had enough sense to keep off the bottle, especially before interviews and rehearsals. Nowadays it hardly seemed to matter, and Terry, for some reason of his own, encouraged his drinking, for all he hardly touched anything himself: he always brought bottles with him and saw to it that he was well stocked with anything he fancied.

Gerard thought for a while of Terry, a little hazily. He had by now finished a quarter of the bottle, and he said aloud, "That will do. You are not to drink any more, do you hear? You have had enough." And then he took another pull.

Terry. The beautiful boy. He was indeed the most beautiful boy Gerard had ever seen. Then in a sudden gust of alcoholic clarity Gerard saw plainly for the first time that Terry would not be good for Sally at all. It was imbecile to believe he ever could have been, for all the young man was urging him to kidnap her. The little fantasy of the three of them together in sentimental companionship was nonsense. Gerard at that moment was frightened of Terry, for all he loved him, and for all the boy was almost young enough to be his son. He was not much of an actor, though from time to time he got small parts on his looks, and he had appeared once or twice on television. Yet for all his youth and the slender beauty of his appearance he was a formidably strong character, and in all the battles between them, it was Gerard who usually lost.

Gerard groaned aloud. The groan was dramatic, but the emotion that prompted it was genuine. The vague thought nagged at him that this handsome boy who resembled the ideal Nazi of Hitler's dream, was proving to be his damnation, yet even thinking of him reduced him to such frantic, devouring adoration that the idea of being without him was insupportable.

And Sally—

"Oh, it will work out," said Gerard aloud again, another couple of swigs for the worse, then he saw from his watch that it was just on five. He stepped out of the car, walking perfectly steadily despite all he had drunk, and made for Curran House. Yet even there he hesitated, and that hesitation, if he had known it, was to prove his undoing.

Lulu, back from her movie, and waiting for her mother who was coming back with both of her sisters for supper, heard the footsteps coming up the stairs. She opened the door happily to greet them: it was quite an occasion to have Monica and Amanda together. If Gerard had not hesitated, she would not have seen him, for she had been changing into sweater and slacks and had only just come out of the bedroom.

He stopped on the landing to stare at her.

Lulu could smell the drink on him then, looking up into that handsome, weak face, knew immediately that he meant mischief, that he was here to harm poor Rose.

In that moment a kind of crazy courage overwhelmed her. She forgot how frightened she was of him, that he was a powerfully built man, that it was the most all-fired bloody cheek to interfere in his business. She was only a schoolgirl, both her parents were out, and there seemed to be no one within call. None of this seemed to matter. She took a sharp breath, then cried out in the quick, high, runaway voice of panic, "You shouldn't leave incriminating letters lying around, you know."

Gerard's mouth fell open. He could not believe his ears. For a second he simply did not know what she was talking about, but the tone of her voice convinced him that she meant mischief, and then he remembered the letter he had lost, the letter he had believed to be so unimportant.

It did not seem unimportant now. In the strange fashion of memory recall he could see sections of it, as if it were a part he had to learn. It was almost as if Lulu, now white with terror, had communicated the words to him. He had always had an exceptionally good memory, drink or no, it was after all an integral part of his profession. There floated before him Terry's firm, small, neat handwriting, so very clear, so very

231

determined, that the words might have been printed in front of him on a screen.

Make sure you get the little girl to live with us . . . Get hold of Sally if you have to kidnap her . . . If we have your daughter living with us, it is bound to make the menage seem right . . . Force Rose to let her come . . .

He turned on Lulu a face that seemed to her straight out of hell. Gerard was not a good actor, he had never been a good actor. His love scenes were so disastrous that producers had been known to grow hysterical. His only potential lay in crude farce with knickers and suchlike, and even this he exaggerated so grossly that whatever humour, whatever meagre laughter lay within, was destroyed. As a very young man his beauty had been such that susceptible producers of both sexes had been decoyed into giving him a chance, but even then he was wooden and stupid, emphasising the wrong things, throwing in passion where lightness was essential, becoming frivolous when he should be serious. He thought after all only of Gerard Menusier, and was incapable of translating that monumental ego into anything else. But now for once he was playing the murdering villain in such a way that Lulu could not so much as move, her legs seemed turned to jelly. She wanted to call out, to scream, to bring someone down, even Rose who should know nothing of this at all, but nothing came out but a gasping croak, and her dilated eyes were fixed on a countenance that would surely have appalled even Sherlock Holmes.

He said in a thin, hoarse voice, "So you did come to spy after all. You came for that letter."

This was palpable nonsense, for Lulu could under no circumstances have known of the letter, but it was true that she had come to spy, so she did not deny it. She still could not utter a word, only clasped her hands across her breast as if somehow to ward him off.

"You took it," said Gerard.

He moved a little nearer her. He seemed to Lulu at least seven foot in height. The flesh of his face had sunk in, and he looked to her quite mad. It was true that what with emotion and the whisky he had drunk, the realisation of the awful

232

thing he had been planning to do and a strange feeling that Terry was somehow egging him on, he was at that moment mad, his senses had left him, all he wanted was to obliterate this little monster who had the power to destroy him.

Then Lulu found her voice again. It soared and wavered, it was a shameful give-away, but then she was shaking from head to foot, and he must smell the fear on her as she could smell the whisky on him.

"It won't go down well with the solicitors," she said, the frightful words pouring out as if nothing mattered any more. She was sunk, anyway, she might as well have her say. Heaven knows what Rose would think, but she was committed now, she was not going to be terrorised by this beastly creature. "All about kidnapping and—and your menage. I saw you kissing. It was disgusting. You're a revolting man, I hope you die. You'd kill poor little Sally. I daresay you wouldn't care. You don't care for anyone but yourself—"

She broke off with a gasp that was almost a shriek. Gerard was almost leaning against her. He said in a whisper, "Where is that letter? I want it, please. Give it to me."

"It's locked up," said Lulu, backing away from him, then in a gabble, "It's not here, it's posted to a friend of mine. If you hurt me, she'll hand it to the police." Then she shouted at him, "Go away! How dare you threaten me? You're the nastiest person I've ever met, you're a blackmailer, you're a— a bastard—"

Gerard saw her now through a mist of despairing rage. To him at that moment she was simply an amorphous thing that could destroy everything that meant life to him. He was long past all reason. The whisky had suddenly seized hold of him so that it was almost as if his brain did not function. Whether he could really have committed murder, no one could say, he was not by nature a physically violent man, and he had never so far contemplated killing any living thing. But his hands shot out towards her, and no producer could have faulted the action: for once in his life it was perfectly timed.

He did not at first hear the footsteps coming up the stairs, and neither did Lulu, petrified with shock and terror. But as the person came on to the landing, he did hear, and at last sanity, provoked mainly by sheer self-preservation, returned to him: his hands dropped and he swung round.

Mrs. Parsons was returning from her visit to the cemetery. She had spent a most enjoyable day. She had laid flowers on the graves of Ted, Maria, William and all the others who lay there: she had walked around, noting the various inscriptions, and remarked with satisfaction that her family were as well cared for as anyone else. She had then spoilt herself with a nice cooked meal in the little café across the road where she always went: egg and chips, a cream cake and a large pot of tea. She felt very pleased with herself. She had done her duty, and now she could relax till the next outing. It was always a little like a family reunion, for though she had never particularly cared for the departed, she had a strong sense of family feeling and, when they were alive, had always visited them regularly. It seemed only fitting to do the same, now that they were dead.

She gazed without particular interest at the odd tableau on the landing. The little Fielding girl looked very peaky. Perhaps she was not long for this world, she was as pale as a sister-in-law who, many years ago, had died of anaemia. She was certainly too fat, and fat people were never healthy. Her eyes shifted to Gerard and she saw that he too looked awful, white and drawn, with eyes sunk into his head. Mrs. Parsons at that moment had a professional interest in death, and she automatically turned the pair of them into headstones: she thought with satisfaction that they were unlikely to be as well looked after as William, Maria and Ted.

As she was thinking this, Gerard, whose nerve was now broken, suddenly turned and dashed past her: if she had not been a substantial person, holding firmly on to the bannister, he might have knocked her down.

"Really!" exclaimed Mrs. Parsons in outrage. She saw him flying down the stairs, three steps at a time. The front door banged after him. She looked at Lulu, expecting the child to offer some explanation, then saw that she was now not so much peaky as ashen.

She seldom concerned herself with her neighbours in Curran House, but was compelled to ask, "Are you all right, girl?"

Lulu did not answer because she could not. She managed to stagger into the flat, shut the door behind her, then, for the first time in her life, collapsed on the floor in a dead faint.

Mrs. Parsons heard the crash, hesitated, then continued firmly on her way upstairs. After all, the door was shut, and there was nothing she could do. As her mind was largely concerned with birth and death, she wondered if the girl were pregnant. This did not surprise her, girls being what they were nowadays: the Fielding child always wore such ridiculous clothes and made up too much, she was undoubtedly one of the fast ones. In any case she could hardly be expected to batter down a locked door, and the mother would be back soon.

Mrs. Parsons opened her own front door, took off her hat and coat, put the kettle on for another cup of tea and settled cosily in front of the television.

Mrs. Fielding returned a quarter of an hour later, accompanied by Monica and Amanda: the latter had just informed her that she was expecting a third child. She was delighted with the news, and happy to have both girls in her flat at the same time, though she hoped that Monica was not in one of those naughty moods in which she enjoyed shocking her sister. It was a pity that Amanda was quite so humourless and censorious. It was true that Monica's way of life was unfortunate, but one had to take people as they were, there was no point in being constantly disapproving.

She chatted away as she looked for her key. Amanda, she thought, was looking very pretty in the new mink coat her husband had given her for her birthday. It was lovely news about the baby. Amanda always did the right thing. Monica, though wearing a long, trailing skirt and rather too many beads, looked charming too in her odd way. Mrs. Fielding reflected that her daughters, however difficult, were a credit to her, and opened the front door.

She nearly tripped over Lulu as she came in. The three of them crowded round, exclaiming in genuine dismay at the sight of their little sister sitting there, recovered now from her faint but too overcome to get up.

"Darling, darling, what has happened?" cried Mrs. Fielding, then with Monica's assistance raised Lulu to her feet and half

235

carried her into the sitting-room, while Amanda ran to pour her out some brandy.

For once the family was completely united. Mrs. Fielding, quite pale herself, hugged Lulu to her, Monica knelt at her feet, clasping the cold hands in her own, while Amanda held the glass to her lips. Lulu, sobbing on her mother's shoulder, thought how lovely it was to have such a nice family and gulped down some of the brandy, warmth, love and liquor flooding through her.

She managed to say at last, a little obscurely because of the brandy, "I don't really know what happened. I just felt funny, and everything went black. I suppose I fainted. Oh Mum, don't ring the doctor. There's nothing wrong, really, I feel fine now. I expect it's the usual. It makes me feel a bit queer sometimes."

But it was too much to keep all this extraordinary story to herself and when Amanda and her mother had gone into the kitchen to unload their shopping and make some tea, she whispered to Monica, "Gerard tried to murder me."

"Gerard what? Lou, what the hell are you talking about?"

"I can't tell you now. Please don't say anything. But it's true. I'll tell you all about it later."

Then Mrs. Fielding came back into the sitting-room, and Lulu shook her head, putting a finger against her lips in a mysterious way. She could not feel very proud of herself, it had all been too scary and she had behaved, as it seemed to her, like a trapped rabbit, but it would be a relief to talk it over with Monica, and it was nice for once to have all the dramatic news.

Then she thought of Rose, and all the elation left her. If she had hurt Rose in any way, she would never forgive herself. I must go up and see her this evening, Lulu thought rather miserably, and she lay back on the sofa, quiet now, and still a little pale, while her family fussed over her, joined now by her father, delighted with Amanda's news but upset for his favourite daughter.

It was not until a couple of hours later that Lulu managed to slip upstairs to Rose's flat.

Rose, after the disturbed morning, spent a strangely happy day in the flat. She felt filled with an extraordinary peace. It was as if a burden had dropped from her. She rang the solicitor at his home, for he was after all a family friend: he had seen Diana through vast complications in his time, and she thought he would not mind.

She said simply, "I'd like to come and see you. I want to divorce Gerard."

And she looked down, a little unhappily, at the small pile of letters she had taken from the cutlery drawer.

He said, "And about time too." He added, with a hint of laughter in his voice, "That's off the record, Rose. But I'm delighted. You can't go on like this. Apart from anything else, it's not good for the children."

"No, it isn't," said Rose, and could have added, It's not good for me either. But she did not, only talked for a while about Tom and Sally, asked for the family news, then made an appointment.

It was in most ways an ordinary day. Sally produced an exercise book filled with her own compositions. The class teacher plainly believed that flattery was essential for the young, for at the bottom of each piece of writing—Sally still muddled her d's and b's, Rose noticed—was some commendation—Fascinating, Terrifying, Interesting, Very good indeed. Then after this Rose put on some records, and being in such an exhilarated mood danced the Charleston for the children—

"a bit before my time," she assured them—but then they would not have cared if she had danced the polka: the sight of Mother flinging her arms and legs about was so delightful that they begged for more and more until Rose fell into the nearest chair, exhausted.

She made the supper, and prolonged the bath. She suddenly realised that she was behaving as she had done when very young: she was postponing the delight of going up to see Dr. Macek. She knew he was in. She had gone halfway up the stairs on no pretext at all, and saw the light under his door, heard a small clatter in the kitchen. The flat belonging to the Photiades seemed to be in the process of being dismantled, which did not interest her, and Mrs. Parsons as usual had her television on much too loud.

She came down again, supervised the bath with its usual accompaniments of celluloid fishes and a small car that Tom refused to part with, which would shortly grow rusty beyond repair. Then she settled down to the routine of songs and stories, only by now the excitement was pulsing within her and she found it hard to concentrate—"You're not paying attention," Sally said indignantly, no doubt quoting her teacher at school.

When there was a knock at the door, she ran towards it, thinking the visit might be reversed and that Dr. Macek had come to see her.

It was Lulu. Rose for a second showed both annoyance and disappointment, for Lulu was almost the last person she wanted to see. But then she saw that the child looked miserable and rather ill: in her dressing-gown and without make-up she seemed very young and somehow very lost.

Lulu said in a rush, "I don't want to disturb you, and Mother doesn't know I'm here so I can't stay, but could I come in for just one moment, please, Rose?"

"Of course. The children are just ready to go to sleep—I hope. Come in with me and say goodnight. Would you like a cup of coffee or something?"

"No. I really can't stay more than a minute. Amanda and Monica are here. Amanda's expecting another baby, and Monica's got a new boy-friend."

238

"As long as it isn't the other way round!"

"Mother'd have a fit if she heard you say that. There's something I've got to tell you. You're looking awfully pretty, Rose. You're looking better than you've looked for ages."

"Am I?" Then Rose laughed and patted Lulu on the shoulder. "Come on. The kids will be delighted. They're so fond of you. Tom always wants to call on you when we come up past your flat. He calls you Luly, but then you've so many names, one more won't matter."

Lulu followed her into the bedrooms. She really was unusually pale, not at all her bouncy self. But she said goodnight to Tom and Sally, kissed them and tucked them in, then trailed after Rose into the sitting-room: she looked so guilty that Rose realised a confession was imminent.

She said soothingly, "It can't be as terrible as all that. What have you been doing with yourself? You look a bit under the weather. Are you all right?"

"Yes," said Lulu, pleating her dressing-gown into folds.

Rose said, "It's about that visit to Gerard, isn't it?"

"Oh, you know—"

"Yes. He told me." Then she had to smile, though really, it was not very funny. "He said you upset the urn. Did you really?"

"Oh my God, yes," said Lulu, looking more her old self. "It was frightful. Those ghastly ashes were all over the floor. I expect pieces of her are permanently missing."

"I hope so," said Rose with vigour. "It's always given me the creeps. I think it's horrid keeping a person's remains in a little pot on the mantelpiece. I'm delighted you spilt it. I wish I'd done it myself." Then she said gently, "Why did you go? Gerard thinks I sent you down to spy on him."

"Well, if he thinks that, he's a complete idiot," said Lulu. There was a little more colour in her cheeks, but she looked to Rose as if she had suffered some kind of shock, for her eyes flickered, and her hands were never still. Then Rose saw with dismay that the tears were beginning to trickle down. "I didn't mean any harm to you, Rose. I wanted to see if I could find out something that would help you."

239

"Find out what? Oh don't cry, Lou. Please don't cry. It doesn't matter. I don't mind. I admit that when Gerard told me about it, I was a bit cross because I thought you were on his side, but that was silly of me, I should have known better. Wait a minute. I'll get you a tissue. Man-sized. I keep them for Tom. Small boys are such wet little things. Now tell me what you thought you'd find out."

"I don't know," sobbed Lulu, blowing her nose with a great trumpeting sound. "Only I was so upset about Gerard's being nasty to you, I thought I might see something that would give me a hold over him and stop him molesting you. I know it sounds crazy. It seemed a super idea at the time."

Rose said in genuine astonishment, "Do you mean you thought you could blackmail him?"

Lulu only sobbed the harder. Before her eyes was still that terrible face, the face that had meant murder, the hands stretched out for her throat. The super idea had turned into a dreadful nightmare. She could only pray that he was frightened enough to keep out of Rose's way.

Rose, jumping to her feet, said in despair, "If only I could give you something to drink—I did have a bottle, but Gerard finished it. Perhaps a nice cup of tea—it's probably much better for you."

Lulu managed at last to stop crying. She said in a choked voice, "I'm okay now. I'm glad you're not cross with me. It was a daft idea, but—" The sobs changed to a gulping giggle. "They all hated me. Claudine could hardly bring herself to talk to me at all, and that Trudy with her mini-skirt—"

Rose, sitting down again, said, "I can't imagine what you hoped to find out. But you're sweet to bother so much about me, Lulu. I expect you'll be relieved to hear that I really am doing something about the divorce at last. It's about time too. Perhaps Gerard will marry Trudy."

Lulu said in a gasp, "He's in love with—with someone called Terry."

Rose did not answer this, only said, "I'm sorry they were so nasty to you. Didn't they even give you a cup of tea."

Lulu said in a burst of confidence, "Claudine gave me a cup, and I poured it all over the roses."

"Good God! You do seem to have had a day. And you didn't find out anything sinister?"

"No, no."

Rose glanced at her sharply, but really, it was impossible to imagine that this poor child, her face all swollen with crying, could be capable of anything devious. She said, "I think the crisis is over anyway. The divorce will be pretty nasty, divorces always are, but it'll be an enormous relief to me when it's over, and perhaps it will be to him too. It can't be much fun being lumbered with a wife who isn't a wife. Anyway, Lulu, thank you for bothering so much about me. You're a good friend, you really are." Then, with a brief sideways glance at her watch, she said, "Well, I've got rather a lot to do, and you look as if you're all set for bed. Where does your mother think you are?"

"Having a nice lie-down."

"Oh. Then you'd better get up, hadn't you? Good night, love." Then she said, as if she were speaking to one of the children, "Come on, give us a kiss. When I've sorted myself out a little more, you must come and have dinner with me, then we can watch the telly."

Lulu to her surprise flung her arms round her neck and hugged her. Then, without another word, she ran from the flat and downstairs to her own.

Rose stared at the closed door. It was plain that Lulu had certainly been up to something, that the afternoon in Chichester had not consisted entirely of upsetting urns and watering roses with tea. And that remark about Terry—but she could not concentrate on this now, she had more important matters on her mind. She looked in on the children, then leaving the flat door slightly ajar—this time she remembered to take her key—went quietly upstairs to Dr. Macek's flat.

Gerard reached the small hotel about eight o'clock. It was a miracle that he arrived at all. He was drunk, emotionally disorganised and frightened to death. He drove there much too fast, cutting corners, twice ignoring traffic lights and zigzagging across the road. It was only by sheer luck that he did not run into a police car, and even greater luck that he ran into nothing else. There were so many near misses that he lost count of them, but they hardly impinged on him. He heard the horns and the angry shouts, but these noises, coupled with frenzied brakes, were as nothing to the screaming noise in his own mind. When at last he came to the hotel he skidded up the gravel path, stopped with a jerk that nearly shot his teeth through his head, and half collapsed over the wheel.

Terry was waiting for him. In the glare of Gerard's car lights that he had never troubled to dip, and which were still on, he appeared clearly to Gerard's bloodshot vision, sauntering down the path, his hands in his pockets.

He was as always beautifully dressed. A large portion of his father's money must have been expended on the Swiss shirts, the tailor-made trousers, the French silk scarves tied Western-wise about that long, elegant throat. The ash-blond hair gleamed in the lights, the face was plainly visible. It was a face that could still, perhaps always would, reduce Gerard to an almost fainting passion of love: it was a beautiful epicene face, of a pure beauty that was neither male nor female, with the deep blue eyes and flawless features.

That face was now a little twisted. Terry looked at that moment entirely the young Nazi he so resembled. There was anger and contempt in the tightened lips. He opened the car door, and stared down at Gerard, slumped in his seat. He said, "So you've made a cock-up of it, after all. I might have known it. Where's the child?"

So he knew—but it was the way he spoke. Not Sally. Not your daughter. Simply the child. It would never have worked, said the small, sane portion of Gerard's mind, yet he ached to have Sally beside him: he wished her no harm, in his own way he loved her. But no love for Sally or indeed anyone else could compare with the violence of his feeling for this boy who looked at him now as if he completely despised him.

He did not answer. He briefly raised his hands, then continued to droop over the wheel as if he lacked the strength to move himself.

Terry said in a razor voice, "What the hell has happened? What have you been doing? You're as pissed as a newt."

Gerard at last raised his head. He looked raddled and old.

He said in an exhausted voice, shaking with self-pity, "I couldn't help it."

"You couldn't help it! What the devil do you mean? When we discussed it, you said it would all be so easy. You knew exactly how to do it. You were just going to take her for a walk and not come back. What could be easier than that? That bloody wife of yours could hardly object if you took the boy as well. She knows you can't abide him. Well? What went wrong? When you asked me to meet you here, I took it for granted you'd have the child with you. I suppose you were drunk to start with."

"Oh, stop nagging at me!" Gerard's voice shrilled out at him almost in a shriek.

"I want to know what happened," said Terry. He had one foot on the running board. The eyes staring into Gerard's were relentless and hard.

"All right. Can I have a drink first?"

"No. You stink of it. Have you driven down from London like that?"

"Nobody stopped me," said Gerard sulkily.

"Well, they bloody well should have done. Now what happened? Come on. Tell me. I want to know."

Gerard told him. He was too drunk, too shocked, to conceal anything, even the fact that he had almost murdered Lulu. When he recounted this, Terry backed away, the contempt on his face replaced by a more natural expression: he did not like this, murder was a bit much, this was no longer funny. Then he cried out in a fury that held hysteria, "Why the hell did you leave that letter lying around? Have you no sense at all? And what a place to leave it—oh well. So that's that then."

"What do you mean, that's that?" Gerard in a sudden panic stumbled out of the car. One of the men from the bar was standing in the porch watching them, but he did not even notice.

Terry stepped back even further. He said in a chilly voice, "I'm going home."

"But I thought—"

"I'm going home. I've had enough. I gather you're broke as usual. Here's your drink."

243

He pulled a fiver from his pocket and dropped it on the gravel. It fluttered in the breeze, and Gerard automatically put his foot on it. He looked despairingly at Terry, now moving away from him: it was as if everything were retreating, as if he were isolated in some icy vacuum.

He stooped to pick up the money and he heard Terry, now a shadow moving swiftly towards his own sports car, laugh.

He called after him, "Terry!" And, "Oh come back. For just one second—"

There was no answer. He heard the car starting up. He staggered into the bar, ignoring the derisive looks that were cast at him, and ordered himself a double Scotch. This made him feel better, and he ordered another.

The barman said, "Are you driving, sir?"

"What the bloody hell do you mean, am I driving? It's none of your fucking business. I want another drink."

"Sorry, sir. I'd prefer you to get home in one piece. Would you like me to ring for a taxi?"

Gerard looked at him. He saw that there was no point in making a scene. He stalked out of the bar. He heard the laughter behind him. He longed to go back and knock someone down, to salve his battered pride, but had just enough sense not to do so.

Then he drove home. It was a twenty minutes' drive, and it took him an hour. Fortunately, the roads were reasonably clear. When at last, after this appallingly unco-ordinated drive, he turned into the Close where his bungalow stood, he turned off the engine and for a while remained in the car, motionless, his hands still on the wheel.

Terry would come back. Terry always did come back. There would be a magnificent reconciliation. Gerard saw dimly in the fuddled depths of his mind that the intervals would grow longer and the reconciliations less magnificent. One day, sooner or later, Terry, who was so young and so beautiful, would grow tired of this lover so much older than himself, who was a failure in everything but his looks, and those eventually would leave him too.

One day this would happen to Terry.

Gerard pushed away from him confused thoughts of Rose,

of Sally, of Lulu, of all the people who had interfered in his affairs and ruined his life. He came at last into the bungalow, a defeated man. Tomorrow he would be victorious again, the handsome Gerard Menusier with a grand career awaiting him and no family any more to hamper him, but now he was simply a bitterly lonely, beaten human being, who wanted to drown his shame in Scotch and more Scotch, then huddle into the pillows in his room.

Claudine heard him come in. She was in bed. She knew from his footsteps that he was drunk. She pulled the shade down over her bedside lamp lest he should see the light and come in. She grimaced and sighed. She had had a difficult evening, trying to explain to a tearful Trudy that she had better go out and find herself a proper young man.

"But I don't understand," Trudy wept, "I don't know what you're talking about," and Claudine, who was practical and no fool, saw that this was so, and gave it up.

She heard Gerard opening the door of the sideboard cupboard, and the clink of a bottle against glass. Then she heard him stumble into the hall and take off the telephone receiver. She could hear the low rumble of his voice. The receiver was replaced. But the hoarse sobbing that followed this was more than she could bear. She at once put out the light and buried her head under the bedclothes: so she remained until the morning light filtered through the curtains.

Rose knocked on Dr. Macek's door.

She saw to her pleasure that he seemed to be expecting her. She said, "Would you mind if we left your door ajar? The children are asleep, but I'd like to keep an ear out for them in case Sally has a nightmare or Tom goes wandering. I think I'd hear. In any case I'll have to pop down from time to time. I don't really like leaving them on their own, but I wanted so much to come up and see you." She added, "You'll be relieved to hear that I have my key in my handbag."

He left the door open and led her into his sitting-room.

"It is very bleak and bare," he said, but Rose exclaimed with genuine approval, "I like it."

It was certainly sparsely furnished. The landlord did not

worry too much about the furnished tenants, such as Dr. Macek and the Photiades. He bought cheap, secondhand remnants picked up at auction sales: the carpet was worn and did not match the curtains. The statutory television stood in one corner, and Rose suspected that it did not work very well, for it was an old model and had a battered appearance. But then Dr. Macek probably hardly ever used it. He did not seem to her a television type. There were, however, books on the shelves that were nothing to do with the landlord, pictures on the wall, including a print of Prague, and photos on his desk, amid a pile of papers. One of the photos was of a small boy. There was in the far corner a record player, with a stack of records underneath. It was open, and there was a record on the turntable. And she liked it because it was not simply a bare, cheap room: it was Dr. Macek's room, it bore his imprint, and he, seeing the look on her face, began to see his desolate flat through her viewing, so that it became warm and human and comfortable, the desolation gone.

He sat her down in the one comfortable armchair, and poured her out a whisky, without so much as asking her if she wanted it.

"I drink very little," he said, "especially when on my own. This is necessary because recently I could learn to drink too much. I daresay you understand me."

"I drink very little because I can't afford it," said Rose frankly. "I sometimes think that if I were able to afford it, I'd become a right old soak. It's my world, after all. I was brought up among theatre people, and Diana was always liberal with the drinks. If I wasn't always so broke, I might be lying in the next bed to Veronica."

And she fell silent for a moment, thinking not of Veronica but of Diana, whose man had done her down, and who must be finding the bottle a sorry substitute.

Dr. Macek did not seem unduly disturbed at Rose's alcoholic prospects. He said calmly, "No. You have the children to safeguard you. It makes a difference. I have my children to safeguard me. I could not arrive at my consulting rooms, smelling of drink. These children are after all largely my responsibility."

"Did you manage to tear up your messages before your receptionist found them?"

"Oh yes. I took all the torn pieces home with me."

"You seem to have a great respect for her."

"She is a most formidable lady. She is also most loyal and devoted. It is a shame that no man will ever dare to marry her. But I knew that I would not have a moment's peace until every trace of my so foolish confession was removed. Still, I admit it was an odd hour for me to go there. When I came out at five in the morning, I was nearly arrested."

"No!"

"Yes indeed. A policeman was most interested in me. He asked me what I was doing, in my consulting rooms at such an hour. He called me 'sir'. Your police are remarkable people."

"I think," said Rose, "they are really like policemen everywhere, except that they don't carry guns. I went to the States once with my parents. I was quite shocked to see all the holsters. But here it's not really so different, only it's fine as long as you speak with the right accent and look as if you've been to the right school. You have of course a slight foreign accent, which is not in your favour. But you look very respectable, so I daresay he let you go without too much argument."

"We parted on very friendly terms," said Dr. Macek, "and he told me all about his little boy who is top of his class at school."

"Is that photo there of Pavel?"

"Yes. Would you like to see it?"

"Please."

He took the photo down for her, and she gazed into the face of a small boy who bore little resemblance to Dr. Macek. It was a pleasant, round, cheeky face, and a couple of teeth were missing in the smiling mouth.

"He must be about five," said Rose. "He's not very like you."

"It was taken three years ago. It is the only photo that has been sent me. He is like Marika, and not only in looks. He does not take life too seriously."

247

"And you and I do," said Rose, handing him back the photo. Then she said, "What have you decided to do, Dr. Macek? That is really why I have come up to see you. I had to know, I couldn't wait any longer. But hang on just a moment, will you? I'd like to make sure the children are okay."

She was out of the flat for a few minutes, then came back to sit down again in the armchair. She said, "I'm sorry about that. They're perfectly all right, of course, both sound asleep. They usually sleep right through till about seven. Tom occasionally gets one of his wandering fits—but you know all about that. Now let's forget about the kids. I want to hear about you. I think you've made up your mind, haven't you? You have the look on you. You look—please forgive me if I'm being impertinent—but you look somehow at peace with yourself."

"You too, Mrs. Menusier. I have never heard you sound so lively and so well. You seem quite a different person."

"Oh," said Rose, "you don't really know me. You've seen me at my worst. I used not to be such a dreary creature. But it's true, I feel marvellous. It was as if something happened this afternoon, I felt as if a vast burden had dropped from my shoulders. Trumpets sounding on the other side—"

He did not know what she meant by this, but he surveyed her with approval, noting the colour in her cheeks and the ready smile. She was, he thought, really an extremely pretty woman and now that she had stopped worrying she looked years younger. He said, "And the eyes—they are better, I hope?"

"Oh yes. I obviously need glasses, but most of the trouble was in my imagination. I suppose I've always had a horror of going blind, and when you're told—but it doesn't matter any more. I propose to forget all about it, and wear nice horn-rimmed glasses that will make me look all academic. Diana will be furious. I think she'd rather never read again than wear spectacles."

"You'll only need them for reading."

"That's fine then. But what about you? Please don't keep me in suspense any more."

"I am going home," said Dr. Macek.

"I see. I thought you would, somehow. I suppose you really have no choice."

"I shall probably be going within the next few months. I know you are afraid for me, but I think there is no need, no need at all. I have been to the Embassy and talked it over with them. I do not think they will put me in prison. I am a precious commodity, Mrs. Menusier." He smiled as he said this. "I am too valuable to them. Probably I am more valuable in my own country than I am here. There are a great many spies, and most of them far more competent than me, but there are not so many doctors. They have even offered me a job in a children's hospital. I shall of course be supervised. I shall not be permitted to leave the country, not now anyway. I daresay there will be certain unpleasantnesses. My phone will be tapped, I'll have to report to the police, my letters will be opened. These things happen in our countries, we learn to accept them as part of the daily living. They are inconvenient but quite endurable, and I shall not after all be indulging in any political activity. And I shall have my work. A spina bifida child is a spina bifida child, whichever side of the Iron Curtain he comes from, and my job is to look after him and do everything I can to help. It makes no difference that once I voted for Dubcek. It is of course a great black mark against me, but then you see, I know how to deal with spina bifida children, and most people do not. It is my great advantage, and it is an even greater advantage that it helps the State." He paused. Then he said, "I shall miss you, Mrs. Menusier."

"I shall miss you terribly," said Rose, looking at him steadily. She said, "Why did they give you such a name, Dr. Macek? You're not a tom-cat. My husband is, but you're not. It's not fair. What is your first name?"

"Stepan."

"I can't help being sorry you're going. We're just beginning to know each other. The children will miss you too."

He said, "Will you write to me?"

"As often as you like."

"I shall like that very much."

"I write rather good letters," said Rose. "And I'll be very careful. It won't be much cop for them if they open them. It

249

isn't necessary after all to write about politics. There are other subjects. You may get a bit bored with Tom's shutting doors and Sally's temperament—"

"I shall not be bored."

"Well, I'll make sure that not even the fiercest hard-liner could complain. And there's something else. This morning I came to a decision in my bath. I always come to decisions in my bath. I have decided," said Rose with the air of one proposing to reorganise her whole life, "to learn Czech, though it really is the most frightful language. Then one day I'll come over and see you. I don't see why I shouldn't. If you would like me to, that is—I can't see why anyone should object. I'm a pretty harmless sort of person, and rather inefficient, politically. I mean, I vote Labour, but I don't think about it much between elections. The party could hardly call me a stalwart supporter, but I am loyal and occasionally address envelopes. I even pay my subscription when I think of it. I don't know why I'm telling you all this, it's very boring, but it's just to show you that your government couldn't really pin anything on me, and after all, I'm entitled to see Prague just as much as anyone else."

He said, "Certainly. It will be my privilege and pleasure to show you round."

Rose looked at him, wanting both to laugh and cry. The stilted words, the formal phrasing, the fact that even now he did not call her by her first name, were more endearing to her than any loving phrases: the warmth glowed through the stiffness, the formality was a kind of sweet-talk.

He went on, "I owe you so much, I can never thank you sufficiently. You have made me see things clearly again. I have grown unused to people, I have almost forgotten how to talk. I have shut myself up, refusing to make friends, refusing to go out. I know what a foolish, barren kind of life it has been. Alone in my room or scurrying around, frightened of my own government, seeing ghosts and goblins in every corner. It is no life for any man, certainly not for me. I do not make a good spy, but I do not make myself a rabbit either. And I am tired of being afraid. When one gets to the stage of contemplating suicide as the only way out—oh, it's such a nonsense. Such a nonsense. I love your country very much, but it is not mine, so now I must go back to my own."

"What about Marika?"

"Oh, that is over. She is after all married to someone else. It is over for me too."

"Don't you mind?"

"Not at all," replied Dr. Macek cheerfully, and he looked at Rose in a fashion that for the first time brought tears to her eyes. He said, "And what exactly are you going to do, Mrs. Menusier?"

"What I should have done a long time ago. First I am going to try to divorce my husband. Then I shall reorganise myself, get myself some proper work. It can be done, even with the children, only it requires an effort and lately I just haven't had the spirit for it. I think like Tom I've been shutting doors on myself because I was afraid to come out into the open. You say you were afraid—oh God, so was I, I can't begin to tell you—but I did tell you, didn't I? You poor man, I gave you a real earful."

"I think I returned it," said Dr. Macek.

"You're not quite as garrulous as I am. Never mind. It didn't really matter, did it? We had to talk. I think there comes a point where people have to talk or die. And now you're going away. I'm sorry to repeat myself, but I really shall miss you."

He said, in his formal manner, "We will miss each other. But do you know, I do not think it will be for so very long. And we still have a little time to know each other better. I am not after all going immediately. These things take time. And then you will take your little trip to Czechoslovakia."

"You make it sound like Southend," said Rose. She was silent for a moment, contemplating the little trip to Czechoslovakia. Dr. Macek would meet her at the airport. It would be all very strange. She said, "You tell me you'd almost forgotten to talk to people, that you were too much alone. It's been just the same for me. I'm always with the children. I hardly ever see anyone else. I love them very much, but one can't pretend that their conversation is intellectually stimulating. It does tend to bring talk down to its most basic. If this had gone on much longer, I too might have forgotten how to hold any kind of conversation. Gerard lost me a lot of my friends, but it was my fault too, I could always have gone back to them. I suppose I was too proud. So that was how it was. I don't see much of Diana, the people in the other flats tend to dodge me, so I'm left with children and school and meals and nappies. And very nice too, but not enough, not nearly enough. I can't go home, because I am home, but I must see about a proper job and meet people again, if it's only on business terms. How long have you lived in this house, Dr. Macek?"

"Two and a half years."

"And until a few days ago you were simply a name on the plate above the door. I must go down now," said Rose. She stood up, brushing down her slacks, but did not walk towards the door. She said, almost shyly, "Will you come and have dinner with me some time? I'm not a bad cook."

"It would give me the utmost pleasure," said Dr. Macek. He made her a little stiff bow.

She smiled at him, and thought he understood why she was smiling. Formality for him had become a protective armour, it was his way of hiding betraying emotions. One day perhaps she would remove that armour from him. She said, "I read a verse the other day. It caught my fancy. I used to quote odd verses rather a lot. Diana says it's terribly dreary, and I haven't done it for a long time, but I don't see why I shouldn't, really. It's by an American. It's something like this:

'I do my thing and you do your thing,
I am not in this world to live up to your expectations,
And you are not in this world to live up to mine.
You are you, and I am I,
And if by chance we find each other, it's beautiful,
If not, it can't be helped.'

It's a bit obvious, but I like it, what with everyone insisting that you live up to their silly expectations and being furious with you when you don't. But sometimes you really do find people, and it's never really too late. It's unfashionable these days to even consider there can be a happy ending to anything, but I cut serials for women's magazines, and I'm going

252

to let myself be corrupted, even if it turns me into syrup."

Dr. Macek made no comment on the poem, only said, "We will make ourselves a story. We will contrive a happy ending."

Rose looked at him in silence. God knew what he was going back to. Not death, not prison, but what kind of life was it going to be? He was still, as age went these days, a young man, he had spent several years in a comparatively free country. How would he adapt himself to a police state, to bugging and spying and perhaps worse? But she thought that he would manage. He was the kind to survive dictatorships and revolutions. The world, thank God, was full of Dr. Maceks, quietly going about living their lives and doing their jobs.

And herself? She thought, I could marry this man if he wants me to do so. I could live with him, I could be happy with him. It might just possibly be heavy going at times, but I do not know, I think we would do rather well together.

Mrs. Fielding said once, When you find a good man, hold on to him.

I think I'll hold on to you, Dr. Macek, Stepan, sir.

She said almost pertly, "If you knew what I was thinking, you'd be shocked to pieces."

He surveyed her for a moment without replying. His mouth flickered into a smile. He said, "If you knew what I was thinking, Mrs. Menusier, you would have run down to your flat a long time ago."

Rose was utterly taken aback. It was the last kind of remark she would have expected from him. She flushed a little. Then she said, "I think I am right after all. I think it would work very well indeed."

And what he made of this she had no idea, but it was somehow as if he understood her, for he continued to smile, and he looked at her in a fashion that she had not met for a very long time, that she had almost forgotten existed. She drew in a sharp breath, then went towards the door.

She said, as Tom might have done, "Bye-bye!"

"Good night." This time he did not use any name at all. He did not even kiss her hand. He simply stood there, his eyes following her, and Rose too looked at him until the door closed between them.

253

She came slowly down the two short flights between his flat and hers. She could hear Mrs. Parsons' television, even from the top landing. She always had it on full blast. Perhaps it was her way of getting back at the landlord. The Photiades' flat was still empty, with the door open. Andreas and Nina were gone, heaven knows where, into their limbo of debt and other people's money. It must be strange to lead an existence permanently in the red. Veronica, sedated in her nursing home, would not be back for a long time, and the Fieldings, briefly a united family, were gossiping in their sitting-room, with Lulu, now quite restored, the centre of attention.

Rose paused for a moment on her landing. She thought of them all with great warmth and love. She felt enclosed, protected, at peace. Then she went into her flat and quietly closed the door.